HOW
I MADE
$3,200,000
FROM MY
HOBBY

The
Max
Brown
Tetralogy (+1)
#1

ALSO BY MICHAEL BERNHART

FICTION

How Ornithology Saved My Life

How Speleology Restored My Sex Drive

How Existentialism Almost Killed Me

Night Sweats: How Moral Philosophy Failed

NON-FICTION

Quality Assurance: Theory and Practice

Quality Assurance: A Textbook

Information Channels for Colombian Exporters

Sustainability: An Organizational Assessment

Strategic Management of Population Programmes

Health Management Appraisal Methods

New Methods for Assessing Developing Country Health Services' Management Needs

Computer BASICs

COMING SOON

How to Fly an Airplane with your Eyes Closed

What God is Really Like

Some After-thoughts on the After-life

HOW I MADE $3,200,000 FROM MY HOBBY

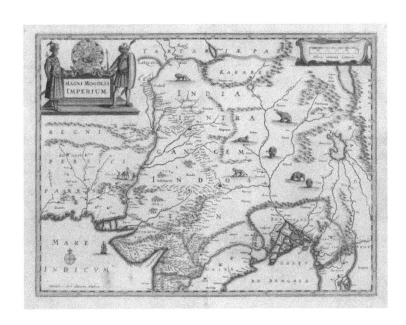

MICHAEL BERNHART

HOUGH PUBLISHING JEWELL MOUNTAIN, GA

This is a work of fiction. Names, characters, events, organizations, places and incidents are either products of the author's imagination or are used fictitiously. Any similarity to real persons, living or dead, is coincidental and not intended by the author. The exceptions are the names of the three men mentioned who died in a pointless war: Tom Walsh (Panel 10E, Row 85 of the Vietnam Veterans Memorial), Chuck Jacobs (Panel 8E, Row 17), and Bill Bare (Panel 24E, Row 4). The author knew the first two personally, both very fine men, and heard only good things about the third.

Constructive criticism is always welcome and, given that current publishing models allow constant revision, will be acted upon. Send your feedback and suggestions to MaxBrown@HoughPublishing.com. Trolls, flamers and other dipshits whose aim is to hurt, not help? Keep your sad little thoughts to yourselves. If you can't, be forewarned that your emails may be published, with full attribution to their authors. Every effort will be made to portray you as pathetic and illiterate as you are. Seems fair.

Published by Hough Publishing, LLC at Jewell Mountain, GA.

Inquiries to Hough Publishing, PO Box 811, Hiawassee, GA 30546, USA. Or, contact@houghpublishing.com.

www.houghpublishing.com

Published in the United States of America

ISBN: 978-0-9976160-7-1

Cover and title page map, *Magni Mogolis Imperium* by Henricus Hondius. Amsterdam, 1636.

Table of contents – *How To* sections

How to become an instant aristocrat 7

Coping with a pretentious name 8

Introductory Theodicy 13

How to become a football star 19

Capitalizing on a pretentious name 23

The manly art 24

How to hustle chicks 27

How to survive a war 53

How to deal with survivor's guilt 60

Dealing with the brass 60

Would You Like to Be a Hero 69

How to get into graduate school 72

How to survive graduate school, I 73

How to survive graduate school, II 83

How to get a faculty appointment 85

Higher education explained, I 89

How to swear 91

Higher education explained, II 92

How to get laid 111

How to fart 138

Grantsmanship 142

Bordello etiquette 183

How to read a newspaper 348

How to deal with boredom 354

Glossary 411

¹ Then the Lord answered out of the whirlwind, and said:
² "Who is this that darkeneth counsel by words without knowledge?
³ Gird up now thy loins like a man; for I will demand of thee, and answer thou Me."

Job 38

0

Jane Austen said it all comes down to love and money. That sounds about right to me (I'll introduce myself in a moment). One small clarification, Jane: Speaking on behalf of the 51.2 percent of the world's population that's male, from our perspective the love part has a significant physical component.

That isn't necessarily a bad thing. Our species would have sputtered out long ago had men not been driven to take insane risks to sow their seed far and wide and often. But that drive has outlived its usefulness. Humankind is now threatened by over- not under-reproduction. And yet men haven't adapted.

Are we that programmed? Of course we are. Even the noblest among us can't keep his fly zipped.

It's disheartening to learn that Gandhi was a horn dog and the saintly Nelson Mandela "was no saint" according to the women in his life.

Founding Father Thomas Jefferson fathered six children with his slave, Sally Hemings.

FDR went to Warm Springs to improve circulation to his crippled legs through some one-on-one physical therapy with his secretary, Lucy Mercer.

You get the idea.

Money? Not as interesting to read – or write – about so we'll hold it to one example:

It's been drilled into us from first grade onward that George Washington was honest to a fault. He was also a wealthy man and he declined the salary offered by the Continental Congress, asking only for reimbursement of personal expenses. What a noble and generous gesture! Actually, it wasn't. He quickly ran up a bill of $449,261.51; that's $4,250,000 in today's money. His monthly liquor tab often exceeded $9,000 in current dollars.

We can take two things from this sampling of the misbehavior of great men: 1) It's getting harder every day to hold on to our heroes. And 2) Ms. Austen stands confirmed. Men are quick to set their principles aside in the pursuit of sex, and our pursuit of wealth never ends.

This is the story of how I got both.

Section I

Formative years.
Why and how I became a smartass.

From a 1940 Johnson Smith & Co. catalog of practical jokes.

How to become an instant aristocrat

My name is Maxwell Smythe Brown IV, a name that's remarkable only because no forebear bore it; there was no MSB I, II, or III. This leap directly to a numerical suffix that bespeaks continuity, tradition, and old money was a sign of the times: an instant pedigree. In the year (1941) and place (Pocatello, ID) of my birth all the proud parents had to do was write IV on the application for a birth certificate.

The ease with which an infant Idahoan could be thrust into the upper crust invites the question: are you limited to a simple Roman numeral? Consider the possibilities: M.D. is an obvious choice; an Anglophile could add OBE; devout Catholics could put the infant on the Right Path from the very start by tacking on SJ or OP*; even a senior management title such as CEO might be fair game. It's surprising there aren't more of us sporting fraudulent titles.

The IV was my father's idea. Perhaps a joke – wayward humor runs in the family – or perhaps he was in his cups when the paperwork was filled out at the hospital.

The origins of Smythe are in dispute. When asked, dad unfailingly referred me to my mother. Her stock reply was that the name was the product of her husband's desire to inject some hitherto absent class into his lineage. The IV wasn't enough? The evidence is on her side. Dad was an avid student of the *Reader's Digest* feature, 'It pays to increase your word power' which promised mastery of 20 new words every month. He'd opt for the Latinate – "sesquipedalian," he would say – over the simpler Saxon word whenever he could.

Whatever the motivation, the appeal of highfalutin names was short-lived. My younger sister escaped with a common moniker.

---

* One legacy of a career in academia: a penchant for the unfamiliar or unusual word. We even make them up. Among university faculty those competitive displays of erudition are the equivalent of comparing penis sizes. A hard habit to shake. There's a glossary, if a term is unfamiliar.

Coping with a pretentious name

A fancy handle can cut both ways; for a boy – as you may remember from your own childhood – the prevailing direction tends to be negative. Max Brown has a sturdy lumpenprole* quality to it; as a child, I tried to pass as Max Brown as often and as long as possible, but there's no refuge. Teachers, scoutmasters, pastors, and other natural enemies of young boys are quick to expose you to the ridicule of your peers. "Which one of you is Maxwell Smythe Brown the Fourth?" the teacher asked with a thin smile on the first day of each and every blessed school year. Broad grins and smirks break out around the room as new classmates marvel at their good fortune. Before their chairs are even warm, the scapegoat, the butt, the outsider has been identified. There were three lines of defense:

The first was actual fighting to establish Max Brown, Tough Guy, rather than Smythie the Fourth (aka Smythie the Fart by my hilarious classmates). These fights ended when the recess bell sounded, by which point I'd been holding my adversary in a headlock for several minutes. It would be pleasant to tell you that my success as a playground gladiator was due to innate ability. No, it was because I had the most practice.

The second line of defense – and a natural complement to pugnacious Max – was smart-ass Max, taunting authority figures and an eager participant in any prank. These reached their zenith with a buzz-bomb under the hood of the principal's car that detonated with dazzling pyrotechnics when he turned the ignition key. The presence of 20+ kids arrayed along the parking lot sidewalk should have alerted him. The pranks reached their nadir when we tipped over one of the few remaining privies on the outskirts of town, revealing the assistant manager of the hardware store, occupied with a girlie magazine.

There's a drawback to this line of defense which you may have spotted already: If your motivation for pranks and practical jokes is to be widely known as someone who does that sort of thing, you're going to get caught a lot.

---

* As promised, there it is: a made up word. Don't judge too quickly. Shakespeare minted 2,000 new words, many in use today. George W. Bush invented several dozen, although none seem to have taken root.

The third line of defense was to divert attention to the names of others by giving a twist to the names of unfortunates who were born Lemprecht, Pithanski, Hotchkiss or Lacocque. For those of you with a squeaky clean mind, they were rechristened Limp Prick, Piss Ants and Crotch Kiss. Even the most sheltered should be able to work out Lacocque on their own.

Some years it was easy, like the fourth grade when Harry Lipshutz was a co-new arrival at school. The next year I struggled unsuccessfully to get Dick Breath to stick to Richard Prath.

If you're thinking these were the acts of a shrewd ten-year-old tactician, they weren't. They were the instinctive responses of a little boy who wanted to be accepted – maybe occasionally admired.

———

The perennial struggle over the name provided early evidence that the cosmos might be unfair – that caprice was as common as divine justice – an observation inconsistent with instruction received in Sunday School. In my case, lots of Sunday School.

Don't get me wrong. Sunday School wasn't all bad; the singing was great. Today, as church attendance plummets, too few are exposed to this wonderful music. It deserves a wider audience. In tribute I've appropriated hymn titles as section headings. Nostalgia.

But the relentless indoctrination at Sunday School takes us to the second preoccupation of my childhood: Who, exactly, is God? And why isn't He doing a better job?

Precious Lord Take My Hand
 - T. Dorsey, 1938

As you might expect, a boy who often came home bruised and scraped from a closely contested fight, or had been chased home by the howling victim of a prank, would arouse the concerned attention of his parents. My mother interpreted these incidents as evidence of a genetically transmitted moral defect that had been passed down from her husband, a defect that would doom the recipient to a life of misery, substance abuse, incarceration, and then early death. No such predisposition was evident in dad, but who knew what turbulent currents roiled beneath that placid surface? To forefend such an unhappy outcome, mom looked to the church for inoculation against the temptations of quotidian life. There was a tendency to outsource my upbringing whenever possible. Compliantly, I applied myself to the task of developing a warm and personal relationship with God.

There were other paths by which to approach God. Dad shared his sense of awe at the splendor and vastness of the Maker's creation with his daughter – not with me – through star-gazing. The two of them would stand in the backyard on clear nights, he describing the constellations and the myths they represented, Debbie asking which of the stars were angels. "Where does God live?" she would ask. A precious moment for them; dad's eyes would be damp when they came in.

For incorrigible Max the job was left to the church.

If you were raised in a Good Christian Family, you also may have been set on the road to redemption early in life. The way this played out for most kids was that they would, in their teens, drift away from theological pursuits, finding the opposite – or same – sex a more compelling object of study. Not me. Whenever I seemed to be losing interest in religion, something or someone would come along to nudge me back onto the path. Three examples:

Example #1. *Bring It to the Lord in Prayer*
- J. Scriven, 1855

"Maxwell, have you felt the presence of God in your heart?" The speaker is Mrs. – although a spinster – Friggenbotham, our Sunday School teacher. An imposing fortress of a woman, we were so in fear of her we didn't apply the obvious twists to her name. Not at first. Later we liked to mess with her.

"How can I know, Ma'am?"

Her large features morphed from beatific to annoyed. "You'll know when the Holy Spirit embraces you and suffuses you with Its light."

"Can you give me a clue? Is it like needing to burp?" Annoyance morphed to indignant anger. We boys in the class wondered if we could get her so worked up she'd swear. Someone reported overhearing her cussing a blue streak in the church parking lot.

"Or would it be lower down, Ma'am? Kind of like the pressure you feel bef . . ."

"Enough!" She was chewing on her lower lip. "Class, let us pray for Maxwell that he may become more godly and less a trial for others to endure."

Small heads bowed around the room. The girls seemed to be sincerely entreating the Almighty to intercede and rescue a lost soul – or, alternatively, take him off somewhere else. The boys were grinning. A couple of drawn out fart sounds were heard.

All very entertaining – to a point – but was my behavior evidence I'd strayed so far that the most powerful force in the universe, the Almighty Himself, had to be enlisted to pull me back onto solid moral ground? The class had never been asked to pray for the soul of a sinner before. I knew I was a smart-ass. Was I teetering on the brink of eternal damnation? A concern, once implanted in a ten-year-old, that's hard to shake off.

And what did this say about God? He's a warm fuzzy feeling? Daily and prolonged prayer hadn't resulted in a suffusion of warmth and light nor any other manifestation that the Holy Spirit had embraced one – if that was what God was supposed to do. The only physical sensation was sore knees or backside, depending on whether I was praying by my bed or in a pew. I redoubled my efforts and scaled down expectations. Still nothing, and this sets even a child to thinking about the rest of the message.

Example #2. *When You Receive No Answer to Prayer*
- C. E. Breck, 1911

"Hey, Max, got a minute?" Here the speaker is minister-in-waiting, Reverend Al. We boys weren't sure exactly what Rev. Al's status was, or even his last name. He was young, perpetually in need of a haircut, and his clerical outfit would have benefited from more frequent laundering. His standard approach with boys was to lure us onto the basketball court where, apparently, salvation awaited.

Hoping Al's question wasn't a prelude to a game of HORSE or 21, my reply was guarded. "Um, yeah, a minute." Let me add, I was a little on edge having just spent a productive hour with Phil Hanson sneaking embarrassing items into shoppers' carts at Albertsons, then enjoying their discomfort as they explained to the checkout girl that the ribbed condoms, stool softener and Preparation H weren't theirs.

"I just wanted to chat."

Good. No basketball. Not busted for the grocery store caper.

"You want a Coke or something?"

Intriguing. Al, who reeked of near poverty, was going to spring for a soft drink? An investment of this magnitude signaled something big. Had Frau Friggenbotham arranged this? The minister, Dr. Hauterre? My mother? Being singled out for this kind of attention is unsettling. It re-stoked the concern that my personal defects were extraordinary and required extraordinary efforts to contain, if they couldn't be corrected. But at least there was a soda in it.

"Sure, sir. What do you want to talk about?"

"Oh, nothing special. Just wanted to see how you're doing." We went to the drug store's lunch counter where, a month earlier, I'd fallen three rotations short of breaking the record for spins (47) on the counter stool. The record attempt was aborted when I sprayed a semi-circle of vomit on the counter, floor and spectators.

As we took our seats the soda jerk eyed me with unmasked loathing. I made a gagging sound and he backed off, perhaps hoping that supervision by a man of God would forestall problems.

Al ordered malted milks for us, a rare treat for the younger members of the Brown family. While I slurped noisily, he blathered on about his journey to God in words that went straight over a ten-year-old's head. Losing interest, I surreptitiously experimented with the bolts under my seat. Could they be backed out to the point where they'd release at the right moment and send an overweight victim sprawling? No. Too tight. Being a smart-ass is a fulltime job.

Well into the second malt, I was starting to feel their effect as well as pressure to contribute to the conversation. Al paused: my cue to participate. "Well, sir, I've been thinking about God a lot lately." This was true; I had. "I mean, what do you think He's like?"

Wouldn't you expect an apprentice minister, fresh from seminary, to have a canned answer to a question like that? Al's brow furrowed and he started off with some claptrap about creation; then he switched to the ever-present protective God; then he dropped that and moved to the future with some disjointed rambling about the redeemer.

I was vacuuming the last flecks and foam out of the bottom of the glass when Al threw in the towel and asked, "More importantly, Max, what's your view?"

"I don't know, sir. There's just so much rotten and bad stuff going on. I thought God was supposed to be good. I thought He was protecting us and if we obeyed His commandments, then we'd be okay."

No one would have accused Max Brown of being a deep thinker. But, fueled by sugar, chocolate, and a desire to repay a gift of two malted milks, I'd confronted Al with one of the great conundrums in Christianity – and perhaps other major religions: theodicy.

I won't tax your patience with Al's convoluted efforts to square a world racked with evil that's presided over by a benevolent and protective God. There was something about free will, mysterious ways, and testing. But even young Al had to recognize he was getting nowhere and he terminated the conversation with a throwaway line that was all too familiar, "Well, Max, that's where faith comes in."

That's the best he could do? A verbal shrug? I signaled for a third malt.

Introductory Theodicy

Anyone conscious of the mayhem abroad in the world (in 1951 Stalin's handiwork was in the news and Hitler a fresh memory) would have to conclude that God couldn't be omni-benevolent, omniscient, omnipresent, and omnipotent. The churches were obviously wrong on at least one of those points. I reluctantly acceded to the view that when it came to defining the nature of God, the mainstream religions were pretty much at sea.

The splendor of the universe provides compelling evidence – to a ten-year-old – that some larger force is at work. But, if God isn't all-knowing, all-powerful, and – most importantly – all-caring, what's God like? In unwitting imitation of many a theologian and philosopher that had preceded me, I created a God in my own image. I figured God for a practical joker.

O God, I Cried, No Dark Disguise
- E. St. V. Millay, 1928

The Bible, and the world, make more sense to a ten-year-old boy once he's embraced this image of the top deity. Job covered with boils? Clearly a practical joke. Abraham circumcising *himself* on the Lord's instructions? Explain *that* any other way. And how else can you interpret the hijinks surrounding the departure of the Israelites from Egypt? Lice, frogs, locusts? Can it get any cooler?

The evidence just kept pouring in. An older boy directed us to Exodus 33:23.

𝕬𝕟𝕕 𝕴 𝖜𝖎𝖑𝖑 𝖙𝖆𝖐𝖊 𝖆𝖜𝖆𝖞 𝖒𝖎𝖓𝖊 𝖍𝖆𝖓𝖉, 𝖆𝖓𝖉 𝖙𝖍𝖔𝖚 𝖘𝖍𝖆𝖑𝖙 𝖘𝖊𝖊 𝖒𝖞 𝖇𝖆𝖈𝖐 𝖕𝖆𝖗𝖙𝖘.

God had mooned Moses!

That clinched it. The Big Guy was a screw off. The clergy might prattle on about the Hand of God shaping our destiny, but I knew better; it was only His middle finger.

I didn't, by the way, share these thoughts with sub-Reverend Al or anyone else.

As a practical joker, omnipotence, omnipresence and omniscience could still be part of God's makeup. Omnibenevolence? Nope. Not if your reference point is the behavior of a ten-year old practical joker.

Human pranksters – particularly those aged ten – are held in check by other humans who set limits on how far a prank can go. But who will rein in the Lord Almighty?

Cosmic Dribble Glass - Picture your friends' surprise. The life of any party. Holds enough to rain for 40 days and nights.

World-class Whoopee Cushion - Remember Krakatoa? Folks will erupt with laughter as the dupe sets off his own earth shaking eruption.

Attributing to Him the challenges I faced, where did He get his ideas from? Does He have a catalog of practical jokes and devices? I made one for Him after mine was confiscated.

Example #3. *Alas Dear Lord, What Evil Hast Thou Done*
            - J. Heermann, 1630

"Can I sit in front now?" The speaker is Deborah Brown, my younger sister by two years. She'd ridden alone in the back seat for the last two hours on our annual winter trip to southern California. Knott's Berry Farm was the destination.

"No, Debbie, I get to sit up here because I'm older and, in case you haven't figured it out, I'm going to get there before you do." That's me speaking, of course.

"But that's not fair. I want to get there first sometimes too."

I was indifferent on the seating arrangements. There was a certain cachet attached to sitting in front with the adults, wedged between them on the bench seat of our Nash Ambassador, fleeing Idaho's bleak winter to palm trees and gentle breezes. On the other hand, in the back seat I could stretch out, if Debbie wasn't there, and read comic books.

"It's not fair that Max always gets to sit in front."

"Debbie, you're so short you can't even see out. I mean, the front seat is *wasted* on you." The view from the center of the front seat was better than on past vacations; Nash had introduced a one-piece curved windshield for the 1951 model.

"It's not fair." Her expression clouded up; her lower lip started to tremble. I had only a few seconds to make a gracious gesture before a parental edict would consign me to the back seat.

"Alright! Let the baby have her milk. You can sit in the stupid front seat." That, my friends, is a ten-year-old boy being gracious.

At the next wide shoulder on US 6 dad pulled over and Debbie and I switched, quickly, as the wind was driving the light snow with chilling and surprising ferocity. A semi hurtled by, spraying my legs with slush and salt as I dove into the back seat.

While I went through the stack of comics, looking for one not yet committed to memory, Debbie perched on her folded knees in order to not waste the view. As evidence that the front seat was not wasted on her, she read passing roadsigns and billboards out loud. "Don't take . . . a curve . . . at 60 per . . . we hate to lose . . . a customer . . . Burma Shave."

Trying to tune her out, it was hard not to consider the advantages of being an only child.

"Daddy? What's 60 per?"

Thirty minutes later Debbie lay still in the dirty snow, a halo of glass crumbs glittering around her, the only one of us seriously injured in the accident.

Six days later Deborah Lee Brown, age eight, was declared dead and her small body was turned over to the embalmers.

Fair?

Faith of Our Fathers
- F. W. Faber, 1849.

Life changed in the Brown household. My parents who'd previously shown no interest in church – other than its hoped for potential to steer their son away from trouble – became regulars. First, Sunday morning worship; then the Wednesday evening service was added; Monday night Bible study went on the schedule a few months later; and finally our lives had to accommodate an occasional Saturday event that couldn't be missed.

Why this religiosity? It wasn't going to bring her back. Did they think a super-zealous display of piety would ward off a revisit? My lengthening Sunday School attendance pins hadn't protected us. Did they think they'd find an explanation? Absolution? The message to their surviving child was unambiguous: Fear God. Make every effort to placate Him. Eleven-year old Max was fully on board with that.

Activities associated with Debbie's death were banished. There were no more winter vacations. We would never revisit the scene, and, when possible, we made long detours to avoid entering the state where the accident had occurred.

As tangible evidence of his renunciation of the frivolous diversions that had attracted the Almighty's malign notice, dad burned his road maps.

Dad took Debbie's death the hardest. He'd swerved off the road into the ditch to avoid being hit by the oncoming white pickup that was passing on a curve. No one thought it was his fault, except maybe him. On Debbie's next birthday I asked, "Dad, I don't understand?" He shook, a sharp cry escaped him, and he clung to me, convulsing. Then he abruptly pushed me back and walked away. Had the wrong child survived?

On the first anniversary of her death he disappeared after dinner. There was no ignoring the significance of the date and the house had been growing quieter each day as it approached. That night conversation during dinner was sparse. Even grace was offered in silence; unprecedented. I wasn't immediately aware, after the meal, of dad's absence until mom started hunting through the house, increasingly frantic. I watched, unobserved, while she checked the top shelf of the hall closet. The disused shotgun was resting in its place.

I knew where he had to be and went out to the backyard where my father stood, staring up at the cold remote canopy of stars, tears frozen on his cheeks. I reached for his hand, afraid I'd be rejected. He took it and we walked into the warmth of the house.

2

How to become a football star

"Hey, you with the fancy-pants name . . . yeah," checking his clipboard, "Smythie the Fourth – take another lap. Get that blue blood of yours pumping."

If you played high school sports you'll recognize that as the voice of a high school coach. The handicap of the fancy handle had accompanied me to high school, unchanged. The coping mechanisms, however, had to evolve.

It's okay for elementary school kids to tussle on the playground; not so for teenagers. Fighting, unless for honor – a girl, a slight – wasn't cool, and certainly not because someone teased you about your name. Plus, the potential to inflict serious injury goes up with increasing age. That may explain why we've created institutionalized combat for older boys: football. Being a starter on the high school football team provides all the tough cred a teenager needs.[*] His name can be Percival Poindexter Fauntleroy Throckmorton Crumpet the Third, and he can wear his hair in a flowing golden pageboy; as long as he starts on Friday night, no one doubts him.

The coach had decided that my primary skill was catching a football – despite no evidence to support this – which meant I was the poor punching bag who would cut across the middle, leap up, and struggle to bring the ball under control. That was the problem; while I was batting the ball around my adversaries were regrouping. I'd latch onto the ball just as two or more psychopaths tried to atone for their failure to cover better with a display of unbridled savagery. I hit the ground as the Greek chorus in the stands moaned, "Oooooh!"

The radio announcer reported these collisions the same way: "Oooooh! The Fort took a real shot . . . He's slow getting up . . . Now he's shaking it off and heading back to the huddle. There's a relief."

Relief my ass! Who would want to go to the huddle where they'd be assigned another suicide mission? I didn't belong on

---

[*] You had to be a starter; bench-warmers were essentially groupies; and when has 'second-string' ever denoted anything positive?

the football field, especially buried under 300 – 600 pounds of linebackers, cornerbacks and safeties. This was a heavy price to pay for a pretentious name.

The Fort? You may have already figured it out. Smythie the Fourth had been rechristened The Fort for his seeming impregnability. This was flattering and I encouraged it, responding cheerily to salutations of 'Fort Max' and 'The Fort,' until it became clear that the nickname was a public challenge, including to *my own idiot teammates!* Even they, during practice scrimmages, thought they could prove something by putting a dent in The Fort. This was also known as 'Taking it to the Max.' What colossal assholes. Fort Max was continuously hurt from mid-August until Thanksgiving. But tough guys, especially those with sissy names, play hurt. A cloud of Mentholatum vapors follows us through the school halls.

That was the tough-guy defense mechanism. There was still the wise-ass mechanism which came in handy on the gridiron.

It's not a secret; most football players are not Mensa prospects. Just look at the nicknames: 'Moose,' 'Hulk,' 'Meat.' I could get open with any of the following lines, delivered as I ran directly at the defensive back as he started to backpedal:

"Careful, man. Your shoe's untied." The genius would look down and I'd make my cut.

"Holy shit! Check out that cheerleader! You can see her beaver!" No teenage boy is going to pass up the chance – no matter how implausible – for a glimpse of snatch. I'd sell the act by keeping my head turned toward the sidelines as I shouted. The dope would look and I'd cut to the middle.

If the pass route was straight down field, any number of taunts would work as the backpedaling began:

"I fucked your sister last night."

"My dad says you and I are probably brothers."

"Don't step in that dog shit."

"They say you have the tiniest pecker on the team."

The hesitation – sometimes he even stopped and headed toward me – allowed me to run past him into the open. Being fleet of foot is good, but if you're not, you can compensate by being quick of tongue.

A Precious Truth to Us Is Giv'n
- U. Phillips, 1949

Of course you've heard – and probably dismissed – the malarkey about sports building character. Justifiable skepticism notwithstanding, there was a life lesson to be taken from football:

We, as humans, have multiple objectives and it's important to remember which are the higher priority ones.

That seems pretty self-evident. How could anyone act otherwise? Here's how –

Objective: Avoid ridicule about a sissy name, and, in the worst case, ostracism.

Means to avoid ridicule/ostracism: Be a starter on the football team.

What's wrong with this? Nothing. Except there's another objective not taken into account: NOT LIVING IN CONSTANT PAIN. I worked this out in my senior year. Too late, but a useful lesson. Later you'll see how this lesson – *Remember What's Important* – is applied to stay alive.

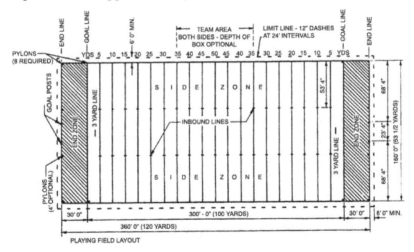

PLAYING FIELD LAYOUT

Will the Real God please stand up

God? The search for answers about God was put on hold to allow for the more pressing study of females and how to access their withheld favors. Sad to report, being a gridiron gladiator doesn't provide that hoped for access; it just allows you to try – and fail – at a higher level than do non-athletes. I know this because in college I found myself dating in the minor leagues again. Lower value prizes; same unsatisfactory result.

And I was still pretty steamed at the Almighty. He expects to be venerated for His compassion when, in Debbie's case, He'd failed to exhibit any? *You can't have it both ways, God.* It wasn't hard to lose interest in a deity that hypocritical. Although I felt uneasy about it.

I Hear Thy Summons From On High
- J. Milton, 1725

Course selection in college can be pretty hit and miss; I'm assuming this applied to many of you as well. When we entered as freshmen we were genuinely interested in the content of the courses, but, in the name of providing us with a broad education – and ensuring continued employment for the faculty of influential departments – we were herded into a full schedule of required classes. By the time we were allowed any real choice our enthusiasm had waned and course selection had become a function of a) which classes were still open because we'd only belatedly bestirred ourselves to register, and b) of those courses still available, which were easiest.

I remark on this because from this haphazard approach to course selection a curious pattern emerged: A high proportion of the classes I landed in dealt with God and religion. Not my intention.

> Mid-term exam question, *Anthropology 216: Magic, Witchcraft, and Religion.*
>
> "There is no explanation for evil. It must be looked upon as a necessary part of the order of the universe. To ignore it is childish, to bewail it senseless."
> W. Somerset Maugham
>
> Discuss
>
> (Right up my alley. I got a B+)

Was I being called? At that age (18-21) when, in rare fits of introspection, you're looking for direction and meaning in your life it's possible to entertain the conceit that your current circumstances – often hung over, rarely prepared for class, pulling mediocre grades, striking out with women – are a test of character to prepare you for greater things.

If so, I wouldn't be the first to turn it around after a shaky start. Just look at this sampling from a long list of flawed men who still made their mark:

- David committed adultery and had the cuckolded husband killed.
- Adam was a blame shifter.
- Noah was a boozer.
- Lot – you might not believe this, or want to believe it – offered up his daughters to be gang raped.
- Jacob was a pathological deceiver.
- Moses threw violent temper tantrums.
- And Solomon puts even NBA stars to shame – 1,000 sex partners. He had a thing for foreign women.

By these standards I didn't look so bad; maybe there was cause for hope. I'd been able to forget about God. Was He trying to re-establish contact? Was *I* destined for greater things? A friend gave me flying lessons and I wore a t-shirt –

Pilots.
Looking Down on
Everyone Else Since 1903.

Capitalizing on a pretentious name

If life hadn't gotten simpler, it was at least less painful. No football in college. Boise State was midway through a thirteen consecutive conference-titles run; there was no place on the team for a receiver of low ability and zero enthusiasm. And that demonstration of toughness was no longer as important.

Increasingly, people took the name as an indicator of noble lineage, although it couldn't be parlayed into anything useful. Rather than granting easy access to the parlors and billiard rooms of old-wealth Boston and Philadelphia families, the name attracted low-born social climbers from Detroit and Houston. Worse luck, it attracted Tiffany.

Tiffany Pratiloma plays an unsupporting rôle in this story. Curiously, we both assumed that the other was to the manor born. I assumed as much on the strength of her dazzling patrician looks and reserve. I misread her taciturnity as sagacity; actually, she just never had much to say. Until later, when she took it upon herself to keep me fully informed of defects in my character, manners, appearance, and friends.

For her part, she initially assumed that anyone with my name couldn't come from the rank and file. Further, she was impressed, when we met, that I was in the process of becoming an Officer *and* a Gentleman (USAF model). It was near the completion of this seventy-seven day transformation that 'destiny brought us together' – as Tiff and I referred to it during that brief early period when we still believed our encounter had been fortuitous – in a San Antonio bar.

The manly art

Let's set the scene here. This wasn't a bar like you find in other parts of the country: dark rooms where a few broken men sit on stools, stare straight ahead, and get drunk. No – and although *The Reverse Cowgirl*'s[*] name vastly exaggerated the amorous possibilities – this was a perfect Texas bar. It was big and noisy, illuminated by neon signs that flashed beer logos and clocks featuring guys in red hunting coats. Coming through the blue air and country music the click of pool balls was balm to a troubled soul.

Unfortunately it was populated by imperfect Texans. At the next table two sailors from Corpus Christie were engaged in a belching duel. Unable to control the direction of pressure, they'd occasionally fart by mistake. Their reaction to these mishaps signaled that this was the height of humor in the Navy.

At the other near table two young women with their backs to us were being subjected to a string of witless double entendres from their beaus, Larry and Ralph. We picked up the names quickly as the women exclaimed "Larry!!" or "Ray-alph!!" in response to every rib-tickler these two merry jesters ground out. Sample: "Ah find it *hard* to make love to a woman; y'know wad Ah mean Lar?" Snickers from Lar; "Ray-alph!!" from one of the women.

Jeff, my roommate, and I hadn't come for beer or atmosphere. We'd come to get laid. As the evening slipped past I sat

---

[*] We can assume that the lifers in the Texas state office that registers business names were unaware of the meaning of the term.

immobilized by the growing conviction that any overtures I might make to a female would result in rejection and quotable rebukes that would quickly circulate through our squadron. This deepening despondency wasn't helped by methodical Jeff who was cheerfully cataloguing every woman that entered the bar, "Good face . . . dumpy bod . . . with a guy . . . could be her father."

After fortifying himself with Lone Star for an hour, Jeff announced that he was ready to go into action and, lurching to his feet, tilted in the direction of a pair of animated girls seated at the far end of the room. That precipitated the Great Bar Fight.

It really wasn't much of a fight, but it had lasting and lamentable consequences. Here's the summary:

As Jeff passed the next table one of the sailors tripped him. Arms wind-milling as he went down, Jeff cleared the drinks off the two couples' table and into their laps.

Muttering apologies to the couples, I confronted the tripper.

The offending swabbie came up into my face, hands on hips, feet spread. That seems like an invitation, doesn't it? I kneed him in the nuts.

Later we were cautioned in hand-to-hand combat training that the crotch kick is a risky play. The effect isn't immediate, giving your adversary a few seconds to retaliate before the pain sets in. Not, however, in this case. Groaning, the swabbie sank to the floor, and his companion rose to his feet.

The second sailor bordered on caricature: he was big, his hands hung almost to knee level and he breathed noisily through his mouth. I took refuge behind the table Jeff had just cleared, to the protests of the two men seated there. "Naow look here boys, don't go gettin' us caught up in yer troubles," while one of the women whined, "Jaysus, Ray-alph, do somethin'." Ralph looked unwell.

You'd think that public-spirited citizens would intervene, wouldn't you? Don't count on it. The men at the other nearby tables were studying the contents of their glasses. Meanwhile the big sailor across the table shifted left and right and, with a grunt, made his move. Jeff chose this moment to rise as the big swabbie stepped over him and they both went down, sweeping the ashen Ralph out of his chair and onto the floor with them. There was much pummeling – it was difficult to determine who was fighting with whom – and then – surprise – Jeff succeeded in tying up the big sailor in a headlock.

This freed Ralph to get to his feet, but his resurrection was ill-timed. He caught a haymaker to the mid-section, delivered by the tripper who'd managed to rise to his knees. The punch looked weak but Ralph buckled forward, convulsed once, and puked on the head of his assailant. It was not a pretty fight.

I circled behind the kneeling tripper – he was drenched in a heavy coating of the undigested contents of Ray-alph's stomach and distracted – and kicked him in the nuts again. He resumed the fetal position as Ralph collapsed on top of him.

So far, so good. Four guys brawling on the floor, and Max floating like a butterfly around them. But it seemed inevitable that the tide of battle would turn against us, when – as proof that fortune does sometimes smile upon the just – two cops burst through the door – they must have been parked outside – blowing whistles and shouting in alarmed voices.

"Boy, am I glad to see you guys; these dipshits are wrecking the place." The cops interpreted my greeting as that of a peacemaker and without pausing for questions hauled off Ralph and the groaning tripper, the two most visibly incapacitated combatants. The big sailor looked alternately truculent and pensive – exhausting work for him – but left when one of the officers returned to inquire whether anyone needed medical attention.

O Mystery of Love Divine
- T. H. Gill, 1864

Ralph's date was gorgeous. She had flawless skin and jet-black hair that curled out over her shoulders. A classic beauty: high cheek bones, small nose and her wide mouth framed perfect teeth. She sat erectly with one arm resting across her lap, the other on the table. I checked her breasts, which weren't large, and decided that they were firm and flawless. She looked slender, more so than I'm normally attracted to, but a black dress tends to shrink a figure. Her face was slightly tipped up and her large dark eyes were fixed on me questioningly.

"Hi. I'm sorry about this. I'm Max Brown."

"The Fourth," added helpful Jeff.

She was Tiffany. I was in love.

Cue the violins. Our eyes locked in an ocular embrace seen only on the worst soap operas. Larry broke this clinch with the announcement that *someone* should try to bail out Ralph. Getting no takers he muttered sullenly that the girls had their own 'whales' (Texan for automobile, possibly derived from wheels?) and, recovering his cowboy hat, made an unsteady departure. Leaving Jeffrey and me, flushed with our recent victory over the unsavory navies, and two awestruck cupcakes waiting for us to make our move.

The point of recounting the Great Bar Fight is that it explains a lot about Tiffany's and my subsequent marital difficulties. There I was, Max, Vanquisher of Scurvy Swabbies, giddily smitten with myself and, as a consequence, quick to fall in love with anyone else. From Tiffany's standpoint, I must have looked pretty good. Confident – no, make that cocky – meting out justice, not a mark on me, a movie musketeer.

It could only go downhill from there. I've often thought, with teeth grinding, had Tiff and I met in normal boy-meets-girl circumstances I would have passed her by. Or, more likely, she me.

How to hustle chicks

I know I said my name brought me no advantage – and ultimately in this instance it did not – but any moron could have seen that Tiffany was intrigued by the possibility of a pedigree. Her questions about my lineage were easy to evade and I didn't go out of my way to discourage visions of baronial halls, obsequious servants, early morning hunts with the hounds, vast acreages grazed by the occasional thoroughbred, and global financial interests. It's remarkably easy to project false modesty by couching the truth in words that imply the reality is far grander.

"The fourth? You mean like you're number four with the same name?"

"I'm afraid it's most likely due to a lack of creativity, masquerading as respect for tradition."

Isn't that a great line? Delivered with just a bit of clip to the speech that one might associate with New England wealth. You should read it again.

I have my moments.

Jeff and I took the two recently vacated chairs as names were exchanged. Tiffany was even more fabulously beautiful at eye level. "I'm also afraid your dress is ruined. And your drink gone. Will you permit me to replace both? You were having?"

"Um. White wine spritzer. And don't worry about the dress. It'll clean right up."

"I can't do that. The family would never forgive me. Look, there must be a Neiman Marcus in San Antonio. We may not have an account there, but if you could pick out something you like I'll arrange the billing."

This was going overboard. Jeff leaned forward; a look of incredulity – or maybe indignation – signaled he was about to blow the whistle. "But, Jeffrey," I continued, "while I'm ordering drinks, what can I get for you?" Good old Jeff. He'd let this whole monstrous lie go unchallenged for a Lone Star. "Another beer?"

"Actually I think I'll switch. Get me a twelve-year single malt, would you, my good man? Laphroaig would be first choice, but I trust your judgment should that be unavailable. Make it a double."

Greedy fucker.

What I told Tiffany that evening was that for most of my years I'd been an only child (the one indisputable fact she picked up all evening), my parents were getting on (aren't we all?) and family tradition demanded service to our country (not a total fabrication; my father had been a WWII Seabee in the south Pacific where he made Japanese flags from parachutes and sold them to sailors as genuine war souvenirs) before I'd be called upon to manage the family's business interests (also not completely without basis: a Dairy Queen franchise in Pocatello, ID). She bought it.[*]

---

[*] I would pay dearly for this deception over the coming years.

Tiffany was perfect. You could show her off at a function; engage her in intimate talks, knowing that her participation would be limited to understanding nods and smiles; she came equipped with the carnal appetite every young man prays for; and she always laughed at my jokes. She continued to believe that I'd temporarily descended from a higher station in life – although I belatedly tried to impress upon her the humbleness of my origins – and she interpreted my fondness for beer, rude noises, and vulgar language as simply an attempt to fit in. We eloped – in observance of another venerated and conveniently economical Brown family tradition – two months after the Great Bar Fight, just before the start of pilot training. Tiffany had only one question about our future lives in the embrace of Uncle Sam: how much did it pay?

3

Ah, marriage. The transformation was instantaneous. One minute a nubile nymphomaniac and adoring companion, the next a middle-aged virago, a harpy, a harridan, a shrew. A new husband anticipates an effort will be made to domesticate him, but Tiffany's transformation went beyond anything imaginable. I was stunned by the change and considered a variety of explanations: hormones, the move, change of role? The common element in all of these was that they were based on the tenuous hope that this was a transitory condition; Tiff would soon return to normal. And she did, thanks to a grand and timely gesture which is all too rare these days, especially among medical professionals.

No Gurlz Allowed

Shortly after our arrival at pilot training the flight surgeon, a physician of fine character and deep understanding, summoned the wives of the student pilots for a friendly confab on the important rôle of the student pilot's wife. I and two other guys witnessed this virtuoso performance through a half-opened door. [*]

"Ladies, thank you for coming. I wanted to talk with you about how important your part is in your husbands' success – even his survival." The young wives all froze to attention at that last word. "I don't want to alarm you. After all, military aviation becomes safer every year. But I don't want to keep the truth from you either. In the coming year your men will be learning how to fly temperamental aircraft at speeds approaching five hundred miles an hour just a few feet above the ground. Similarly, they'll be flying in close formation with three other aircraft at speeds well above 600 miles an hour with wingtips only a few inches apart. Obviously a steady hand and clear concentration are vital."

---

[*] This has little to do with the larger story (how to find love and money) but it does speak volumes to the culture of the USAF. It's included because it's a great speech; up there with the Gettysburg Address. Perhaps required reading in college speech classes?

A pretty brunette in advanced pregnancy had started to tear up and the flight surgeon hastened on.

"But, despite the challenges, we have never – I repeat, *never* – had a student death on this base. Why?" He looked around for dramatic effect, but paused too long and one wife raised her hand to answer the rhetorical question. Ignoring her, "It's because we all do our part as professionals. The instructors were selected for their experience and training. My job is to make sure no students fly when their health might affect their performance. Your job, and that's why we're here today, is to send them off to work in a positive frame of mind, a mind that's free of domestic problems that might be a distraction as he's attempting an engine-out landing or bad weather approach."

The women looked stunned. How do you do that? Domestic life means domestic problems. Kids get sick; the car breaks down; the dog urinates on his dress shoes; your mother announces she's coming to stay for two months. Domestic life happens. The good doctor had answers.

"Let's start with the basics. Half the time these guys have to be out here before sunup. Make sure they arrive well fed – some protein like eggs or bacon would be a good idea. For variety maybe an occasional breakfast steak. Brain food.

"We have studies that prove the obvious. The more a man bonds with the other pilots in the squadron, the more likely he is to do well, and, on the down side, the less likely he is to have an accident. Loners don't do well. While on the face of it you might think that hanging around the stag bar is inconvenient while you're wrestling with diapers and house cleaning, for the student pilot it's part of the job."

Now let's stop right there. That's just pure unadulterated horseshit. Hanging around the stag bar only translates into hangovers and mistakes in the air. I've been there. But this physician, this master of oratory not seen since Mark Antony stood beside Caesar's grave, had them lapping up every crumb. He finished strong.

"Ladies, I don't need to tell you we live in an unfriendly world. For almost two hundred years men like your husbands have kept us safe and strong. You are now partners in protecting our democracy and I know that, like the women who've gone before you, you'll step up to this challenge and provide the support and understanding that will keep your husbands safe and able to provide the protection our country depends on." I wanted to barf, and cheer. How can he get away with this? But get away with it he did.

The meeting broke for refreshments. The wives, eager to enlist as active partners in defending America's freedom, approached the great doctor with questions about optimum hours of sleep for a pilot, the best distractions when he seems worried, and one aggressive wife, slightly older than the others, raised the most fundamental question of them all – from my perspective: "What about sex, doctor? I've read that some athletes avoid sex before important games because it takes away from their concentration or performance. Would that be true for a pilot?" Side conversations died; my two buddies and I moved closer to the door.

"Well," said the great doctor, "that's an excellent question." *Oh oh. That's an excellent sign you're stalling, doc.*

Not to worry. He furrowed his brow, stroked his chin, looked over the heads of his audience, pursed his lips and gave every indication he was searching for a delicate way to frame an answer that was known and accepted by all in his profession. That's how good this guy was.

"Athletes are notoriously superstitious." He paused for this self-evident truth to sink in. "In medicine we have to base our advice on what science tells us. I can assure you there's no evidence to suggest that the minuscule change in hormonal levels resulting from ejaculation has *any* effect on concentration or mental skills or motor skills. On the other hand, our colleagues in psychiatry are pretty clear on the negative effects an argument over sex would have on the same set of attributes that are important to safe flight."

He turned toward the woman who had asked the question, "I thank you for raising – courageously – one of the most important issues there is. I never know how to introduce it and I'm grateful to you, ma'am, for getting this out into the open." The woman blushed and, for a moment, it looked like some of the others might applaud.

Hot diggety dog! Pretty fucking clear: Sex is not at all bad for you. Withholding sex is bad for you. Could not be clearer! My two buddies and I would have linked arms and broken into a jig had not fear of discovery prevented us. This was my introduction to the boys club known as the United States Air Force. The doctor, by the way, rarely had to pay for his drinks in the Officers' Club or stag bar.

The making of a misogynist

We student pilots couldn't believe our good fortune. The effect of the lecture was immediate and, in my case, especially welcome; in the space of an hour Tiffany the Termagant had been transformed into a Stepford Wife.

Alas. It couldn't be permanent and as the months rolled by the effect wore off. Our wives noted, with relief (to give some of the tougher women the benefit of the doubt), that none of their husbands had bought the farm. In fact, we seemed to be having the time of our lives. Had the dangers been overstated? Tiffany – and every other student pilot's wife – began to question the emotional benefits of the long hours spent in the stag bar or at late night poker parties. Tiff also seemed perplexed that we weren't moving in an elite group of chic and daring jet-setters whose conversation glittered as brightly as their jewelry. Our social outings were the antithesis of what she'd expected. The men would take in volumes of beer while executing flight maneuvers with their hands; the women talked of their infant children and cast disapproving glances at their husbands. No clever repartee, no tinkling laughter, no champagne, no yachts.

Tiffany, as it turned out, would have no need for the information exchanged on the distaff side of the room, information that was limited to toilet training, feeding schedules, and formula preparation.

She gradually lost her taciturnity, her reserve, and her reluctance to criticize. By the time our class had progressed to advanced instruments she was on my case night and day. This led to my first law of marital relations: Despite all the Oedipal nonsense about a man marrying his mother, he doesn't; he marries his wife's mother.

Tiffany's mother appeared to be a genial woman, but one who'd found much to fault – perhaps with reason – in her husband. Apparently she believed the poor sod could be salvaged, and in that spirit generously shared with him her many insights into the defects of his character. The effect of this negative feedback on my father-in-law was hard to determine, but the effect on Tiffany was obvious. Her rôle model and image of a married woman was to be middle-aged, waspish, hypercritical, and sarcastic.

Compounding the impact such an unfortunate example would have on her married behavior, Tiffany was an only child, same as myself from age ten onwards, but, unlike me who had felt marginal to the family, Tiffany had been the unwavering focus of attention. She acknowledged that she'd gotten away with murder. As she grew to become a stunningly beautiful woman she encountered no pushback to the same high-handedness – from men, anyway – and the behavior was cemented in place.

As graduation from flight training approached, my home life became unbearable. If she prepared a meal, I never helped out. If I prepared a meal, I always did it wrong. If I was away from the house, I was never there when she needed me. And if I was home she never had time to herself. The reliable inclusion of those two adverbs – never and always – elevated the *annoyance du jour* up to the category of Ingrained Character Flaw.

This steady onslaught took its toll. The criticisms became self-fulfilling and I was soon stumbling and bumbling about the place, burning food, unable to deliver a perfectly reasonable and accurate explanation for my late arrival, making simple driving mistakes, and painfully aware that in less than three months I'd gone from a self-confident, cheerful lad to a middle-aged burlesque of the hen-pecked husband. Pathetic Max.

I came close to formulating a second law of marital relations: that we create the mate we either expect or want, I couldn't decide which, and then scrapped it. It seemed possible – no, it was likely – she was creating what she expected, but I was damned if Tiffany bore any living resemblance to someone I wanted to cohabit with. Until, of course, I was face-to-face with her and found myself instinctively eager to please a beautiful woman. Perhaps that tendency to melt in the presence of beauty could be expressed as another law of marital relations.

Take Courage
- J. H. Johnston, 1907

As the end of the thirteen-month training program neared, the partying picked up. A hallowed Air Force tradition was the Wing Dining-In, or WingDing, for which everyone would bedeck themselves in a ridiculously modified tuxedo, sit stiffly at long tables in the O Club, and get falling down drunk. There was a strong culture of alcohol abuse in the Air Force at the time.

Clutching bottles of wine, at around midnight we took the party outside to participate in another hallowed tradition: jumping up and down on the rooftops of officers' residences. After several dramatic but not fatal mishaps the party wound down and I drove home – covering one eye to kill the double vision – where a welcoming committee eagerly awaited my arrival.

"Just where have you been? Huh? Do you know what time it is?"

With the courage that comes from a) immoderate amounts of alcohol, and b) surviving a fall from a roof into a rhododendron, the retorts, counters, jabs and rejoinders that had been long queued up came out. This new resolve may have been bolstered by the fact that Tiffany didn't look as intimidatingly beautiful as usual; her face was contorted with anger and the doubled features – two noses, four eyes, etc. – didn't do her justice.

"You know exactly where I've been, Tiff. If not, doesn't the silly uniform I'm wearing tip you off? And time. Let's just see here. The little hand is between the three and four so maybe 3:30?" This sarcasm would have been more effective if I hadn't had to cover an eye again to read the watch.

"Don't you be smart with me, mister." God's great swinging willy. She was talking to me as if I were a child. "Your forehead has a scrape and there're leaves under your collar."

"Smart? Golly, ma'am. You know I ain't smart. Least wise, that's what you're always tellin' me."

"What are you talking about?" She looked worried; maybe thought she'd overplayed her hand?

"What am I talking about? For months you've been telling me I'm incompetent, unable to carry out small tasks, a bad driver, and basically a second rate human being. Here's a surprise: I DO NOT FUCKING LIKE IT!"

Can you predict the reaction to a raised voice? Sure you can: tears.

"How (blubber, sniffle) can you say those things to me?"

"How can I say them? The mystery is how I've kept them bottled up so long." The response to this was more snuffling and sobbing. The tears were getting to me and I was about to apologize when I caught her sneaking a look to gauge my reaction. Calculating bitch.

"The tears aren't working, Tiff." I had no idea I could be such a good debater when dead drunk.

"Well I don't think I want to stay with a man who gets drunk and abusive."

With nothing to lose at this point, "That's your decision to make. I've thought for some time that your talent for fault-finding might be better applied to the reform effort your mother's making on your father." That was a mistake. A general rule, men: Never bring her mother into the argument.

"You don't dare bring my mother into this!" See how that went? "You don't hear me complaining about *your* mother although, God knows, there's plenty to complain about." I arched an eyebrow menacingly, but it had no effect. "My mother is a wonderful person, and she . . ."

"I'm sure she is," I cut in, "but getting back to the central topic. If you want to be a constant nag, a common scold, be it somewhere else. I want to be happy. I want to feel I'm useful in the relationship, and I really, really, really don't want every goddamn thing I do second-guessed and criticized."

"I didn't know you had such thin skin."

"Maybe I do. I hadn't thought about it. But, new rules: If you want this to work, then you have to get off my case. If you can't do that, let's call it quits because I can't deal with the non-stop carping and complaining."

Damn, I was good! Firm, clear.

Her response was to stomp into the bedroom and lock the door behind her. Just in time. A sinking spell sent me scrambling for the bathroom to disgorge the poisons churning in my stomach. I figured I'd have to be sharp in the morning..

The message must have gotten through because things started to improve. At first Tiffany couldn't conceal that it required a near super-human effort to hold her tongue and she'd often interrupt her own critical statements with, ". . . I forgot; you don't like to hear these things."

After a few more months this gave way to, "You know what?" Pause and scowl. "Never mind," leaving the clear impression that she was editing out criticism. But eventually even these vestiges of her former voluble displeasure disappeared and within a few more months she'd settled into the position that she maintained throughout the rest of our marriage: an (usually) unvoiced disappointment with all that I was or would be.

Coincidentally, the less she criticized me, the less she seemed to like me. Was the carping a pressure-relief valve? And when that was blocked, all her displeasure remained bottled up inside? Just a hypothesis. I'm not the best guy to propound on the caliginous recesses of the female psyche.

I studied "It pays to increase your word power" too.

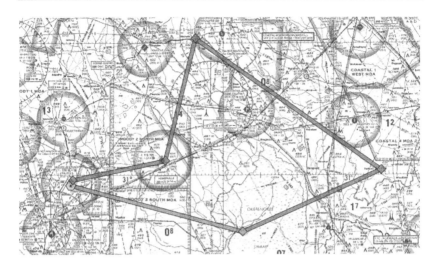

Aeronautical chart, military training areas. The heavy lines are a high-low route I flew for a check ride of navigational ability. The magenta segment was flown at 39,000'; the blue segments 75' above the surface.

Section II

War is rarely a good idea
and
this one was an especially bad idea.

Vietnam War Memorial, Washington, DC

4

Something you may have noticed is the unwillingness of many – perhaps most – Vietnam war vets to talk. Are the memories too painful to recall? Do the inquiries seem voyeuristic? Or is it that they simply did nothing worth talking about? For me it's the voyeurism. What I'd like to say is, "You want to know what war's like? Well, Gomer, you won't have to wait long. Our political leaders, those with tiny peckers and short memories, will land us in another one soon enough. Then you can find out first hand." But none of us say that. We say as little as minimal courtesy demands. Will writing be easier?

I've 'Listed in the Holy War
- J. Macmillan, 1835

For most vets of that era their military service began and ended with Vietnam; they joined to fight or, more likely, were drafted knowing they would have to fight. For me the war was an unpleasant surprise. I joined the Air Force to fly, not to fight, and emphatically not to die. Vietnam was an unwelcome interruption in the barnstorming. What happened is this:

We were refilling beer mugs during a break in a marathon game of liar's dice, and my flight instructor was waxing nostalgic about past planes he'd flown. "Ya' know, Brown, I think you'd make it as a 101 jock. It's a hell of a plane and the reconnaissance job is the greatest. My squadron was in Fontainebleu. Most clear days we'd go out and buzz nudist resorts in the south of France. Got some great pictures." He closed his eyes and chuckled. Apparently they were great pictures.

"A good bird, sir?"

"Out-fucking-standing! Held speed records 'til the 104 came along. Hot. Has a pitch-up tendency so we couldn't climb out in afterburner in the suds, but that just shows you what a strong machine it is."

I was in the market for a good job. Several of our instructors had *Einbahnstrasse* shoulder patches, a remnant of a past assignment. The 'one way street' was to Moscow. These guys had been flying F-101s that carried enough fuel to deliver a nuke deep in Soviet territory, but not enough to come home. Their

survival kit included a few small gold coins with which to purchase cooperation during the long walk back through Russia.

Then there were the 106 jocks. Their patches identified
them as the *6th Missile*. The plane carried five air-to-air missiles
and was, itself, the sixth. Their orders were to ram in-coming
Soviet bombers when all else failed.

You'll agree that taking pictures of naked women was better. France was no longer open – the French had kicked the yan-
quis out – but there were other choice European bases. It
sounded good.

The Air Force employed the felicitous device of permitting
graduating student pilots to select from available assignments in
the order of the students' class standing. I was third in my class;
I got third pick. As luck would have it there was one RF-101C
on the list of available assignments and I took it. My instructor
was proud, I was excited, and Tiffany was laying in Michelin
guide books.

How short-lived our joy. As 101 training was nearing completion it became evident that everyone was going to Asia.
Tiff's disappointment at missing out on Europe was leavened
by the news that combat pay would ease our financial straits.

Comfort was briefly taken in the fact that we reconnaissance
pilots wouldn't be bombing clinics or strafing orphanages;
hence, the argument ran, we'd be less interesting targets to our
adversaries. That hope foundered on a stunning statistic printed
in the *Air Force Times*: The mortality rate for RF-101C pilots in
Vietnam was a whopping 55 percent. If the significance of that
statistic escapes you, let's spell it out: a 101 recon jock stood
less than an even chance of completing his tour alive.

The implications were clear to me and I began to look for an
escape clause in my contract. I called an old family friend at the
CIA to see if I could transfer to Air America; if you're going to
die, do it for the right money. He said he'd never heard of Air
America. I applied for every advanced course in the book. No
luck. During the pre-deployment physical I informed the flight
surgeon that I'd developed an unnatural fondness for little boys,
recently revealed to me in dreams. He closed his eyes to register
his despair and told me to cough.

I didn't share the dismal statistic with Tiffany; others did. She elevated the probability of my imminent demise to a certainty and sought protection by progressively distancing herself. Her conversation became more formal – light topics, fully formed sentences. She looked surprised when I kissed her as if a casual acquaintance had taken a minor liberty which didn't merit a full rebuff but could scarcely be encouraged. She stopped notifying me of her daily plans and expressed mild annoyance if asked. When I finally boarded a chartered TWA plane for Vietnam my thoughts weren't focused on the perils ahead, but how to get even. The possibilities ranged from dalliance with an Asian beauty to infantile satisfaction at the prospect of Tiffany's sorrow when the chaplain came with tragic news of her heroic husband's fiery end.

Tell Me the Old, Old Story
- Birdie Bell, 1909

The tropical heat was a staggering surprise as we stumbled, dazed, out of the plane and onto the tarmac at Cam Ranh Air Base. Dragging our duffels, we were herded across the ramp to a large Quonset where an Army staff sergeant was tapping a pointer on a desk at the front of a long room of folding chairs.

"Sit down, gentlemen. First, I wanna be clear. I'm not a REMF." He pronounced this as a word. A few of our group nodded; most looked perplexed. "REMF is rear echelon mother-fucker. I've seen more action and wasted more gooks than any of you are likely to see in your lifetime. I'm here to tell you what it's gonna be like." At this point the aggressiveness went out of him and he launched into a thirty-minute briefing, delivered on autopilot. There was something in there about respect for local traditions; the ARVN were our partners; an assassin lurked behind every bush and beaded curtain; we were fighting for democracy and freedom; and then I dozed off as did many of the others.

The Defense Department's attention to the hazards of cultural insensitivity didn't end with the briefing. We were handed a pamphlet that informed us we were there at the invitation of a freedom loving government 'for the deeply serious business of helping a brave nation repel Communist aggression.' There were some tips on culture, a few phrases in Vietnamese, and, since Vietnam was on the metric system, charts for converting miles to kilometers and gallons to liters. Thus armed, we sallied forth to win the hearts and minds of our hosts.

Between Two Worlds
- J. Gill, 2014

War was not like the movies. The USAF pilots lived a starkly bifurcated existence. You were either in Little America – specifically at the country club – or some asshole in black pajamas was trying to kill you.

The fighting part was all too real. We heard about 105 and F-4 flights that might lose one-fourth of the planes trying to take out a single target. The survivors would look around the debriefing room and confirm their fears: not everyone had made it back. Then, the next morning they'd head out to the flight line, saddle up, and take off toward the same goddamned target.

The rest of the war was surreal. A swimming pool, Officers' Club, air conditioned hooches – many with a bar, videotapes flown in from the US to ensure no one missed an episode of *Bonanza*, and other comforts of home that made you wonder – but not forget – how you could've been peeing in your pants two hours earlier.

Some of the men took this cosseting as their due and protested loudly when their preferred brew was unavailable (someone in procurement had an incomprehensible and unshared liking for Falstaff). These tended to be the same men who were either in the O Club or on a mission. Did they even use their rooms? They also tended to be the True Believers who talked about their plans to finagle a second tour in order to continue killing commies for Christ. I certainly didn't belong among those zealots.

Compared to the disjointed life of the Air Force pilots who went from country club to combat and back to country club every day, the grunts and jarheads lived more consistent, if more brutal, lives. The differences between their circumstances and ours were underscored by strict segregation. At the top of the hill sat the Air Force housing and facilities. Down one step and behind a barbed wire fence, the Army had a few permanent buildings, but slept in tents. Further down the hill, and behind another barbed wire barrier, the Marines had the most primitive facilities. Fraternization across the services was not allowed.

The conscience of a USAF pilot was never troubled by this unequal treatment. We were America's most valuable and talented (and smart, and courageous, and handsome, etc.) defenders. We were entitled to better treatment. But you couldn't help notice that there were more dark-skinned men on the Army's side of the barbed wire. Did that have anything to do with it?

We did have one thing in common: no one had a guarantee of going home alive.

Tell Out the News
- N. A. Davidson, 1908

You had to spend time in the O Club to know what was going on, rumor, innuendo and hearsay being more credible than Armed Forces Radio Saigon which was heralding the steady advance of the forces of truth and enlightenment. The news reports in the O Club were at odds with the AFRS's sunny dispatches.

"Hey, Ng. Hand me the whole fucking bottle. No, the Black Label." The speaker is the left-seat pilot of a C-130 who flew the shuttle from Japan (and who would probably appreciate anonymity).

"You guys want to know how the war's going?" Ignoring the absence of interest from those of us hunched over our drinks along the bar, he continued. "I'll tell you how it's going. This morning I went out to the bird and a forklift is shoving covered pallets in. I could see the struts were already compressed and this guy just kept piling the shit in. I asked, 'What gives?' and two ARVN officers came over – armed to the teeth – and told me to file a flight plan to Jakarta. They said this was the personal property of General Nguyen Thanh. I said, sure, and went into the cargo bay to see what was up. I couldn't fucking believe it. Every fucking pallet was piled with gold ingots. Shiny fucking gold bars, just like in the fucking movies. I said there's no way this plane can get off the ground with this load. The ARVNs said it was the General's wish that his cargo leave immediately. I thought the fuckers were going to shoot me, right there on the flight line. So I filed, we closed up and set off on what I figured would be the shortest and last flight of my career. There were six ARVNs along for the ride – all majors and up – I guess to prevent us taking the gold to Brazil. Anyway, it took full fucking power just to roll forward. At first I thought the chocks hadn't been pulled." He paused to sip his Scotch. There were now expressions of interest up and down the bar.

"Never thought I'd be grateful for the lousy taxiways those Seabee pussies poured. First good ridge we hit, the left gear collapsed. End of trip. The ARVNs took this pretty hard and were probably wondering if the General might go lighter on them if they shot me and the rest of the crew right there.

"Hey, Ng. Can I get some ice for this shit?"

Meanwhile, AFRS was broadcasting rapturous accounts of the inexorable advance of ARVN and allied forces as Charlie fled in terror. Was General Nguyen – at that moment the 'president' of the freedom loving country we were fighting for – tuned to another station?

Something else you didn't pick up from AFRS: Who were the players in this game? An A-1E jock came in who'd bailed out near the DMZ.

"Here's a weird one for you guys. I was flying close support at Ia Drang and took a coupla' rounds. Thought I could nurse the bird back, but the oil pressure went tits up so I went over the side. Didn't get fucked up in the landing and was gathering up my 'chute when I heard the VPA crashing around on all sides. Then the weirdest thing happened. This really bizarre black chopper showed up, laid down some suppressing fire and dropped a yoke, so I climbed in. It couldn't get worse, right? But here's the really freaky part. The crew were wearing ski masks – how fucked up is that? I could see the skin on their hands was really dark, but they didn't have light palms like Africans would. But their skin looked too dark for Asians. I don't know who the fuck they were." He sat in wonderment while we waited for the answer. "They never spoke to me and after maybe twenty minutes they dropped me off in a clearing where a Jolly Green picked me up later. I just spent an hour looking at pictures of choppers over in the intel office. That thing that picked me up is definitely not a bird any of our guys know about. Or are talking about. Who the fuck were they?"

Good question. Who else was fighting in this war? Several of us listened to Hanoi Hannah for clues. She didn't seem to know either. Well, of course the CIA was there. They couldn't walk away from a fun war just because the Cavalry had arrived.* That said, some of the best information came from the spooks who were frequently in our Club, probably for the cheap drink. We were most interested in hearing what these guys would only hint at until they got drunk enough to open up: the black missions, especially those that took out ARVN units that Saigon feared might have developed wavering loyalties. There seemed to be a lot of ARVNs that were switching sides and we wanted to gauge the ebb and flow of the defections.

Among all the pilots who passed through the O Club, the CIA freelance pilots were the most tight-lipped; they were practical men. When informed there was a mission they'd go out to their B-26 or A-1 and open the Manila envelope on the seat. The envelope contained a description of the mission and a wad of cash. The pilot would count the money, read the mission, and decide whether he wanted to take it. Practical men.

You can see that there were lots of reasons to spend time in the O Club: refreshment, camaraderie, news, and a sobering perspective on the 'deeply serious business of helping a brave nation repel Communist aggression.' And, there wasn't a whole lot else to do.

---

* The spooks were fond of repeating, "It's not a great war, but it's the only one we have." Not funny the first time. Spook humor.

I'll Fly Away
- A. E. Brumley, 1932

It could get hairy and seemed destined to get hairier. Since nothing appeared to be slowing Charlie down, more ambitious targets were selected and the air war moved steadily northward where anti-aircraft defenses were better. Here's an example. Okay, not typical; actually one of the worst days.

As I finished a photo shoot and banked hard left, afterburners belching flame to accelerate, my head swiveled looking for telltale signs of MiGs and SAMs. The SAM warning box started to rattle indicating SAM radar tracking was looking for a target. Worst fears confirmed: There was the signature mushrooming of yellow smoke on the ground that indicated a missile was on its way.

The SA-2 relied on radar to find its quarry and radio guidance to shoot us down, but there was a rumor that they'd recently been outfitted with heat seeking sensors to improve their accuracy and overcome our countermeasures. If that was true our evasive measures would have to adapt.

You can twist and turn, but these dudes are pretty agile and they'll track you until doomsday – literally. With perfect timing you can dodge out of the way, but you have to keep doing it and at some point your luck will run out. The best recourse is to get the missile interested in some other target.

I threw out chaff to confound the radar tracking system and, since it was a clear day, headed toward the biggest heat source of them all, the sun. This put the plane in an unsustainable 60 degree climb. As the airspeed approached stalling, I shoved the nose over and to further reduce my attractiveness to the SAM's suspected heat sensor, shut both engines down. Now diving directly at the ground, the missile was coming up at me, and me down at it. There was enough airflow over the control surfaces to dodge, and the SAM passed 100 yards to my left. Wishing it a pleasant journey to the outer reaches of space, I was about to restart when another yellow mushroom blossomed directly below. I released more chaff.

Remember those high school algebra problems? Two trains leave distant cities, traveling at X and Y miles per hour. Where will they meet? This was the same problem, but with immediate practical implications. There wasn't a lot of air left between me and the ground. If I started the engines – and it takes time for them to light and spool up – that might signal my presence to the new SAM before it opted for the chaff or the sun. Plus, I would need room to pull out of the dive. Here's the algebra question:

Will the SAM accelerate quickly enough to get past before I went below the minimum altitude required to restart and pull out of the dive? Show all your work; there will be no partial credit awarded on this one.

Well, yes, obviously it did work out or you wouldn't be reading this. But the larger lesson was that the war wasn't getting any easier.

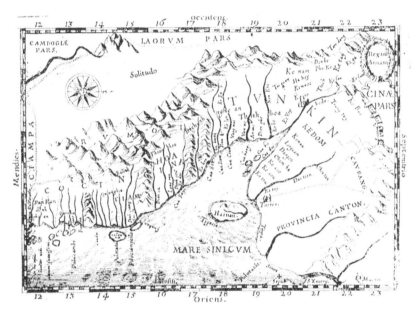

Vietnam , Alexandre de Rhodes, S.J., 1651.

5

How to survive a war

Max Brown's name is not among the 58,195 on the Vietnam War Memorial wall who died, nor was I among the 303,644 who were wounded, and that's because I was more devious than some and luckier than others.

Recon pilots were dying on the damage assessment flights because the enemy knew where and when we were coming. The Johnson White House was much concerned about public opinion and international political complications should a bomb fall on the wrong target or the wrong clinic be napalmed. To preclude such incidents, the Joint Chiefs were running the war from Washington. Targets were sent out, as were routes pilots were to fly to and from the targets. Damage assessment recon pictures were to be snapped exactly thirty minutes after a bombing raid as the JCS had concluded – on the basis of what evidence? – that this provided enough time for the smoke to clear but not enough time for Charlie to conceal the damage.

Now, picture what happens in the bunkers surrounding a bridge as American F-105s paste it with 750 pound bombs: everyone checks their watches because they know that in half an hour they'll have their chance for revenge. And they always mounted some form of attack. When Charlie didn't have SAMs or anti-aircraft guns, they'd deploy in a large X formation and everyone would fire their rifles directly upward as the clock wound down to 0:30. Sure enough, thirty minutes after the bombing run, here comes the Lone Ranger, shutters blazing, anus puckered, and prayers rising. Our motto was *Alone, Unarmed, and Unafraid.* What a crock.

> *Charlie invites you to a barbecue*
>
> **Where?** Phuc Yu Bridge
> **When ?** 0:30:00
> **Dress ?** Fit to Kill
>
> **No reply necessary**

In introductory psych classes they teach you about Skinner's superstitious pigeons. B. F. Skinner starved his pigeons to get their attention and then provided a pellet of food for a particular action, say two scratches with the left foot. He only had to do that a few times for the pigeon to make the connection. Then he'd select another meaningless activity and another until the pigeon would go through a lengthy routine of scratching, pecking, and cooing in an effort to win a pellet. As a variant on that, Skinner just let the pellets drop in at random intervals and the pigeon quickly started repeating nonsense sequences that – to the pigeon's thinking – were associated with the appearance of food.

That 55 percent figure is much like near starvation: it concentrates the mind. After a relatively quiet mission a pilot would review what had preceded it, what he was wearing, where he'd placed his feet as he walked out to the plane, and so on. After a lousy mission – two or more brushes with death; the two SAM incident above would qualify – he was likely to add things not under his control such as the date, the phase of the moon, and the silt content of the river off the end of the runway.

The upshot of all this analysis was that every pilot had a lucky pair of undershorts, followed the same path every day to the plane, conducted the pre-flight check in the same order, muttered the same words of self-encouragement during taxi out, and would pray for a credible mechanical problem that would scrub the mission.[*] Then, incredibly, the reccy pilots would try to get to the target exactly thirty minutes after the bombs had gone off.

The only explanation I have for this suicidal behavior was that punctuality was the one challenging part of the job. Anyone could find the target; if you could get to the general neighborhood the dissipating smoke would take you the rest of the way. We all knew how to fly – and bail out when that became necessary. And any fool could turn on the cameras. The only thing – aside from surviving the run – that presented a challenge was

---

[*] Pilots, for all their talk of personal invincibility, are pathologically superstitious. Some WWII jocks flew with animals, others urinated on the wheel of their plane to show the contraption who was boss, one B-29 crew flew with a boomerang because boomerangs always come back, and the Good Luck Boot Shop sold a *lot* of boots to pilots in Vietnam.

arriving precisely on time. Such are the follies that arise from professional vanity.

I Saw the Light
- H. Williams, 1948

I bulls-eyed the thirty-minute mark once – the first mission – and never did again. (*Remember What's Important.*)

When you considered Charlie's habits it was better to be a little early than a little late. So accustomed was he to our punctuality that he didn't seem to set up to bag the recon plane earlier than 25 minutes after the strike. But Charlie had wonderful patience and wouldn't give up easily if you were tardy.

The best defense, of course, was not to arrive over the target at all. This could be accomplished by a mechanical abort (an air abort was preferable as it took so long to get back on the ground and airborne again that a hapless standby would be dispatched if the mission were deemed important enough) or by failing to find the target. A mechanical abort usually, but not always, required a reproducible failure. I calculated that for every three actual mechanical problems that I experienced I could fake one. "I dunno, Sarge. The landing gear wouldn't come up and I was pumping the fucking handle like I was jerking off Harry Reems. And now you say the mother works?"

Outright inability to find the target wasn't credible. I claimed that once and used up my quota. However, there was another avenue to avoid harm that I learned of – where else? – in the O Club bar.

"Hey recon weenie," the person addressing me was a major wearing an F-4 Tactical Fighter Squadron patch. "I don't know whether to thank you for a milk run or kick your ass for wasting our time."

"Explain?" His expression darkened, so I added, "Sir."

"You ever hear of Lang Giai bridge, Lieutenant?"

Of course I had. Just a week earlier I'd been dispatched to take the pics following a strike. What I'd found, and photographed, were a few concrete pylons standing in the river; the rest of the bridge was gone.

"My last visit, sir? Lang Giai no longer existed. The remnants were still pretty well defended so I can't recommend it as a tourist stop."

"No shit! We took that sucker out and lost two planes doing it. But lo and fucking behold, the brass thought it was still standing so we paid another call on it yesterday."

"I flew the post-strike recon, Major. Shot three carts. Anyone could see the bridge was down and I can't believe the film didn't show the same thing."

"Yeah, well you hang onto that story, Lieutenant," and he returned his attention to his Scotch.

No arguing with a half-drunk senior officer and fighter pilot, but what was amiss here? Was the film bad? Or did the brass pay no attention to what we brought back? If you lean toward the second option you're about to get further support. Two other guys in the squadron had similar stories to tell. They'd done photo shoots on demolished targets and learned later that another strike had been ordered. The REMFs weren't paying attention to the reconnaissance that was exacting a 55 percent toll on our pilots.

After a few days of simmering indignation, I accosted the squadron commander, Lt. Colonel UTMEC (Unable To Make Eye Contact), as we came out of the evening mess together. "Sir, I'm hearing from different sources that our intel is ignored by the brass." The CO continued to look straight ahead.

"What makes you say that, Lieutenant?"

"Three of us have done post-strike assessment runs on obliterated targets in the last few weeks. Then we learn that another strike was ordered." There was no reaction from the CO. "They're sending the Thuds and F-4s out to bomb rubble," I added, to ensure the message was clear.

Colonel UTMEC didn't shift his gaze from the darkness ahead. "Well, first, you have to wonder about your sources. If, and I repeat, *if* this is true, the brass are probably ordering insurance strikes. It's possible for the VC to rebuild these structures if we don't take them out completely."

Unsuccessful in changing the management of the war, I directed my attention to how this new information could be used to reduce my own peril. If no one was paying close attention to the film brought back, would it be possible to photograph a look-alike target, especially if the weather were bad? The major problem with this ploy was that you had to have some idea of what the assigned target looked like before you could select a plausible substitute. It took time and research to acquire a portfolio of lightly defended and photogenic buildings, bridges, footpaths, cisterns, dams, etc. In the guise of professional improvement I studied the photos brought back from easy missions in the hope that someday the opportunity would arise to substitute one of them for the assigned target.

As a side benefit of this study, I was able to hang around base ops and monitor the return of the 101s. The more I tried to reduce my own risk, the more I worried about someone else being shot down on a mission I'd weaseled out of. Grief is bad enough without the added burden of guilt.

Of all these stratagems – maintenance abort, look-alike target, lost – the one consistently available subterfuge was to miss the appointed hour. It was often possible to sneak into the air a few minutes early, climb to an unauthorized high altitude where I could make tracks without using up all the fuel, dive in supersonic, and then slow at the last instant to turn on the Brownie for the photo session. When everything went well I could arrive twelve to sixteen minutes ahead of schedule.

For distant targets you had more room to play with, especially to arrive late. My best effort included a ground abort, change of aircraft, a ground speed of 280 knots (450 was nominal), and a few lazy turns over a scenic area. I was two hours ten minutes late.

All of these stratagems became more difficult when the JCS decreed that two 101s would parade out together on each mission. It was suspected this was dubbed Double Exposure as the Joint Chiefs were more interested in getting film back than pilots. The squadron commander, however, called it Double Coverage and explained – while looking away from us – the advantages of having a buddy there to locate the spot of your crash for the body baggers. We pilots called it Double Jeopardy. Charlie probably called it Two-For-The-Price-Of-One.

Teaming up confirmed my worst suspicions. The boasts of the other jocks were based on fact; they did prize punctuality. I'd hoped that everyone was playing the same games I was; they weren't. Rather than fly with these misguided zealots, I tried to pair myself as often as possible with the new pilots. Given the high mortality rate, there was a steady stream of new boys.

The conventional wisdom was that you paired with an old hand who'd proven that he was both lucky and less likely to do something that would get you in trouble. My thought was that pairing with a new guy provided two advantages: First, I flew the lead airplane so I set the speed, the route, etc. Second, the new guy would assume that my disregard for punctuality was the norm and would follow unquestioningly as we rushed or dawdled to the target.

Meanwhile the 55 percent rule remained in force:

Tom Walsh died. His plane exploded over the target. Survived by a pregnant wife and two small children. Best guy in the world. Declared MIA against overwhelming evidence of his death to permit his family to continue receiving his regular paycheck and benefits.

Chuck Jacobs died. His plane rolled inverted as it went into the jungle. Survived by a wife and four children. Best guy in the world.

Bill Bare. You couldn't find a better guy. He never came back and no trace was ever found of him; his aircraft was discovered years later. Left behind a nice family, I understand.

Does every war have a special appetite for the good? This war claimed decent men who held doggedly to their integrity and values in the face of senseless barbarism.

The same war took carousing unfaithful drunks and made them decorated heroes. An F-5 jock who spent his hours either holding up the bar or at a whorehouse is a case in point. His plane was hit by ground fire immediately after takeoff and lost power. Gliding – dropping, really – toward an elementary school, he stayed with the plane to try – according to him – to clear the school. His path took him into a grove of palm trees which stripped off the bombs and external fuel tanks. The plane, now much lighter, was able to glide further and he cleared the school and bailed out safely. The Air Force PR people were delirious and the decoration machine went into overdrive. Probably not a bad guy at heart, but not a Boy Scout.

Will the Real God please stand up

Participation in the Vietnam war prompted reexamination of the nature of God. Killing the good while glorifying jerks goes way beyond bad taste and low pranks, a position I'd moved away from when Debbie was killed. God was perverse. God was nuts. Forget the flowing robes; picture a wild-eyed old man in a strait jacket.

Patient: *'God', real name unknown*

Observations: *Third session with 'God.' Aggressive behavior reported by orderlies. Pt rambled during session; told of childhood torture of small nations. Now imagines self omnipotent/beyond retribution.*

Clinical Diagnosis: *Textbook Theomania, extremely hostile, potential for violence.*

Treatment: *Continued p/a. 0.5cc melazine daily. Isolation from other pts.*

There may have been no atheists in WWII foxholes, but participation in an a- or im-moral war quickly undercuts your unquestioning belief that the God at the receiving end of your prayers gives a good shit. He's probably just toying with you. Maybe He enjoys seeing how you rationalize each new betrayal of your expectation that He'll reward the just and smite the unjust. Maybe He's a prick. Maybe just nuts. We can keep omniscient, omnipresent and omnipotent; scratch omni-benevolent.

Meanwhile: Tom, Chuck, Bill? Look them up on that cold sad wall on the DC Mall and say you're really sorry they died in a criminally stupid war. Don't be afraid to say it out loud. It's the least we can do. I'm serious. I, the writer, Max Brown, am asking you, the reader: please do this. We don't owe them thanks. We owe them an apology. [*]

How to deal with survivor's guilt

There is no way to deal with survivor's guilt.

Dealing with the brass

My junior wingmen went along unquestioningly with my disregard for standard procedure for three weeks and then I was summoned to the CO's office. He was standing, staring out the window when I entered, but he looked directly at me, briefly, which indicated that he felt emboldened by the presence of Right on his side.

"Brown," with a note of exasperation in his voice.

He paused for so long that I finally said "yes?" just as he resumed. "Do you have a watch?"

"Yessir." Good. I was never bothered by sarcasm. It was the red-faced, top of the lungs' ass-chew that got under my skin.

"Do you know what the little hands stand for?"

"Absolutely, sir."

"And although this exceeds the number of fingers and toes you have, you can count to thirty, right?"

"Can I ask what you're leading up to sir?"

His nerve failed him and his eyes swept quickly across me as he shifted his gaze from the window on one side of the room to the other. "Dammit, Brown. I want these new kids to do things right. We're s'posed to be over that target thirty minutes after the strike – or pretty close to it." A pleading quality had entered his voice. "They take their cue from you older heads (I was 23) and if they think you don't give fuckall they won't either." You had to feel sorry for the guy. He knew what was going on and he knew it was apeshit. "Do you understand what I'm telling you?"

"Sir, the system is apeshit."

---

[*] Thomas Walsh (Panel 10E, Row 85), Charles Jacobs (Panel 8E, Row 17), and William Bare (Panel 24E, Row 4).

His head snapped up. "I'm telling you the system is ape-shit?" He sat down heavily and placed his palms on his desk. His eyes fixed on his wedding ring. "The system is apeshit?" He almost sounded hurt. "Brown, don't tell me that."

The request was probably sincere. He didn't have the courage to oppose the system, even tacitly, and he was lousy at dissembling. He was being asked to acknowledge the moral corruption of the war, which he couldn't, and he was having trouble insisting that we go along with it. Poor bastard.

"I'm sorry sir. I spoke out of line. I'll try to improve my time accuracy." The CO smiled with relief and his right hand started up to shake mine before he caught himself.

"Okay Brown; a word to the wise and all that." I saluted and left.

That's the way it was in 'Nam. Only the delusional bought into the 'deeply serious business of helping a brave nation repel Communist aggression.' For the many who were not in that camp, attitudes and opinions splintered. Some were just following orders, others were protecting their career opportunities, and a few assumed there was a defensible rationale that had not been shared with us. But the majority seemed too exhausted – mentally and emotionally – to wrestle with the basic question of why they were putting their lives in jeopardy in a failing attempt to prop up a string of ruthless kleptocrats.

The Caterpillar Club

The next flight was short but eventful. Immediately after take-off the fire warning light on the left engine lit up, the little red bulb assuming the size of a number ten washtub. I shut down the left engine and, presto, the overheat light started to flash on the right. I pulled the plane around to a loose downwind and extended the gear and half flaps. "No visible smoke," said my wingman.

Entering the turn to final the controls seemed to be getting less responsive. "You got smoke now," crowed the tower, sounding pleased to be the first to announce this discovery.

Here's the problem: I don't like to make snap decisions. Definitely not a 'rip the bandage off' kind of guy. On paper you could safely eject above 900 feet in level or climbing flight but I was *descending* through 1,300. Already late.

"I'm going to land it. Roll the fire trucks."

"Negative, Brown. Bail out!" Easy call for my wingman. His ass wasn't on the line.

I pulled the nose up and the plane started to buck. *Đi tiêu!* That's it. I reached for the yellow and black striped ejection handles on both sides of the seat. The left handle seemed to be missing and the right one came up so easily it caused an instant of panic that I might have wrenched it off. Will it work? Dropping through 1,100 feet. Not good odds. Squeeze the trigger.

The force of the ejection snapped my head down on my knee before the wind blast whipped me back against the seat. A half somersault in mid-air as the butt-snapper threw me out of the seat and then I was wrenched back by the opening 'chute. In time?

Let's pause in the action here to consider what's happening. A young pilot who's taken comfort from the familiar and cozy confines of the cockpit has, after potentially fatal dithering, abandoned that familiar habitat and entrusted his fate to a Rube Goldberg concoction of straps, rockets, and exploding bolts. You think I'm exaggerating? Take a look at the Flight Manual description and you'll understand a pilot's reluctance to reach for the handles.

Ejection Seat, Operation.

The ejection sequence is initiated by raising either of the handles positioned beside the seat. This arms the seat and exposes the triggers. When either trigger is squeezed explosive bolts on both sides of the canopy fire and the canopy is released. One-tenth of a second later the rocket motor in the seat ignites and ejects the seat from the aircraft. Two seconds after rocket ignition an exploding bolt in the seat belt fires, releasing the pilot from the seat belt; this occurs simultaneously with rapid retraction of the center strap in the back of the seat which pulls the rear of the

seat pack up, forcing the pilot clear of the seat.
Full parachute deployment requires two seconds
at airspeeds in excess of 155 knots.

In the odds-defying event that this sequence occurs as planned in equipment that's old, misused, and never tested, what's the predictable reaction of the pilot? I'll tell you mine:

*"I'll be a motherfucking sonuvabitch!
The cocksucker works!"*

It works, but it also exacts a price. The designers of the seat had selected a fast-burning rocket that produced a 17 g kick in the pants. This wallop often caused lower-spine injuries known as Martin-Baker Back in honor of the pioneering British manufacturer of ejection seats that had acquired a reputation for inflicting lower back injuries.

As I made the brief descent earthward I reflected on these things and wondered if my own back might not be injured. Would the disability bar me from further flying? Yet not be so serious as to impair my rumba? Luck was clearly with me that day – I'd survived a low-altitude bailout – perhaps this could be parlayed into something more. My back felt bad . . . but so did my neck, my head, my left hand which had brushed against something on departure from the aircraft, and other parts of my body which would be too tedious to catalogue. Better to take the cautious course and allow time for my back to heal, if in fact it needed healing.

Landing in a soft field, I rolled onto my side and awaited the fire truck with composure and an expression of deep pain. This carefully orchestrated reception was spoiled by the misjudgment of the driver who applied the brakes too late and I had to scramble out of the way as the fire truck slid past, all six wheels locked.

Send the Tidings of Salvation
- F. J. Crosby, 1894

The flight surgeon held the X-ray in front of the window and scowled. "I don't see anything out of whack, Lieutenant. See these bones here. That's where Martin-Baker usually hits but the spacing between them doesn't seem compressed which would indicate that you'd blown out a disk. Can't see any compression fracture either." He gave the film further scowling scrutiny, his mouth pursed. Reaching a decision, he smiled, "Good news. Probably just tense muscles."

Good news my ass! I leaned forward gingerly, wincing audibly, to examine the area he was pointing to. "Well great, doc. How soon can I get back in the air?" If you can't get out of it, sound gung ho.

"I suppose in theory you could launch this afternoon but I'm going to keep you on the ground for a week just to be on the safe side."

Well, a week is a week. Maybe Ho Chi Minh would cry uncle within the week. Maybe LBJ would find another macho sport and call this game off. Maybe we'd even be replaced and shipped out.

And, *mirabile dictu*, that's what happened. When I got to the Officers' Club from the hospital the floor was awash in beer and booze. "Hey Brownie. Come 'ere you shorry shack of sheepshit and have some bubbly. We're goin' home."

The redoubtable 101 was being replaced by RF-4Cs. The new squadron wouldn't start arriving for another two weeks but since I was grounded for one week . . .

As it turned out I drew only one more mission before we were shipped out. My wingman aborted on the ground so I flew to an abandoned look-alike target, snapped some pics through the mist – looked kind of like smoke – flew back to the base, kissed the tarmac, burned my lucky skivvies in the waste basket and nursed a fifth of Cutty Sark.

In a parting nod to Professor Skinner's pigeons I packed up the aeronautical charts. Had they been good luck totems? They were, at the very least, fellow survivors.

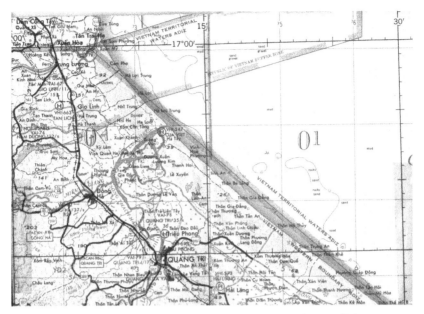

Tactical map. DMZ, Dong Ha, Cam Lo, Quang Tri

Section IIIa

Higher education.
The view from below.

Most Improved Student

This certificate of award is presented to

Maxwell Smythe Brown IV

For outstanding scholastic effort

From the period of _____ to _____

This _____ Day of _____

_____
Signature

6

Would You Like to Be a Hero
- H. E. Nichols, 1921

Relief at escaping a combat zone (alive) was tempered by un-ease at the prospect of returning to Tiffany, my wife. That's a hell of a note, isn't it?

How would she react to the premature repatriation of her husband? The messages had been mixed. There was the frosty departure, but once I was out of town – a surprise. She'd written weekly two page chatty letters. These unfailingly contained 1) a weather report, 2) at least one news item about an acquaintance (sick, moved, pregnant, etc.), 3) a sagacious statement of her mother's ("She said that the best thing I can do now is not have you worrying about me.") and 4) a closing that spoke of her af-fection and pride.

Expressions of affection were novel and welcome – and long overdue. Expressions of pride? Unwarranted. I was, against all standards of good judgment, taking pictures of busted bridges, bending the rules, and, when the rule-bending failed to confound the opposition, scrambling to dodge missiles and bullets. All this in a war that was a moral disaster and a military catastrophe. I wasn't doing much anyone could be proud of.

It quickly emerged that she'd been cast in a rôle that she and her mother understood and could attach value to: the strong wife of a warrior away at battle, a knight on a crusade. Was she dressing like Guinevere? You had to wonder if she wouldn't be even better suited to the rôle of unflinching war widow. What nobility, forbearance, and quiet strength she could exude in the face of that calamity.

She'd probably resent my return and her demotion to com-mon wife.

Another surprise.

Tiffany made a great parade of my war heroics. Like many others in the Air Force who went to Vietnam, I was over-decorated upon return to the US. I even received a Bronze Star – with V for valor! – for the bailout 'due to enemy action,' although the cause turned out to be birds, probably pigeons, ingested in the left engine. Since these medals took differing lengths of time to process, I could count on receiving a token of the service's gratitude every few weeks for several months. [*]

Tiffany stood beaming proudly at these ceremonies, whether in the Wing CO's office or on the parade ground, and regardless of the size of the crowd, she attracted the approving looks and nods of the assembled. It was the way she applauded: gloved hands held chest high, arms extended, head back, face radiating pleasure. And – in case you missed earlier references – Tiff was a knock out. After the last medal had been awarded and the final clangorous echoes of the *Air Force Song* had reverberated off the hangar walls, people gravitated toward her. Annoyingly, no one talked to *me* after the ceremony.

"It must have been very difficult for you, dear . . ."

"How I admire your courage, worrying about your husband . . ."

Granted that few of the decorations were deserved.[**] But dissonance reduction is a wonderful thing and I soon came to regard these minor displays of official recognition as fitting tribute. The contrasting absence of unofficial recognition began to fuel an irritation that boiled over the morning I received a DFC. A reporter, sentenced by his editor to cover the decorating ceremonies, muttered in my direction as he sauntered toward Tiffany, "You must tire of being the center of all this attention. I think I'll probe your wife for her angle." That was the straw.

Hostile Vet Lashes out at Reporter
(Bergstrom AFB) - A reporter from this newspaper was verbally attacked yesterday by Air Force

---

[*] Apologies to those of you who were *under*-decorated; I know at least two of you guys whose contribution went unnoticed and there must have been thousands more.

[**] Editor's note: Mr. Brown's propensity for self-deprecation does him a disservice. He was awarded the Distinguished Flying Cross for flying cover for his downed wingman, rapidly depleting his fuel supply with supersonic low-level passes that distracted and pinned down enemy ground forces until armed aircraft arrived. His plane flamed out immediately after landing. Mechanics counted 17 bullet holes.

pilot Captain Maxwell Smythe at a decorating ceremony on Bergstrom AFB. Smythe responded hostilely to questions, and, resorting to vulgarity, would not allow his wife to be interviewed. Psychologists have warned that these aggressive reactions are typical of battle-weary veterans of any war and may be particularly common among those who served in Vietnam.

Professor Donald Bogswell, when reached for comment by phone, stated that reactions, such as Smythe's, are in part a function of the immaturity of the veterans and deep-seated conflicts they may have about the propriety of their own conduct in the war. Bogswell, a psychologist who conducts research on stress and violence stated, 'We know that many of our servicemen commit acts that, in saner times, we would label atrocities. They are torn between justifying these atrocities as rational responses to a brutal and dehumanizing war on one hand, and trying to square them with their Judeo-Christian values on the other.' (Disturbed Vet, p. 8)

All that news coverage for snarling at the reporter, "Look Ace, only one cock is going to probe the lovely Mrs. Brown." And war atrocities? The closest I came to committing an atrocity was to gently copulate with a plump whore in Saigon, for which service I overpaid her two cartons of Marlboros. [*]

It was while driving home from this ceremony that Tiffany offered a rare compliment, "You know? I bet you'd make a great college professor. You already talk like one with your big vocabulary."

Well, my my! Where did this positive attitude come from? Not to worry; she pulls the rug out in the next sentence. "Like, you know, being a pilot's kind of the same as taxi driver or bus driver."

---

[*] I only did it because I felt sorry for her. She needed the business. And I was dead drunk. I'm still embarrassed.

Taken by surprise – first time I'd heard my profession wasn't well regarded – I lamely came back, "Um, Hibiscus Hips, the D in DFC stands for Distinguished."

I mean, come on! There I was, crammed into my dress blues, ribbons festooned all across my left chest, and a new medal in its box on the seat between us. First the exchange with the reporter, and now this? The conversation continued downhill. Maybe mentioning her hips was a mistake.

Nevertheless, Tiffany's strong upward social ambitions prevailed over my weak career ones. When Congress, in a surprise move, cut the budget for active duty pilots, Tiff intensified her lobbying that I request early separation and apply for graduate school. In fact, the heady life of a junior birdman had started to pale. Two pilots in our squadron had already received their orders to training in the RF-4C, after which they would, inevitably, be sent back to Vietnam. Civilian life looked better every day and I put in a request for separation.

The Air Force, while demanding another year's service, seemed happy to show me the door. You'd think they'd try to talk me out of it. I was a damn good pilot; just a little indifferent to the whole military thing. And the dying part.

Tiffany was convinced that prestige and universal respect (and possibly money) were accorded those with advanced degrees. Although having no strong thoughts of my own on the subject it was still easy to become caught up in the game of embellishing applications and flying off in the Air Force's jet – in the name of maintaining proficiency – to interviews with admissions officers and those faculty that would see me.

How to get into graduate school

"And why do you want a doctorate? It's a long slog." The speaker is a sociology professor I'd ambushed in his office.

"Well, sir, you have a lot of time to read between missions in 'Nam. Did you know there are almost no scholarly works on Vietnamese culture in English? I had to read the Army's *Country Studies Handbook* for information." The professor looked unimpressed so I rolled on, "And the great French anthropologist, d'Andrade, is almost Delphic in his treatment of the ancient Dong Son culture." Squinting, he looked at me with new interest. "In fairness to Professor d'Andrade, my undergrad French is so weak that I was into the dictionary every third paragraph. But it's not the opaque French that bothered me. There we were, Americans, dying by the tens of thousands in a country we'd made no effort to understand."

That statement may raise two questions in your mind. Here are the answers: Yes, there was a Dong Son culture way back in the day. No, there's no French anthropologist named d'Andrade. I was only half faking it. And while on this topic, do you like the use of 'Delphic' in place of 'obscure' or 'puzzling'? Tiff said I had the vocabulary. Why not cash in?

The trips also put me beyond the sound of her voice.

To my surprise I was accepted into Cornell's doctoral program in sociology despite a lackluster* undergraduate record. It's safe to assume they let me in because I was the first applicant they'd seen in years whose primary motivation wasn't to avoid the draft. Tiffany wasn't surprised. In a puzzling mixture of disdain and admiration she always assumed I could accomplish anything I really wanted and my failures were due entirely to a lack of will.

How to survive graduate school, I

King Solomon said that whoever increases his knowledge, increases his sorrow. I came across this inspiring message while killing time between leaving the Air Force and entering grad school. If Solomon's right, higher education screws you coming and going: If you do learn, your personal sorrow deepens. Don't learn and you flail around in agony and despair until they kick you out. Why would anyone do this? Or, more to the point, why would a dedicated slacker like myself do this?

Solomon's warning aside, there was one incontestable downside to graduate education: A college campus didn't offer a congenial environment for a Vietnam war veteran. There were two schools of thought among the students:

1) the vet had dined with gusto on the flesh of his innocent victims, or

---

* A magnanimous description.

2) the vet was the victim.

No middle ground; you were either despised or pitied. Even in the latter case it was made clear that you were being extended the king-sized benefit of a king-sized doubt. The first group couldn't bear to speak with you. The second would tolerate brief verbal exchanges – nothing extensive – as my interlocutors would talk around the issue.

"So, like, you were a pilot in Vietnam?"

"Yeah. Reconnaissance." Did he understand recon planes don't carry bombs or guns?

"Heavy." He chewed on a corner of his drooping moustache. "It must be crazy, being here now."

"Basically the same job. Over there I was trying to collect info. Here, the same."

"Yeah, but, being part of the war effort? Heavy."

Long silence. How much unspoken curiosity should I satisfy? Had I killed anyone? Not directly, but you have to wonder about the wider effect of my consistent flouting of the rules. Did another pilot die completing a mission I'd blown off? Something I try to not think about.

Increasingly I offered self-justifications. "Yeah, well, military justice falls on dissenters from a great height and with great weight. An F-100 gunnery instructor at Cannon in New Mexico announced he wasn't going to train any more pilots headed to 'Nam. It took the Air Force only a few weeks to sentence him to twenty years hard labor." [*]

"Whoa. Heavy!" Then the conversation would end, as most of them did, with some variant on, "You must be carrying a lot of baggage, man."

This got really old, really fast.

---

[*] Here's something that should set you on edge: The swiftness with which the Air Force dealt this guy a harsh sentence was all over the military news in 1967. The message was clear: don't make waves. Now there's no record of him. Internet searches come up blank. He never existed. Spooky, no?

I've Got a Newborn Feeling
- G. Hardison, 1955

The whole 'personal baggage' thing was part of the self-exploration movement in vogue at the time, taking form in the sensitivity training groups – commonly called T-groups – that bloomed throughout the land. For a grad student in the social sciences there was no avoiding them. For starters, many courses in social psych and sociology had a T-group component, included on the thin justification that to understand others one must understand oneself. Then, if we hadn't already gotten a snootful of self-exploration on campus, we were remanded to off-campus T-groups to bask in the reflected glory of a group leader who'd achieved some small notoriety.

This was all new to me. The US military did not – and I suspect still doesn't – encourage introspection.

One of the norms of these groups was that every member would spend at least one session in the spotlight, talking about their 'feelings'. I suggested to the group that we might take our cue from the label; if we were supposed to talk about our emotions, then they'd be called 'talkings'. This earned perplexed looks.

I'd hoped I might be exempted from this requirement and strove to project an image of insularity and detachment. I didn't participate in the probings of others; I didn't take part in recreational weeping with some overwrought soul (others did join in the sob-athon) who was detailing her (usually a female) struggles to establish an identity separate from her mother/father/sister, etc; and I definitely did not respond to the group leader's probes, "How does that make you feel, Max?" or "Does that strike a chord with you, Max?"

I knew exactly how I felt. For most of my life I'd usually considered myself the brightest bulb on the tree. Now, thrown in among ambitious graduate students freshly arrived from Ivy League schools, I felt unprepared, scared and a little dumb.

It took me longer to read the assignments and I often arrived in class unprepared. The quantitative methods courses were a nightmare of late night cramming and coat-tailing on every study session I could find. For seminars I learned to choose and rehearse my interventions with care lest I reveal, a) my lack of preparation, b) my failure to grasp the salient points, or c) my inability to describe those points economically with the right combination of admiration and skepticism.

On the eve of general exams Glib Max was stammering and stuttering.

I didn't belong. As a lecturer would drone on, I was back in the cockpit, bending through lush jungle valleys, feeling the increasing tenseness as the target came into view, rolling the cameras, bracing for the impact of a missile or AA shell, and then shooting up into clear air out of the hell of bullets and smoke, reveling in the rush that surviving a run always brought, and barrel-rolling around the first available cloud.

I actually missed Vietnam. I actually dug out the aeronautical charts I'd brought back and mentally retraced the missions. How fucked up is that? Which is exactly the question I asked myself every time that insane feeling hit. To be back in the midst of an immoral war where people were trying to kill you? A war that was scything through my buddies?

I didn't need sociology to tell me the answer. In Vietnam I was a warrior. At Cornell I was a school kid.

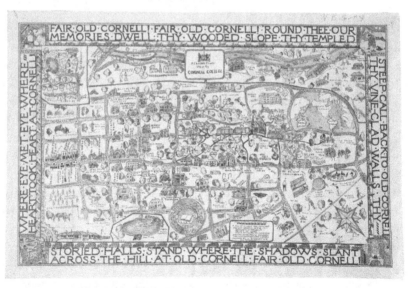

Created by a Cornell student, Eva McCalley Heefner '33.

7

"You know, you're no better than any of the rest of us." The speaker is a short bespectacled brunette, one of fourteen members of a course-related T-group.* Taken off guard by her comment, I was still able to muster a puzzled look which I fixed on her. She had nothing more to say, but the group leader picked up the challenge.

"That's pretty direct, Max. You must have some reaction." Then silence. That's how peer pressure works; you can ask any sociologist. Where there's a well-established norm – in this case, everyone has to spill their guts – all you have to do is place the holdout in the center of the circle and wait him out. No badgering; just patient silence.

"Reaction? I'm sorry Shareen feels that way." I carefully opened a notebook to signal that I was moving on to other things. Do you think that's going to work? Of course not. The class smelled blood. Every face was turned toward me.

After a long silent minute I caved. Closing the notebook, "Alright, Shareen. I feel I'm different. My path to get here has been different from yours or anyone else's in the room." Will that satisfy the mob? Of course not. All eyes still on me; expressions souring.

Darryl, a preppie from Yale, chimed in, "Is that why you're so judgmental?"

"Judgmental? I rarely speak."

"Exactly. You don't participate. Can't you see that an unwillingness to engage is a judgment that what the rest of us are doing is of no consequence." Darryl spoke well, for a prep school twit.

"Maybe you can start," offered the group leader, as if he were rescuing me, "by explaining how you see yourself as different."

There are three problems with that statement: 1) It assumed that I would have to 'explain' why I felt different. Isn't it obvious that combat affects a person differently than do frat parties

---

* As irony would have it, in her case I did think I was better.

and panty raids? 2) My first response will only be a 'start'; we'll be fucking around with Max for some time. And 3) I took the bait.

"Alright," pretty much in the tone of, 'you asked for it!' "three of my best friends were killed in a war for which there's no excuse. I know of six occasions where I was nearly killed, and there may have been others I was unaware of. Most mornings for five months my waking thought was, will I still be alive when the sun sets? Or will I be captured and disappear into the torture dungeons of Hỏa Lò Prison?" I paused briefly to allow the torture reference to sink in. "And when I was released from this daily hell and came home, no one said 'good job, Max.' The Americans I was told I was protecting spit on me. Sometimes literally. So, yeah. I'm probably different."

That would have been the perfect time to stand up, collect my backpack, and march out of the room. A dramatic exit by a wronged patriot and warrior. But I didn't.

Shareen was quick to speak. "I learned my mother tried to abort me three times. Does that make me better than others, Max?"

A student whose name I didn't know offered, "My brother was gunned down in South Boston." This was followed by other tales of crisis, danger, loss and bereavement.

What had I started? Apparently a competition to establish oneself as the most pitiable victim.

Some of these stories smelled like complete inventions and others were clearly embellished, but they did send the mob up a different trail. In the end Shareen's prenatal traumas presented the most intriguing case and the rest of the session was spent dialoguing with her on how that had affected her life, how it made her feel about her worth as a person, her subsequent relationship with her mother, and so on.

The group leader gave me a long look as we filed out. The message was clear: 'You got away with it today, fella', but I've still got you in my sights.'

The next group meeting, one week later, was April 30th, 1975. This is a date that probably means nothing to you, or almost anyone else, but you might remember Operation Frequent Wind, aka the fall of Saigon. The newscasts and papers were full of pictures and videos of desperate Vietnamese scaling walls, climbing ladders, huddling with their families in the US Embassy compound, and, most memorably, being kicked off the helicopter skids they  were clinging to and falling to their deaths.

Yes, that's an actual photo taken on April 30th. Those are actual human beings falling through the air.

If you read about the events of those two days now you'll find them rendered in heroic tones – packed with statistics of the numbers safely evacuated. The mind-searing pictures of GIs stomping on the hands of the Vietnamese who'd bought into our bullshit have become very hard to find. You could, however, see them on April 30th, 1975.

Should I go to the group meeting? If I didn't, how would my absence be interpreted? Shame? Guilt? Sorrow?

I walked in five minutes late and the leader, for the first time, acknowledged my arrival. "Max, we were hoping you'd show up. We were wondering how you're dealing with the news out of Vietnam?"

I scanned the room. The one Asian student *was* absent. Those images must have had him on the verge of homicide.

"Why do you ask?" hoping to put the ball back into the group leader's court.

He was too good at the game to fall for that. He simply maintained a patient and expectant expression. So I tried, "I have to wonder why my feelings on the matter are more important than anyone else's?" That was an easy one to knock down and Darryl did.

"You're closer. You told us last week that the experience made you different from the rest of us. You were part of the game and your side lost."

My side? Of course. These snots, whose presence in grad school was owed to draft deferments or parental influence, weren't responsible for the disaster that was the Vietnam War. In fact, they'd be quick to point out that they'd marched to protest the war, if the weather had been pleasant that day. Those of us who'd landed there out of happenstance, bad luck, misguided patriotism, or lack of influence would pay the full price: both the heavy down payment *and* a mortgage which we'd service for the rest of our lives.

I thought about a response for a long time – time that I had, since it was clear the floor was mine. Did those shameful pictures mean nothing to these pampered pricks? Likely. Growing annoyed, I asked: why should I be the only one feeling miserable today?

Hands spread on the table, I looked up through the window as if I were addressing a higher audience. "This puts me in mind of those clueless television reporters who corner someone whose home has just burned to the ground, or whose family has been blown away by a tornado and they ask, 'Describe for our viewers how you feel.'"

Pacing was important; a pause.

"There are times when feelings should be private. Those are the times when a man can justifiably deny the voyeurs that titillating glimpse into his inner turmoil." Another pause, and I finished quietly, "A time when the desire for privacy should be respected." I looked first at Darryl, then the group leader. Then I *did* pick up my backpack and headed toward the door, stopping to add, "I trust the news will bring a new topic for discussion next week." To satisfy my own voyeurism, I stood in the hall near the door, listening. Silence. They were in shock.

I still think back on that farewell speech with pride. And here's the icing: there were no negative repercussions. I received a good grade (A), was treated with deference, and Darryl apologized. "Look, old man," a curious occasion to invoke his preppie bloodlines, "sorry if I was insensitive. No hard feelings?"

A side note: I did miss classes the next day. Second worst hangover I ever had. There's more to it than just being on the losing side.

Everyone Needs Compassion
- B. Fielding, 2006

"I don't know if this is a good idea," she snuffled into a tissue. The speaker is a forty-ish woman who had dropped into an off-campus T-group we'd been strongly encouraged to participate in. Finally she looked up, "I need to tell someone." Another long hesitation, then speaking low and haltingly, "He made me have an abortion. He threw me down, spread my legs and started poking around in there – I don't know what he was using, I think maybe his drumsticks. That was my husband, you know. Fucking bastard. But God help me, I still love him. I bled for three days and then the rotten smell started up from my vagina and I knew I had an infection. My friend Shirley took me to her doctor and I passed out in the car going over from the fever."

The group facilitator slid a box of tissues down the table toward the distraught woman.

"Can you believe it? I still want that bastard. Can you really fucking believe it? I feel like puking now when he plays his fucking drums." Face dabbing.

"I'm sorry." She shook her head back and forth in support of her apology for burdening us with her troubles. Then she squared her shoulders. "You've been really kind to listen." Exeunt stage left, suppressing sobs.

The eyes of the other group members followed the woman out the door and then turned toward me. I was feeling miserable; what a terrible experience, and the woman's future didn't look all that bright. Then I realized what was expected. *Ah fuck!* I hadn't bargained on becoming the conscience and spokesperson for the group. Sensitive Max? Bringing solace to the oppressed? There's a fine irony. Where had he come from? Apparently the combination of taciturnity and the Fall of Saigon speech had transfigured Baby-killer Max into Messianic Max. They expected me to do something to comfort the poor woman. Their confidence was flattering, but misplaced. I was wondering if I'd be able to beat up the husband.

I looked into each face in turn as if asking for approval to represent the group, but really I was stalling for time. After receiving the silent blessing of every member, I slowly rose and walked out into the hall. By this time, of course, the woman was long gone, but I had to play it through. I walked quickly and noisily down the hall as if in pursuit of the aggrieved victim, then ducked into the men's room. If I was going to be absent from the group for a while, I might as well take the opportunity to relieve myself.

A minute later I came out of the john just as the forced abortion victim emerged from the women's room. She'd washed the tears away and was dabbing excess lipstick from the corners of her mouth. She offered an obligatory social smile and stopped.

"Hey. Weren't you just in that classroom with me?"

"Are you okay, ma'm?"

"Sure. Why shouldn't I be?" She studied my distressed expression and laughed. "Oh that! I was just messing with you kids. The looks on your faces were great. I thought that one girl was going to soil her panties. And you looked pretty bummed yourself."

God's bunions! "Do you mean that was all an act?"

"Of course. You don't think anyone would tell a bunch of strange college students something like that?"

"But, uh . . . um . . ." I wasn't holding up my end of the conversation very well.

"You kids take yourselves so seriously in those groups. Me and my friend Shirley – yeah, she's the one real part – hit one or two of these groups every week. It's a blast. Beats mopping the kitchen floor." She looked me over. "Do you want to have a drink or something?"

Pranked! I'd been pranked! Hoodwinked! Hornswoggled! Me, Smart-ass Max who'd spent his childhood stretching Saran Wrap over toilet bowls and couldn't walk through the teachers' parking lot without shoving a potato into at least one tail pipe. The Prince of the Pranksters. I'd been duped. Staggering.

"No. No drink." She wasn't that good looking, for one thing. And for another, I was really pissed.

I went back to the group which had put all business on hold pending my report. I gave them a serious smile and a small hand wave to signify the matter had been dealt with, then turned toward the group facilitator indicating he could resume.

Guilt, Lord, Deep Guilt Is Mine
- W. Allen, 1835

"Max, hang back for a second, would you?" That's the group facilitator, as he wrapped up the session.

When the others had cleared the room he asked, "She was faking, wasn't she?" I nodded. "You know, I'd heard about these gals. Probably bored housewives out for fun. But why didn't you tell everyone it was all a put-on?"

I considered several answers and settled on, "And rob them of the experience?" That noble sentiment concealed the real reason: I didn't want to acknowledge to the world that I'd been taken in. I'd always been the prankster; not the pranked.

"That's thoughtful of you, Max. No one likes to think they've been made a fool of."

Ouch. To Gullible Max, let's add Mean Max.

He wasn't done. "I've never understood what drives some people to take enjoyment from making others feel small and foolish. I read somewhere that it's because they're basically insecure. You're studying sociology, aren't you? Any ideas?"

I was having another, larger problem with the T-groups. All of the other group members seemed to be plumbing profound depths of their own characters and the insights were making them better human beings with each meeting. It wasn't working for me and I wondered if I had no depths; maybe my character was only a few millimeters deep? Shallow Max.

How to survive graduate school, II

I wound up a practicing sociologist – after four anxiety filled years as a doctoral student – because the subject matter appeared, from the outset, intuitively obvious.[*] But, of course,

---

[*] Sociology at Cornell was coasting, but two social psychologists at the school were about to make a major contribution. If you don't

that's why I applied; it was the one discipline I thought I could master. Stripped of the arcane language authors in the field hid behind, sociology seemed little more than illumination of the self-evident with a singular and lamentable focus: a fascination with those on the periphery of middle-class white society. The literature – maybe beginning with *Street Corner Society* – on marginalized groups grew at such a rate that it seemed inevitable every college in the land had, or would soon have, a sociology course informally called *Nuts and Sluts*. This sustained attention to the powerless members of society seemed to undermine whatever legitimacy the 'science' might lay claim to.

Although alive to the peril of being identified as a malcontent, this cynicism surfaced in a department symposium. When asked to reflect on our experiences as students, I filled the awkward silence with, "I can't help but notice all the attention sociologists pay to these subcultures, and almost nothing to the behavior of the 'mainstream.' Is that because," I continued with growing unease, "we believe our middle-class white male behavior is readily interpreted as a rational response to the world, and therefore merits no inquiry?"

That seemed well-phrased, but self-congratulations were suspended when it became clear that the question had struck a nerve. One senior professor stomped out of the seminar; another favored me with an indulgent, sickly smile. The students nearest whispered that my goose was, for once and for all, cooked – a view that I was quickly coming to myself. Three and a half years down the toilet. Once again, I'd opted for cleverness over prudence. I spent the rest of the meeting thinking about a) alternative careers, and b) how to break the news to Tiff.

As we left the room my advisor came over and said, "An excellent comment, Max. You did yourself proud."

This had to be sarcasm. "Yeah, thanks."

"Really. You still have a few things to learn about the sociology of your discipline, sociology. But, that fleeting display of brashness was probably taken as a positive development by most of my colleagues."

---

know about the Dunning-Kruger effect, check it in the glossary. It's wonderful. You'll want to work it into conversations.

Could still be sarcasm. "It was?"

"I hope I'm not being untrue to my profession," he glanced around and continued in a conspiratorial tone, "but, you see, a sociologist's enduring fear is that he doesn't have a whole lot to say that's useful. That, I hypothesize, is behind the tendency of so many in our discipline to occasionally propose something mildly outrageous to attract attention and combat these deep fears of irrelevance. Then," fixing me with a stare over the top of his half-moon reading glasses, "before too much attention focuses on them, they'll retreat into silence or mumbling." He stroked his chin as he reconsidered what he'd said. "Maybe it's not just sociologists. Maybe this neurosis infects all social scientists?" At this point he was talking to himself as he wandered away.

That one naive outburst was interpreted as evidence I was approaching fledgling status. When I passed this news on to the other doctoral students, they competed to outdo one another in provocative declarations. They overdid it. Several of them later encountered unusually hostile grillings during their orals and theses' defenses and failed to graduate. Lucky Max.

How to get a faculty appointment

Not as lucky in landing a job after graduation. For starters, military service – an asset with admissions committees – was a liability with faculty selection committees. If the American public at large didn't believe we were all war criminals, that conviction remained firmly rooted on college campuses. Members of faculty hiring committees tended to believe that the My Lai massacre was only the tip of a very large and bloody iceberg. To give you a sense of the tenor of the interviews, here are some of the questions asked:

"With your background, how do you expect to fit in?" Answer: I just spent four years on a very liberal Ivy League campus, you sanctimonious shit.

"An important part of the educational process here is to impart a set of humanitarian values to the students and to show them that non-violence can be a productive approach. How can we be sure you share those values?" Answer: Make love, not war. At least that's what your wife said as she wrapped her legs around me and howled with pleasure.

And, most aggressively, "Given your war record, why do you think you'd be comfortable on our campus?" Answer: Go fuck yourself.

You realize I didn't say those things out loud.

As a further obstacle to landing a job – and despite Cornell's strong reputation – it's always been a buyers' market in sociology. Only after submitting numerous applications I was offered an appointment in the sociology department of a large urban university in the Midwest.

The notice of selection came just as Tiffany, who'd been manning a cash register at K-Mart to keep the rent paid, started sending signals that she thought she might do better on her own. Curious; despite her unremitting dismay at my myriad shortcomings, Tiff seems to have considered bailing out of the marriage only when I stumbled as a breadwinner. And, if you can't guess her one and only question about the job, you haven't been paying attention: "What's it pay?"

Section IIIb

Higher education.
The view from above.

Pomp and Circumstance
- Edward Elgar, 1901

8

Higher education explained, I

"Mark! Glad to have you on board. Your Department Chair has told me good things about you." The speaker is the Dean of Social Sciences who, without looking up, continued to search through papers on his desk while I wondered if I should sit, stand, or whether he'd notice if I took a leak on his dying ficus. His gleaming false teeth added a sibilant undertone to his greeting.

"I know you're going to flourish here. I've got to run in just a second but I wanted to welcome you." Before I could acknowledge what was shaping up as the most tepid welcome I'd ever received – he still hadn't looked at me and the parched ficus was calling out – he pressed on. "A couple of quick things I wanted to mention: First, you'll find our students remarkable for their high motivation and seriousness about their studies." This turned out to be a patent fiction. "And second – and especially important for your professional development – our senior faculty are as good as you'll find anywhere. Look to them for guidance; they won't let you down." Hoo boy.

―――――――

You may have picked up on the refrain, 'Max didn't belong.' With that in mind, consider the oddballs, posers, humbugs, charlatans, bores, boors, and frauds in whose midst I'd just splashed down.

You've met the dean and already achieved as close a relationship with him as I did over six years. In my several encounters with the man, I don't think he would have been able to recall whom he'd just been talking with if challenged.

The leadership picture doesn't improve as we move down one rung. The chairman of the Sociology Department, B. Samuel Wagner, had distinguished himself by scaling the heights of mediocrity. You'd think it a contradiction that anyone could stand apart from the crowd solely on the strength of his singular lack of distinction, but B.S. Wagner was living proof that it could be done. He never expressed an original thought in the years that I knew him; he had no interests; could point to no scholarly contributions; was a weak administrator; and it was difficult to sustain a discussion with him on any topic more intellectually challenging than the optimum class size (he had theories). Actual conversation:

"Sam, could you invest some of your vast influence and persuade the Maintenance Department to repair the window in my classroom in Sieg Hall? My entreaties have produced nothing."

"I heard about that. Apparently pigeons are now nesting in that room as well?"

"They're not ideal roommates. Some students won't enter the classroom. And it's colder than a well-digger's willy."

"Ah, Max, you're new. Those students are just using the pigeons as an excuse to skip out. I'd wager they would find another reason if the window were repaired."

"No doubt. However, it's not a good learning environment when the temperature hovers around freezing and we're welcomed by a fresh dusting of snow on the floor and desktops."

"It must seem quite an experience for you. I won't try your patience with accounts of the privations I suffered as a student."

And then the SOB did just that. For the next fifteen minutes we relived his childhood hardships in northern Minnesota where it was commonplace to lose half the students to wolves or polar bears every winter. Okay, maybe not exactly that; I tuned out early on, but that was the general drift.

"Oh, poop! Look at the time. I'm keeping the Dean waiting." And he bustled out.

This was his standard response to any request that he perform the minimum functions expected of his position, but I guess you could, with misgivings, say it was an administrative 'skill.' He'd hog the floor and take the discussion off into unrelated areas until he'd worn his petitioner down; at that point he'd escape without having addressed the issue at hand.

To compensate for his lack of intellectual substance the chairman attired himself in tweed jackets (with leather elbow patches), a Phi Beta Kappa key crossed his necktie, and an unsuccessful Van Dyck sprouted from his receding chin. When called upon to read in the presence of others he'd extract a pince nez from his vest pocket, and, wedging it across the mid-point of his pitted nose, would lean back and squint at the document in his hand. This elaborate ritual, enacted several times at every departmental meeting, always irritated us because we all knew the old humbug wore contacts. He complained tirelessly of the demands of administration which prevented him from pursuing the rigorous research and publication schedule appropriate to a man of his gifts and prayed that the Dean might one day allow him to turn his full intellectual energies once more to advancing the frontiers of knowledge. But I think his most irksome characteristic was his inability to swear.

He didn't swear often, but, perhaps given my service background, he would frequently throw in a four-letter word when I was present, and then look hopefully toward me for approval. The effect, sadly, was to establish him as a potty-mouth, not a member of my, or anyone's, circle. Wagner's embarrassing example justifies a brief detour.

How to swear

Swearing is a ubiquitous feature of daily life – and it helps define a person – but so far hasn't been the object of serious academic scrutiny. You'd think it would be a popular area of study for sociologists.

Let's assume you talk proper; then you need to swear proper as well. It's one of the signs of good breeding. Anyone – except for Chairman Wagner – can swear casually to signify his inclusion in a group (Army, street gang, sports fan) and anyone can curse with pain and anger (hammer + thumb). None of this counts as real swearing. What's going to establish you as a person of quality and refinement is your ability to swear inventively and with detachment. Here are a few quick ideas off the top of my head. If these resonate, maybe I'll become the trailblazer who builds an academic career on smutty talk.

First, style:

> Swear like you intend to swear and not because you can't help yourself. Swear calmly.

Avoid common vulgarity, unless you've established yourself as unquestionably posh. As a simple matter of statistical probability, you're almost certainly not, but if you were . . . Imagine Queen Elizabeth telling us Prince Phillip is an asshole.* For QE2 that's effective swearing. For you? No.

Do not, whatever else you do, look around to gauge the effect. Bush league.

Words. There aren't many. The Motion Picture Association of America lists only seventeen words that will earn a movie an R rating. You have to move beyond the top three – fuck, shit and cunt – if you're going to engage in memorable swearing:

Archaic is good. I, personally, like God + body part. This goes way back; Shakespearean vestiges are still found in the UK in words like 'odsblood' (God's blood), 'odsbodskins' (God's little body) and 'zounds' (His wounds).

Similarly, use of Latin derivatives lifts your swearing out of the gutter. Compare 'fuckin' cunt' to 'oft-poked pudendum.' Better, right? But be careful with alliteration; it's easily overdone.

Be creative; make up words. Turn verbs into adverbs: fuck => fuckingly. Nouns into adjectives: twat => twattish. Verbs into adjectives: shag => shagworthy, shagable.

Are we on the right path here? Write and let me know.

Researchers tell us that the incidence of swearing is on the rise. Please join the campaign to ensure that quality is not sacrificed. Don't be like Chairman Wagner. Put some thought into your swearing.

Higher education explained, II

Returning to our taxonomy of the phylum *professor academicus,* at the next level we have the –

Full professors. Of the five full professors in sociology, all but one had long since cashed in their careers. They talked of

---

* Not farfetched; there's plenty of evidence that he *is* an asshole.

their past importance and of books forever in preparation. Apparently they believed that eccentricity was a sufficient substitute for scholarship. This was demonstrated in dress and the expression of unconventional opinions. One wore suspenders, another bow ties, a third was never without a plaid vest. As sociologists their opinions tended to be principally on the future of society where they predicted radical departures from current norms ("The family will cease to exist by the end of the century"); however, they recognized no boundaries on their wisdom and would just as readily pronounce on international economics, classical music, or the fate of upper atmosphere ozone.

Although the full professors were of one mind regarding dress and a penchant for controversial opinions, they were divided on how to disguise their lack of productivity. Some were often found dozing at their desks; the honest response. Others dashed in and out of the office in an unsuccessful attempt to project urgency and non-stop activity – which was never supported by scholarly output.

The full professors were joined in their idleness by those associate professors who'd been granted tenure. To a man – and one woman – they believed that they'd labored long and hard for tenure and now deserved a brief respite – a chance to rest momentarily on the oars – before again committing themselves to the race. This period of recuperation could extend for years and they were infrequently found on campus.

With tenure also came an inflated sense of position.

"Hey, Max. There's a curriculum committee meeting in an hour. Something came up and I can't go. Would you represent the department for us?" The speaker is a recently tenured associate professor.

"Short notice, Dennis. Did the clinic reschedule your treatment for undescended testicles?" Two passing co-eds snickered.

"Cute, Brown," asserting rank by using my last name. "We really need someone there to defend our turf. I'd appreciate it if you'd step up and do this for the department?"

"You know, Dennis, I'd go to any lengths to help you out, but I've got a leg-waxing appointment and I've been waiting ages to get onto Mr. Phyllis' schedule. Try Tom. I think he's awake."

Dennis and I didn't get along.

Will the Real God please stand up

Observation of these senior colleagues suggested an inverse relationship between intellect and power; stupidity, it appeared, was one of the hallmarks of rank. If this relationship is extended, the most powerful will be the least able. You know where we're going, right? Yes friends, could it be the Top Banana, Jehovah Himself, is the all-time Cosmic Cockup?

A popular image of God is that of a mad, but brilliant, scientist. Okay, granted that the image of a wild-eyed hirsute coot in a lab-coat has appeal. But the world viewed from a university campus invites other explanations. Just because you're in charge doesn't mean you know what's going on. It could mean the opposite. Tell me I'm wrong. How many of your bosses have *not* been nincompoops?

The more we learn about the universe, the more likely, it seems, that the Supreme Intellect might be a dullard, always a few steps behind a rapidly-moving process. He'd set forces in motion which operate in a haphazard and unpredictable fashion. We can keep omnibenevolence and omnipotence – although it scarcely matters; omniscience drops out. And, conveniently, this new formulation distanced me from the angry and dangerously blasphemous denunciations provoked by Vietnam. God's not a brutal sociopath. He's just not very bright.

TO: Jehovah

FROM: Committee on Research Funding

RE: Review of your proposal to create a 'universe'

The Committee has completed its review of your proposal for the creation of a universe. We regret we will not be able to fund your project at the present time.

To recap the Committee's understanding of the basic elements of your approach –

You plan to start, essentially, with a void in which hydrogen molecules are drifting around. You propose to allow them to collide randomly which will create the element hydrogen$_2$. A second collision with this element will form more complex elements and in this laborious fashion matter will be created. This process brought a laugh from Committee members. Perhaps you were unaware that the half-life of H_2 is less than a millisecond – a very brief envelop for the second collision to occur.

Certainly there is a more expeditious way to create matter and life.

This takes us to a second criticism of your proposal: The absence of even the most cursory review of the literature is a surprising omission. To list a few of the major contributors to current creation research that you might profit from:

- Brahma has been experimenting with the possibility of repeatedly splitting himself in two. The early results merit your attention, especially in that you propose cell subdivision as one mechanism for reproduction of lower life-forms.

- Amen-Ra, via masturbation, has created a divine son and daughter who are now in the process of creating a race of gods. If you do contact Amen-Ra, please remind him that his last progress report lacked the promised annex containing the materials used during masturbation.

- P'an Ku has taken a different approach and has, for 18,000 years, been manually crafting an 'earth.' P'an's experience may occasion you pause as the committee's last correspondence from him indicated he was exhausted from his labors and near death.

In contrast with these straight-forward attempts to create matter and life-forms, your proposed approach seems unnecessarily complex and slow.

It was the consensus of the committee that your talents might be better suited to a different field than creation work. Please do not interpret the constructive recommendations above as encouragement to re-apply.

Oafish as they were, the senior faculty didn't have a monopoly on foolishness. Every encounter with two of our untenured colleagues, Frick and Frack, brought to mind a wonderful anecdote attributed to Clausewitz. It was said that the great military strategist described his personnel staffing policies to a group of journalists as follows:

"All recruits to military service can be categorized on the dimensions of intelligence and ambition; they are smart or dumb, and lazy or ambitious. If a man is smart and ambitious, we will make him a line officer. If he is smart but indolent, he may still be fit for a staff officer position. The dumb and lazy, who make up the great majority of the recruits, become common soldiers."

An attentive journalist noted that one combination hadn't been mentioned and asked the Prussian leader what was done with the dumb but ambitious. Clausewitz's reply was immediate, "Those bastards, we shoot."

Frick and Frack richly merited such a fate. They were a menace to themselves and to all around them. How much trouble, you ask, can a college teacher create? Listen to this. Frick, in an effort to demonstrate the power of communal action, encouraged a group of his students as they organized a protest; this mush-  roomed into the strike that closed the university for ten days.

Frack tried to enliven the section of his introductory course dealing with deviant behavior by bringing some real live deviants to the classroom. The session climaxed, so to speak, when one of the guest lecturers performed fellatio on another.

These were the people who strolled through the groves of academe. I didn't belong. But – here's the kicker – *with each passing year I became more like them.*

~~80~~ ~~90~~ 99 percent of success is showing up

I didn't belong, but Tiffany was in her element. She wrangled an invitation to every social event connected with the university, no matter how remote or tenuous the connection. Thanks to her looks Tiff was a welcome adornment at any social occasion.

Since the majority of these invitations arrived in my name I would find myself trailing Tiffany at a cocktail party for new faculty members in the English Department on Thursday evening, at a reception for inductees into some student honor society Friday afternoon, milling with throngs at the Provost's house Friday night, lunching with junior civic leaders – *real* junior – on Saturday, entertaining 'colleagues' in our apartment Saturday night, and chasing flyballs Sunday afternoon with the college's softball team.

We soon learned we didn't have to provide clever repartee to be welcomed into the homes of Academia's Grandees. We just had to be there. The more senior the host, the more urgent that there be a good turnout as evidence of his or her importance. Who would have thought that an academic career could be built on choking down soggy canapés and sipping watery cocktails?

We also bought our round. Tiffany was one of those rare people who could entertain effortlessly and graciously. And the unexpected thing about it was this: our social visibility was sufficient to advance my career. I published nothing; I soon became bored with teaching and invested as little effort into it as I could without precipitating student unrest; and I avoided college committees as if they were a dread social disease. Despite this disinterest in professional activities, my appointment was renewed, my salary increases were slightly above average, and I was promoted to associate professor on schedule. The only thing standing between me and nirvana was tenure which I began to regard as inevitable.

The formula for this success was not the traditional publish/teach/service troika that propelled the efforts of my colleagues, and, no doubt, competing explanations for my success found their way into the political theories developed by my peers. I wonder if any of those theories recognized the self-evident: Tiffany and I had become fixtures of university life.

Although I tried not to brood about it, my success seemed to rest mainly on Tiffany's participation and she was, if anything, more beautiful than when we'd met; a few well-distributed pounds had moved her from the svelte to the voluptuous category.

Her stunning appearance stood in stark contrast to the women on the faculty who'd proclaimed their defiant refusal to take part in the ongoing American beauty pageant. As unwitting proof, they highlighted their worst features in dress, hair and cosmetics.

Faculty wives? No better. Where female professors subscribed to a 'this is how I look asshole, get used to it' ethos, the faculty wife actively aspired to an *American Gothic* dowdiness.

Tiffany found this unforgivable. Blessed by nature with great beauty herself, she assumed that the absence of the same attribute in others was a sign of God's disapproval.

Her low regard for the other faculty wives led her to communicate with them economically; this was initially interpreted as natural reserve, and subsequently elevated to graciousness. Her developing hauteur was put down to refinement. Have you noticed that disagreeable traits are given a positive label when found in a beautiful woman?

But, to give Tiff her due, she was a regular: she was always there and she did, to her credit, put in many hours dialing, stuffing envelopes, and making casseroles. If anything, I was a negative quantity in the equation as I was unsuccessful in disguising my disdain for the charlatans, frauds, and pretentious humbugs that populate academia. Tiffany's contribution exceeded my own and I occasionally experienced a fleeting pang of gratitude for the way she'd made my professional life easy and carefree.

What stopped me from expressing that gratitude was that she was also an unending pain in the ass.

9

The main problem: boredom

Who would have thought that boredom would be my undoing? Well, Kierkegaard perhaps; he said it's the root of all evil.

After five years as a faculty wife Tiffany was growing restive. She'd reached the summits of all the social molehills in our neighborhood. She'd taken advantage of the tuition waivers for faculty dependents and, after completing several liberal arts classes, had acquired an archness in her speech that went well with her high-born looks, but poorly with our relationship. She wanted more from life and talked of travel and more prestigious schools.

As for me, after five years as practicing pedant, mild mannered professor, sociological savant, I could barely muster enough enthusiasm to make out a course syllabus and I'd not read a scholarly article, much less written one, since my third year on the faculty.[*] With this record we weren't destined for any universities higher in the academic pecking order and we lacked the money for travel.

And after thirteen largely unrewarding years of marriage to Tiffany I had to acknowledge that we weren't going to fall in love again and I started to consider when might be the best time to unload her. The pragmatist in me argued that after receiving tenure her usefulness would be diminished.

I know, I know. That sounds calculating and mean but a gradual transformation seemed to be occurring in our marriage: our personalities and behavior were converging.

For her part, she sounded more like me every day. Her Texas twang had been replaced by the hard R's and flat A's that characterize the dialect colleagues in the Linguistics Department referred to as Inland North. Her sentences now sported subordinate clauses, occasional and correct use of the subjunctive, and those sentences were packaged in fully formed paragraphs.

---

[*] The only vestige of the days when I did write is a penchant for footnoting. Had you noticed?

For my part, I'd come to view the marriage as less an emotional bond and more as an expected accessory of modern life. This, I assured myself, was why I viewed the continuation of our relationship in basic utilitarian terms. But I didn't dwell on it.

"The unexamined life is not worth living"

Socrates said that. Socrates was a dick.

"Who do you want to be, Max?" Tiffany had been lunching with her lady friends and, as was too often the result, had come home with a new issue to discuss.

"What are my options?" She would certainly have some thoughts on this question.

"Well, on the one hand you speak like a professor, but you still have the posture of a soldier (soldier?!) and your attitude toward your job seems to be more like a goldbricker." I was debating which epithet was more offensive, soldier or goldbricker, as she resumed.

"My mother said something interesting." I tensed; nothing constructive had issued from Mother Pratiloma yet. "She said you never seem to like who you are. You didn't like being a military pilot." Half true; I loved the pilot part. "You hated being a student. And you don't seem to enjoy being a professor. You certainly don't like the other professors." She had that right. "So, who do you want to be?"

That's a pretty large question to spring on a guy who's watching baseball on TV and into his fourth beer.

It's also something that a grown man should have figured out. An answer was expected. Without an opportunity to think, I said the first thing that came to mind.

"I want to be a homing pigeon."

Her hands flew into the air. "Can't you be serious about anything, Max?"

Serious? There's a difference between serious and somber. I'm the most serious person on the globe. I was about to explain the difference but her question was rhetorical and she quickly continued.

"I'm trying to be helpful here and you give me some nonsense about birds?"

Challenged, I'm about to make a mistake: I'm going to explain myself to someone who will use the information against me.

"A homing pigeon knows where it's supposed to be – where it belongs – and it always knows how to get there. I don't know either of those things."

This explanation brought a look of withering scorn. "I didn't ask where – like Pocatello. We're talking about *what* you want."

The discussion didn't go anywhere – Tiffany kept repeating the same questions/accusations and I resumed deflecting them – but it touched a nerve. My life had been that of a journeyman actor, playing whatever rôle had been offered at the time. Sometimes the good guy – gridiron hero, hot pilot, the conscience of our little T-group; and sometimes the bad guy – duty shirker, wise-ass, prankster. Now I was technically an intellectual, another rôle I'd signed onto without forethought. The constant? Few of these rôles had been rewarding, and they'd all quickly become boring.

Commercial and military carrier pigeon routes, 1890s.

Will the Real God please stand up

Looking for an escape from what was becoming a dangerous descent into introspection, I wondered, can any of this be applied to God? Maybe He's bored and restless too. I mean, 14 billion years at the same post? Your focus is likely to drift a little from time to time. And God's absolutely stuck in His job. That might explain His inattention, His negligence, His failure to intervene when needed. You can't be omniscient and omnipresent if you're not paying attention. God's not immature or malicious or dumb; He's just seen it all too many times.

Celestial Date: 1.478326-E17

Dear diary. Haven't written lately. Certainly nothing else to do. What a drag. If just one of them would do something different. I gave up peeking into the future in the forlorn hope that would introduce an element of surprise. Noooo. Predictable. Boring.

What a laugh to think of the energy I invested into populating the universe, expecting that would lead to interesting diversity. Hell, you can't swing an archangel around this place without hitting an inhabited planet. 31 million flavors of mush. Boring. Balls! What am I going to do to while away the millennia?

Tried something last week. Presented myself, naked, in the form of Idi Amin to a housewife in Bismarck, ND. "I am the Lord Almighty," I announced. She looked skeptical, but I think the alrighteous rogering put her on the road to the light. At a minimum she has a clearer picture of what the Coming of the Lord means.

Broke my own rule - why not? everyone else breaks them - and peered into the future to see how the progeny turns out. Disappointing; she names the kid Fred. Not a promising start for a Messiah. Still, you never know when one of them will catch on. Who would have thought that noodge Jesus would take hold? Simpler times then. But what a long-shot! Airhead for a mother. Father was a semi-senile old goat. Why else would he take a vow of chastity? Joseph wasn't missing much. Gabriel says Mary was no firecracker in the sack.

What irony, diary. Here I've plumbed for goodness from the start. And it turns out the only entertainment is to be found in the great villains. Rasputin stirred things up at least — seems a pity his reward is to be spitted over Lucifer's hibachi.

Maybe Fred or one of his half-siblings will start up a real church. Something that captures the true spirit of the universe — the Ecclesia of Eternal Ennui. Not great as a title but it captures the drift. And please, anything to knock off the prayers. All day long they rise up, this great effluvia of pious whining, ass-kissing, toadying, favor-mongering. When was the last time I answered one? If, purely by coincidence —

*because it won't happen any other way —
some putz receives what he's prayed for he
broadcasts the news and hope is rekindled
in this forlorn and odious practice. Did I
ever say I wanted prayers? Maybe. It's hard
to keep track.*

*Balls! Boring. Nothing to do. It was better
before I decided to set a good example
and turned my back on my Old Testament
ways. There was some fun. Chatting it up
with bewildered old men in the desert.
Messing with Job on a bet with Beelzebub.
Maybe that Swiss fart-head, Jung, was
right. I, me, the real capo de tutti capi,
have been going through the same growing up process as humans. Wouldn't that
be a pisser?*

*Isn't there one of them down there doing
or thinking anything original?*

The antidote to boredom is new experiences, right? Given the
setting, my attempts to break out of the routine were predictable: I took up a hobby, moved into a new academic area, and
dallied.

10

Resolution attempt #1, the hobby

"I don't get it." Tiffany was scowling over my shoulder as I thumbed through an atlas.

"Don't get what, Fern tip?"

"The maps. Back in grad school when you should have been studying you were looking at your old maps from Vietnam. Now you should be writing scholarly stuff but you spend more time going over that old map of Utah than you do trying to make a career. Not to mention all the National Geographic maps you pore over as if you're about to set off on safari. Does this have anything to do with your homing pigeon yearnings?"

"It seems a normal interest."

"But, Max, you're the guy who says he doesn't know where he belongs. What good is a map if you don't know your destination?"

A clumsy bit of sophistry and I could have pointed out the flaw in her argument. Maps are about journeys, not necessarily destinations. Or, maps help you visualize where you *might* like to be.[*] But, debates with Tiffany aside, I did like maps, despite the unhappy event that led to the first one I'd kept. From the time of Debbie's death forward I'd been an indiscriminate map accumulator; I was about to become a discerning map collector.

Have You Ordered Your Map
- O. Webb, 1940

The survival chances of a very old map are slim. Just take a look at the odds facing a navigational chart produced in the seventeenth or eighteenth century: In the first instance very few were drawn because very few people had any idea of what the world looked like. In the second instance, of the few that were developed, only a limited number of copies were printed; the charts had commercial and/or military value which shouldn't be

---

[*] And, of course, they're educational. Here's a dispiriting statistic: one-fifth of all Americans are unable to identify the United States on a map of the world. These are probably the same lardheads who shout 'America's number one' – with no idea of where America is.

offered freely to a rival. Third, when the map was proved to be inaccurate – as they all eventually were – their inaccuracies became liabilities and they were withdrawn from circulation and destroyed. Finally, if any of the few in existence survived these perils, remember that they were made of a highly perishable material, paper, and could easily succumb to water, fire, and acids from proximate materials or acids in their own composition. Consider these challenges the next time you see an old map. I do. It was because of the enormously unfavorable odds they'd faced that I liked old maps from the start.

The start was a booth at an antique show in a local mall.

"Can I help ya' find something?" The speaker is the booth's proprietor, a short jowly man with thinning hair and two inches of dead cigar clenched in his ocherous teeth. Not what you'd expect for an antiquarian.

"The maps are all originals?"

"Look, bud. Would I put 'em out here if they wasn't?"

"How about maps of this area?"

"You get around much? The reason I ask is that the local rubes snap up the local maps. Beats me, but they want to see the name of their hometown – which is like Dry Heaves, Missouri or Dreary, Indiana – on an old piece of paper. But, a sale is a sale. If you want a good deal on an old map from around here, go to one of these antique fairs a little ways off. I mark my local maps up 100 percent and I'm sure the other sellers do more."

I was upgrading my opinion of the guy. "What would be a good buy, then?"

"If you know what you're doing," his expression conveyed absolute certainty that I did not, "you should be hittin' the estate auctions. Price of a map is about one-fourth what I have to get for it. If you don't know maps, forget about it. They ain't crooks at the auctions. They just don't know the business and they'll confuse a reproduction for an original every time."

He had pretty ordinary stuff, as I look back on it, but I parted with $150 for some nineteenth century maps, probably as a perverse response to his gruff anti-marketing behavior.

The Midwestern United States is not a hotbed of old map dealing. London is; Amsterdam and Utrecht are; the bank of the

Seine is on Sundays; but the corn belt is not. Fortunately there was a lively mail-order business conducted by dealers in London and Holland and it was through those that my collection increased.

Hat trick

There are four reasons for collecting old maps: dilettantes collect them as wall decorations and to impress their acquaintances; investors collect them because the value of the rare and semi-rare editions tends to increase steadily; sentimentalists collect them to preserve, and touch, a piece of the past; and aesthetes collect the elaborately embellished ones as works of inspired artistry. I fall into the first category; I like the way they look on the wall and the envy they inspire in guests.

So, there you have it, the trifecta:

- Pretentious name? Check.

- Pretentious theological pursuit? Check.

- Pretentious hobby? Check.

Tiffany was quick to point out that our household budget contained no line item for antiquarian maps. The problem with map collecting, as with many other hobbies, is that as you become more knowledgeable about the field, you inevitably want older and better and rarer maps. And they're more expensive.

Eight months into this hobby our walls sported the finest collection of ancient maps of Ceylon, known also as Taprobane and Serendib (to which we owe *serendipitous* of Arabic derivation), in the Midwestern United States. This was an expensive antidote to boredom. I totaled up the size of the investment in anticipation of a showdown with the fiscally vigilant Mrs. Brown and was dismayed to find that $1,300 had been squandered on old pieces of paper with inaccurate drawings on them – a vast sum in light of my paltry salary. As you'll see later, however, this modest investment ultimately paid a handsome return.

Petroglyph/map created by Native Americans. Pocatello, ID

11

Resolution attempt #2, a new academic area

Not all departments at the university were like Sociology. The Psych departments occupied the two floors beneath us, and a different planet. You've certainly heard that all psychologists are certifiably insane. In fairness, that's probably not true; however, it's no exaggeration to say that some are skating close to the boundary. On our campus the most entertaining subspecies of psychologist was the clinical. Every month a fresh tale would circulate regarding who was screwing or buggering whom in Clinical Psych. These stories were received with wonder as the Clinical Psych faculty had been shorted in the looks department, some of them severely so. It was generally believed that they publicly seduced so many, including one another, in order to demonstrate the power and utility of their science and not out of an excess of libido.

Let's stop here and ask: Are you getting enough sex? I hear a chorus of predominantly male voices crying back, "Hell, no!" That justifies another detour. Based upon what you've read so far you might question my credentials as an authority on this topic; however, an examination of the improbable success of the Clinical Psych faculty may teach us something.

How to get laid

Those of our colleagues who followed Carl Rogers would seduce a vulnerable individual by empathizing her, or sometimes him, into bed. They'd listen attentively to every asininity their prey might bleat, and they'd ooze compassionately, "Wow, I see where you're coming from," or "Uhuh," or "Yeah." These inarticulate Lotharios were easy to spot as their brows were prematurely creased from constant furrowing, a staple among their gestures of empathy. Their quarries, of course, were convinced that they'd encountered the one caring and spontaneous human being on the face of the earth. Who wouldn't want to hop into the sack with someone as wonderful as that?

The transactional analysts also did well. Riding on a wave of popularity generated by two intuitively appealing books (*Games People Play* and *I'm OK, You're OK*), the mark had usually been pre-sensitized to the message. And what was the message?

a) *I do not play games* (ha!).

b) *We are both OK*. She's not certain that she *is* OK; that's why the line is effective.

c) *We are both adults*. As opposed to acting like a scolding parent or petulant child. This is a key and complex point; it helps if she's read up on the underlying theory.

d) *Let's go to bed*.

That's a stripped down version, but I've seen it produce results. Try it.

A group of neo-Freudians held that patients in psychotherapy – which included not only those who came voluntarily for therapy but those who needed it but hadn't yet recognized the fact – should work out their problems directly with the therapist. Since so many problems derived, by their lights, from an underlying sexual conflict, they urged those who came under their spell to work for emotional wellness with them on the counseling couch.

There were also behavioralists, disciples of Reich and Janov, rational-emotive types, and more drawn from the vast and perplexing array of frauds and fads that populate psychology. Not all of these groups subscribed to philosophies of promiscuity, but probably felt that to be credible they had to play – and score – in the same game.

Pride Ugly Pride Sometimes Is Seen
- Armstrong, 1810

A different neurosis gripped our friends in the business school. Where the psychologists wanted to be known as lovers, the business faculty wanted to be thought of as social scientists. We 'true' social scientists, who were paid less and taught more than the business school faculty, were incensed by these pretensions.

The defenders of the faith fought an annual jihad over this issue when the faculty intramural softball season opened. Our team was unimaginatively – if accurately – named the *SocSci*

No-Stars.[**] A lengthy roster of overweight non-athletes from the social science departments and a smattering of business faculty signed up every year. The high turnout of social science faculty was to ensure that the identity of the team be preserved and the elected team captain would be a genuine social scientist. At the organizational meeting there would be at least one speech decrying the mongrelization of the team due to participation of faculty from a school that was labeled professional, applied, or trade, depending upon the meanness of the speaker. This always made the business teachers uncomfortable and the dimmest among them would rise to the defense.

A second reason for the good turnout of social science faculty was that this meeting provided an opportunity to show off. If there was discussion – and of course there always was – dismal options were presented as Hobson's choice. Logical arguments were said to have been constructed in accordance with Occam's razor. One of my colleagues would work in a reference to Potemkin villages. And if the discussion grew heated someone from our side might suggest the business teachers were guilty of glossolalia. [*]

What a bunch of jerks. The objective, if it's not obvious, was to let the business teachers know they had no business on a university campus where erudition was the exclusive purview of the liberal arts.

After these preliminaries and one dispiriting practice, the politicians would melt away and the team would limp through the season with no certainty that enough players would appear Sunday to avoid a forfeit.

———

"We didn't have a great record last year (two wins – both thanks to forfeits – and eight losses), but I'm confident that if

---

[**] Frick, who played second base, petitioned tirelessly to change the name to Nads in the expectation that our wives and sweethearts would cheer "Go Nads!" from the stands.

[*] If you don't recognize these terms – and there's no reason you should – there are shorthand definitions in the Glossary.

we all pull together we can improve on that." The speaker is Team Captain Dennis. In the apparent belief that a demonstration of leadership on the softball field would improve his chances for promotion, Dennis perennially sought the position of team captain. Since I was untenured I had no vote on Dennis' career advancement, but I was pretty sure of my leanings. He was an asshole. Here's a sample of his leadership style during a game:

"Come on, Brown. Don't stand there with the ball in your hand. It was *not* a gift bestowed on you by the batter. After you're through bobbling it, you're supposed to throw it to someone in the infield."

What was annoying about his criticisms was that there was an element of truth. I did frequently struggle to bring a fly-ball or grounder under control – rarely dropping it, but often juggling it – and then I would frantically look from base to base, undecided where I should throw the thing. Someone in a T-group had told me I seemed unable to let go of things. Even a softball? Perhaps so. Once it's thrown there's no withdrawing the decision.

The most reliable player, as measured by attendance, was the chairman of the Management Department, John Hall, one of the few genuinely endearing people on campus and someone who moved my career in an unexpected direction.

John was a large florid man with only a fringe of white hair that made him appear ten years older than his actual age. His team nickname was Swish – not for his effeminate walk but for his performance at the plate – and he was only allowed to play substitute right field.

John and I were swilling down beers[*] on the bench one warm Sunday while our team was at bat and I put a proposition to him. "John, any chance of me teaching in your department?"

---

[*] Frick reported that the trend line for beaned players on our team was 0.38 over seven innings and the correlation coefficient was 0.55, evidence of a strong association between alcohol consumption and deteriorating coordination. To the relief of all in the department, the reviewers of three journals failed to find adequate intellectual merit in the research and rejected it.

John studied the pull-tab on another Schlitz and without looking up asked, "You ever study management?"

"No."

John pulled back the tab; "Do you have any practical experience in business."

Deciding that summer help at the Dairy Queen wasn't what he meant I forced out a casual, "No, not really."

"How about research in business or on business organizations?"

This wasn't going well. "No."

"Well," drawled John, and he looked out at the mound where the opposing team's pitcher was scratching his crotch, "you seem as qualified as anyone else in the department." He sipped the foam bubbling up onto the top of the can. "Could you pick up an OB course fall semester for us?"

Absolutely! Without inquiring what OB meant – obstetrics maybe? – I checked with our chairman who confirmed what was widely alleged. We had too many faculty for the dwindling number of students still interested in our offerings. He regarded my finding employment elsewhere as a service to the department and went to the extraordinary length of penning a memo to the Dean of the Business School applauding the decision of that group to import a fresh perspective and some intellectual rigor. This put a chill on the reception but it didn't sink the deal.

A little contextual information here: OB stands for Organizational Behavior, a bastard offspring of sociology and social psychology, but with a welcome focus. The objects of study were usually middle-class white males, the group that traditional sociology had largely ignored. OB researchers, rather than preoccupy themselves with the formation of gangs in prisons or the normative basis of pimp-prostitute relations, sought to describe how alliances were formed among managers or what factors were associated with career success.

I embraced this new discipline in the heady expectation that, now aligned with a field that addressed practical questions, great wellsprings of motivation would be released within my long dormant intellect. Yessir! No longer a voyeur peering into the lives of the less fortunate from my academic cloister. As soon as I had a grasp of the central issues in OB I'd be a fount of research productivity.

Do I have to tell you how that played out?

The B school faculty were, with a few happy exceptions, no more likeable than the sociologists. Equally pathetic, but for different reasons.

Social science professors play to the fractious, heckling audience of other social science professors. In contrast, the business professors try to please two audiences: A university administration drawn largely from the liberal arts, and, secondarily, the business community which indulgently allows business professors a seat at the table, but rarely takes them seriously. The upshot was that our business faculty, with an eye on the business community, were forever trying to disprove George Bernard Shaw's dictum, 'those who can't, teach,' by consulting, running a small business on the side, or playing the stock market. The university administration viewed these activities with alarm, as distractions from scholarly endeavor, and was ever vigilant for a business professor who used the university as a base of operations rather than the center of his universe. In this the administrators were joined by the liberal arts faculties, possessed of a knee-jerk reaction to their business school colleagues as the hand-maidens of corporate America. "Red in tooth and claw," someone would mutter whenever the topic of business education came up.

Thanks to their split academic identities, the business teachers were a trial to be around. Several sought me out assuming that our association was evidence that they, like me, were true-blue academicians (if only they knew!). Others viewed my tilt toward professional education as acknowledgement that the disciplinary boundaries were disappearing and they wanted me to testify to that. And still others wanted to socialize with us for no larger apparent reason than to stare, jaws aslack, at Tiffany.

Have you anticipated the punch line here? Of course you have. Max didn't belong.

The students in sociology and business differed as well, but in a potentially useful way. The sociology students enrolled for an enormous variety of reasons, none of which was a desire for personal advancement; that, however, was the predominant motivation for the graduate students in business. This was especially true of the females who, I noted, were prettier than the sociology students. The business students were there to practice being tough-minded and practical. They affected deep voices, they often wore suits to class, and they tended to issue pronouncements rather than make simple statements. Their view of business was that it was amoral, single-minded, and efficient. Again the women tended to be the more extreme and sounded as hard-bitten as drill instructors – when they weren't flirting shamelessly.

It was that last, the flirting, that nourished the hope that exciting possibilities awaited just over the departmental divide.

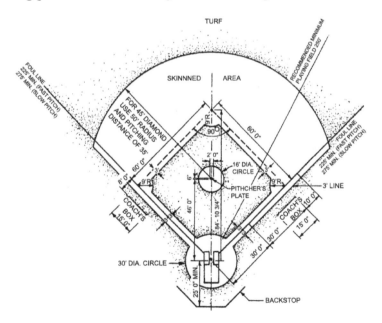

Softball diamond.

12

Resolution attempt #3, dalliance

Did I say the problem was boredom? Let's be honest. It was sexual starvation. One of the reasons for moving closer to the business school was that there seemed to be more action over there – action in the colloquial sense. Colleagues daily pointed out gorgeous coeds in the cafeteria who were rumored to be sleeping their way to a degree.

"See that one in the red sweater, Max?" Shoving her tray along the food line, a curvaceous brunette couldn't escape notice. "Guess who's boffing her?"

"Careful, Dennis. I'm the jealous type and could easily go on a killing spree if I learned she were unfaithful to me – starting with the messenger bearing the news."

"You wish. The word is she's involved in a steamy three-way with two guys in Marketing. Kinky, huh?"

"It makes you wonder what bedroom arrangements a double major might lead to. But, speaking of sex and marketing, we noticed as you walked in that you're prepared for action."

"Huh?"

"Your fly is at half-mast, Dennis." He stared blankly into space, his hands slipping below the table to verify and correct the problem. "We were discussing it and concluded it's a form of advertising. Always a good investment, especially when peddling inferior merchandise." The other two professors at the table guffawed – more than the line deserved. I don't know what it was about Dennis. I couldn't resist a shot.

It was all a man could do not to sob out loud at these tales of unbridled coupling; why should such good fortune elude me? The accounting faculty, fusty and oldish, were reportedly the heaviest scoring group because their courses were difficult and the exam content unpredictable. There were witless attempts to contrast 'hard' courses with the others, but aside from the frenzied couplings of the clinical psychologists, the business school had the reputation for the most activity.

Some of that activity would have been most welcome. Nothing was happening at home. Tiffany took the unnecessary precaution every evening, when not in menses, of starting a small fight just before bedtime. This precluded any amorous advances from me but they wouldn't have been forthcoming anyway since I'd thrown in the towel long ago. Occasionally we got drunk enough or something titillated us and sex would follow. But the glow would be gone by morning. Her transparent gambit of starting a fight over some non-existent slight was doubly irritating since it ensured that I'd go to bed both horny and ticked. I often rehearsed how I'd tell Tiffany to knock this off.

"Buttercup, knock off the cheap shit. I harbor no carnal intentions." Too curt and stilted. And the 'no carnal intentions' wasn't credible.

"Lotus lips, there's no need to argue (said soothingly). We're married (said earnestly). I love you deeply (said brightly). AND I WOULDN'T TOUCH YOUR INVIOLATE LILY WHITE BODY WITH A FUCKING TEN FOOT POLE!" (said at the top of my voice).

You can see the problem. I was so incensed by years of her behavior that if I started out on the subject I couldn't trust myself not to really get going. I often wondered if maybe I wouldn't wind up smacking her. And then I wondered if that was such a bad idea. Of course it was a bad idea. Without even getting to the ethics of the matter, she'd use the incident against me for all time.

So you might anticipate a slavering receptivity to the possibilities that professorial contacts with female students might provide. Receptive, but unprepared.

Happy Be Devoted Teachers
- S. Michael, 1882

It's an understatement to say that my courses were easy. Continuous respiration for three consecutive months was all that was required to earn a passing grade, and this was true for the bulk of my colleagues. It wasn't that we didn't have standards; we did. I deeply felt that over half of the students in every class should be failed and a few of that group be required to display a warning to alert the world of their profound stupidity, perhaps a Scarlet D for Dumb. But it was just too much hassle to mete out the marks deserved.

A low grade almost insured the student would protest and the chairperson would have to review all relevant material. His or her opinion was only advisory; the University Senate had seen to that – academic freedom, the specter of Hitler. If you didn't cave at that point, the student would take the case to the Dean who would also have to review everything. The upshot? Although the school administrators decried grade inflation, not a one of them would thank the faculty member who assigned a low grade that would launch this tedious process.

Did you know this when you were in college? I wish I had.

I failed one student in five years. I misinterpreted his poor attendance record as disinterest; actually he'd been killed in an automobile accident the second week of the term.

Given these grading practices you wouldn't realistically anticipate that any nubile vixen would offer her fair body in exchange for a passing mark. Would you? It caught *me* by surprise, despite months of wistful longing.

There were several comely lasses who staked out the front row of the class, ample leg on display. But what male with a pulse wouldn't be attracted to the redhead who sat in the last row, her desk moved so that she was fully visible? And she was smart, although it was never clear that she'd prepared for class. Her hand was never the first one up, but she had a knack for joining in late, as class discussion stalled, and summarizing or drawing out the conclusion I'd hoped to extract from the session.

Unfortunately, none of these lovelies had shown any amorous interest and the prospect of carnal encounters became a fading fantasy.

Wasted Opportunities We Can Ne'er Regain
- T.D. Lemmond, 1894

As the students filed in to take the final, spring was in the air, but romance was not. Each student who passed through the door represented another joyless half-hour of grading. The adorable redhead waited with me outside the classroom and when the corridor was empty she fixed her gaze on my belt buckle – or was it my fly – and said earnestly, "Professah Brayown, Ah'd do anythang fo' a passing grade in yoah course." She looked up, and seeing my bewildered expression repeated, "Anythang," and went into the room.

I didn't believe it. The proposal was at odds with her looks and demeanor; she was the picture of corn-fed wholesomeness. Clearly she meant additional course work, perhaps a report on a book that I might assign her. What professor wants to have to grade another report? Maybe she intended to do library research in the mistaken belief I was a practicing academic. I didn't want that either.

I couldn't take my eyes off her. First I checked the eyebrows to determine if the red hair was authentic. It seemed to be and there were a few freckles for corroboration. Weren't redheads supposed to be passionate? Then I tried to imagine what she would look like undressed. Pretty good. And where had the broad southern accent come from? Hadn't noticed that before.

This went on for the full two hours of the exam and I was in a wild-eyed state when she turned in her blue book with the rest of the laggards. What should I say? I wanted to keep my options open until I could think clearly about this. What would *she* say? Nothing, but she looked at me inquiringly and I announced to the class in general that the grades wouldn't be submitted for another ten days. That would give her time to clarify her intentions. This was her problem, right?

Back in my office I pulled her exam booklet from the pile. She'd carefully copied each of the exam questions on a separate page but had written nothing more. On the bottom of the final page she'd printed her telephone number and address. That seemed to clinch it – the address.

For two days I thought of little else. She was too young. What was the age for statutory rape? No, I was okay there; her class registration card showed her to be 26. She looked younger. Married? Probably not and what difference would it make. Carrier of some nasty social disease? Possible, but that's what rubbers are for.

At the end of the second day I called. Perhaps I'd read too much into her statement. "Sally, this is Professor Brown. I've looked at your exam. Did you have in mind doing some compensatory work?" That much had been rehearsed.

"Compensatory?" and silence. Damn, a sociology student would have understood the word. I had no more prepared lines and the ball hadn't left my court.

"Something to make up for not completing the test," I explained lamely.

"Well, Ah do know the meaning of the word." she sounded confused. "Ah thought you'd understand. After all, Ah put down mah address."

Indeed she had. What game was I playing? It was evident that the decision was mine to make and I shouldn't badger her for any clearer declaration. What did I want: A price list? A printed menu? I envisioned one, bound in leather.

Appetizers	Price
Strip Tease	D
A sensuous treat that will whet your appetite for more.	
Served to the accompaniment of swelling organ music.	
Vigorous fondling	D+
An especially exotic dish spiced with secret ingredients.	
A tonic for both body and spirit.	
Deep kissing while fondling	C-
A specialty of the house combining two of our favorite	
offerings. You'll want to tell your friends about this one.	

"Yes, I guess I did understand. Perhaps we should discuss this – but not here." Christ, that sounded avuncular and I was still jerking her around. "Sorry. I don't mean discuss. I think I know what you're offering and I accept that offer."

Holy shit! Was I buying soybean futures? I accept your offer? Now it was her turn to give me the treatment; she was silent. When had I decided to go through with this? I hadn't. I'd assumed it would dissolve and I could anguish over the lost opportunity. "Sally, are you there?"

She waited before responding. "When do y'all want to do it?" It? That sounded awful. Fulfill the contract. I *was* buying a commodity. But scheduling meetings is a more normal topic of discussion and the conversation started to go better.

"My schedule is pretty flexible except for an exam that I have to give tomorrow."

"The next day then? In the afte'noon? Ah get back off work at two."

"Three o'clock then?" I said, trying to regain some measure of control over things.

She agreed and signed off with a cheery, "Bye-bye."

I'll spare you the agonies I went through for the next 47 hours. But one thought hit like an exploding horse turd. What if she was setting me up for blackmail? Or just wanted to ruin a professor in retribution for all the evils done to her in the name of education. Entrapment! Jolted out of the throes of passion by exploding flash bulbs. Or a videotape, shot from behind a one-way mirror, delivered to the president of the university. I could back out and not show up, but that might be worse. She could have taped the telephone conversation and would use that with a vengeance if I stood her up. But why attribute such dark motives? Her exam booklet looked pretty incriminating and I'd heard this stuff went on all the time. Why couldn't it be my turn?

The appointed hour arrived and I thought of driving, but discarded it; how to explain the presence of my car anywhere but in the faculty parking lot? So I took a bus and, absorbed in a final internal argument over the wisdom of this course, inadvertently rode two stops beyond the one nearest Sally's house.

The neighborhood was what you'd picture for a struggling student: rows of small clapboard houses, fronted by untended yards where weeds and broken toys provided the only relief from the dead brown grass and unraked leaves. Most of the houses had burglar bars on some, but never all of the first story windows. As I walked, a late spring shower broke, justifying an umbrella for protection against the elements, but also conveniently tilted to conceal my identity from the occupants of passing cars. My mind flashed headlines in the student newspaper:

Soc. Prof Diddles Bus. Student
Prof. Brown — Pants Down
Violated Coed Seeks Legal Damages
Dallying Don Dismissed

Only the headlines would matter. The articles themselves would be incomprehensible, testimony to the fine work of our Journalism faculty.

Sally's address was on a small white house, the vinyl siding of which had started to warp and pull away from the plywood sheathing beneath. The house had been awkwardly converted into apartments; the location of the doorbell button with Sally's name above it suggested her apartment was on the second floor. She'd had few recent visitors as evidenced by the coating of pigeon poop on the button. I pressed the bell with the tip of the umbrella and waited. Would she be wearing a feathered boa? Or a long slinky nightgown? Should I be offended if she'd gone to no evident pains in anticipation of my arrival?

I rang again. No one answered. *Fuck!* It *was* a set-up. She was somewhere laughing her ass off at my expense. I felt old. I felt foolish. After all it had taken to get that far it was difficult to go back down the porch steps. The rain picked up. Murderous thoughts replaced those of humiliation. Was there a grade lower than F?

As I reached the sidewalk a yellow Vega careened around the corner, rattling and belching blue smoke in the great traditions of the mark. It came jerkily to a halt and Sally could be seen wrestling with the driver's door. She slid across the seat and emerged from the passenger's side and called out, "I'm so sorry. I wanted to be here and have everything nice for you and this damn shitbox car wouldn't run. I tried to call your office but they said you'd left so I told them that I might be late if you called in."

"You called my office?" I bleated. In the shock that my philandering could now be public knowledge the fact that her southern accent had disappeared was slow to register. "You left a message?"

"Yeah, but I gave my name as Shelly. I figured you'd figure it out. So no one's any the wiser."

Great, they'll think I'm porking some nymphette named Shelly rather than Sally. I started to frame an explanation of the ineffectiveness of her ruse, but abandoned it and, sharing the umbrella, helped her with the shopping bags in the trunk. They were filled with jug wine and party food.

"Having a party?" She hadn't serviced me yet and was already laying on the next fête.

"Us, of cou'se," she said brightly, the southern accent back in full force.

There was a half-gallon of wine and I wondered which of us she thought needed that much lubrication to get through what loomed more as an ordeal than an orgy. "I'm a light drinker," I lied to no purpose. She looked crestfallen and I was sorry I'd said it. When we got into her apartment, complete with two posters (the *Jefferson Airplane* and a stern *Uncle Sam Wants You*) and an enormous off-brand stereo, I turned paternal and sat down opposite her. "Sally, are you sure this is a good idea? I'm afraid that you're going to do something that you're not cut out for." Annoyed at the patronizing way this had come out I continued in a more colloquial vein, "I'd really like to make it with you but I don't want to mess up your head in the process." That was better and she nodded solemnly.

"It's nothin' like that. Ah've really liked you. Don't get me wrong. Ah'm not a collector or promiscuous or anything. Ah just figured you'd have a lot of experience – you know, your name and the way you talk and all – and," she looked embarrassed, "it could solve a problem with mah grades." I wondered if this was my cue to say something, but she continued. "It's not like Ah want to be in this situation. Ah've had to work extra shifts to catch up since Ah lost two weeks to the flu in March. Natcherly the courses turned out to be harder than Ah expected and Ah was so far behind Ah knew Ah could never finish all the papers and study fo' the exams. So Ah made a decision and came on to you. You're far away the best looking teacher in the faculty, and the way you talk makes you sound sexy."

That was great to hear. Tiffany said I talked like I had a 54 ounce Louisville Slugger up my ass which doubly pissed me off. Beyond the insult, that was Babe Ruth's bat and I felt I should be the sole custodian of baseball trivia.

"Well, I have to tell you, Sally, I've certainly noticed you. Great looks and a strong intellect. I'm surprised someone as smart as you got behind in your studies." *Wait a minute. This sounds like verbal foreplay.* Were we trying to convert a shoddy transaction into something bordering on romance?

We drank some of the jug wine and I tried to dispel her inflated notions about the superiority of professors – wasn't my presence there disillusioning enough? Then very matter of factly we went to her bedroom and did it.

'It' was pretty disappointing. She opened with a coy undressing routine – very good figure, cute round rump – and then she performed an unnatural act on me the effect of which was opposite that intended. To overcome the embarrassing flaccidness I focused my attention on her smooth undulating backside and my interest was renewed. I hastened her to the main event, hoping there'd be no request to stop, find, and put on a condom. And then to my chagrin I was finished before we really got started. I thought of explaining that this was the first accompanied orgasm I'd had in over a month but noticed that she seemed pleased. "Am Ah really that good?" she beamed. "Ah mean Ah don't have much experience but Ah've nevah satisfied a man that fast befo'." The comparison made me feel even worse but I was grateful to be let off the hook.

"That was just a little release of steam," I explained grandly. "Now we can get on with things."

Such promises should not be lightly made. We got on with things but there were too many distractions. Her movements seemed awkward. The bed didn't feel right. I kept getting her hair in my mouth. She scarcely made a sound. As we bumped and thrust at one another I realized that one of the values of orgasms is that they're a universally recognized signal of when to quit. Finally, fearful that I might detumesce, I faked it. She couldn't know the difference.

Some more wine, some stale cheesy crackers and out the door where remorse and guilt mugged me on the steps. The closest we'd gotten to intimacy was sharing an umbrella, which I'd left behind and was now unwilling to go back for despite the continuing rain.

Poor Esau Repented Too Late
- Unknown, 1791

I was testy with Tiff. Wasn't it her fault that I'd been driven to depravity? And I anxiously waited for the mailman to deliver a copy of a compromising tape or photo. When none had arrived after three days I moved on to what grade to give Sally. An 'A' for enterprise? It was a management course, after all. A 'D' for performance? Not fair. Consider my own performance on the occasion. Wouldn't a high grade encourage her to sink further into a life of sin and licentiousness? But wouldn't a low grade violate the unwritten contract between us? At one point I jotted down and weighted all the elements of her performance -

Undressing	10%	A-
Kissing	10%	B
Blow job	20%	D+
Screwing	30%	C

I tore up the paper and later worried that I hadn't burned it.

When the grade rolls were due and with the department secretary hovering over my shoulder I scratched in a C+ for Sally. That seemed safe.

13

A Day of Reckoning Is Coming
- F. Rich, n.d.

Safe? How wrong can a person be? John's secretary called two weeks later to tell me John wanted to see me as soon as possible. The urgency was surprising; certainly congratulations for the fine teaching job could wait.

John had laid claim to one of the larger offices on campus, a claim he buttressed by filling the office with books and papers, boxes bulging with, presumably, more of the same, two small tables that looked like they'd buckle under the load, and a large desk turned inhospitably toward the wall. The total effect, and presumably the one John was aiming for, was to make visitors uncomfortably aware that they were trespassing on someone's work area and the work was crying out for attention. John always scheduled leisurely chats in other places as few visitors were likely to remain long in his office.

Nodded in by his secretary, I approached John's round back as he hunched over the desk, stepping carefully through stacks of journals and federal publications. "Trouble", John said as he half turned and waved a typewritten letter.

```
Dear Chairman Hall,

I am writing to you because I don't know who
else to turn to. I am a graduate student in
your department and I am working my way
through school. I just started graduate work
last year but hopefully I will finish next
semester. Last semester I took Intro Mgt
from Profesor Brown. I thought I did pretty
well but Profesor Brown said I was failing
and I would have to do something special to
pass. I will not spell it out for you since
I know you will understand my meaning. He
told me to just come to the final exam and
not write anything except where we could
meet later. At the end of the exam he said
very meaningfully that the grades would not
be decided for ten days which told me how
long I had to "pass" the course.
```

Passing the course is very important to me
for my career. My parents are no longer living so I have to work to pay my tuition
which is also why my grades are sometimes
not as good as I know they could be. I felt
I had no choice so when he called me I had
to go through with it. I have been tormented
by this thing ever since and I am writing to
you to see if you can do something so that
other women like me will not be forced to do
things against their will. I will not tell
you that we women are at a disadvantage in
business already.

To show his total disregard for me Profesor
Brown gave me a C+ for the course.

                    Sincerely yours,

                    Sally Taylor

"Holy shit, John, the bitch is trying to ruin me!"

"You're referring to the copy she sent, I assume?" I wasn't
because I hadn't noticed it.

"Holy shit! God's great dangling balls!"

There at the bottom:

cc: Prof. Wagner, Chairman of Sociology

"John, it wasn't like this at all!"

"I know, Max. For all the sophistication you project, you're
still a clueless bumpkin under the surface. You fucked up." The
admonitory lecture over, "The letter came this morning so you
should be hearing from your chairman soon. I'd like to help you
but you really put your dork in the wringer on this one."

Christ, what a fix! Then I brightened, "Wait, wait! There's
hope. Wagner went to his 'cabin'." Mention of the chairman's
cabin always conjured images of a rodent infested shack or a
small trailer on cinder blocks. "He may not be back yet. Save
the ass-chewing for later while I see if I can contain the damage."

There is Constant Joy Abiding
- F. J. Crosby, 1896

Summer's heat and humidity had arrived prematurely. By the time I'd raced the 200 yards to the soc sci building, scattering the quad's pigeons that waddled indignantly out of the way, I was perspiring freely. Climbing the stairs to the fourth floor in order to continue burning adrenaline, I followed the well-marked path to the chairman's office. A large wooden arrow near the elevators bore the message **Chairman - Sociology.** A plastic sign over the door to the outer office where his secretary lurked announced the same. A metal sign on the inner office door said grandly

```
B.S. Wagner
Chairman
Sociology
```

and a triangular shaped tube on his desk confirmed, in inlaid pieces of broken glass, '**B. Samuel Wagner, PhD – Chairman.**' Who could fail to be impressed by the multiple media employed: wood, plastic, metal, glass?

Controlling my breathing I stepped into the outer office and met, with sinking heart, the malevolent stare of Wagner's secretary, misnamed Joy. My immediate concern – that her expression bespoke discovery – waned as I recalled she always looked at me as if I'd just dosed her grand-daughter with clap.

"Joy, any sign of Dr. Sam?" delivered as off-handedly as possible – given the circumstances.

She waited to answer as if trying to decide whether it was a trick question. Pursing her lips she finally favored me with, "He should be in later to pick up his mail. Why?"

Pick up his mail? Later? He's coming *later* to pick up his mail!! *Thank you dear Lord. I have sinned and in Your mercy You have bestowed upon this unworthy servant a second chance. See You in church on Sunday, Big Fella!*

"Oh, I just wanted to discuss something with him but it can wait until he has some free time. Keep smiling."

I retreated to my office. How to get past the charmless Joy and to the mail which was certainly on Wagner's desk? Easy. I dialed the bubble-headed receptionist in the Anthropology Department, one floor up. "Could you get me the secretary from Sociology? Their lines seem to be tied up and it's pretty important that I speak to someone." She said yes, as no request ever seemed too inane to her.

Half a minute later she flounced by and then returned with a grumbling Joy in tow. Congratulating myself on the success of this ruse I eased into the hall and sidled to the chairman's office while keeping the hall under surveillance over my shoulder.

Quickly to Wagner's desk. There was the pile of correspondence. *Oh happy day; my salvation at hand. My redeemer liveth . . .*

Oh shit! Oh fuck! Forget the Sunday rendezvous God; You've got one sick sense of humor. There was Sally's letter on top, slit open by the efficient Joy, and bearing a note,

I think this one is urgent. J

O That My Load of Sin Were Gone
- C. Wesley, 1873

"That's it John. I'm done for. There was no point in taking the letter since his secretary had already read it. Sam will blow this thing to the sky and Joy'll put it into the gossip mill so it's only a matter of time before some malicious dickwad, claiming their only motivation is a desire 'to save the family,' will tell Tiffany."

John rested his chin on his fingertips. "Wrong and right," he finally said. "Wrong. Your chairman won't blow this up. By the perverse logic that governs this place, your errant ways reflect on his leadership; he'll want this to go away as quickly as possible. His big problem – the same as yours – is his snooping secretary. Right, however, that Tiffany will get wind of it sooner or later. I'm always amazed at how fast bad news travels around this place, so probably sooner. Some mean SOB will pass it on to Tiffany, that's a certainty; probably some drab little sparrow envious of Tiffany's extensive connections and fine manners."

Like the practiced management consultant he was, John paused and shifted in his chair to indicate his analysis of the situation was complete and the next section would deal with recommendations.

"Now here's what you have to do – and you owe me your closest attention because you deposited this turd in my department:

"First, send in a grade change to the Registrar giving this woman an 'A.' A rational blackmailer quits when there's nothing more to get. She wants the grade changed because she brought up the 'C+' at the end of her letter, and there's nothing more she can get from you than a grade.

"Second, put on your sack cloth and ashes and crawl on bloodied knees over to your chairman and give him an award winning performance in contrition. Promise me you'll rein in your smartass inclinations." He paused; he wanted the promise.

"Of course, John. Reined in."

He didn't look reassured, but continued.

"Third, get Tiffany out of town for a while. It's summer. Keep her away until this becomes old news. A better story will come along to keep the busybodies occupied.

"Fourth, and this is the big one, I think you should consider moving to another school, at least for a while."

"What? I can *consider* moving John, but it'd be real hard. I have no connections and no leads."

John looked impatient. "Watch my lips boy, *word gets around this place*." I watched his lips. "Our Bible quoting chancellor would love something like this. He won't get an official complaint so he won't have to take any formal action and that leaves him free to adopt a much stronger position in private. I can hear that sepulchral voice going on in meetings." John tucked his meaty chin into his neck in imitation of the second-ranking officer in the university. "'It has come, unofficially, to the notice of the Chancellah's office that junya faculty in some unnamed depahtments' – and he'll look at Wagner or me or both of us long enough to make sure everyone in the room knows which departments are unnamed – 'have been engaged in the most despicable, the filthiest, the most reprehensible behavya it is possible for anyone entrusted with guiding our youth to stoop to . . . ' and on and on."

"But, wouldn't . . ." I interjected. John, his impatience resurfacing, cut me off and resumed.

"This isn't the kindest moment to bring this up, Max, but your acerbic ways have earned you enough ill-wishers to guarantee the story will not only stay alive, but will grow new chapters and colorful embellishments. You can't do yourself any good here. Picture a piñata at a biker gang birthday party. That's you."

Alarmed by the unbidden appearance of an Old Testament deity who exhibited zero tolerance for even minor infractions, I really didn't want to turn tail and run. My crime, I reminded myself, was not that great. That, however, wasn't what John, my lone ally, wanted to hear. "You're right, John. I really appreciate your advice. I'll get busy on points one and two right now. Not sure what I can do about moving, but let me think."

Did I already say that this was a prince of a man? Driven by the urgency of my dilemma and the inhospitable ambience of John's office, I took off again.

After forging Wagner's signature on a grade change authorization for Sally and dropping it in the campus mail I went to plead for an audience with the Great Scholar himself. Joy received this request with her customary stoniness and instructed me to wait. She was sure, she sneered, that the chairman would want to talk to me. So I sat across from Joy in the outer office and waited. As I waited I catalogued the injustices that had brought me to this point:

1. My record had been spotless for almost six years and this was my first offense.

2. And what offense? I'd made no overtures to this woman. I was the victim, not the predator.

3. At that very moment, probably right there in the building, a professor and a student were doing something naughty. So, what's the big deal?

4. Finally, she was making out like a bandit and I stood in peril of losing my career and my marriage. Never mind that I considered divorce weekly.

I kept going over these points and with each review became more incensed at this gross breach of fair play. Wasn't it time to take up arms against a sea of hypocrisy? Wouldn't the justice of my case be evident to any fair-minded person? Is it not the duty of an academician to stand up to sham morality?

But self-deception crumbles under its own weight at some point. Yes, faculty–student couplings might be going on all around, but certainly with better motives than I'd had. Perhaps students and teachers were hooking up out of mutual attraction. Maybe mutual loneliness. Maybe a mutual need for reassurance. I'd engaged in the lowest form of prostitution. As a john I'd paid in a currency that wasn't even mine to spend. The only thing preventing further descent into self-recrimination was that I despised Joy and Wagner more.

At this point Joy cleared her throat and tilted her chin in the direction of Chairman Wagner's door.

Humbly Now With Deep Contrition
- A. C. Cross, 1901

Wagner was pretending to work on some papers and my arrival was a surprise. It occurred to me later he'd kept me waiting so he could rehearse the dressing down he was about to administer; such opportunities are rare in the faux collegial atmosphere that pervades the ivy-covered walls. He stacked the papers; with ex-aggerated care he straightened them; he looked up at me, then returned his attention to the stack of papers, and squared them again. I was ready to punch the pompous shit.

"Well, Max, we have a problem here. A very serious prob-lem. It seems there has been a complaint made against you. A very serious complaint." He didn't signal that I should sit.

"I feel terrible, but it's not quite as the young lady described in her letter." Wagner ignored this and continued haltingly with some perfunctory remarks about the 'calling' of teaching, our responsibility to guide the young, and some BS about rôle mod-els. At this point he fell into his accustomed rhythm and droned on without pause.

Out of deference to John I kept my head down and weaved slowly from side to side as if in wonderment at my own failings – although I still wanted to plant my fist on his bulbous nose.

Wagner seemed to draw courage from this display of self-abasement and before embarking on the next chapter of his discourse paused to inquire sharply, "Do you follow what I'm saying, Brown?"

That was too much. "I can manage the small words," I mumbled. Then, alarmed that I'd blown the whole bit with one smart-ass remark, I shrugged and gave him a hang-dog grin as if, deranged by the enormity of my self-inflicted problems, I could do no better than try to inject levity where it was least appropriate.

Perhaps he bought that as he resumed with some asininities about morality and codes of conduct, written and unwritten. This segued into a homily on a man's responsibility to curb his appetites and not prey on those weaker than himself – pretty racy stuff for B. S. Wagner.

The monologue droned on for a few more minutes until Wagner decided it was audience participation time again. "So, Brown. Considering what we've just discussed (we?), what is it that we men have to acknowledge as a fundamental truth?" He looked at me intently, his head cocked slightly. He expected an answer. A fundamental truth known to all men? The emphasis seemed to be on men. How about this:

'No matter how you shake and dance, the last two drops go in your pants.'

There's a fundamental truth for you, known to all males over the age of ten, but I didn't have a chance to deliver it. Joy's announcement from the outer office that the Dean was on the phone snatched away the opportunity.

Dean Poligrip knew about Sally too?

Apparently not. The conversation seemed to be about a curriculum proposal.

"Yessir, I received it and read it first thing."

. . .

"Absolutely. I knew it had to be your work – all the hallmarks were there."

. . .

"I especially liked your suggestions on core courses; you certainly cut through the chaff on those."

. . .

"I know it's selfish, but I wish we could have the benefit of your guidance on all our problems."

I fought down the urge to make kissing noises. I'm in the stocks and this braying jackass, this rump-bussing sycophant was taking liberties with *my* patience and self-esteem? Dangerous sentiments were stirring again.

At that moment I recognized what one of my clenched fists, both dug into my jacket pockets throughout the ordeal, held. With elation I drew it out while the chairman purred on. It was a chapstick left over from the winter. Should I? Not the best come back, but it was what had presented itself. I turned the little tube slowly; Wagner, distracted by these movements, looked up. With a slow sweep of my arm I presented him with the lip balm and my warmest smile. It was only a small measure of retaliation, but self-regard demanded some response.

He hesitated and took it and . . . smiled back. A man too obtuse to insult. Now what?

Then another more direct and less ambiguous means of delivering the message presented itself. The cafeteria management, as a low practical joke, had decreed that Wednesday was Mexican Day. One result was that, weather allowing, every classroom window was open on Wednesday afternoons. I'd been containing the pressure for over thirty minutes. What better time than the present to find relief *plus* issue a clear declaration of contempt for the current proceedings? Wagner's eyes were now on me as he tried to decipher the lip balm gift.

Should I do it? What if that long contained back pressure only produced a comical little *pfft*? Could I sell that as an indication my contempt for this unworthy adversary was so absolute that I would expend no more than a faint zephyr?

What the hell. I smiled, raised my right leg and produced . . . a trumpet blast!

No need to explain that to Wagner. His face turned brick red.

"Why, you shit fuck! You . . ."

. . .

"No, Dean, I didn't mean you."

. . .

"No sir, it was something else."

. . .

"Tourette's? Of course not sir."

This was fun to watch but, the exit line having been delivered, it was necessary to carry through. Touching my brow in a small salute, I walked out, pausing by Joy's desk. Unfortunately the supply of ammo was depleted.

You're expecting self-congratulations. No, this was due to luck. It could have all gone wrong: Smelly but inaudible => has Max shit himself? Burbling and moist => yech! A pathetic toot => pathetic.

The fact is, few people have, or are likely to gain, adequate control over their own flatulence. That's not to say that we can't start laying some ground rules. Bear with me for another quick detour:

How to fart

There are occasions when a well-timed fart is an effective, yet woefully under-utilized form of communication.

When to fart. Apart from dealing with a pressing ana-
tomical imperative, the properly executed release of back pressure may be used to signal a) your emphatic disagreement (see above), b) your disdain for present company (same again), or c) your self-confidence and sense of superiority. In all three instances the act must be audible; otherwise, what's the point?

In the first and third cases courtesy may demand that audibility not be accompanied by smellability. Stand downwind, by a fire, open door or window, etc.

Timing is everything. Since a fart is such a strong state-
ment, it must be employed sparingly. Don't become known as the guy who can't hold it in. When a fart-
worthy occasion arises, wait until the room is quiet.

The mechanics. Rock up on one cheek. This helps with the release and signals that the act is intentional. That's important. Your flatulence is not an embarrassing loss of control; it's a statement. Contract your lower abdominal muscles and relax your sphincter. Hope for a drawn out and audible release. Practice at home.

Prepare for all contingencies. Since it's impossible to predict the volume and duration of the emission, have cover lines prepared for statements that are less bold than hoped for, or – it can happen – far exceed what might be appropriate to the occasion. For example, in the latter case you might say, "I hope I've made myself clear" in a tone that signifies your target audience is composed of idiots who need every message delivered in high relief. Then you should leave, walking with dignity and in measured paces.*

Sell it with a smile. If your intention is to signal disagreement, finish with a solemn smile that indicates solidarity with those present who share your view and endorse your response. If your purpose is disapproval of present company, grin broadly and disdainfully. If you're breaking wind to underscore the fact that normal social conventions don't apply to you – in fact those present are privileged to inhale the byproduct of your digestive workings – you can even pat your stomach.

Do not apologize.

Back in my office I dialed John. "I've considered your fourth point – the one about leaving here. Upon reflection I find your arguments compelling. I'm ready to go."

----

* Should a woman fart? Of course. The statement may be even more powerful when delivered by a woman.

14

You would have thought Tiffany would jump at the chance to travel during the summer recess.

"Rose petal? I feel like doing something wild and crazy. Something spontaneous . . . mad."

"Is this your way of telling me you've already bought the map, or just have your eye on it?" Even though we were into our second bottle of wine, her guard was still up.

"No maps, Fern tip. Travel! See a bit of the country. New vistas. An empty two lane highway stretching before us to the distant purple horizon."

"How about an empty bank account yawning beneath us? We can't afford to go to the movies right now, just like every other night. And forget spontaneity; you know I have a dozen events to go to in the next two weeks."

I knew, I knew; it's what fueled my desperation to get her out of town.

"Actually I had family in mind." That was a lie. "Your folks won't be around forever and it occurred to me that we should drive out and spend some time with them." A sure sign of desperation; visits to or from her parents were agony. Mother Pratiloma chipped away relentlessly at father Pratiloma who looked helplessly to me for a distracting intervention – we ran out of those early – and Tiffany regressed to age five and became a willful demanding child. "Your father just retired and it must be a tough adjustment. I'm sure they'd love to see us – I'd enjoy seeing them (hoohaw!) – and it would only cost us gas for the flivver."

Tiff eyed me suspiciously over her wine glass, deciding correctly that there was another agenda somewhere. She appeared to be digging in, so I played my trump card. "Of course, another possibility is to invite my mother to come spend some time with us. . . I'd just like to do a family thing this summer," I trailed off with a half-smile as if this sudden rush of sentimentality were a little embarrassing.

Tiffany choked on the mouthful of wine; resistance collapsed. She was as crazy about my parents as I was about hers.

She'd forgotten for the moment that my mother could go no-where during the summer – business was heaviest at the DQ – and shrank from the prospect of bedding, boarding, and enter-taining someone who made her as uncomfortable as my mother did. We agreed to set out for small town mid-America and the elder Pratilomas the next day. Reeling from the Pyrrhic out-come to this step (#3) of John's plan, I opened a third bottle of cheap wine.

Too drunk to pack, we fell into bed. I think Tiffany may have suggested some horseplay as I was passing out; her sullen expression the next morning seemed that of a woman scorned. But, who can tell? Her dissatisfaction could arise from a thou-sand different sources. While she washed clothes needed for the trip I hied back to the campus to follow up with John on a sug-gestion he'd made concerning a Fulbright award.

Grantsmanship

"Isn't it late to apply for anything like that, John?"

"In sociology, yes; in business, no. Probably because of the miserably low stipends Fulbright pays, few business teachers are interested in these awards and I understand many go unfilled every year. No offense, Max, but you guys are so poorly paid that you don't recognize a bad deal when you see one."

It didn't sound bad at all. Images of sun-dappled British campuses had entertained me since John mentioned this possi-bility the afternoon before. "The bad deal is if I hang around here. Do you really think there's a chance of landing a Ful-bright?"

"Easy to find out. Call this guy in DC. He'll give you nine yards of nonsense about application dates, too many applicants, materials not ready for next year – if you might still be inter-ested then – and so on. Hang in there and make sure he under-stands you teach management. If anyone looks at this schmuck's performance at all they must rate him on how many applicants the program generates and whether he fills all the positions. Mention my name; we were on a proposal review committee once."

I called from my office. John was right; the twerp launched directly into a spiel that would have disheartened anyone not forewarned. Wrapping up this lengthy and droning counsel of despair, he concluded with what was unmistakably intended as the farewell line. "So, you see, it's very late for this fall. And we've had a large number of excellent applicants this year so the positions in the social sciences have been filled. But thanks for your interest."

I almost responded with my own farewell, when Joy waddled past the office door, reminding me of the stakes. "All filled? That's excellent – pleased to hear it. I would certainly hope the program would be well subscribed, and nothing less than what's expected of a program as prestigious as yours.

"But, back to the purpose of my direct call to you. John and I were discussing how I could marry my background in sociology with my current teaching in management. It was his thought that an international position would allow me to capitalize on my earlier experience in East Asia and a sociologist's perspective on culture, but with the ability to teach in professional areas such as management and marketing."

Probably against his better instincts he allowed the conversation to continue. Or maybe he thought he'd found a stopper. "Experience in East Asia? Did we sponsor that? I'm afraid we almost never make a second award to a scholar."

"I wish it had been you people. No, my field research was sponsored by another arm of our government."

The simple act of prolonging the conversation seemed to be working in my favor. He'd said 'goodbye' once and probably didn't know how to say it again without appearing rude. "Well, there are still a few business programs that are looking for someone. We're able to provide Scholars to teach the survey and intro courses fairly easily, but demand for instructors of advanced operations management and finance usually outstrips supply."

An opening, which I incautiously went through.

"Really? A happy coincidence. Ops management has long been an interest. I've been at pains to point out to my quantitative colleagues that the training in quant methods is pretty standard across the disciplines. Math is math." At this point the frustrated academician in the man kicked in. I'd noticed his secretary had referred to him as 'doctor' when she put the call through.

"You know, Dr. Brown, that's been my own position all along. Our Advisory Board is unconvinced, but when I think of the stat and probability courses I endured at Harvard[*] I suspect I also would encounter much that's familiar in the production management literature."

"Exactly. The tendency to pigeon-hole us by graduate degree is a disservice." I would have continued but the poor guy couldn't wait to jump back in.

"More than that. It's incomprehensible to me that we speak in awe of the 'renaissance man' who is, by definition, a person whose interests and abilities span multiple disciplines, but when someone tries to move outside the confines of his or her discipline, they're punished for it."

What had happened to this guy? He'd picked up a doctorate from Harvard and now was pushing papers in a bureaucracy. Perhaps he'd had the temerity to step outside his discipline.

We were on a roll. More exchanges on the failure of specialization, the need for generalists to reassert control of policy, and – his contribution to the conversation – the rôle of Fulbright in encouraging a cross-disciplinary perspective. Carried away by how well things were going, I, unfortunately, added new areas of teaching experience to strengthen my credentials as a renaissance man in formation. Providence stopped me from laying claim to nuclear engineering. Then something snapped at his end and he reverted to bureaucratic mode. He told me where to find application materials on our campus, warned me not to expect much, and disengaged.

Whatsoever Is Honest
- V.R. Raye, 1966

The application forms were forbidding. I leafed through them, expecting to encounter an item asking for a listing of Nobel Prizes received. With Tiffany waiting there wasn't much time to develop a strategy, but made reckless by the hangover and the certainty that my luck would have to change, I hastily embel-

---

[*] You've noticed how they always work that in?

lished the responses to strengthen my case and bolster the claim to management. For example, a forthcoming article in the *ASQ*, 'Social Control and Rate Busters: A Study in Six Manufacturing Plants.' The breadth of my international interests and contacts was demonstrated by inclusion of an article on the adoption of western managerial practices in Yugoslavia, co-authored with Milos Djavlovic and published in *Nvoya Studjes Slovenjes*. Both the co-author and journal were invented; perhaps too many j's? Six publications were created in this fashion; they demonstrated broad interests and sound scholarship. I debated whether to include my one and only legitimate publication – a byproduct of my doctoral dissertation – and decided against it. Somehow it didn't belong.

15

The Lord Created Families
- M.E. Leckebusch, 2005

During the day and a half drive to her parents I told Tiff about the application for a Fulbright. The news went over well. This positive attitude wasn't dampened when I interrupted her rhapsodizing about Paris with the reminder that my impoverished linguistic skills restricted us to English speaking countries.

Noteworthy: her usual priority question about salary was well down the list.

We rolled into the senior Pratilomas' driveway late in the afternoon, not expected, and found May and Lyle taking the air on their front porch.

Join us now for an abrupt temporal shift to the middle class of the 1950s: The lawn is trimmed an even height and weedless; large rhododendrons flank steps which have been recently swept; window shades are all drawn to the same level; the gutters, although not visible, have certainly been cleaned; and water at the foot of the driveway signals the family sedan has recently received its weekly bath.

I hesitated, expecting Rod Serling to appear by the car and say, "Maxwell and Tiffany Brown don't realize it, but they've just arrived at an address that doesn't exist in time or space. They've just made a one-way journey to . . . The Twilight Zone."

The first audible words were not Rod's; they were May's. "Now you see what I been tellin' you? Company, and you settin' there lookin' like a bum."

After a rondo of greetings, delivered with much false heartiness on all parts, we settled into the guest room while May Pratiloma commenced preparations of mountains of bland food, pausing only to issue useful correctives to her husband.

We caught repeated references to a lodge meeting and May's gloating insistence that Lyle could now not possibly attend. But Lyle no doubt felt differently so at dinner I led with, "We don't want our surprise visit to interrupt your normal routine in any way. We'd feel terrible if we upset your socializing or meetings with your friends."

Lyle looked up from his pork chop, hopefully, but May was quick to counter, "Oh no. We see so little of you we want to spend every minute you're here doing something together."

A ghastly prospect.

Alternating words with eating Lyle chimed in in his own interest, "Now dear, (chew chew) the children may just want some time (swallow) to themselves. They can't spend (bite, chew) all of their time with a pair of old fogies like us." He dabbed at the corners of his mouth with a napkin and suppressed a small smile.

This was no counter to May. "Nonsense. Don't go on about old fogies. These kids have come a long way to see us. If they wanted to be by themselves they wouldn't be here and I'm sure they want to spend time with us just as much as we want to be with them and that settles it."

Checkmate. Gin. Game, Set and Match to May. Sometimes the most unassailable arguments are the crudest ones. May had declared herself winner and I started to nod agreement when Tiffany assumed the rôle of arbiter.

"That misses the point, Mom." It did? But I gave her a supportive smile. "Max and I won't be able to relax and enjoy being here if we force ourselves to be with you constantly. It would be too artificial." May started to protest the reference to 'force' but Tiffany rolled on, "Now what had you planned to do tonight, Daddy?"

Daddy, unprepared for this turn of fortune, couldn't answer and sat with a spoonful of lima beans suspended below his open mouth. May, however, could always answer. "Fool lodge meeting. That's what he wants to do. I think they drink and gamble – I wouldn't put it past some of 'em to have women there – and then he comes home late and gives me some mumbo-jumbo about keepin' the secrets of the lodge if I ask him anything. Like little boys with a 'no gurls allowed' sign on their clubhouse door."

"How interesting," I ventured. "Have you been a member for very long?" I followed this up with a series of questions about the frequency of meetings, what sort of person belonged, how often he attended, and so on until I recognized that I was conducting a sociological interview. Tiffany interrupted to suggest that since I was so interested, perhaps I should go with her father. I tried to think of a disqualifying condition but could do no better than mumble that I really shouldn't impose. This only seemed to confirm my interest.

A final warning from May: "I hope you 'boys' don't let that Francis DiVitale back in. I heard he was released this week." My expression must have signaled a request for more information. "Frank is one of them anger problem fellas. A little liquor and he's throwin' chairs and punches. Every time he's hauled in the judge gives him a longer sentence. Ninety days, was it this time, Lyle?" Lyle nodded. "That judge is too easy on him. Put a guy in the hospital, I say throw away the key. He's not gonna be there, is he?" Affirmation was written all over Lyle's downcast face. "You're all nuts to even be near him. I got enough to worry about you gettin' hurt through your own stupidity, much less someone else's."

Our departure for the meeting was marred by my playful question to Lyle, "No funny hat?" assuming those were found only in television skits. He crimsoned as May brought a be-spangled fez from the closet and placed it ceremoniously on his head. "I've seen worse," I volunteered and the trip to the lodge hall started in silence.

I interpreted the silence to mean that Lyle had taken offense at the remark about hats but was wrong. He was rehearsing.

"Uh, I know it's not our business, but May and me were wondering if you've thought about children? We're getting on and if there's going to be grandkids, we could enjoy them more – and help you with them more – if we still had our health."

Poor old guy; he'd certainly been short-changed when it came to the quality of his primary relationships.

"I'm counting on you being around for a long time, Lyle." That didn't do it. He continued to look at me, waiting for an answer. I added, "We'd like to have children, but it's not ours to decide."

Like many unwise couples in an unhappy marriage, several years earlier we'd tried to rescue the relationship by adding children to it. How's that supposed to work? Pile the stresses of child-rearing onto an already stressful relationship? A popular, but very bad idea. And, I'm not sure I was fully committed to fatherhood. My little sister Debbie had demonstrated how vulnerable a family is to the loss of a member. It leaves a hole that's never filled.

"I'm afraid we found out that I was the victim of an involuntary vasectomy as a child[*] and the vas can't be surgically reconnected." We rode in silence.

————

The lodge hall was a long one-room cinder block building located on the outskirts of town. A familiar sensation descended on me as we walked though the door: Another place where Max didn't belong. Fezed heads turned as we entered and my heart sank at the prospect of sustaining conversations with these paunchy representatives of middle-aged, middle-class, mid-America.

But I'd failed to realize that professors enjoy a standing disproportionate to their contribution. I was a minor celebrity, addressed haltingly and with respect. This was rather pleasant and I began to regard these deferential men with growing fondness. They seemed modest and well-behaved – almost abstemious – as only occasionally a Frater would venture to the bar that occupied one long wall of the building for a Hamms.

The trained sociologist started cataloguing behaviors. For example, when I put a question to a Frater, he'd stick a finger in his ear and swivel it back and forth (stimulate thought? wind up the brain?), his brow would furrow slightly, and then a reasonably cogent reply would issue forth. So while they weren't a barrel of laughs, the evening was going better than expected when a rippling commotion accompanied something that was being dragged across the floor from the rear entrance. It turned out to

————

[*] The consequence of an accident involving a bicycle chain and sprocket, an accident best not visualized.

be a bathtub, squealing along on lion feet fitted with casters, and half-filled with a frothy gray liquid.

It transpired that for every meeting one of the Fraters was charged with the responsibility of providing the drinks. In recent times this had been accomplished by concocting a tub-full of an original libation. "I call it El Grando after a drink I had like it once in Tijuana," the inventor explained. Several eyed the brew skeptically; it was murky but gave off no strong aroma.

"Here, professor, have an El Grando;" one of the Fraters pressed a large paper cup into my hand. I smiled thinly and took a sip. Would I be able to see in the morning?

A second mobile commotion started at the front door. "That's Frank," whispered Lyle. A tall, barrel-chested man with a crew-cut was surrounded by Fraters, each timidly offering his welcome. Frank/Francis looked in our direction and spoke to the Frater nearest him who glanced uneasily our way while replying. They both turned toward us, Frank sneered, then headed for the El Grando tub.

The party picked up momentum. A game of buck-buck was organized – I was excused by dint of profession, although we'd played this regularly in the Air Force – and continued until a slight man, probably an accountant, was crushed to the floor by a construction worker, requiring attention from a chiropractor present.

Banquet tables were then lined up in two parallel rows, covered with black construction Mylar, and coated with vegetable oil. The fraters formed teams for the competition, some putting on plastic aprons. The game turned out to be indoor luge races, without the sled. The contestants ran at the end of the row of tables and belly flopped on them. The contest was to see how far down the row a person could slide. Most crashed off the sides before traveling more than two tables and some had painful encounters with the end of the first table.

The obvious perils notwithstanding, it looked like a fun challenge so I put down my second El Grando to try my skill. The dive went well and I'd sailed down three tables before my journey was interrupted. A poor sport from the other team – I suspected Frank – had separated the third and fourth tables by three feet, the gap concealed by the Mylar. I crashed through and wound up entangled in the metal legs and braces of the next table. Bruised and disoriented I lay there inventorying the damage until the anxious faces of my hosts appeared; were the penalties stiffer for injuring a learned man? In reply to their inquiries I moaned, "Feeling no pain." This reply was greeted as capital humor and was repeated often throughout the evening. I got unsteadily to my feet and sought comfort in a fresh El Grando.

Deference often masks resentment so it should have been no surprise that some of the Fraters began to bait me. They appeared tipsy but I ruled out drunkenness as the El Grandos had been circulating for less than half an hour. "Hey perfesser! When are you guys gonna come up with something practical?" This was supported with a chorus of "Yeahs" and just audible comments were made that ten minutes in the mill taught a person more than ten years at college.

Frater Frank seemed especially persistent so I asked him to specify the problem with which he wanted some practical help from the academic side. Frater Len broke in, "Explain to him why his old lady won't put out for him anymore." This brought apprehensive laughter.

Lyle whispered, "Jesus, is Len nuts? Frank'll kill him." Frank's neck muscles started to work; he clenched and unclenched his fists; he looked like he was trying to bring himself under control – and failing. To break the tension, I spoke up.

"Wait," I said magisterially. "Alright. I'll do it. A practical theory of why not necessarily Frank's sex life, but any married man's sex life becomes unsatisfactory." This was received with murmurs of approval and a much larger audience than I wanted began to gather. Frank appeared to be relaxing and someone led Len off, presumably for precautionary counseling. "First, however, another El Grando;" this to buy time in which to invent the theory that was expected by forty critical listeners.

16

Piled higher and deeper

"Could I have a napkin or two?" Why not napkins? Wasn't that the medium that launched Arthur Laffer on the lucrative lecture circuit – and with a topic of less universal human interest?

Pressed in on all sides by fraters, the nearest of whom were slopping their drinks on my pants, I casually wrote

$$S_s = f\{S_r - (F_c + F_a)\}$$

Those closest stared intently at this formula, apparently expecting that it would reshape itself, as in a cartoon, into something intelligible.

"Satisfaction with your sex life – that's the S sub s," I explained, "is a function of the *recency* of sex minus the quantity current frustration with sex and accumulated frustration with one's sex life." I wondered if I needed the big f in the formula but decided it would be a bad thing to start correcting myself. A crash at the far end of the room sent everyone's head swiveling, first toward the noise, then in search of Frank. A table had collapsed; Frank was standing quietly with the rest of us. His presence kept everyone alert.

"We all know – or dimly remember – what recency of sex is (laughter) so we don't need to examine that. The two frustration components of the formula are different." I added

$$F_c = S_e - S_a$$

to the napkin. "Current frustration is equal to the sex you expect, S sub e, minus the sex you actually get, S sub a." Murmurs of comprehension.

Someone explained to Frank, "Yer frustrated if yer getting less than ya' think ya' should."

"You think I don't see that?" snarled Frank, and cocked his fez forward. Why bait Frank? Death wish?

"Finally," I said triumphantly, and wrote

$$F_a = \sqrt{\sum F_{c_{1-n}}}$$

I inspected this formula for a moment, realized it was either meaningless or wrong, and further realized that I wasn't going to improve it. "Accumulated frustration is equal to the square root of the sum of current frustrations . . . you know, added up over time?" I reached for my El Grando to indicate school was out.

"See," said Frank, "a bunch of academic bullshit. Put some letters on paper that no one can figger out so no one's the wiser and call it knowledge."

He was right. Maybe I'd taken the wrong tack with the phony posturing and specious formulae. Others picked up Frank's refrain until I held up a hand for forbearance. No turning back.

"Alright. This is too theoretical a way to put it. I'll draw some graphs." What the hell was I saying? Draw graphs? Where would the inspiration for those come from? "More napkins," I ordered imperiously, "and could someone top up this El Grando for me?"

At that point something rushed past my ear. "There's an El Grando for you, perfessor." Frank had hurled the drink and just missed my head. I turned and found him advancing menacingly. He stopped a foot in front of me, his mouth working.

"Here's how I see it, perfessor. Some of us work our asses off trying to make a living. We go to war for our country and get pissed on while candy-ass perfessors fuck their students and go to protest marches." The Fraters spread out in a circle around us, reminiscent of the ring of elementary school fight fans that formed whenever I tangled with another kid to defend Tough Max's fighting credentials. What sentence would the lenient judge give Frank for putting me in the hospital?

"We, uh . . ." His mouth had outpaced his thought processes. An opening.

"What unit?" I demanded.

"Huh?"

"What unit were you in in 'Nam?"

He studied me. Wondering if I was laying a trap? At length, "First Cav. An Khe."

First Cavalry(Airmobile) was the real deal; my respect may have shown in my expression. He retreated half a step. "Was you there?"

"76th Tactical Recon. Tan Son Nhut."

"Fuck me! You're not a candy-ass perfessor. You're a candy-ass zoomie!" He considered this new information. The circle of fight fans drew closer. Frank walked around me as if he were conducting an inspection. Inspection completed he stopped by my side and threw an arm around my shoulders. Broad smiles of relief broke out.

"Listen up. You had to give one thing to the zoomies. They were pussies but they were smart enough to live in air conditioned hooches while the rest of us were wallowing around in paddies. Maybe this one is smart enough to teach us something. Go on, perfessor." My stature was enhanced. I had the endorsement of the PTSD poster child.

After two false starts due to indecision on how to label the axes, I drew –

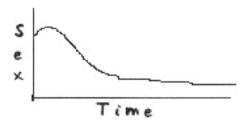

"Now this wavy line represents sex. The higher the line, the more sex you're getting (a chorus of 'right on's). Moving from left to right is time beginning with the start of your relationship with the woman and continuing on for years ('and years and years' someone added). See here at the beginning sex actually goes up briefly (more 'right on's and a wolf howl). Then things drop off. First slowly and then faster and then they sort of level out after a few years. But at a very low level" (cries of anguish rent the air). I was fearful that Frank would realize this didn't address the original question, *why* does it drop off, but then saw that he wasn't paying attention. He'd discovered a comrade in arms, even if only an Air Force pilot. I quickly continued. "But this is only half the story. The other half is expectations." I added a second line, descending, to the graph.

"This line, S with the little e for expectations, shows how much sex you *expect* to get. See here at the start it's lower than the sex you're getting. That means that things are better than you expected them to be and you're as happy as a pig in shit. But then as actual sex falls off, your expectations stay pretty much the same and now there's a negative gap – you're getting less than you want and you're frustrated (grunts of affirmation). You scale your expectations down some but still they don't get as low as the actual poontang delivered and this gap remains and so does your frustration. Think of the distance between the two lines, actual and expected sex, as the frustration gap. Only very late in the relationship do expectations get down to the point where they equal action. Your frustration with current sex is zero at that point."

Long silence. I was quite pleased with myself for extemporizing so glibly, half-assed as it all may be. Frank had wandered off to the bathroom. The inventor of El Grando cleared his throat and spoke thoughtfully. "That all seems okay and I would like to thank the professor for this illuminating presentation but it doesn't quite fit. I don't expect much from my old lady anymore and, by God, I don't get it, but I'm still a little teed off."

"Very perceptive," I said supportively. "Even after things are going about as you expect them to, still you're a little honked off. That's where the accumulated frustrations come in. The accumulated frustrations are made up of all the past and current frustrations added together but you tend to forgive and forget (every face wore an expression of compassion) so they aren't the full total of the old frustrations – they're something less than that. Here, we can draw that on another chart where this line, which I'll call F sub a, shows accumulated frustration."

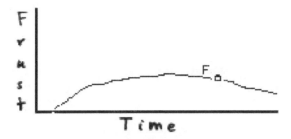

"Now, if we add current frustration – we'll label that F sub c – to accumulated frustration, we can see for any point in the relationship what total frustration, F sub t, is going to be." I sketched in the last two lines of the final graph amidst reverent silence.

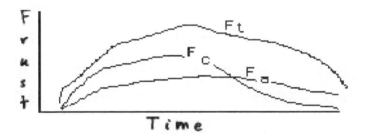

Frank was emerging from the bathroom and I acknowledged his return. "There, Frank, how's that for something academic that bears on a practical problem?" Before Frank could reply – I was afraid he'd realize how far we'd strayed from the original question or might notice how absurd my presentation was – I swept my arm toward the bathtub, "Drinks are on me!" Shouts and whistles greeted this announcement; then I was honored with a formal ovation as the fraters put down their cups and clapped politely.

"You were great professor. How ya doin"?"

"Feeling no pain!" I replied and hoisted an El Grando in toast. The fraters started drifting away, most of them in the direction of the bathtub.

"Wait a minute. I can't leave it there. You know what the real problem is? The bitches just don't have the sex drive we do. Forget all that bullshit with the graphs and formulas. It all comes down to us wanting it more than them. Go all up and down the food chain; the male is always looking for it; the female comes into heat once every blue moon. Sometimes I think that's sad for bulls and stallions and boars, and other times I think that they're lucky to have two things going for them. They know that sooner or later they're going to get a little and in the meantime they don't interpret her disinterest as a comment on their appeal or performance. We're all in the same boat. The man who tells you his wife tears his clothes off him every night is lying."

This candor fell on deaf ears. Conversations had started while I was speaking. They were happier with academic BS than with a truth they'd resisted because it meant things were never going to improve. Is this what the layman wants from academicians: arrant bullshit? We seem happy to provide it.

———

Frank brought me a replenished El Grando and we exchanged the usual information: dates of deployment, duty stations, time in country. He'd arrived in 'Nam an E-3 and left an E-5 – better than average advancement in rank – and had fought in one of the most celebrated battles, la Drang Valley.

"So, you recon jocks took some heavy losses. Maybe half your guys were shot down?"

"More. And we were over-represented on the guest register at the Hanoi Hilton." We both tried to think of something more to say. Frank broke the silence.

"You been to the fuckin' wall on the fuckin' mall?"

"I can't, Frank."

"Same. I got up to a hundred feet of it and had to leave." To our mutual surprise, we were starting to tear up at the image of 58,000 names engraved on the two long slabs.

Choking with emotion Frank snarled, "Fucking sunsabitch cocksuckers hid the fucking wall below ground level. Don't that say it all? Fuck!" and he turned away.

That's the way it often goes when the survivors meet. No reminiscences, no real camaraderie. Who wants to relive a tragedy?

———

I was surprised Frank and I had gotten emotional so quickly. What was different? I sought out the drink purveyor and learned that he was a pharmacist. He explained that he used only pure alcohol in the El Grandos which was a departure as the other fraters were obliged to rely on branded liquor. "How much pure alcohol," I asked uneasily.

"Twenty quarts. I needed to save some for my work and that was all I could spare." Thank God for that.

"That means," the calculations seemed unusually difficult, "that every man in this room will drink on average one half of a quart of alcohol."

"Yeah, I guess they will."

"Do you know how many bottles of whisky that's equal to?" He didn't. "A fifth of booze is only 40 percent alcohol, so . . ." I was struggling with the math, "what you put in there would be equal to fifty quarts of booze. God's pickled liver, man. That's more than a quart of hooch for everyone here." Then, incongruously, I shouted, "Feeling no pain," a cry that was picked up throughout the hall.

The news that I should be drunk made it a reality. I sat down heavily and nursed the El Grando; after all, if I wasn't dead yet . . .

Some of the events at the lodge hall were later indistinct but I recall Frank putting his pickup into reverse by mistake and slamming into the wall of the building; he accepted this mishap philosophically and, squinting determinedly into the night, drove forward into the creek. A Frater named Phil finger jammed up the cinder blocks in one corner of the building and pulled himself onto the roof. He appeared to be stuck there until someone suggested he jump down onto the roof of a car. Phil acted on this proposal immediately and dropped through the cloth roof of a Dodge convertible parked under the eaves.

The party alternated between the lodge hall and the parking lot, depending upon where an antic was in progress, until a police cruiser arrived. I expected the worst but the policeman summoned three taxis and the four cars started efficiently chauffeuring the Fraters home. Lyle and I departed to cries of "Feeling no pain" and after dropping off an incoherent Frater, motored toward Casa Pratiloma. We tried to work on a story – it was three AM – but broke into giggles at every suggestion.

Jiggs and Maggie

The house was dark when we arrived. We surveyed it uncertainly from the sidewalk. "Shoosh," slurred Lyle, "we'll tiptoe pasht the witches." And giggled. I removed my shoes and motioned for Lyle to do the same.

"You know," I said, suddenly teary, "you're a hell of a father-in-law. No," I raised my hand to stem the anticipated protest, "if a guy hash to have a father-in-law he could do a lot worsh than you." Lyle's knees buckled and he sat down heavily on the grass. I sat down with him and he threw his arms around my neck and sobbed gently. "There, there," I comforted, "a good night sleep and like new." Whoosh. The world was spinning and my speech sounded distant and slurred.

"I'm sorry I asked about the grandkids. It's not any of my business. And since we live so far away we probably wouldn't see them much anyhow." This brought more sobs. Then he asked a question that apparently had been troubling him all evening. "You know with that damage and all that keeps you from having kids. Are you able to . . . you know . . ."

"Sex?" How many fathers-in-law inquire into the bedroom performance of their daughter's partners? Should I tell him it scarcely mattered, given the rare opportunities his daughter provided? "Yes. All that's normal."

We got unsteadily to our feet, and holding our shoes in one hand at shoulder height in imitation of an old cartoon, climbed the porch steps and entered the house. All quiet. How far would we get? Arm in arm – for physical support as much as out of comradeship – we lurched up the stairs. No creaks. Lyle had the banister on his side and I pawed at the wall for balance. The top of the stairs seemed to never arrive. . . I could have lain down on a step right there and passed out . . . maybe we'd be able to sneak into bed and work out the explanations in the morning . . . finally reached the top, we were going to get away with this after all . . .

Holy Mother of God! Sweet Jesus in Heaven! A demon from hell jumped at us snarling! It was wrapped in red terrycloth, face covered with brown grease, wire rolls on its head! So great was my fright that I didn't realize the vile apparition was May as Lyle and I cried out and recoiled backward off the top step. My younger reflexes gave me the faster recoil so I went down the stairs first with Lyle heavy on top of me. We rolled down some of the steps, we skidded down others, and we bounced painfully on the rest, most of the time Lyle a passenger. The long ride ended with a crash against an umbrella stand in the entryway.

Lyle rolled off me; I lay there motionless and made a conscious decision not to move to see what effect that might have on the welcoming committee. Tiffany cautiously came down the stairs and edged toward me as if approaching a corpse. Leaning forward she asked, "Are you okay?"

I couldn't resist. "Feeling no pain!"

17

Breaking up is hard to do

The X-rays showed one broken rib and a fractured bone in the left hand – a metacarpal. But pain? Think back to the last time you had the dry heaves. Now add a broken rib. And that wasn't the worst of it. The worst of it was getting those two gleeful bitches, May and her spawn, to move out of the way so I could get some medical attention.

Let's pick up the narrative at the point where my broken and battered body lies at the foot of the stairs. Tiffany responds to my selfless attempt to allay concerns about my state.

"Feeling no pain? Why you sonuvabitch! Momma and I were half crazy with worry and you come in drunk as a lord. I should give you some pain right now!"

I'd never seen her so worked up. Perhaps she assumed I was in no condition to defend myself and she could be extravagant with her threats. She was wrong. I reached out and caught her ankle. "C'mer' you little fire brand you. . . You saucy temptress. . . You sloe eyed vi . . " I stopped there because after struggling against my grip Tiff lost her balance and came crashing down on top of me, first contact being her knee with my chest. Maybe that's where the broken rib came from.

She was incoherent with rage but I wouldn't have understood her anyway because I resumed. "Throwing yourself at me, huh? Oof! Can't wait to get into my trousers can you. Argh. No screwing here in front of pater and mater but perhaps a . . . aagh . . . subtly executed dry hump might be pulled off." Tiffany battled free and stepped back, wild-eyed.

"That's it Max. You've humiliated me for the last time. You're leaving in the morning but I'm staying here. I never want to see you again so get your shit and yourself out of my life." To emphasize the irrevocability of this ultimatum she stormed upstairs and started throwing my clothes down the steps.

Lyle and May were mute spectators to all of this. Tiffany's tirade may have spared Lyle considerable grief; it was a tough act to follow and May probably knew that any reproach she might hurl at Lyle would sound feeble by comparison. Upstaged by her daughter, May stood fuming, then snorted at Lyle in disgust, picked her way up the stairs through my undershorts and socks, and with a slam of distant doors both harpies were gone.

I lay there afraid to assess the damage. It had been a longer night than planned.

"Lyle? Best father-in-law in the world? I think I'm hurt." Lyle's expression turned to alarm. Had he spotted some dreadful condition on my person – perhaps one or more bones protruding through flesh? He turned and fled. His alarm had been triggered by a warning flashed ahead from his stomach; retching and pleas for divine deliverance could be heard through the open door of the downstairs bathroom. No help was forthcoming from Lyle.

With a fortitude for which medals should be awarded I pulled myself on all fours to the couch. It was good I acted when I did; the last words I heard before unconsciousness were Lyle's. "Where am I going to sleep now?"

Relieving Suffering, It's All I Care to Sing
- S. Michael, 1872

The next morning was difficult. Tiffany had postponed the hour of my expulsion, not out of concern for my wellbeing, but to enjoy my suffering. Her surveillance proved a welcome distraction. When one is clinging to the toilet, deep in self-loathing and despair, the sound of a foot slowly tapping at the door and a contemptuous, "Uh huh?!" dispels remorse and replaces it with a bracing anger.

"Lily pad? Could you get the number of your parents' doctor for me?"

"Doctors have better things to do than minister to drunks and louses." It always interested me that Tiffany spoke with only her lower teeth showing when she was mad. I was unable to imitate that. Her English also improved on these occasions.

"Pet, your loving helpmeet needs medical attention. I think I need to go to the hospital. Something's broken." I'd found that nothing stoked the smoldering ire of my spouse during an argument as much as a tone of sweet reasonableness.

"Look asshole," I knew I had her going when she stooped to common vulgarity, "the only place you're going to is the bus station and the only thing broken is this marriage."

Was this it? I'd often wondered why she'd stayed in the marriage. Hypothesis: Our relationship met her expectations: a long-suffering woman enduring a clueless and annoying man. That's what she'd grown up with.

I was pretty clear on why I'd stayed with her: a wife that beautiful enhanced my own stature and she was, sometimes, actually nice to me to the point of (rare) affection.

Lyle hadn't been seen yet – midday was approaching – and I wondered whether May had offed him in the night. If so, he'd gone to a better place. Nothing to do but make my own arrangements. Clutching my pounding left side with my throbbing left hand I dialed 911 and asked the operator to connect me with the emergency room of the hospital; the town couldn't have more than one. In due course a meat wagon arrived and two white-jacketed alumni from the mud-wrestling circuit strapped me on a gurney and started to roll me out.

Tiffany was incensed at the prospect of any amelioration of my suffering and tried to set the record straight. "He's just drunk – the jerk. He's . . ."

The more officious of the two white-jackets cut in with a statement that seized both our attentions. "He may be drunk lady but he's also spitting blood." Something I'd not noticed to that point.

The blood turned out to be from small vessels in my stomach that had ruptured under the strain of the heaves. I never bothered to tell Tiffany. Now concerned – or morbidly curious – she followed in the car and waited outside the emergency room while bored people in white – one splattered with blood – exchanged stories of their own revels the previous night and manifested total indifference to my suffering.

After two hours of x-rays, injections – for the hangover, I assume, as one of them was given with a wink – and a lot of lying around feeling conspicuously ignored, the spokesman for this disinterested group made public my condition and announced that I would spend the night for observation. I doubt that the stay was necessary but he may have sized up what awaited me at home; Tiffany seemed to be still vacillating between feelings of guilt that she'd treated me so badly when I was really, actually, almost mortally wounded, and feelings that my injuries were too light a sentence.

I spent two nights in the hospital. Not a great place to hang out but the deductible on the health insurance policy was absorbed by the first night so the second was on Aetna.

Time to think – always dangerous. With the remorse that accompanies a hangover came a visit from Tom, Chuck and Bill. Funny, isn't it? Living friends drift off, never to be seen or contacted again. The dead ones hang around your door.

———

No longer in danger of death from alcohol poisoning I tried to make sense of my performance at the lodge hall. At what point in recent years had I decided I was better than those men? There I was, strutting and preening; making up lame bull shit as if it mattered. What a horse's ass! I struggled through an academic program, came out the other side with three letters behind my name, and now I'm on a frigging pedestal? Come on!

But, wait. Is there a larger lesson here? The fraters colluded to put me on that pedestal, and where do we find a parallel? Exactly. Mankind has gone along with the deception that God is all-knowing, etc. We put Him on that pedestal, and He buys it. He's not really up to the task, but He – and we – expect that He knows what's going on and how, if He's so inclined, to fix things.

At which point I acknowledged this was just an attempt to avoid the main topic: I'd behaved like an asshole and I had to come to terms with the fact that every day I was becoming more like the academic colleagues I despised. Do they have the same self-doubts? Let's hope for all of our sakes they do. Pompous Max.

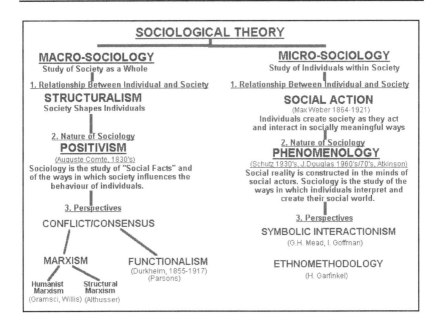

Map of concepts in sociology

18

On the morning I was discharged a smiling Tiffany appeared with a fresh change of clothes. I'd expected to find my belongings in a cardboard box at the cashiers. After all, she'd not been seen since I was admitted.

"There was a phone call for you this morning. It's the Fulbright guy." That explained her change of heart. "He wants to speak to you right away."

And indeed he did. "Dr. Brown? Glad I could track you down. Fortunately a mutual acquaintance, John Hall, knew where you were. Say, I was quite impressed by your resumé. Do you, by chance, speak any Slavic languages that you were too modest to put down?" I answered accurately that modesty had played no part in completing the application. "Well then, an English speaking position it would have to be but I think we still might be able to work something out. I'll put your qualifications on the telex to several universities that have – belatedly – indicated an interest in a Fulbright Scholar this year and see what turns up." Brief chitchat about the beastly weather, over 90 again in DC, and he rang off with the promise that he'd be back in touch within ten days.

During the conversation I repeated every positive comment for eavesdropping Tiffany's benefit. . . . "Glad you think I'm qualified." . . . "English speaking country would be fine." . . . "Pleased to hear you're so optimistic." . . . "Ten days then; I'll look forward to good news."

Tiffany sat forward on the sofa and looked at me questioningly. *Got you now. How far dare I take this?* Could she be made to beg me to stay in the marriage? Did I want to stay? An unsettling development: Sally had begun to feature in my dreams.

I waited a moment for the upbeat mood of the phone conversation to dissipate. "Tiffany? This is tough old girl, isn't it. Where are my things so I can get them together?" She looked stricken. I masked my glee with an expression of deepening sorrow. "Could I use the suitcase? I'll send it back to you."

It took her a minute to find her voice, "Wait Max, don't be silly. You can't travel in that condition. I heard the doctor tell you to rest."

"Of course. I'd overlooked that. Mind is elsewhere, isn't it? Just have to stay in a local hotel until the bones knit." I lengthened my features in a simulacrum of fatigue and pain.

"Not a hotel Max." She was scrambling and not doing a very good job of it; was I pushing her too hard? "Think of the cost. We don't have the money for you to just lie around in a hotel when there's a comfortable place for you here."

"We?" I asked ruefully, and then with a shrug, "That's what the Lord gave us credit cards for Daffodil." The use of a pet sobriquet was well timed; she was struggling against tears. "What's this? I thought you'd be better prepared for this moment."

She gave up. "Max . . . I don't really want you to go. I was just mad at you when I said those things." Her features tightened at the recollection.

"You mean," I asked grimly, relishing the moment, "that you let me spend two days in a hospital bed nursing broken bones and believing that my marriage was finished? And you were only *mad*?" She looked like she was starting to get ticked again but checked the impulse to fire back.

"I'm sorry Max. It's just that when you said those things in front of Momma and Daddy and grabbed me so roughly . . ." she trailed off. "I want you to stay." I gave her a skeptical look. Boy, did I have her where I wanted. "I'll try to control my temper better." It was evident this was terribly difficult for Tiffany; a large part of her wanted to kick me in the shorts.

"Alright," I said warily; it was important that she understand she was going to be on probation for a while. "It was never my idea to break up the marriage – certainly not over a night on the town with my wife's own father." We stood and embraced; I milked my advantage by emitting a slight 'oof' of pain as we hugged.

I should have gone to a hotel. I had Tiffany where I wanted but enjoyed no similar advantage with May. To her I was a corrupter of harmless old men – a premise Lyle was reluctant to dispute – and her husband's fall from grace was attributed to my malign influence. Additionally, my treatise on the course of conjugal relations was being repeated by husbands to wives all over town, with embellishments designed to strengthen a debating position that had little to do with the lecture. I learned this from Tiffany who reported that her mother shared with her some new bit of scandal that had come in daily about *Dr. Brown's* sermonette. I was being quoted as having borne witness to, among other things, the general frigidity of women, their indifference to the frustrations of their mates, and their contribution to the spread of prostate disease in the world at large. The napkins had been preserved in some unspecified location and were referred to as secular writ by my unbidden disciples.

One more thing about May. I think she deeply resented the fact that I had the Indian sign on Tiff. Our relationship, me smug and swaggering for the moment, Tiffany cringing and obedient, was an aberration, a reversal of the natural order of things. There was not, however, much that she could do about this breach of the laws of nature as Tiffany was quick to intercede on my behalf whenever May started to tune up. But her glares got me down and I dreaded the hours when Tiffany wasn't around.

May's seething displeasure reinforced my desire for a speedy recovery and departure, and it was with deep relief that I received John's call that the coast was clear.

"Max, I think your peccadilloes have been upstaged by the latest act."

"Does that mean it's safe for Tiffany to go abroad in the streets?"

"Absolutely. The word is that our Bible-brandishing chancellor has tested positive for AIDS. No one's interested in your penny ante philandering at the moment."

"God's pancreas!" I'd always despised the sanctimonious prick but this was too harsh a sentence.

"If he doesn't have AIDS, he sure looks like he does. He makes only an occasional appearance, where, needless to say, people shrink from him, and he's about as grey and unhealthy looking as I've ever seen a man look."

"Further proof that God does have a sense of humor, I guess, John." I told him of the Fulbright prospects before hanging up. Then I went upstairs and quickly packed, while urging Tiffany to do the same.

———————

As it later turned out, the chancellor did not have AIDS. Evidently there was a high rate of false positives reported by the lab, and this glad news was welcomed throughout the university community. The rejoicing was not because he would live, but because we could all gossip about the bastard without guilt. Why had he gotten tested in the first place? What indiscretion made him fearful that he'd been dosed? Many theories, competing in salaciousness, addressed these questions.

No call from Fulbright within ten days but I remained calm. Did one expect efficiency from the Feds? After fifteen days my patience gave out and I called Fulbright to learn that my contact was on vacation – and would be for another two weeks. The secretary was unwilling to help until my name finally registered in a dim recess of her consciousness. I imagined a nail file clattering to the floor as she said, "Oh, that Dr. Brown. Let me look at the file. Could you spell your name for me?"

Do questions like that inspire confidence?

A minute later she was back. "Yes, you're going to be one of our Asian Scholars." My heart sank. "I think you'll be going two places but it would be better to wait until the Coordinator gets back from vacation and he can go over the details."

I invented some reasons why any delay in revealing the destination would place my participation in jeopardy; she finally relented and left the phone to find another file. "Ah yes. . . hmmm. . . I wonder why they did that? . . . Okay, Dr. Brown. You're going to the Thai Institute of Technology in Bangkok."

TIT? Not bad; not Oxford, but still a place with possibilities. Bangkok was a popular R&R destination for GIs in Vietnam and it was universally agreed that no town had ever been so aptly named. I wondered if there was any significance in the school's acronym.

"Do you know anything about the school you can tell me?"

"No, but it won't matter because you won't be there long. The course you'll teach runs only for four weeks and, with preparation and exam time, you'll be there for seven weeks."

Unwelcome surprise.

"I applied for a full year award. I can't just drop my job here for two months out of the school year." Peevish and whiny, Max.

"Nooo," drawn out to signal exaggerated patience, "I said you were going two places. This is just a kind of a bonus, Dr. Brown. We rarely fix up something special like this." Silence followed this statement until I realized she was waiting for an expression of gratitude and perhaps contrition for the fleeting ungrateful thought.

"I'm sorry; I couldn't have known. I can see that I'm lucky." That should be enough for her. "And the other place?"

"Well, I think we had to pull some strings to get you this." I was to learn in the coming months that the Fulbright people viewed the simple performance of their minimum assigned duties as a personal sacrifice which could never be repaid by the Scholars, although we were expected to try. They condemned a Scholar to a year of poverty and diarrhea as if they were dispensing largesse from their personal fortunes. "It hasn't been firmed up which is why I really shouldn't go into it but apparently there's a program in administration in Rome which is taught in English and they wanted someone this fall. We just don't have the details although we've notified them of your availability."

Rome!! Hot damn! Tiffany is going to kiss my feet and any other anatomical appendage I specify. Rome!

And she did. She accepted the news about Bangkok with less enthusiasm than I thought warranted but was ecstatic about Rome. She collected guide books and tapes that taught idiot-level Italian. She was frantically busy preparing for our departure. She was transported. She even seemed ready to reconsider her long-held low opinion regarding my prospects. She was amorous.

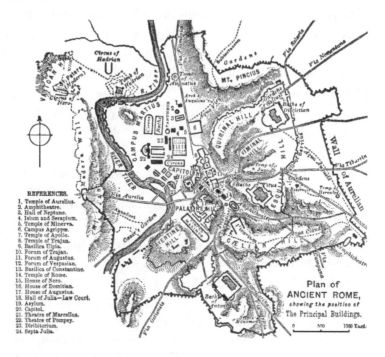

REFERENCES.
1. Temple of Aurelius.
2. Amphitheatre.
3. Hall of Neptune.
4. Isium and Serapium.
5. Temple of Minerva.
6. Campus Agrippæ.
7. Temple of Apollo.
8. Temple of Trajan.
9. Basilica Ulpia.
10. Forum of Trajan.
11. Forum of Augustus.
12. Forum of Vespasian.
13. Basilica of Constantine.
14. Temple of Rome.
15. House of Nero.
16. House of Domitian.
17. House of Augustus.
18. Hall of Julia—Law Court.
19. Asylum.
20. Capitol.
21. Theatre of Marcellus.
22. Theatre of Pompey.
23. Diribitorium.
24. Septa Julia.

Plan of
ANCIENT ROME,
showing the position of
The Principal Buildings.

Thou to Whom Revenge Belongs
- William Allen, 1835

You're familiar with the growing anxiety that a run of good fortune can produce? Things were going too well. Would the news break about my tryst with Sally? Anxiety nurtures anger which, in turn, is the catalyst for thoughts of revenge. The upshot? I wasn't unprepared when, passing the Registrar's office, I saw a familiar student pecking at a data entry terminal. "Hi Rolf. Been working here long?"

It turned out that Rolf worked on student files and, as luck would have it, right at that very moment was entering grades. In the obsequious manner practiced by successful students he explained the procedure for getting the student's record on the screen, inserting or – important knowledge – changing a grade, and saving it for posterity. Problem: how to get Rolf away from the terminal for a few minutes? Good fortune intervened again and Rolf was summoned into the next office.

"Not to worry, Rolf my boy. I'll keep an eye on things." I pulled up Sally's record and dithered over how low I should drop her grades. All F's – tempting – wouldn't wash as that grade point would have been picked up earlier. But she was already on the margin so any lowering of her grades would now be noticed by the system. I finally settled on a combination of D's and F's that should result shortly in a letter dismissing her from the program, F's in the courses of faculty no longer around to slow her attempts to sort things out.

"Oh, Rolf, you're back. Just browsing through the records to see how some of my old students have fared. It's good to see them getting what they deserve." Before I departed Rolf gave me the cheering news that the records were about to be culled again for students with low grade points.

That had worked so well that I returned to my office, called the telephone, gas, and electricity companies, and, in a quavering falsetto, cancelled Sally's utilities, instructing that the returned deposits be sent to an invented address in Moosejaw, Saskatchewan.

Will the Real God please stand up

These rapid turns of fortune will force even the most cynical man to reconsider his earlier preoccupation with the downside of human existence: the evil and suffering. What could be learned from focusing on the upside? Notably, pleasure. After all, Hedonism had been a respected philosophical position during several periods in history and there was even a Christian offshoot. God didn't have to be bored, vengeful, psychotic or immature. God could be a roguish fellow who admires the daring and picaresque. God might even be a swinger.

> This month **Playboy** interviews the universe's premier bon vivant, God Himself. We met with God in His celestial condo on the upper side of the Firmament where He received us dressed in plaid slacks, sandals, and a natural cotton pullover open at the neck that revealed a gold chain mounted with a diamond too large to fit in a D cup.

PB: As the creator of sex, has it turned out the way You anticipated?

God: More or less. I tend to take the long view and there are ups and downs – and ins and outs I might add * – but I would rate sex one of my more successful inventions.

PB: More successful? That suggests less than total satisfaction with the result.

God: Yes, well, that's true. If I were doing it over again I might have introduced more variety in the size of the male organ, just to see how the short-changed coped. And testicles should be re-designed. Look at 'em – like two marbles in a laundry bag. I should have made them really ugly or else attractive – not the semi-ugly appearance they have now.

PB: Beyond anatomy, what would You change.

God: Oh, lots of things. You know, for me, there's no such thing as an unnatural act. Another thing that's definitely underexploited is sex between the species. The uptight way things are now, a guy has to travel to Tijuana to see a donkey making it with a woman. That restricts it to only those with the free time and money for travel. And the poor women . . . I don't know where a woman could go to get fixed up with a donkey for herself.

PB: Can we take it from that that You have no problem with extra-marital sex?

God: It's the best kind. Hell, it's the only kind I get. I never figured out where the prohibition on adultery crept into the Ten Commandments. I always suspected that Moses slipped that one in on his way back down the mountain. He was insecure about his lady, probably because he had such a pronounced lisp.

---

* Just because I redefine God from time to time doesn't mean I'm obliged to give him a good sense of humor. Look around. You may find evidence of humor in God's creation. It isn't subtle.

PB: We don't usually ask this but it seems appropriate in Your case. Are You good in bed?

God: I'd answer that the same as anyone else: You'd have to ask my partners. Being who I am I have a certain advantage with chicks. Though not as great as a minor rock star.

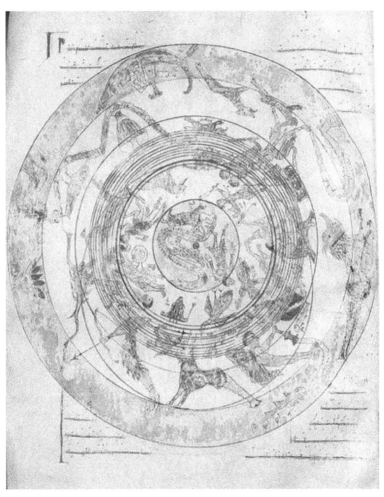

Map of heaven with zodiac. Burgo de Osma, 12th century.

Section IV
How I found wealth.

Treasure Island, from Robert Louis Stevenson, 1883

19

The mysterious orient

Bangkok. The official name is *Krungthepmahanakhornboworn-rattanakosinmahintarayuthamahadilokpopnoppratratchathani-buriromudomratchaniwetmahasathan*; the natives have prudently shortened this to Krung Thep, or City of Angels, for use in everyday parlance.

If you haven't been there, here are some questions you might want answered:

• *How big is it?* Six million of the globe's most laid-back homo sapiens disport in the sweltering heat on the banks of the Chao Phya river.

• *If they're so laid back, how do they get anywhere?* Were it not for the relentless entrepreneurship of the Chinese minority, the society would lapse into a terminal revel.

• *Does their religion allow that?* The Thais have developed an inordinately permissive strain of Theravada Buddhism. For example, where the Lord Buddha said no hooch, the modern Thai has determined that Buddha really meant firewater should be taken in moderation – or something close to moderation; the important thing is not to lose control of oneself – or total control. And bear in mind that Buddha was really after an end to suffering; maybe he meant for us to get shit-faced after all?

• *Tell us something cute or quaint that they do.* Animistic vestiges abound. House spirits are a common problem; if the infestation isn't addressed the rascals can carom around your house causing endless mischief. To draw them away from one's home, a 'spirit house' is provided outside. It's a small ornate dollhouse that the little dummies are lured to. They have to be fed every morning.

• *What makes a Thai mad?* Touch his head, the site of the soul.

• *What makes a Thai happy?* He's already the happiest person in the world; you can't make him any happier.

• *What do they do to make a living?* The principal business of Bangkok is sex. Seven hundred thousand employees in this industry toil on their backs and in other positions to serve a clientele of 1.5 million sex tourists per year – predominantly Germans and Japanese but with increasing numbers of Arabs turning up – plus the much larger and seemingly insatiable domestic market. Total revenues exceed $1.2 billion which rivals the take from the drug trade up country.

• *How does one get around?* The city has only a few main streets, nearly all of them wide one-way affairs, which are clogged with traffic; the ratio of vehicles per mile of paved street is the highest in the world. A tricycle scooter, known as a *tuk tuk*, conveys three passengers in discomfort, danger, heat, and noise at high speeds when the streets are clear. Their continued use may be owed to a desire by the Thais to test their kismet.

• *When is the best time of year to come?* The average daily high temperature is a muggy 91° F. and the climate is never pleasant at any time of year.

I really liked the place.

I didn't know any of those tidbits when I arrived but I was taken in hand by my new-found colleagues at TIT, particularly Professor Terd P. who made a special effort with *farangs,* and they set about completing my education in the mysterious ways of the East.

TIT was located in central Bangkok and occupied three floors of a large office building. I was never sure who the students were or what they wanted from the place – I couldn't understand what I guessed was English in their mouths and they obviously couldn't understand me – but they seemed an affable group and the girls were uniformly cute.

Classes were usually over by two o'clock at which time small groups of faculty would retire to a bistro to wax philosophic and put away beers. I was graciously included. The conversation veered back and forth between Thai and English, with English losing ground as the beers went down. One of the revelers would make a vague proposal to return to work midway through the drinkathon but it was never acted on during my stay. The region was moving into the rainy season so a convenient excuse to continue drinking was often found in the knee-deep water that filled the streets following the daily torrential downpour. Impassable streets are a justifiable reason to stay put in the bar; however, it seemed improbable that the afternoon bacchanal was ever interrupted for something as inconsequential as work and the excuse to keep drinking was modified to fit the season. In truth, there's something chummy about getting wasted with your workmates while a deluge as intense as Niagara pours off the protective canopy.

Tiffany was initially curious about what led to my chronically exhausted and disheveled state as I reeled in but she accepted that the heat took its toll and the alcohol on my breath was the result of a harmless glass of collegial sherry taken with the other dons. She seemed content with the apartment provided by TIT and spent the days roaming shopping stalls and temples.

Bordello etiquette

One afternoon toward the end of the third week, as the Singha beer sat heavy, I was preparing to excuse myself from the daily drink-'em-up. A long and evidently off-color joke was in progress in Thai; it's always a challenge to adopt the proper facial expression when everyone else is convulsed with laughter and you have no idea what it's about. Perhaps prompted by the subject of the joke, Terd abruptly asked, "I don't know how you feel about such things, but do you like to visit massage house?"

Hoohoo! I'm not your average rube; I'd seen the signs all over town and knew that there was more going on at those massage places than met the eye. Next thing, we were rocketing along in a *tuk tuk* toward Soi Nana in search of the Ultimate Massage Parlor. I admit to a touch of apprehensiveness. What, after all, was a good Christian boy like me doing, headed for a certified den of iniquity?

"This place mostly for tourists," Terd explained apologetically. "Next time we go to real Thai massage house."

A doorman admitted us to a large foyer with chairs on one side and a glass wall on the other. The chairs supported three seedy looking Europeans, judging from their haircuts and general air of dissipation. If they'd already been serviced they were lousy advertisements for the restorative power of massage.

Behind the glass sat twenty or more beautiful women on a three-tiered bleacher. Their attention was fixed on a television set although they would occasionally glance up at the glass to see if any business was developing. They were dressed in identical outfits, white blouse and dark blue skirt, and each woman wore a large button that bore a number. Tasteful, no need for the client to point.

My heart ached for number 47. She was the cutest girl I'd ever seen. Would she be attracted to my western wealth and savoir faire and accept a proposal of marriage? Would I get along with my foreign in-laws? Was it true that these girls were turned off by body hair? Electrolysis will fix that in a jiff.

But 14 was also fetching in a very different way. Very exotic looking with full good lips and hooded eyes – and boobs. If 47 wouldn't elope with me maybe 14 would. I wanted one of those girls for my very own. How to choose between these two wonderful women who were waiting to fall in love with me if they only got to know me? If we got that far. And then how far would things go after that?

Let me interrupt the narrative right here and point out that I'm not an habitué of cat houses, massage parlors, and singles' bars. Perhaps I tarried in the occasional meat market when I was young and collecting experiences, but that was then and I've never felt comfortable in these places. Which makes no sense. Why should a person feel awkward and ill at ease in dives that cater to the feckless and classless? It should be a point of honor that one is unfamiliar with the rules in sleazy joints, should it not? Why, then, the raised shoulders, the rapid breathing, the damp palms? Why the apprehension that I'll be found out, a naïf from middle-class America?

"You like girl?" The questioner hovered like an obsequious maitre d', waiting to take an order.

"I like them all," followed by an uneasy laugh. I needed to look like I knew what I was doing.

Then, dropping the pretense, "Um, how do things work here?"

"If you like girl you say number and what you want and then go to room."

That much I'd figured out for myself. I shifted and looked at my feet. *Relax, Max. You're a man of the world and so is this gentleman.* And just because the clientele was weighted toward Germans with major sexual dysfunctions and/or perversions was no reason to feel out of place. "Well then, how much do things cost?"

He nodded toward a green board high on the far wall that listed prices. "Massage cost 100 baht. Full body massage cost 200 baht."

Interesting distinction: full body massage vs. a massage. "Do they rub more of you when you get a full body job?"

This question got a patronizing smile. "No, full body mean she massage you with her full body. Regular massage she only use hands."

Well, imagine that! I did so, right then and there.

"Also have Sandwich for 400 baht. That two girls give full body massage."

As luck would have it I had 400 baht with me. I'd intended to pick up some wine at Foodland and party with Tiff but that could wait for another 400 baht to come along. This neat solution to the dilemma of choosing between 47 and 14 was most welcome. I could have both!

Terd, who was studying the rows of girls, turned, "If you want sex you must arrange that for after girl gets off duty. Usually they let her go right away if she has customer. Separate prices. Usually 200 baht for quickie." Eight bucks? A bargain. Too bad I'd already committed all my money . . . but then, my last foray into fornication had ended badly.

Numbers 14 and 47 were summoned and they disappeared through the back door of their brightly lit showcase. I would have to assure them that I loved them equally. They reappeared in the foyer and we proceeded single-file down the red-carpeted corridor to a small room that contained a shower stall and a slightly elevated firm bed. The girls stepped behind a screen and emerged almost immediately wearing long loose fitting shirts –

and nothing else I hoped. What, I asked myself, was I doing here? Had a conscious decision been made?

14 indicated that I undress. When I stopped at the boxer shorts, the girls looked at each other. Don't get the wrong idea. It wasn't modesty, nor was I embarrassed to display my regalia.[*] I thought that by leaving my shorts on I would signal that I was there only for the therapeutic value of massage; no hanky-panky for Max.

14 – she seemed to be in charge – motioned for me to lie on the bed; then both girls began to vigorously rub oil into my skin, starting at opposite ends and working toward the middle. Pretty harmless; nothing to store up for confession yet. Instructed to roll onto my back they resumed the lube job and reached a crescendo as they arrived at the boxer shorts; such kneading and gentle pummeling my genitalia had never experienced as the girls reached inside the shorts to ensure that everything was coated with oil.

Detecting an unsurpressable response from my loins I brushed 14's hands away and pointed to my back and moaned to indicate a need for attention to that region. This request to deviate from routine slowed things only momentarily. Placing me on my side, both girls pulled off their shirts, revealing flawless bodies which made me moan again. This seemed to alarm 47 who may have thought I was in distress. Then 14 lay down in front and 47 in back, both facing me, and started the Sandwich.

Not every one of you will have this experience but I can recommend it as good value for the money. The important thing seems to be getting into the right rhythm and there are several to choose from: It can be a top to bottom squeeze; this is the simplest to execute as the girls first press their breasts into you, then their stomachs, then hips, thighs, knees, and finally run their feet around your ankles and calves. Next most complex is something I called the Ripple; same motion but one girl starts first and the second follows when the first has half completed the cycle; sort of like singing rounds beside a campfire. Deserving comment is the Gyration. Here attention is focused on the

---

[*] You don't have to spend much time in locker rooms to know where you stand in the rankings.

chest and back; the attendants rotate their upper bodies, alternating the amount of pressure so that their breasts sometimes brush your skin lightly and other times are buried hard against you. The ball-bearing action provided by the supple nipples on 14's firm breasts made it difficult for her to immobilize them totally until considerable pressure was applied. And there was the Bump and Grind: This starts in a well choreographed and coordinated fashion with pressure alternating between gyrating breasts and hips but the coordination between the two girls gradually breaks down as they enter their own erotic rhythms.

All of this was causing me considerable difficulty. My member kept poking through the fly and 14 would stop to take it in hand and inquire, "Do this?" I would shake my head no and the massage would resume. Not that I didn't want, and eventually need, it 'done' but what were the financial consequences? My cash had already been committed. What was the tab for ejaculation? Terd said that sex was extra. Was he still around to lend me money? "Hey Terd, I splattered it against the wall. How about 100 baht 'til payday?" And if a customer couldn't pay the bill, what happened? Was there some analogue to washing dishes in a restaurant? Perhaps servicing all the girls whose passions were still inflamed at the end of their work shift?

47 behind me had her hands in my shorts and was trying to work her fingers between my legs. I was in agony. An explosion was imminent. I thought of Mao Tse Tung. 47 had my scrotum in her hand and was slowly stretching it while massaging the perineum. I pictured Mao leading thousands of his followers in a swim in the Yangtse. 14 started to ride up and down on my hips until I signaled for her to stop and pointed at my back again. The girls conferred briefly and rolled me on my stomach. If I thought there was going to be any abatement in sexual stimulation I was mistaken. They both straddled me and worked their muffs up and down my skin in slow sweeping arcs, 47 handling my back and neck, 14 my legs and buttocks which had been exposed by pulling my shorts up tight. I focused on Mao addressing the multitudes in the Great Hall of the People. 47's thighs were around my neck and pulsing slowly. All reactionaries are paper tigers! My nuts were aching as I was rolled onto my back and the pussy sweep was resumed. Shifting leaders, I pictured Abraham Lincoln and was groping through

the Gettysburg address . . ."whether any nation, so conceived. . . can long endure, uh . . ." when the girls slipped off the bed and pulled on their chemises. I was dazed. It's over? Thank God. Just lie quietly for a moment to detumesce, collect wits, rinse the oil off in the shower and out of there.

Terd was waiting by the cashier. Noticing my hunched walk he asked, "They hurt something?"

I handed over the 400 baht. "Worst case of lover's nuts I've ever had."

"You didn't come?" asked Terd incredulously. "That must have been a challenge for the girls. I wonder why you take so long; you've been in there almost an hour while they tried to make you pop." I didn't speak but must have looked sore afflicted. "Well, your wife can relieve you when you get home."

Fat lot he knew.

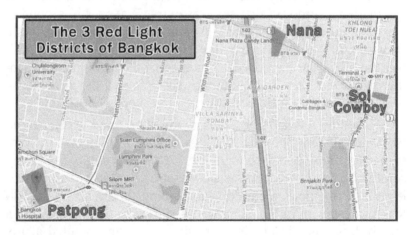

When Threatening Enemies Assail
- W.H. Bathurst, 1831

At the beginning of the fourth week a letter arrived at the school for Tiff marked 'Personal.' I opened it, of course.

```
Dear Mrs. Brown,

It pains me to have to write you this letter
but I know that one day you will thank me.
Your husband has been unfaithful to you. I
know that for a fact because I was the one
he did it with and I am pretty sure there
are many more. In case you think I was try-
ing to wreck your marriage, I did not do it
of my own free choice. He made me or I would
not have passed his course. This has been on
my conscience a lot and I finally decided
that if my husband did such a thing I would
want to know it myself so I could decide
what to do. As one woman to another, I hope
that you can work things out and have a
happy marriage.

                         Sincerely,

                         S. Taylor
```

Good old Sally. You had to admire her persistence. I wondered if a duplicate had been sent to another address and examined the letter to see if it was a photocopy.

How to divert this one-woman wrecking crew? The obvious solution was to give her a victory: Write back, over Tiff's name, and announce that thanks to Sally's timely and welcome intelligence the marriage was over and Max had been carted off in a canvas camisole to the funny farm where a team of psychotherapists were working around the clock to bring him out of a suicidal depression caused by his belated realization that he was an utter wastrel. Couldn't do that, of course. I wrote:

```
My dear child,

I have received your letter denouncing my
husband's "infidelity" and we have discussed
```

the best way to respond to it. As you will learn, we discuss everything as we have what was recently heralded as an Open Marriage.

Max tends to be more sympathetic in these matters than I. As "one woman to another" I think you should be spanked for presuming on another's relationship. Had Max and I a different relationship, you could have done irreparable harm. Your motives are not the selfless ones you declare; rather, they reek of vindictiveness and a childish disdain for the welfare of others, in this case mine.

Max and I talked at great length about you before he went to your apartment. He was deeply concerned that you had painted yourself into a difficult corner: you were failing out of school and you had made an improper suggestion to a faculty member. Max thought, and I agreed, that the least dishonorable way out for you was for him to accept your proposal.

Twice you have repaid his consideration with malice; you have tried to undermine both his career and his marriage. Sally, this is not the behavior of a rational adult. I urge you to avail yourself of the excellent counseling services at the university. If you do "I know that one day you will thank me." With hopes for a happier future for you,

Sincerely,

T. Brown

With hopes that you don't take seriously the advice to seek sanity among the crackpots in the Counseling Service,

Kiss my ass,

M. Brown.

Pretty good response, don't you think? For good measure I sent off another letter to the CDC, Sexually Transmitted Disease Division, reporting a dose that was resisting every antibiotic in town, and urging them to get on Sally's case pronto before half the males in the Midwest were blind.

My indefatigable socialite went to work shortly after we arrived in Bangkok and we were soon entertaining in our small apartment. Tiffany was reluctant to have much to do with Terd, perhaps because of his name, which I explained wasn't uncommon in Thailand, or perhaps because he was becoming a pal of mine which marked him as an undesirable. A series of excruciatingly polite and diffident faculty members and their wives nibbled our canapés, sipped our grog, and out of grudging obligation repaid the invitation in like kind. Perhaps in the belief, nurtured by exported American television programs, that we hobnobbed regularly with gangsters, we frequently found one or more of the other guests made their living in illicit trades. Tiffany didn't know what to do about this inverted social scale but she kept tabs against the possibility that cachet would someday attach to supping with traffickers in opium, precious metals, and women.

I felt compelled as a new recruit to the academic discipline of management to quiz these entrepreneurs on the details of their operations. Terd pointed out the obvious: these probings alarmed my hosts and placed my life in jeopardy. The only one who spoke of his business – albeit guardedly – was a large ethnic-Chinese man named Leung who dealt in gold. His was a quasi-legal business so he was willing to offer more information. In effect, he fenced. He claimed he never asked where the precious metals he bought came from and he usually laundered them through one relative or another before taking title and selling the goods on the open market.

O Friend of Sinners, How Blest Am I
- W.C. Dessler, 1692

The corpulent Mr. Leung surprised us with an invitation to dine chez Leung.

"I don't like this one bit, Max. You already told me he's a shady character."

"Poppycock, Snookums. Mr. Leung is obviously a gentle-man of discernment that he should select us to grace his board."

"Right. Which course do you think we'll be?"

"Your imagination is getting the better of you. I'm sure we'll find Leung a hospitable host and the worst that can happen is that we'll spend a few hours, as we usually do, in circumstances humbler than our own."

We revised 'humbler than our own' when the cab deposited us in front of a large gate through which could be seen a fleet of black Mercedes. Admitted by a grave menial, we crunched up the polished stones of the driveway toward the distant mansion.

"I had no idea there were houses this big in the center of Bangkok. God, I'm under-dressed." She was, in fact, having anticipated an evening perched on a vinyl kitchen chair with the women while the men worked through one or more bottles of firewater. "I don't think we should go in, Max."

"Because of your dress? You're the picture of understated elegance."

"I thought as much. Let's get out of here."

What a pain in the ass. We had dressed; we had found a cab; we had invested 120 baht in the fare; the nearest taxi would be a ten-minute walk; I longed to reach the air conditioned sanctuary just a few yards further; and Leung would be offended.

"Let's calmly consider the situation. You believe that Mr. Leung is an underworld figure. The trappings lend credence to that hypothesis. That means he's a man of immense power. A man who makes his own rules. A man who is generous to his friends and ruthless with his enemies. And you propose that we gratuitously offend this grandee?" She shrugged and resumed her march toward the door.

––––––––––

While a white-jacketed minion followed with a box of after-dinner cigars our host guided me away from the other three Chinese businessmen. "Dear Professor, if I may call you that, what exactly is the nature of your undertakings in Thailand?" Does he know about Sally and my self-imposed exile? "Have you traveled much? You seem an inquisitive man who seeks information."

"Very little travel, sir. My duties keep us in the city. And given my calling, I am far too disinterested in information for my professional good."

"I doubt that, Professor. Certainly your superiors would not have sent you here had they not full confidence that soon you would know what interested you. May I ask what does interest you?"

"Maps, sir. And, of course, excellent cigars," while selecting a *Partagas* panatela.

"Maps, that is curious. Of any particular region?"

"The local area. I've prowled the antiquarian shops off Sukhumvit but the quality doesn't warrant the prices asked."

"The local area? I would have thought you would be interested in our borders with Cambodia, Laos or Burma. Or perhaps the 'commercial' area in the north of the country. What you people call the golden triangle."

"Old maps, Mr. Leung. I've had no success finding locally produced ancient maps of the area. A few drawn by British cartographers during the early Raj years, but nothing local."

"Ah, Professor Brown, they say we Chinese are inscrutable; you are the one who wears the mask. I am a simple businessman," he trimmed his cigar with the proffered gold clipper, "and I have no capacity for deceit. If you are what I think you are and you need assistance, please accept my services."

"I'm grateful for the offer but I'm uncertain what you think I am." Confused by Leung's line of questioning, I redirected the conversation, "Your English is impeccable."

"USC, class of '59."

Tiffany approached at that moment, luxuriating in the deep plush wealth.

"Oh Mr. Leung, Ah'm having the most delightful time." Her voice rose on the last syllable. Scarlett O'Hara perhaps? "You have the most cha'min' house and everyone is so kind." It was true; she was channeling Margaret Mitchell. "Ah do hope we keep in touch."

Leung won my undying admiration with his response. This 'simple businessman,' born and raised ten thousand miles west of Atlanta, raised his left eyebrow and intoned, "Fiddle-de-dee, ma'am."

———

"That snotty fat Chink!" Her mood, damaged beyond repair by Leung's remark, hadn't been improved by the long search through dark streets for transportation which culminated in a *tuk tuk* with unpadded seats and a certified cretin at the controls. "You probably thought it was cute, that snotty remark."

"Ah, Pansy Blossom, I took his answer as a light-hearted rejoinder, a compliment almost."

"I was having such a good time talking with everyone and when I sincerely told the host that, he came back as if I were some goofy caricature. If you were any kind of a husband you would have spoken up."

And so we demonstrate once again what marriages are useful for, even bad ones: No disappointment is ever so severe that it can't be ameliorated with a kick to the spouse.

She did dispel the confusion about my conversation with Leung. "Max, you thick shit! He thinks you're a spook."

Arrivederci Roma
- R. Rascel, P. Garinei, 1955

Despite her awe at the wealth of Leung, Tiffany seemed to place less importance on her social contacts than before. Not because she looked down on the Thais; she was quite impressed by the fact that the country was a monarchy, of sorts, and she thought that royalty was more likely to touch those who live under it than those who have no connection at all. But she seemed surer of her social station now that she was headed to Rome and Rome overshadowed our deferential Thai acquaintances.

It was the intangibles of Roman culture, the residue of the greatness that had once been there. She was quick to agree that Italians were moral defectives and the jokes at their expense were too kind. But she wasn't going to Italy; she was going to

Rome. She would walk where Caesar walked. She would meditate where St. Thomas Aquinas meditated.[*] Her creativity would soar free in the same halls where Michelangelo had created his masterpieces. As a consequence, she didn't have to prove anything to the Thais. Although I felt there were one or two things she had to prove to me.

I thought about Rome a lot too. I hadn't heard from the Fulbright functionaries and began to worry about several things: 1) We didn't have onward plane tickets to Rome. 2) We had only ten days left in Bangkok. 3) We didn't even know the name or address of the school in Rome. I sent a telex:

Flbrght. Pls advs re Rome. Brown

I was then billed for a minimum three-minute message in which I could have sent ten times as much. But apparently such parsimony is contagious. Two days later a telex arrived from the ditsy broad at Fulbright:

Appt not cnfrmd. Seeking altrntve.

Bad news. There were over 160 countries in the world. Perhaps 10 percent of them habitable by a gentleman of breeding and standards. No third world cesspools for Max.

I broke the news to Tiffany. Her reaction was illuminating. For years one of my friends, in an effort to appear folksy, had said, "I didn't know whether to shit or go blind." This had never made any sense. What strange alternatives: Shit? Go blind? But the saying fit Tiffany's reaction perfectly. When I broke the news that evening she fell into a stupor; I had to help her get into bed. What, I wondered as I removed her bunny slippers and lifted her legs onto the bed, would a court slap on me in support payments when I divorced a woman who'd lapsed into a vegetative state. That was the 'go blind' part of the saying; the next morning was the other part.

"You mean to tell me we might not go to Rome!!?" she cried for the tenth time.

"'Might' is not the word I would choose, Rose Petal. My money is on 'probably won't'."

---

[*] And came up with the wonderful notion that we'll be reunited with our fingernail parings in heaven.

"They can't do this to me, Max! (Note that she did not say 'us.') This whole thing was accepted in the understanding that we'd be sent to Rome."

"The same thoughts passed through my own mind, Mimosa Breath. But we're only pawns in a cosmic chess match that exceeds our comprehension. Perhaps we're being called to some higher purpose."

"You can blow that higher purpose right out your ass, buddy boy! If these schmucks don't come up with some place pretty fucking good I'm going to sue everyone from that moron president on down to . . ." then she started to cry. Weak moment for me; I felt sorry for her. Here was one of the few people I'd met who knew exactly what she wanted – everything – and lived in the secure belief that it was her due. And now she wasn't getting it.

I'll spare you the extended histrionics, but Tiff's reaction to the first telex was such that I feared for her sanity when I received the second one.

```
Professor Brown, Regret Rome arrangements
not finalized; school does not answer our
inquiries. Have checked with your depart-
ment and learned that you cannot be re-
turned to payroll before next fall. Also
received anonymous letter calling your
moral qualifications into question; will
want to pursue this in separate corre-
spondence. Information suggests you best
suited for men's college. To minimize
travel expenses to program, looking for
position in Asia. Rgds,
```

I didn't trouble Tiffany with the full details of the cable, nor my reply ("Unaware of any moral disqualifications. Have asked my attorney to investigate penalties for officials who discriminate on the basis of unsubstantiated libel.") but I did tell her that we might have an opportunity to linger a while longer in the sun-kissed tropics.

"Look Max, you get me out of this toilet. I've had it up to here with these little wogs with their obsequious wives and that nasal singsong they prattle in. I want to go somewhere where there are real people – and not overweight Americans either. Tell those dildos in DC that they'd better come through."

"Ah, you're overwrought, my pet. Trust in Providence. We're all extras in a vast tragicomedy for which none of us has the script. The Great Playwright in the sky may be penning our lines right now; this could be our big break Tiff."

"Max," she wailed, "you're impossible to talk to."

Which, my dear, is precisely the objective.

I was kind of taken with the Great Playwright idea. Here we were on the cutting edge of civilization, lives thrown into confusion by an unanticipated sequence of events, and a pervading sense that the cosmos was realigning in a manner that would propel my own fortunes in a new direction for the better. Was Sally on the side of the angels? Would some *deus ex machina* descend over the stage and pluck us up. I was prepared for anything. However, I was unprepared for the next telex.

```
Professor Brown, Good news. Have secured
position in major Asian university teach-
ing operations management and mathematic
modeling. Report to Dr. Md Choudhuri,
Dhaka University at conclusion of present
course. Prepaid tickets will be sent to
Biman Bangladesh Airlines; arrange visas
directly. Best of luck,
```

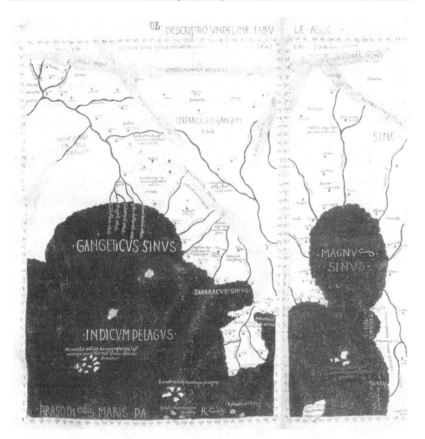

Ganges delta area, after Ptolemy. Circa 1540.

21

Ill Tidings Never Can Surprise
- I. Watts, 1807

"Aaarrgghh . . . nooooooo . . . aaarrgh . . . no no no no nooooo."
The wailer is Tiffany. The news that we were Bangladesh-bound didn't sit well.

"Pansy Petal, don't go on this way. This could work out fine.
What do we know about Bangladesh? It could be a tropical paradise. An opportunity to mingle with a new culture, meet new and different people . . ."

"Ingest exotic and lethal microorganisms," she interjected.
Good. Sarcasm was usually a healthy sign in Tiffany; it was as close to a well-adjusted outlook as she was often able to muster.

"I know about Bangladesh, Max. I've read all about the place on the record jackets of rock concerts where they're trying to raise money to save the place. It's basket case numero uno in the whole dismal world. People go there to discover diseases that are named after them. It's crowded, it's hot, it'll be the worst place I'll ever live in my life." Surprise. I'd assumed that her first response would be not to go. "It's a fucking laughing-stock of a country."

She was wrong, as we found out. There's little to laugh about in Bangladesh. In fact we found only two genuinely humorous things: the slogans of the national airline and the national tourism promotion board. The airline boasted that they were 'always dead on schedule.' This proud assertion elicited a nervous laugh when we encountered it upon boarding our flight. The tourism promotion board's posters admonished one to 'Visit Bangladesh before Tourists Come;' we counted ourselves fortunate on that score. Then the humor runs out. Try these travelogue entries:

• *How congested is it?* 105 million humans live in an area the size of Iowa. Iowa!

• *Will it get any worse?* They breed at an alarming rate so the 105 million will double to 210 million in less than thirty years.

• *Is it really so awful?* It's awful for children. Government statistics say that a baby stands a one in four chance of *not* living to see its fifth birthday; knowledgeable researchers say those odds are far too optimistic.

It's awful for women. They're 100 times more likely to die in childbirth than an American woman and they have the distinction of being rated as the most oppressed women in any country in the world.

It's awful for men who, on a good day, will work for ten hours and make a dollar. And don't believe what you've heard that 'everything is so cheap there.' It isn't. Basic items cost almost the same as in a developed country. How long could you support your family on a dollar?

Poor countries have their own special aroma. It's a bouquet composed of the sweat of thousands of rice-fed workers; not a pungent smell, but a sad stale one. Occasionally the acrid stench of rotting garbage will cut through, but the dominant odor is the product of over-work and under-nutrition. The smell greeted us before we deplaned and caused Tiffany to pale. "I can't go through with this Max. I hate this place and I haven't even left the goddamn airplane."

"A brighter day dawns tomorrow, old girl."

We shuffled through the arrival formalities in a terminal in which less than one-fourth of the lights were functioning. There was no cheer among our fellow travelers; few conversed; only solemn acknowledgement was given to family members waving from behind the window.

"God, Max, I feel like I'm being admitted to prison."

I felt the same. There was a desperate wish to turn and run back to the airplane but that offered no escape. Our sentence had begun. Or perhaps our entire lives were a sentence and the warden had just decreed hard labor for Tiff and me. Is that who You are, the universe's jailor and this planet is the repository for souls who misbehaved in past and better lives? Earth, the cosmos' Alcatraz.

One shouldn't expect an immigration official to be bright. The sharpies are next door in customs where the money is. The immigration officials could understand none of the documents presented to them that night. The transaction between traveler and official was always the same. The official would thumb endlessly through the traveler's passport, brow furrowed, while the traveler alternately held his arms straight out from his body in despairing explanations or attempted to retrieve the passport to speed the search for the sought stamp or visa.

"It must be a better place than we thought, Tiff. They're obliged to use every bureaucratic tactic to keep people out."

Our turn came at last. The official muttered something unintelligible through his betel stained beard. "I'm sorry?" I said, nurturing the wan hope that egregious omissions had been found in our documents and we'd be shipped out post haste.

"Where? Where you are staying?" he repeated, stabbing at the landing card with his forefinger.

Behind him a poster declared the Sonargoan Hotel to be the pearl of the orient. "Sonargoan Hotel," I answered, assuming that we'd be met by someone from the university, but not wanting to burden him with the intricacies of our arrangements.

We collected our bags from an arthritic conveyor belt and waited for a customs agent. The young man in front of us, a Bangladeshi, had been on a supply trip to Bangkok and the customs agent was pulling new shirts for resale from his bag and strewing them on the floor. The importer's precious cargo of cheap polyester was worth less than any one of Tiffany's dresses; we were waved through.

Emerging from customs, small brown hands wrapped themselves around our suitcase handles, attempting to dislodge our grip. Boys wearing only long skirts made from what appeared to be discarded tablecloths competed for our business. "Taxi?" "Foreign money?" "Baksheesh?" Pathetic beggars pushed up to us: women loosely holding limp infants, boys with twisted legs, healthier aggressive young men. Cupped hands were held in front of our chins. "Baksheesh. Foreign money." An infant with oozing closed eyes was presented for inspection.

"Max. I'm going to start screaming."

"We'd like a taxi, please. We're going to the Sonargoan Hotel." The retinue of beggars and ersatz porters followed across the parking lot, the less tenacious falling off as we progressed.

After loading the dilapidated black and yellow taxi I distributed five Thai baht to each of the porters – there were two men for every item of luggage – and we departed.

Tiffany was trembling. "It can only get better Tiff."

"I can *not* do it Max. I know my limits and this is way beyond them. This isn't a country; this is an asylum. And those are not real people. I've got to get out of here." She fell silent, her unfocused gaze directed out the window. Progressively her posture became more erect and her head moved to follow things as we passed them. I interpreted this brightening as a sign that she had decided that her sojourn would be brief. Mine would not and as her spirits improved, mine declined.

———

Things improved, briefly. The hotel turned out to be a luxury establishment with teak paneled walls, a stocked refrigerator, and non-stop flicks and exercise videos on the TV. It was often and accurately characterized as a great luxury ocean liner afloat in a sea of refuse. Inside there was no suffering and want; outside there was nothing other. In the morning we swam after breakfast, returning to the room in time for Tiffany to join Jane Fonda for calisthenics.

The telephone interrupted my shave; Professor M.I. Choudhuri was waiting in the lobby.

———

"Professor Brown, is it you?" Choudhuri was short and prematurely balding. "I waited for you at the airport last night but did not see you arrive. The Fulbright Commission certainly treats its people well, placing them in such an expensive hotel."

"A little self-indulgence, Professor. We look forward to getting settled more permanently."

"That we can do today. My office has performed the needful and your new apartment is waiting for your arrival even while we are discussing."

Begging time to repack, I left Choudhuri in the lobby and interrupted Tiff in the cool down stretches with Jane.

"Good news, Pansy Petal, our new home awaits." Tiff took in the luxury around her and resumed stretching.

At this point I made an uncomfortable discovery: I wanted her to stay. After years of wishing Tiffany gone – or, on a few occasions, dead – it was surprising and unpleasant to fear her departure. Tearing eyes, once a source of mean satisfaction, were now a cause for alarm.

"Hey, old girl. The place is awful but we can do it." No response other than a snuffle. "Look, the trip has been hard. We may never grow to like this place but remember two things: first, our time here is short, and second, uh . . ." Damned if I could think of a second positive aspect to our situation.

Eyes fixed on the TV, Tiffany answered in a distant, flat voice. "You'll say it's just selfishness, but I expected a lot more from this adventure. I really feel I'm due a break. Marriage to you is no bed of roses and I was starting to think that perhaps this travel would be a small reward for staying with you. You know, the fates trying to make up for the raw deal I've had so far."

Un-fucking-believable! How can every disappointment in her life be linked to my perceived short-comings as a mate? This question, and the emotion behind it, was held in by sinking my teeth into my upper lip. Regaining composure. . .

"I'm all for discussing our relationship, Tulip Stamen, but your timing surprises me. Actually I'd hoped that with no other distractions we might begin to see each other more clearly – and positively – here. This experience may bring us closer together." Closeness is something neither of us had wanted for years.

Her face worked. Something was about to break, and did. "You arrogant asshole! I've seen you clearly enough already and I sure as hell don't want to get close to you! You probably think this is all funny. It isn't Max. We should be back home and that's where at least one of us is going." She picked up her exercise towel and headed for the shower.

Abide with Me
- J.E. Rankin, 1896

Decision time. Should her desertion be encouraged? I once kept a daily written record for two months; on 47 of the 61 days I wrote that the day would have been more pleasant without her. A social scientist should respect data and those data argued for freeing oneself from this odious burden. And while this wasn't the best time to go our separate ways, her decamping at that moment might put me in better stead in divorce court. Perhaps a Bangladeshi judge could be bribed to award a divorce in her absence, free of alimony or property division. Why did I ever commingle my community property with hers in the first place?

On the other hand, she might get a divorce in the US and in my absence some barracuda could persuade a judge to strip me clean and saddle me with alimony payments through the end of time. Or she might simply raid the storage locker and disappear with all our worldly goods.

Another consideration came to mind. This was going to be a tough assignment. The social outlet were few. No place for a bachelor.

The decision on when to unload her should be deferred. You've seen that I'm not quick at letting go of things. Besides, Bangladesh was sure to provide future opportunities to drive her out, should I change my mind. To keep her there required an exercise in marital realpolitik.

Tiff was in the shower when I entered the bathroom, the sight of her firm breasts and dark pubic hair through the vinyl curtain was further argument that her continued presence might be turned to an asset. The forlorn hope of sex-starved males everywhere.

Voice modulation would be important. No whining, no hint of weakness. As matter-of-fact as possible. I leaned against the counter. "Alright Tiff, there's no way I can keep you here. But – and listen to this very carefully – if you bail out you can figure out how to support yourself because you'll get fuckall from me. We're in this together. We agreed to do this together. This isn't what either of us expected. But right now it's what has to be done." I left before she could respond, signaling by my measured departure that no response was expected. She had to be considering her only option: moving in with her parents.

All sound from the bathroom ceased and I started to worry about Choudhuri waiting in the lobby. At length Tiffany emerged, wrapped in two towels, an indication she'd decided to stay. Were she leaving she'd be parading around naked, flaunting what I was about to lose. Retrieving her clothes, she retreated to the bathroom to dress. I thought I heard an occasional soft sob through the closed door. When she re-emerged she kept her sullen gaze off me, muttering, "You might at least help get our things together and packed."

Watching the loading of our luggage, Professor Choudhuri endeavored to reassure red-eyed Tiffany. "You will occupy the top-most floor of the building. I think you will find that most delightful as it gathers the most breezes in the evening. Every apartment has two bedrooms so you can perhaps persuade your good husband to allow you one for your hobbies. My own wife will help you find servants. You will want a cook and bearer but I see you do not need an ayah. You must let my wife tell you how much to pay the servants. Americans make the mistake of paying them too much and they do not work any harder for it. A very good thing for you Professor; you will walk only five minutes to our office building. There is no need for a car in Dhaka. Everyone rides by rickshaw or baby taxi; I think you will not go in our buses." The chatter continued as we got underway.

22

Home, Home, Sweet, Sweet Home
- W. Cushing, 1883

At night Dhaka's squalor and ugliness are shrouded in darkness. By day they're fully revealed. The hotel was the last well-painted building we saw as we rode toward the campus. Skinny men in long skirts – lungis our guide informed us – strained to pedal overloaded rickshaws. Squatting expressionless women with their infants slung on their backs reduced bricks to rubble for construction by beating the bricks with a rock. A long smelly ditch beside the road was covered with black Mylar; this turned out to be a squatter settlement and the thin plastic provided cover to the families that lived in the ditch.

Did that register? Whole families living in drainage ditches under black plastic.

Gaining the campus we rolled through a broken gate and down a weed-choked lane between deserted-looking buildings with peeling beige paint.

"Your building is there," indicated Choudhuri, his voice filled with pleasure. He pointed at a five-story concrete structure with peeling walls and several broken windows; two large cracks ran vertically through the concrete from the top to the bottom of the building. Tiffany was wearing her brave face.

The five-story climb dispelled the last vagrant hope that the shabby exterior concealed a polished jewel. Every corner of every landing was splattered in red betel juice, sprayed from the mouths of generations of heavy salivators. Arriving at the top floor, Choudhuri struggled with the keys in the lock and finally declared them to be the wrong ones. As he turned to descend the stairs Tiff tried the doorknob and the door swung open. An overstuffed sofa, two vinyl covered straight back chairs, and assorted Formica veneered tables beckoned us enter. This was the living room.

A single florescent tube sparked and turned black in response to the switch; the problem was easy to diagnose as the wiring was stapled directly to the wall; it appeared that a staple had broken through the insulation and shorted the wires. This was a foretaste of maintenance problems to come.

Tiffany's expression was stony. Saying nothing, she inspected each room while Choudhuri resumed his description of the delightful evening breezes that would bring balm to our souls after the day's heat. Then, revealing himself to be at least minimally perceptive, if overly optimistic, he said, "Your wife will begin to enjoy it here too. Many women are melancholy for some months, but in my experience which is not little if I may say, they do not want to leave. That is true to the very last jack man of them."

This assertion was punctuated by a truncated shriek. Staying Choudhuri with a gesture I went to see what ill had befallen my love slave, imagining that she'd disturbed a coven of cockroaches or somnolent rat. It was better than that.

Sometimes the fates relent and visit upon us a moment of unexpected and delicious joy. Such a moment had arrived for me, a moment I hoped to prolong. The shrieker was, of course, Tiffany (née Pratiloma) Brown. During her tour she'd wandered into the bathroom and, stepping incautiously, placed her left foot through the hole in the floor that the developing world uses for a toilet. When I found her she was steadying herself on the wall, trying to extricate her foot without, apparently, bending her ankle.

"My goddamn foot's stuck in the shitter and I can't get it out!"

Stooping to inspect, I offered this advice. "Straighten out your foot and it should slide right out."

"Can't you see?" she cried. "There's a humongous turd in there. If I straighten my foot to get it through the fucking hole it'll go in the shit!"

The problem, as I saw it, was threefold: First, I couldn't laugh out loud despite waves of glee that were welling within me. Second, this situation had to be dragged out; it was too precious to let slip away only briefly enjoyed. Third, at some point we had to extricate Tiffany, if, for no other reason than that this was the only 'sanitary' facility in the apartment.

"Let me enlist the able services of Professor Choudhuri, Pet. He's certainly dealt with situations like this before." Choudhuri could use a good laugh too.

"Don't you dare, you smirking prick! Get a pickaxe or something and enlarge the hole."

"Too dangerous, Tulip Twigs. One mis-stroke and your severed foot would join the turd in the cloaca."

"Goddammit Max, can't you . . ." and she started to blubber. That made me angry. Here I was, feeling right about the world for the first time in months, and she dampens the occasion with a great rain of tears.

"Alright, hold still." Needless caution. "I'll get something."

By pouring a pail of water down the hole the noisome turd was flushed away and Tiffany – still sobbing – delicately extracted her foot. My mood was restored by the appearance of Choudhuri at the door during the rescue who took in the scene gravely and admonished Tiffany to watch where she stepped.

The following days were little short of a nightmare. Shopping for food was a horrific encounter with flies, foul smells, and small boys insisting that they would guide us through the market. The stove was out of gas; the refrigerator struggled to maintain its contents at room temperature; the mattress was lumpy, made, it turned out, of coconut husk fibers; and the much touted evening breezes transported several thousand voracious mosquitoes to our chambers. Each minor disaster brought a torrent of laments from Tiffany; her evident intention was to insure that my own suffering matched or exceeded her own. I had to endure both the inconveniences and the incessant whining of my helpmeet.

Every effort to find a remedy through the University, the owner of the property, was met with silence. Direct inquiry was pointless; the responsible official was away, not appointed, recently deceased, taking the cure for a blemish discovered on his pituitary, no longer empowered to handle such matters, or summoned to the chambers of a senior official. These excuses were relayed to us by the hapless Department Administrator, Mr. Khan, whose workload had skyrocketed due to our presence.

The behavior of these elusive officials inspired an obvious comparison. God's not immature, psychotic, bored, or a swinger. He's an absentee landlord.

                    Terra Tenants' Union
                      Milky Way Galaxy
                       Solar System

Grand Panjandrum
Firmament

Dear Absentee Landlord,

On the advice of legal counsel our association is serving notice of the following defects on which corrective action is expected
within ten (10) working days of postmark. If
remedial work on all of the following defects has not commenced within that period
we will be obliged to seek other remedies:

1. The dwelling is inherently unstable.
Seismic disturbances, volcanic eruptions,
and climatic unpredictability combine to
render the premises hazardous.

2. Inadequate insulating materials. The
ozone layer should be able to withstand the
occasional spritz of aerosol without falling
apart.

3. Quality of the populace. There are some
endearing species — the otter and some of
the smaller monkeys, as examples — but in
the main the inhabitants are physically un-
attractive (when You viewed Your creation
and 'saw that it was good' did the warthog
escape notice?), intellectually deficient
(the amoeba we understand, but the turkey?)
or morally repugnant (we assume You disap-
prove, as do we, of parents devouring their
offspring).

The list could go on. These are the most urgent items that demand Your immediate attention. Please notify the residents through
our Union of the date on which work will
commence so that they may plan accordingly.

                              Sincerely,
                              President
                              TTU

> Dear Smart-asses of the TTU,
>
> You are hereby notified to quit the follow-ing premises:
>
> Earth, Solar System, Milky Way
>
> and to surrender possession thereof within three (3) days of service of this notice. The reason for eviction is that you have consis-tently violated every provision governing tenancy.
>
> Scram, beat it, vamoose, scat.
>
> <u>God</u>
Owner

The situation did improve, somewhat. Tiffany engaged, with help from Mrs. Choudhuri, a staff of two: a cook and a house-keeper. This dream of every middle-class American housewife having been fulfilled, the downside of servant management be-came evident. They broke things, schemed against one another, and would turn willfully ignorant.

Tiffany had been cautioned not to hire 'sharp customers' as they were probably on the take. Babul and Pushpa were unlikely to be confused for sharpies, but they did prove able, in short or-der, to take over all of the household chores and Tiffany sud-denly found herself without a rôle in the world. She did not cook; she did not buy groceries and other household supplies; she did not clean; nor do laundry; and she was not – nor had she been for a long time – a companion. Free time, and nothing to invest it in.

It's an unsettling experience for someone of our upbringing to become suddenly a drone, making no contribution, consuming and not producing. The books on adjusting to a new culture were replete with advice on which hand to extend in greeting and what gift to bring when invited to dinner. They were silent on this larger challenge: how to cope with losing the foundations of your identity and your place in the world. Poor Tiff.

It didn't bring out the best in her. Poor Max.

Since we were distantly attached to the US government via Fulbright, we tried the 'official' US community which consisted of the Junior Dips, as the second string in the Embassy called themselves, and the American employees of the development assistance mission. After attending two social gatherings with these anointed champions of Truth, Justice and the American Way, it became evident that their preoccupations were two, and only two: 1) the caprices of the Embassy's Housing Committee that assigned the residences under contract to the Embassy in a fashion that, miraculously, failed to satisfy anyone, and 2) the next posting which was decided via a process that was similarly opaque and unfair. Having nothing to offer to the conversations on either of these topics, Tiff and I would find ourselves – for the first time in our lives – visible social failures; we would wind up talking to one another.

23

My Crafty Foe, With Flattering Art
- **Psalms of David (G. Paine), 1793**

Thank the Lord for honest employment. It provides a man the wherewithal for sustenance, a source of dignity, and an unimpeachable excuse to get out of the house. The office shared by myself and a Professor Singh – not yet returned – was shabby, hot, dimly lit, and an unlikely refuge. The only other person consistently around was Mr. A. G. Khan, the Department Administrator. It was he who had secured the choice apartment for us, who promised to extend every effort to make our sojourn comfortable (he did try), who would take upon himself all administrative requirements, and who lost no time in fishing for an explanation for Sally's damning letter.

Dear Director of the Management Dept,

I am writing to advise you that an American professor who will be coming to your school soon has been involved in some morals scandals at his American university. I know this for a fact as I was the person who blew the whistle on him as we say here. The university administration is trying to cover up his problems so they may not tell you the truth if you ask them directly. I can only urge you to keep a close watch on him so that he doesn't try anything there. Since yours is a Moslem country I understand that an adulterer is killed. I think you should warn him of this.

Sincerely yours,

Sally Taylor

"Interesting letter Khan. What do you make of it?"

"Well, Professor Brown, Professor Choudhuri and I do not know what to make of it but I was hoping that you could somehow put me in the picture as to its precise meaning."

"Careful, Khan. That sounds close to an accusation, that *I* am the culprit – a despoiler of youth, a deflowerer of innocent virgins."

"No, no. So sorry to give the impression. Being that you are the only American professor, I thought naturally you would know how such letters come to be written."

"I do indeed, Khan. I know the young lady. I disappointed her with a grade that led to her dismissal from our university. I've asked the courts for protection from such calumny but the legal costs of pressing a complaint are high. It's the kind of vilification that goes with the territory nowadays, Khan. Zealots pressing for the emancipation of women from workplace harassment have provided a safe haven for the demented and mean-spirited, a haven from which they can launch their forays, returning with fresh scrotums tied to their belts. Stick to the administrative side, Khan. Teaching has become a blood sport."

Khan winced as he deciphered the part about fresh scrota. "Has she tried to blacken your good name before, Professor?"

"This is the fourth letter I know of, Khan. Seasoned managers in America are learning to discount these ravings. I doubt that people here have the experience that would make them equally skeptical."

There were three noteworthy things about Sally's letter: First, she knew that Bangladesh is a Muslim country. That knowledge seemed the likely product of special research. Second, she'd failed to mention my name. Did this omission suggest – such is wishful thinking – that her resolve to destroy me was weakening? Third, she didn't wish me dead. Putting these last two points together nurtured the hope: are all her feelings for me negative?

Other evidence didn't contradict that possibility and it might explain her anger and persistence. Why else would she keep up this long-distance harassment? She'd said she liked me, right? And she had come on to me. Human behavior is overdetermined; Freud was right about some things. She propositioned me to get a grade and get her man.

I know: pretty pathetic. But this was such an attractive possibility that I found my thoughts turning to Sally and her undulating backside when I next took solitary pleasure.

A fourth remarkable feature of Sally's letter was that it was postmarked Copenhagen. She'd found the jack, or a Jack, to support travel. This brought an unwelcome pang of jealousy when I thought of her with another man. I wrote:

```
Director, Drug Enforcement Administration
Washington, DC

Dear Sir,

I have been informally advised that a Miss
Sally Taylor, currently traveling in Europe,
plans to return to the US with a quantity of
illegal drugs concealed on or in her person.
I cannot vouch for the reliability of this
information but pass it on for your consid-
eration and action. Given the reputation and
reach of my informant, I regret that I can-
not take the risk of revealing my own iden-
tity.

I pray for your success in stemming the flow
of poisons that are crippling our great
country.

                        Sincerely,
```

Why no search party is looking for the lost art

"Belladonna Breath, I need to unburden myself." Narrowed eyes; did she think a confessed adultery was about to splash down in the punch bowl? "Years of solitary rumination have brought me no closer to the answers. Cosmic questions, Tiff. Industrial-strength philosophy."

"What is it, the wine or the absence of your usual sleazy buddies?" She refilled her own glass, but not mine. "For years you've turned off every conversation I've tried to launch cutely, cryptically, or both. Now you want a deep chat on the meaning of the universe?"

Ignoring the barb, "Exactly! Doesn't this godforsaken place make you wonder what life is all about? Look at these people. No hope in their faces, no reason for hope."

"I try not to notice. When the mosquitoes drive me out of this pisshole we call home I keep my eyes on things, not people. Otherwise I'd go nuts."

"That's what I mean. Their experience with life is so different from ours that it's difficult to recognize them as the same species. Where we Americans have a vibrant shopping mall culture that sustains and unifies us, these poor souls' sole preoccupation is the next meal – which will probably not arrive today."

"Where are we going with this Max? I'm waiting for the zinger."

Her unwillingness to engage was annoying. "What the fuck *does* it all mean, Tiffany? That's where we're going. What does it mean? Why do one-fourth of the little babies in this country die before they see their fifth birthday? Why does any little baby die? A child, Tiffany. A goddamned child! In his bunny pajamas, holding on to a teddy bear. And dying in a fancy hospital. Or here lying silent on a straw mat with his little belly bloated up. What kind of a fucked up world is this? How do you tell a child whose life hasn't begun that it's over?"

What would Debbie's life have been like?

"My, the boy theologian is really worked up. I haven't seen you this upset since you caught Ralph Hanson with his hand on my ass last year."

"This is serious shit, Tiff. Even more so than the infatuation of an aging and acned assistant librarian." She clenched her napkin into a ball. "This place is living proof that God has gone fishing, or that He's bonkers, that madness is reeling out of control across the galaxies." I stopped for a sip of wine and an assessment of Tiff's reaction. She was coiled, her eyes hooded. Perilous to continue?

"Maybe God just got old. Why not, Tiff? Everyone else does. Picture the old coot, half-slipping out of a chair on the nursing home porch. A little spittle trickles out of the corner of His mouth. Latch onto that image. Then the world starts to make sense, see? The boss has lapsed into senile dementia.

Things start to drift, the simple logic that created matter and life from hydrogen becomes random. Where there was once order now there's chaos. There's no justice, no logic. The good do not prevail; more often, it seems, the unjust do. God doesn't have to be dead, He's just . . ."

"That's enough. I'm impressed. Mighty Max Waves Fist under Nose of Almighty." She leaned forward, spitting out the words. "The immediate question is, what's *your* game? Is this an early sign of mid-life crisis? Could be, couldn't it? What quicker path to glory for a punched out bum than to take on the heavy-weight champ himself. Even though he gets knocked into the fourth row in the opening round he'll always tell himself he was a contender."

How could I not hate this woman? "Alright, Tiff. I give up. I'd hoped to stimulate your intellect, not your ire. Should you ever be in the mood for some adult fare, look me up."

Can't we ask the big questions? Even if there's no hope of finding the answers? I'd read Leibniz, St. Augustine and Hick.[*] They'd approached the paradox of evil – lots of evil – that runs rampant in a world that's supervised by a benevolent, omnipotent, omnipresent and omniscient God by accepting all five elements as givens. Then they would come up with some lame-ass rationale, such as allowing for free will, which, in their tortured explanations, reconciled the lot. There were two obvious alternatives:

   1) Misfortune (evil) is divine justice meted out to those who have it coming to them. According to this school of thought, God's okay with this. Has He read Anne Frank's *Diary*?

   2) A more common and less loathsome view – which I subscribe to – is to start by acknowledging that one of those elements, the existence of evil, is experientially undeniable. Shit happens. Then you have to be open to alternative visions of God – He's not omniscient, or not benevolent, or not omnipotent, or not omnipresent (but which?) – that allows evil to coexist with this imperfect God. The metaphors I'd invented – prankster, head-case,

---

[*] Okay, read *about* them.

player, senile – permitted a little whimsy to enter into what has, admittedly, always been a doomed inquiry.

No easy answer. But, come on everybody. There's a grotesque inconsistency here. Doesn't that bother anybody? Shouldn't it?

I carried my dishes into the kitchen and was met by the terrified stare of Babul, our dim-witted cook. Had my rant struck a responsive chord in a nincompoop?

————

Of course there are no cease-fires in the war between the Browns. That night in bed, on a roll after her debating victory, Tiffany favored me with a wet, full-lip kiss. Thinking I was about to get lucky – a consolation fuck? Pride won't get in the way of that! – I reciprocated. She rolled away. "Night, Max."

24

When Faith and Culture Clash
- J. Thomburg, 1993

"Mr. Khan, a pleasant good day to you."

"And you also Professor Brown. I have some good news that I may convey."

"And that is that the Israeli Prime Minister has embraced Islam?"

"I had not read that in our press Professor. What a fine happening. No I was mentioning your passports which are now nearing readiness. I believe that I may persuade the Under-Secretary of the Interior to grant your resident visa this very day."

"Excellent news indeed, and no less dramatic than my own. Please, however, don't exhaust your capital on us, Mr. Khan. You may wish to complete processing my own visa but Mrs. Brown's can wait as she'll be going nowhere."

"I understand, Professor. You will also be happy to find that Professor Singh has returned from his native country and is in your office this morning."

Singh was turbaned and sported a luxuriant mustache and beard; a fierce looking Sikh when seated behind a desk. Unfortunately his body was small and when he stood the overall effect verged on comical.

"Ah, you will be the American professor going by the name of Smythe-Brown," extending his hand.

"The same, Professor Singh. Welcome back from the Punjab. I see that you have already made yourself at home." Some papers I'd been working on at the one serviceable desk had disappeared.

"Not a relaxing holiday if I may say. Many appointments and work in Delhi. Contacts must be maintained you know."

"Indeed I do, sir. And speaking of contact, how do you propose we cohabit in this office without stumbling over one another constantly?"

"Ah yis. Of course an American would be surprised to encounter the cramped space here. We manage, as you know. But for some curious reason, that reminds me that I wish to invite you and your wife to dine with us tomorrow evening if that is convenient. If you can accept I will send a car to fetch you."

"As you might imagine, Professor, our social calendar is unencumbered. We would be honored to join you. At what hour?"

"Ah yis. Seven-thirty for drinks I should say. Not too much fire in your curry I would imagine."

"Don't vary the menu on our account Professor. We're here to quaff deeply from the cup of cultural diversity."

"An admirable attitude. I believe we will get along famously Professor Smythe-Brown." Said with a dazzling display of teeth. "Now I could not help but noticing that you had work in progress when I arrived this morning. I placed it in this drawer – you will find it undisturbed – and I return you the use of the desk."

Perhaps not such a bad person.

O Land of Heroes Dead
- W.W. Fay, 1876

The Hero preoccupies many sociologists. These savants (the sociologists, not the heroes) make a small living out of defining a society by its heroes, explaining man's emptiness by his lack of heroes, and predicting the decline of modern civilization by the base quality of current heroes. As individuals these mavens are at pains to tell us that their own heroes have died. These revelations are made wistfully; an important dimension disappeared from their lives when JFK, RFK, MLK, Gandhi, or their own father was plucked from among the living.

I had several heroes; none of them died a hero's death. Popular heroes go out heroically. Quickly. Violently. Cleanly. Some of mine went quickly; others died by inches; none died painlessly. My last hero died that day in Dhaka.

This is how it happened:

The walk from the University office to the apartment was four dusty blocks long, half of it on sidewalk. One didn't encounter many people on this walk by Dhaka standards, perhaps fewer than a hundred. Of those passed, two-thirds were poor laboring men wearing a lungi and skivvy shirt or no shirt; the remainder were students and women. The people were a study in the conservation of energy; no unnecessary gesture, movement, or animation could be observed. The eyes appeared to register no more than was needed for safe navigation. The blank faces weren't masks, they were simply blank faces which were too tired and drained to carry an emotion. If there was a sudden flurry of activity it almost always meant trouble, probably a fight, and those were rare.

I walked the distance four times a day, striding with purpose to and from my important work. I moved rapidly to discourage beggars from way-laying me and with a slight bounce in my gait to affirm my apartness.

Half the distance between the office and apartment a wide sidewalk appeared for 100 yards in front of the skeleton of a high-rise building. In front of that building my last hero received a mortal blow. A man in a lungi lay across the sidewalk. I noticed him just before I had to step over him. His body was twisted at the waist, the top half turned toward the ground, the bottom half turned upward. A small pool of blood surrounded his head. I catalogued the options:

Passed out drunk and fell. No, can't be that. There were few opportunities to obtain alcohol in that Muslim country without identification documents as a foreigner.

Lightly injured? Unlikely.

Okay, he's in bad shape but the language barrier precludes my providing effective help. No again; language differences matter little when dealing with the comatose.

His compatriots will recognize the symptoms better than I and respond better. But his compatriots were oblivious to him.

He's different from me and not my responsibility. And my last hero gave up the ghost as I walked ahead, striding purposively.

———

"You sure are putting it away tonight, Max. Lose an argument with God?"

"My last hero died."

"And whom might that be, I wonder? I don't mean to sound proprietary, but it took me two hours at Shafir Brothers Duty-Free Ripoff to get that crummy fifth of Scotch." She straightened the cushions on the couch. "But what the hell, we don't lose a hero every day. You didn't just discover the passing of Captain Ahab of *Moby Dick* fame, did you? He was a fellow theomach of yours."

God's hemorrhoids! Does she ever let up?

My last hero was Max the Compassionate. He didn't just die; he probably never existed. He was a fiction. So was Max the Brave who didn't survive Vietnam. Max the Lover vanished soon into his marriage, murdered by the same venomous harridan who sat taunting me. Max the moral? Drawn and quartered when he sold academic credit for sex. And Max the Diligent? I never really believed in him fully; his passing was no surprise. But it was painful to lose Thoughtful Max. And there will be no easy recovery from the death of Max the Compassionate. He was the last hero left in me.

It's dangerous to be your own hero. How many men are? When conventional heroes die we erect memorials to them and dedicate ourselves to their ideals. After a brief period of bereavement their deaths engender renewal and sometimes optimism. For those of us who are our own heroes, there's no renewal, only loss. We are less – irremediably diminished.

Max the Caring, the Compassionate, walked away from an injured, dying, or perhaps dead man and didn't break stride. He didn't pause. Or look for chest movement. Feel for a pulse. He didn't turn the man's head up. Or inquire. He didn't pick up that skinny body and cradle it and cry. God, how I wish he had. But if presented with the same opportunity again, Max would fail the test. My last hero was a fraud.

———

"Here's a cheerful item to lift your spirits this morning, Max. The *Bangladesh Observer* reports that a peasant woman near

Rajshahi cut off her husband's pecker after he failed to give an adequate account of his whereabouts for the preceding three days. Got him in his sleep. I trust you slept well after dispatching our monthly ration of Scotch in a single sitting?" She looked up from the paper with a treacly smile. "The hapless victim was taken to the Rajshahi hospital where expert Bangladeshi surgeons stitched the member in place, although, quote, 'expressing sincerely doubts whether it would retain its full functioning as hitherto', unquote. No more Mrs. Nice Girl. The Sisters are on the move everywhere."

She sounded more like me every day. Only wordier.

"Are we not speaking today? Could I have a grunt? Perhaps a soft moan?"

Tiffany would only attack this way when I was in a weakened state. Had to respond with something before she picked up more momentum. "No, Lilac Lips, I'm conducting a subtle behavioral experiment. You are a participant in sociological history, the details of which you may read when I publish."

"Funny you should mention publishing. You know? It occurred to me that we might enjoy easier circumstances if you'd do the conventional academic thing and write something."

Christ, woman. I'm always writing. How about -

> Dhaka (AP) – Decaying corpse of Western woman retrieved yesterday from Gulshan Lake. Faintly detectable to the eye were marks around the throat where the victim had been strangled. The mouth was open as if the fatality had occurred in mid-sentence. Police authorities say they don't know fuckall.

"I've seen very few thoughts in print that merited the sacrifice of the trees required for their printing." Now it was her turn to be silent. Had she read my mind about the corpse?

With exaggerated care she prepared a cup of tea for herself, sipped at it, then addressed me, separating the words to ensure comprehension. "Successful faculty write. They are admired by other faculty. They get good jobs. They don't get sent to Bangladesh." And she cleared her breakfast dishes.

The only retort that came to mind was "Oh yeah?" I didn't use it.

25

Are Your Treasures on Earth
- W. E. Penn, 1887

Apparently it was possible to live comfortably on a Dhaka University salary. Professor G.I. Singh and family occupied a free-standing two-story house with a tiny yard. The yard itself was little more than a path around the house; in the world's most densely populated country land isn't given to trivial uses.

"Ah Professor, and the lovely Mrs. Pratiloma." How did Singh know Tiffany's maiden name? "Please come in for subcontinental hospitality."

Uncertainly, we shucked our shoes at the door beside several other pairs and entered. Awaiting our arrival, fully shod, were Choudhuri and wife, Khan, and a young man who was introduced as Nawaz.

"Nawaz, you will find, shares some of your interests," explained Singh. What interests could those be? My only leaning revealed to date was Sally's allegation of incurable satyriasis.

"And what interests are those, Professor Singh?"

Red-faced Tiffany retreated to recover our shoes.

"I understand you are a fancier of old documents. And please, you must call me G.I. as do my other friends."

Choudhuri offered that he should be addressed as M.S.; Khan as A.G. Nawaz, presumably content to be known as Nawaz, scratched his armpit.

"Actually my interest is in old maps. But we expect to find little here. The climate, perhaps, is too inhospitable for them to survive."

Nawaz, unexpectedly, spoke. "No. Maps there are. Maybe not maps you know. Different with words, no pictures. Old makers make maps with palm leaves dried and cooked."

"How very interesting, Nawaz." Apparently he'd studied English under Yoda. "Are there many examples of these old maps around?"

"Maybe not so many. I will tell you." And he lapsed into silence, rediscovering the itch that had preoccupied him earlier.

Choudhuri, eager to protect his neophyte American, warned, "You must avoid the antique sellers whose stores are near the Parjatan Cooking School. Many of their goods are fakes and the ones that are real, I will wager, are not legal for sale. The authorities have many myopic laws about protecting Bangla culture and heritage. When there are no sales allowed, there is no market so how can there be any exploration? Our bureaucrats wonder why there are so few antiques and blame the foreigners for taking them away. I will tell you what has happened; the bureaucrats took away the incentive to find old things from our past so no one is looking." Pleased with this defense of free market principles, Choudhuri looked around for signs of approval.

"Tell me then, M.S., is that why no one has found the Salim Ullah treasure? But first, I must attend to my pleasant duties as host. Drink orders? Mrs. Pratiloma, what is your pleasure?"

Tiffany ordered the first of several gin and tonics. Stripped of her usual rôles she was trying out for a new one: town drunk. After the drink orders had been relayed to an unseen servant through a door, Singh repeated the question about the treasure.

"How intriguing," from Tiffany. "A lost treasure here in Bangladesh?"

"Ah yis, fairy book stuff perhaps. The Moghuls were not terribly interested in governing this area after they took it over. I believe the first Moghul governor arrived, built a large bath house . . ."

"A toilet," exclaimed Tiffany, "did you hear that Max? The first foreign visitor built a toilet."

"But the story has an unfortunate twist," resumed Singh. "Shortly after putting up the – toilet, as you say – his daughter fell ill and died. The unfortunate man departed, perhaps leaving the start of a modest fortune behind as a memorial to the child."

"Not perhaps," asserted Choudhuri. "Most definitely, I would say. No one doubts that there is a treasure, my good man. But who has it. That is the question on the tip of everyone's mind."

This was obviously a fun topic as Khan, beaming, had been waiting for an opening to speak. "And just as they think they have found it, it disappears. I, for one, never believed it would be in the safe at the Nawab's palace."

"Explain please?" asked Tiffany over the top of her glass.

Singh laced his fingers. "Ah yis, there was great speculation that the treasure was kept in a safe in the palace of Ahsah Manzil, the Nawab. Records showed – although I do not know of anyone who said they saw such records with their own eyes – records showed that the governor appointed by the British during the 1890s, a Sir Salim Ullah, had collected all of the Moghul wealth found by the British and placed it in a safe in the palace. Some said the treasure was composed of many jewels, others claimed that there were only a few tawdry trinkets. Last year, among much anticipation, the safe was opened and found empty."

"Ah, but was it truly empty?" asked Khan. "I believe that the people who had access to the safe came in early and took the treasure away."

Entering into the spirit of the discussion I asked, "Was the safe under constant surveillance or could the treasure have been removed at any point during the last ninety years?"

"There was no true confirmation that the treasure was ever in the safe," explained Choudhuri. "Some say it never left Lalbagh Fort, the site of the Moghul bath, and is still buried on the grounds. Others say that it was found many years ago by thieves and dispersed. Others who believe that the British did find it express doubt that they would have kept it here. And some gloomy Johnnys say there never was a treasure."

At this juncture Singh's wife entered and, after an offhand introduction by her husband, announced dinner.

Seated, Tiffany and I noticed that we were the only ones with eating utensils. The reason soon became evident. Our hosts ate with their fingers, deftly rolling the rice grains into a small ball that remained intact while it was hoisted to the mouth. The curried chicken was easy and dispatched in the same style as at any outdoor barbecue. Carrots were also finger food. Driven by cultural relativism (or gin), Tiffany began to bulldoze rice grains around her plate with the tips of her fingers.

There was no conversation during the meal at the conclusion of which our hosts leapt up from the table and washed at a sink in the room. Tiffany followed suit.

After we had reassembled in the living room, Singh offered a modest brandy with evident pride and I asked him how he'd learned Tiffany's maiden name.

"Ah yis, these methods are simple but must be practiced." He paused briefly to allow this enigmatic response to register, then continued, "It is a name that anyone from my country would take instant note of. You see the name is a Hindi word and refers to a woman who marries beneath her station."

Tiffany whooped and splashed a few drops of gin and tonic on her skirt, "Just as my mother said." She executed an uneven pirouette, and laid her hand on a chair for balance.

"How would an American lady come to have such a name we were wondering," asked Khan.

"Fate," answered my smirking spouse. Then her face turned mean, "But my stature is nothing compared to Max." Eyebrows rose expectantly all around except for Nawaz who was picking dead skin off of his elbow. "Max talks to God."

"Ah, that is good. Although I am not a devout person myself, I must approve of a man who pays his earnest respect through prayer to Him who is higher than all of us." Vigorous nods of concurrence from Choudhuri and Khan. Nawaz turned his attention to a small pimple on his neck.

"No, that's not it. Don't you understand? He talks down to God. He insults God."

Our hosts looked nonplussed, perhaps trying to decide who was the greater criminal, a man who blasphemes the Almighty or a wife who publicly derides her husband. Evidently Singh opted for the latter and reproved Tiffany, "Your good husband certainly has his own reasons. The faith of all thoughtful men is tested – that is my view – and for some it is strengthened in that wise." Subdued nods from Choudhuri and Khan; Nawaz looked up quizzically. "But, tell me Maxwell, how do you find the brandy?"

———

Tiffany takes her defeats poorly. On the short ride home, "I love it how you men band together. That midget Singh making excuses for you." Slight gagging sound. Was she starting to get sick? "I've been thinking Max and I've come up with some more ideas for you. Build on the books of reckoning at the Pearly Gates; you know, God as Accountant – the Great Bean Counter in the Sky. What do you think?"

Although I was trying to ignore her, I did see the application.

Celestial Ledger

Account: *Tiffany Pratiloma Brown*

Debits	Credits
Arrogance	*Hot looks*
Pettiness	*?*
Meanness	
Insensitivity	
Vulgarity	
Frigidity	

"Or maybe God's a weekend gardener. You know the kind. They devour the Burpee catalog when it arrives in late winter. They envision vast acres of tidy weed-free rows growing without encouragement under the warm sun." She paused; another gagging sound. "Then when the weather breaks they can't find time to turn the soil, a few seeds are planted, one perfunctory attempt is made at weeding. And Safeway provides the vegetables. I like that Max: God the Indolent Gardener. This isn't Eden. This is His Unattended Weed Patch."

I turned my head slowly toward her with an expression of concern, but in the darkness the effect was probably lost. How much had she had to drink? At least six gin and tonics plus some brandy.

"Since you've taken an interest, here's one for you Lilac Lips: God the Carouser. Look at the lousy shape things are in. The place is untidy, things are thrown around. Great works begun on one hand and on the other the simplest things aren't attended to. If our moment in time is just a bubble in God's champagne glass, a night on the town for Him could span millennia. He starts out with a few and enjoys that heady feeling of invincibility. Great plans are made, things are right. A few more tall ones and things get muddled. The horizon recedes; the rosy glow is gone." I was starting to like this idea.

"He no longer cares or knows what happens outside the periphery of His tunnel vision. Rotting corpses may be piling up but He doesn't notice. A few more and He senses He's in trouble but another drink goes down. Now He's unsteady as He lurches to the john; He pisses on His foot and laughs. He's no longer just indifferent to the spreading chaos around Him, Tiff, He's contributing to it."

A passing light shown on Tiffany's pale face. She was in trouble.

I continued, "The bar closes but the room is spinning and He fears for the hangover to come. Should He ralph it up now? Unpleasant choice: minor but immediate pain versus probable major pain in the morning. Then, almost with relief, He senses that He may not have to choose. His great stomach starts to roil. And what's happening to the world during this Olympian pub crawl? Great works are started and come to nothing; petty arguments flare up in which millions are slaughtered; the place physically falls apart through abuse and inattention. Nations are starving, men are killing each other, injustice reigns supreme . . . and where is Mr. Big Time? Hugging the commode, His body arching with each convulsive heave, His mouth filled with phlegm, His nostrils with vomit, His . . ."

"Stoppit Max. I know wha' you're trying to do." Silence again. Did it work? That would be too much to hope for.

"Would you like some fresh air Tiff? It's awfully close in this cab and the jouncing and exhaust smells must be taking their toll." Oh happy sight! She looks stricken.

"Fucking window won't open. Dammit Max, the wog has taken off the window handle. Make him stop the car! Make him stop the . . ."

Too late.

I tipped the driver fifty takas to compensate him for cleaning up the floor and helped my staggering love slave up the five stories to our cozy haven.

"There, there. You'll feel much better in the morning for having gotten that out of you. Good to clean out the greasy meal too. That chicken looked lethal; probably steeped in lizard lard. Now when we get upstairs promise me you won't rinse your mouth with the tap water. Wouldn't want you to go from the heaves to the trots. Especially with our primitive shitter. And if you do have to vomit some more and go into the bathroom, watch where you put your hands on the floor; you know how unsanitary it is. I think Babul uses it when we're away and I shudder to contemplate what diseases and parasites inhabit his intestines. What's that? I can't make you out, you're mumbling. Stop talking? Sure, just trying to create a little distraction to keep your mind off your stomach. Think you can make it? If not, let it go in a corner. The evidence will be shellacked over with betel juice soon enough. Sure . . . sorry . . . stop talking . . . okay. Ah, jeez, here it comes again."

26

An All Sufficient Helper
- E. D. Elliott, 1908

"I am coming here because of Dr. Choudhuri telling me."

"Good, Nawaz. Did Dr. Choudhuri tell you what to do after you'd arrived?"

"He say I assistant to you." Blessings come in strange guises. This one, scratching the sole of one foot against the instep of the other, came in a gaunt and angular package.

"I imagine then, that you are to assist me with this course, Introduction to Production Management." A topic about which I knew nothing and was praying for the intercession of civil war, flood, earthquake, meteor strike, plague of locusts, etc. before I was exposed in the classroom.

"No, I am knowing nothing of such matters." We were well matched then. "I am studying old writings. I am reading old writings." My visible lack of comprehension signaled he should continue. First he removed a minute foreign particle from his neck and examined it. "I am reading Sanskrit."

"A useful skill, Nawaz. Did Dr. Choudhuri indicate to what use I might apply that talent?" Puzzled look from Nawaz. "What will you do for me?"

"I am helping you with old maps."

"Since I have no old maps in my possession worth study, Nawaz, does your assistance extend to procurement?" Puzzled look accompanied by scratching at the belt line. "Will you get old maps for me?"

"Yes. You tell me what map and I am looking."

What map? Perhaps he should be sent in search of the original etchings of Ptolemy. That would keep him and his private infestation out of the office. "Nawaz, I have a challenge for you."

He looked up from the excavation project begun on the cuticle of his left hand. "Yes, Professor?"

"Nawaz, you're a smart scholar. Locate the Moghul treasure."

This request galvanized the classical scholar and he suspended his twitching, scratching, and bodily inspection. "You are telling the treasure which is not finding in Nawab palace?"

"Precisely. And you will have to work on your own as I will be unable to provide you any clues. Initiative, Nawaz! But I know you have it. Don't bother with progress reports until you have something concrete." And I favored him with a smile that bespoke dismissal in any culture. He stood rooted in front of the desk.

I lowered my head as if to resume work but gave that up. "Yes, Nawaz? Something more?"

"I am needing money for rickshaw to make questions of map."

Not only was he an unwanted assistant but he couldn't be gotten rid of cheaply. "Here's two hundred taka. Try to make that last the month." Inspecting the two bills, he left the office. With any luck, I wouldn't see him again for months, if ever.

Now Shall My Head Be Lifted High
- C. M. Victory, 1849

Dhaka University is unlike any other school on the face of the earth. It was usually closed to quell or forestall unrest among the student body. Unfortunately it was presently open and the day of my unmasking in the classroom was rushing forward. The reason for the frequent closures is one of the prices of political pluralism. The two major political factions in the country had armed their student adherents – the precise moment the arms race had begun was in dispute – to the point where gunfire was as frequent in the dorms as hangovers were on a US campus. The stockpile of weapons had grown to the point where they surpassed the immediate needs of the students who had become, in turn, suppliers of firearms throughout Dhaka.

Most of the guns had, I was told, come from Darra in West Pakistan, a town outside Peshawar in the Northwest Frontier Province. The denizens of Darra were masters in recreating almost any firearm, and Kalashnikovs, Uzis, Colt 45s, and about anything else short of a Howitzer, rolled out of the small shops. Guns and politics: an interesting contrast with my previous

campus where sports rivalries, fraternity hazing, and public ine-
briation formed the bedrock of student life.

The classroom language of instruction was either English or
Bangla; the decision seemed based entirely on the whim of the
instructor, irrespective of student ability. If English, that
doomed the educational process as few students understood the
language well enough to follow even a simple lecture. Of course
if the students couldn't follow English, it was unlikely that
they'd embarrass the lecturer (me) with informed questions – or
perhaps venture any questions at all. In that hope I pored over
Harvey Wagner's venerable text on operations management.
Had I been less pressed I might have even enjoyed learning
some of the tricks of the trade.

One morning, in the midst of these preparations, Mr. Khan
appeared in the doorway and awaited acknowledgement.

"Mr. Khan. In light of your remorseless dedication to duty, I
assume this is not a social visit?"

Khan shifted weight. Apparently it was a social visit. "No, I
was only passing by to inquire of your good self and to ask if
there is some small matter that I have been remiss in attending
to."

"My good self lacks only a high colonic to achieve physical
nirvana. And you?"

"I also am feeling well. You have met with Professor Singh.
What is your thinking of him?"

"I hadn't formed an opinion, Mr. Khan. Is there some special reason I should be assessing him more carefully than any of
the other 5.5 billion of our species?"

"No Professor." He appeared to be searching for an artful
way to bring up what was promising to be a delicate topic.
Finding none, "It is said that Mr. Singh has contacts with RAW
in India." My furrowed brow indicated he should elaborate.
"RAW stands for Research and Analysis Wing of Indian Intelligence. They are very difficult and harsh people in RAW. I
would not want to be found in their clutches, if you understand
my meaning."

"The warning is much appreciated, Mr. Khan. In truth,
Singh's stature – even with turban and elevator shoes – miti-

gates the terror of his countenance. But I shall watch my step." Khan donned his trademark embarrassed grin and departed.

The warning was singular. . . in the literal sense as Khan hadn't taken the trouble to warn me of anything else since our arrival. Due to rivalry with Professor Singh? Bangladeshis were infamous for intense professional rivalries that converted the occasional academic conference into puerile slanging matches. No. Khan wasn't in the same professional league with Singh. Something else . . . personal? Singh was a queer duck and had made oblique references to his many high level contacts in India. But it seemed unlikely that a professional spy would be at pains to advertise his calling. These reveries were interrupted by the arrival in the doorway of my able classical colleague, Nawaz, drilling his left ear with his pinky.

"Welcome Nawaz. It's pouring social manna today. You have progress to report? Or you too have an enigmatic message?"

"Perhaps we should not be looking for this map."

If difficulty was the problem, that was what I'd hoped for. One of the under-appreciated academic burdens is supervising research 'assistants.' Any assignment given them engenders unending demands for more precise direction. In exasperation I'd informed one such menial, "If I knew the goddamn answer I wouldn't have asked you to research it, would I?" But Nawaz looked troubled and perhaps frightened – paler than when I'd last seen him, and the acrid smell of vomit came my way with each swing of the wall fan. Had he, in his relentless self-inspection, uncovered some serious pathology? Was the paleness due to overzealous picking and he'd broken open a gusher?

"And why, Nawaz, should we abandon the search?"

"There are many stories. People die when they look for the treasure. Maybe poisoned. One man eaten by dogs." These stories could not be new news for Nawaz.

"Courage man. It's my guess that something has happened recently that's upset you." This was followed by a long silence during which Nawaz examined his fingernails. Inspection complete, he arrived at a decision to let me in on the story.

"Yesterday I talk with Mr. Rahman who knows many sources. He say he have some ideas but the information is very expensive. Today I return to his store. He is dead."

"I'm very sorry to hear that. My condolences to his family. I hope he passed away in bed, surrounded by loved ones."

"He is sitting in his chair. He is holding his head in his hands."

Were we going somewhere with this detailed description? "Expired of headache, then? Tragic. American television would have kept him informed of many life-saving elixirs."

"His head is cut off. It is in his hands."

There's a powerful image for you. I'd been in several of these antique dealer's little shops, crowded with brass gewgaws, pieces of decommissioned ships, a Victrola, maybe some blue dishes the Dutch or Brits had abandoned. In this one, behind the small desk at the back, sat a corpse proffering its sightless head.

"My God, Nawaz. What do the police say?"

"They say nothing. It is always mistake to bring the police. They only come for mischief and to make profit."

"Then you are the only one to see Rahman? Certainly he must have other customers come and go?"

"I am arriving early. Perhaps now others know of this deed."

"I gather, Nawaz, that you think there's a connection between your inquiry about the treasure and Rahman's death. That's hard to believe. In any event, we must report the death."

Nawaz showed no enthusiasm for that. "Police only cause problems. They will accuse me and ask for money."

At this moment Professor Singh swaggered in.

"I must say there are graveside faces all around. Who died?" This seemed to be a morning for gaffes.

"Actually, an antiques trader named Rahman was murdered. Nawaz discovered the crime and we're debating how best to proceed." Nawaz scowled disapproval at letting Singh in on the news.

Singh returned the scowl. "Murdered? Was there anything at the crime scene that would suggest a motive, Nawaz?"

"I am not looking. I am not staying. Mr. Rahman have no head. I do not want to be discovered there." Nawaz had taken in the situation quickly, and skedaddled.

"Ah yis. If you will pardon me, I have some small experience in these matters. I will make a brief call that will resolve everything. But first would it be seeming too macabre to visit the scene?"

Reality couldn't be worse than the mental image. Succumbing to curiosity I asked Nawaz to lead us to Rahman's store. Then, in a nod to caution, "If we're found there it'll be hard to explain."

"Nonsense," countered Singh, "people go into antique shops all the time. It is now business hours. Come along and not be such a nervous Nelson."

Singh drove and parked a block away from the shop – apparently some concern obliged small precautions. We approached the door fearfully; two pigeons were looking through the display window but there was no sign of the police. The birds seemed untroubled by the scene inside which firmed our resolve. Through the door window we could dimly see the corpse, as Nawaz had said. The severed head appeared to be on the desk, cupped in the dead man's hands. Singh's bravado dissolved; he looked ashen. I finally spoke, "Shall we go in or have we seen enough?"

"I fear that we must enter," said Singh. "Nothing we can do for that poor beggar. But we must be sure that there is no evidence that could link us to the murder." A curious concern. What evidence could there be, unless Nawaz had left a telltale scab, booger, or exudate that DNA testing could place him at the crime scene? We soon found he'd left the undigested remains of his breakfast on the floor.

I opened the door and avoided looking directly at the dead man. Apparently the other two did the same for only as we edged near the desk did Nawaz notice, "There is paper in mouth." Extending from the dead mouth was a folded piece of ruled paper.

Rahman appeared to have been mid-forties when he abruptly stopped getting older. He had a full head of hair; his left eye was wide open and the right was half-closed. His expression, while not a reliable guide to his final thoughts, didn't look like that of someone who was being executed.

We looked at the paper, and at each other. Singh finally reached out, and, avoiding contact with the head, tried to pull the paper free. Gentle pulling only made the head rock back and forth in its cradle of hands. Singh gave the paper a hard yank and the head leapt forward and off the front of the desk. We debated later whether we'd screamed or not. I voted that we had.

Now the head was on the floor, lying on the right ear, and the paper hadn't yielded. "I am thinking maybe this is a case of lockjaw," opined Singh. Growing bolder, he squeezed the dead cheeks to force the jaws open. Blood trickled from the neck, but the mouth did open and Singh was able to work the paper free. He smoothed the paper on a glass counter, squinted at it and shrugged. There was writing, but it was indecipherable. Nawaz took his turn with the note and returned it to Singh.

"I suggest we decamp . . . vamoose . . . leave." The speaker, of course, is me.

"Maybe we put head back?" asked Nawaz. This seemed like a sensible thing to do but no one wanted to touch it. Singh's courage had apparently deserted once the paper had been extricated. An unspoken agreement was reached that a severed head on the floor was no more unusual than one held in dead hands and we silently backed toward the door.

Singh answered my thought. "Do not worry about fingerprints, my dear chap – or vomit. No one here is able to lift prints or identify them or match them. I will, however, keep the note."

The first part of the trip back to the university was spent in debate whether we'd screamed when the head catapulted toward us. This distraction helped briefly but we were all occupied with our own thoughts by the time our car rolled through the campus gate.

Singh repeated his intention to set everything right with a single call and departed in search of a working telephone. Nawaz followed me to the office and stared at the floor. He was scratching distractedly at the back of his neck.

"You could read the note, couldn't you?"

Nawaz searched the corners of the ceiling for help with the answer.

"It say not look for treasure which must stay buried. But the Sanskrit writing is not good."

Whoops. This sounded like my instructions to send Nawaz looking for a left-handed monkey wrench had gotten one man killed and the three stooges stumbling around the crime scene. I was less sanguine than Singh about the ineptitude of the Bangladeshi police.

"Two questions, Nawaz: Why do you say the writing isn't good? And what do you think it means that Rahman was killed and we were warned? That event, in modern detective novels, would indicate we were getting close to something."

"Sanskrit maybe someone who know it from Hindi. Some modern words." Nawaz had no thoughts to share on my second question. But why would this poor schmuck get killed – and dramatically so – on the strength of the most casual request to my assistant, a request made just to get him out of the office. Singh returned.

"I have done all that is needed. The authorities can get on with their work and they do not suspect we were ever involved." I didn't inquire how this had been accomplished, as the news had been delivered with a tone of such arch intrigue that any follow-up queries would be met with evasive replies.

"A question for you Professor Singh. I made only the most perfunctory request to Nawaz here. He, in turn, made a hardly more ardent inquiry to Rahman. Then, lo and behold, events are set in motion leading to the death of said Rahman, a death with theatric overtones, you'll agree."

Singh rose on his tiptoes. "You said a question?"

"So I did. I'm distracted by the morning's events and not speaking clearly. The implicit question is: Why?"

Singh took no apparent offense. "It is a simple warning. And a jolly effective one, if you are asking my view of the matter!"

"A warning of what? I was given to understand you couldn't read the note."

"Ah yis. I did not wish to alarm you. I can read some San-skrit and I saw the word treasure clearly. Forgive me for keep-ing you in the darkness."

"Let me put it another way. Unless Rahman had a treasure map ready to deliver, or we were on the verge of discovering the treasure, it makes no sense. I had no expectation this would lead anywhere. Now I encounter a decapitated messenger who intimates we're on the cusp of uncovering great riches. Either someone was convinced we were about to cart away the loot, or they're the worst amateurs alive to encourage us like this."

Singh scowled. "Encouragement? You say a man with no head and a note in his mouth is enticing you forward? I say jolly not!" Pausing briefly for effect, he spun on his small left foot, and turning, made a painful encounter with the doorjamb. His grand exit spoiled, he added, "If you persist with this you will be throwing all the cautions to the winds." His second attempt to find the door was more successful and the click of his heels retreated down the hall.

Nawaz had regained his composure and was fingering a pus-tule on his right temple, deliberating whether the moment to ex-cise it had arrived. Not wishing to witness the event, I hastened, "Is there anything you saw or heard that makes you think Rah-man had something for us?"

After lengthy reflection, "No, Sa'b."

"Nawaz, I'm a weak judge of human moods, but the fact that it took you almost a minute to decide there was nothing means you're unsure. What else has happened?"

More time passed, but mercifully Nawaz refrained from fur-ther excursions in personal hygiene. "Last night my friend in hall say man call on telephone for me. He say man excited but not telling name."

"And you suspect that caller would be Rahman with news of a breakthrough?" Nawaz shrugged. "It still doesn't make sense. If Rahman had a lead on a treasure, why would he sell it, even for a high price, as you said earlier? He'd go dig up the damn thing himself." Another shrug. "You know what I think, Nawaz?" Shrug number three. "I think . . . ah damn, I don't know what I think." After a moment, "Nawaz, can you buy a gun for me?"

27

With Courage Strong
- B.C. Harrington, 1910

If I was unsure on a motive for the murder, there was a separate question I was more at home with: what to tell my helpmeet? Option 1: tell her nothing, thereby giving her no further reason for leaving. Option 2: share the excitement with someone, swagger a little, impress her with her husband's derring-do and sense of adventure.

Sad testimony that I still wanted to impress Tiffany. I blurted out the day's events within two minutes of returning home. All that prevented me telling her earlier was that the climb to our luxury villa takes the spark out of one.

"As I gather from your account – between gasps – it appears that this encounter with the headless mapman has really turned you on."

"No-no-no-no-no." Long pause for breath. She was right; I did find the whole gruesome business rather exciting.

"I saw my share of death in 'Nam, Tulip Twigs. If there's anything to be excited about, it's that my long-scorned antiquarian interests may be about to bear some king-size fruit."

"Don't bait me with talk of king-sized fruits," she sniffed dismissively. "You really think that untold wealth – the riches of the Moghul empire – are within your grasp? Poppycock, Max! And poppycock, because I wouldn't dignify this with a stronger Saxon expletive. A nerdy zit-popping student says he'll help you with maps. You say, 'find the mother-lode.' He asks a dealer. And the dealer winds up dead – and grotesquely dead. Pretty tenuous."

"My thoughts also, Tiff. Without the note there'd be nothing to any of this. Someone must think we're close – or has one sick sense of fun."

"Still seems pretty farfetched. But, in the monumentally unlikely event that there is some connection here, will you watch your back?" This concern was flattering and it must have shown, as she hastily added, " . . . until I check that the premiums are paid on your life insurance."

I did watch my back. Heightened awareness plus the vivid image of luckless Rahman produced a jumpiness – Tiffany would have added, paranoia – that had me spinning toward soft noises, starting at distant creaks, and waking if there was a sound, or perhaps more ominously, if there were no sound.

In this fragile state of mind I received Nawaz to my academic chambers two days later with mixed emotions. He might have news to indicate that we were, through no active effort on our part, close to the treasure, but also closer to danger. Or he might have no news at all, encouraging the faint hope that Rahman's death and the note were bizarre coincidences.

"I have news," he began. I tried to not look pleading, but at that point concern for survival had outdistanced the hankering for instant wealth.

He produced a .38 caliber Smith and Wesson Masterpiece revolver and three hollow-point bullets. The appearance of the gun did nothing to settle my nerves and three bullets were a reminder of how much ammunition I'd had to expend every year to qualify with the same weapon. My wild inaccuracy had brought Air Force firing ranges to a standstill while the instructors waited for me to squeeze off a lucky sequence of shots so they could certify me for another twelve months.

"Rahman have partner who is brother of Rahman wife. Brother come to my room yesterday night and say he know I in Rahman store. He say I cause Rahman death by making questions about map. He say now bad people know Rahman secret."

This trove of information was followed by another long silence. Realizing that some response was expected, I said, "Rahman's secret may have something to do with the treasure. But that still makes no sense. If Rahman knew where the treasure was, why didn't he go get it? He could have been rich."

"Many people believe treasure is bad. Moghul Khan Shaista who make treasure have bad luck. Treasure disappear from safe. Man who open safe die from bus. Two men who . . ."

"Yes," I interjected, before we could hear again about being eaten by dogs, "there are some stories. But, Nawaz lad, buck up! Terrible things happen to people everyday . . ." and then I trailed off. The chain of events was too persuasive:

• Nawaz asked about old maps, specifically anything linked to the Moghul treasure. A man, perhaps Rahman, called the dorm with news.

• Rahman was killed and a warning note left in his dead jaws instructing the reader – presumably us – to abandon the treasure hunt.

• Rahman's brother-in-law surfaced to confirm that Rahman harbored a valuable secret.

"Nawaz, able colleague, we need to make a decision. And I say 'we', not 'I', because our peril is mutual. It looks like someone's convinced we're close to the treasure, but we have no better idea where it is than anyone else in the country. Question number one is: what is it that we know that we don't know we know?" Seeing Nawaz's bewildered expression I rephrased, "Do we have some useful information that we haven't understood yet? Question number two is . . ." I stopped as Nawaz, whose basic frame of reference was that of student, held up his hand to be called on. "Yes, go ahead."

"For question number one, I have idea. Maybe you have old map already that tells part of treasure finding. One time I see cinema. One man have part of map. Another man have other part. Maybe you have part of map already."

Ah, Hollywood. Inspirer of countless farfetched theories. I did, in fact, have an 18th century map of the area that I'd purchased in Bangkok, but the scale was such that Dhaka was no larger than a fly turd. I explained this to Nawaz who countered, "Maybe writing on map. Maybe writing on back of map. Moghul sometime make map with writing, not drawing."

While Nawaz had been growing more loquacious in recent days, his syntax had made no corresponding improvement. Perhaps he was feeling the same pressures I was. Pressures driven by an image that he might wake up before the Pearly Gates, head in hands. Largely to satisfy his curiosity and signal that I valued his continued services and advice, I brought the map back to the office after lunch for him to inspect. It was neither especially old nor artistic so I hadn't paid it much attention. I didn't point out the basic flaw in Nawaz' argument. It was unlikely that anyone was aware of the existence of this map. I thought so little of it that it hung over the toilet in our bathroom. Women might not notice it at all.

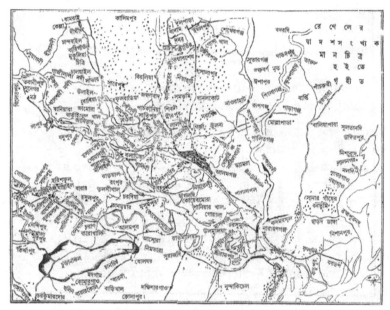

Dhaka, c. 1850 (not the map mentioned above which was later stolen)

Nawaz pored over the map, his expression not changing. He breathed rhythmically through his mouth, his right eye ticking to discourage the interest of a mosquito. The mosquito abandoned Nawaz and circled around, presumably to approach my blind side; it would have to queue up behind the other mosquitoes who were waiting their turn. The arthritic wall fan shuddered with each reversal of direction.

I describe this scene in detail, not to build suspense – he did find something – but because I focused on these minutiae to control my own impatience.

"I find something," he announced flatly. And then didn't continue.

"Would you care to share your discovery?" asked with forced pleasantness.

"This map maybe made 50 years after Moghul here. Map made by Englishman but writing in Bengali." When I looked surprised, he explained, "Here say man who draw map Captain Robinson. I am thinking this Englishman name. But all writing

Bengali. We now say Bangla but almost same language. Writer maybe also Englishman. Many mistakes. I translate important thing: 'Moghul wealth of legend buried behind toilet.'"

"Let me be sure I understand. It says the legendary treasure is buried behind a toilet?"

Nawaz nodded. "Yes. You say same thing." I recalled Tiffany's scornful remark that the first thing the Moghul overlord built was a toilet. "I know this place. Many tourists go to this place to see where Moghul live. But there is much digging during many years. Earth now all smooth. Everything change many times."

"So you're concluding that due to construction and excavation any treasure would have been uncovered?"

"Maybe. Unless maybe not if treasure buried far down in ground."

"I guess that's a possibility, Nawaz. But, what could Rahman have found or know that complements this information? Did he know how deep the treasure was buried? Or maybe he had details on where it was buried, but without mentioning the toilet? And why has no one tried to steal this map of mine?"

"No one have to steal this map," answered Nawaz. "Only read it to get all information."

That was true. Tiffany had continued her entertaining in Dhaka and any one of our dinner guests could have read the inscriptions. They would more likely be male as they would be facing in the direction of the map, and they would have to read Bangla. This second criterion eliminated none of our dinner guests/suspects as they'd uniformly been Bangladeshis, with the exception of Singh, an Indian, who also read Bengali/Bangla.

"Who see this map?" asked Nawaz.

"Probably ten to fifteen people, almost all of them DU faculty and their wives." I mentally went down the list. Inconceivable that any of our invitees would have the stomach for beheading.

"Look," I continued, "things now make a little more sense. Someone saw this map at my apartment. Then you made an inquiry about the treasure map. It turns out that Rahman also had partial information and a few people knew about it – at least his brother-in-law. We don't know why Rahman was killed. Maybe there's some spooky society that protects the treasure?" Now Hollywood was driving my own thinking.

"Nah. There's lots of spooky stuff here, but I doubt anyone would sit on a large stash of money so that leads me to think that we're racing someone else to the treasure . . . without knowing we were in a race. The race would be over if the other side got the information they needed from Rahman but I'm guessing they didn't. If they had the information they *might* be less likely to kill Rahman, but *definitely* less likely to tip their hand by warning us off." Nawaz's expression progressed from puzzled, to bewildered, to befuddled as I rattled on. It settled back to indifferent and I realized I was talking to myself.

"Perhaps something went wrong there. Maybe torture that went too far too fast and Rahman died before he could spill the beans." In the tradition of professors the world over, I'd moved to the worn office blackboard to jot down these points.

"Maybe not leave writing," said Nawaz, rejoining the conversation. "Some person read from board and they know we have idea."

Quite so. We had an idea that there was another map – or something like it – that indicated where 'behind the toilet' the Moghul treasure was stashed.

"Nawaz, would you fancy a touristic outing? I've often wanted to visit the Moghul site and drink in the history, not to mention sniff around the toilet." Nawaz scratched the side of his head, producing a gentle shower of dandruff. This, I took to be assent.

Blessings of Knowledge
- unknown, 1834

At the historic site small boys pressed their services on us as guides. I looked for a more seasoned informant and after rejecting several slick looking touts, settled on a be-turbaned, be-whiskered, chin-be-splattered-with-betel juice gentleman who was distributing crumbs to pigeons.

He began with a recitation of statistics which I interrupted. "Where were the original buildings?"

"Ah my yis. Original buildings by which Sahib is meaning the very same built by the great Moghuls in seventeenth century and . . ."

Fearing another avalanche of irrelevant and probably specious data, I interrupted a second time. "Fascinating, but could you take us to the exact spots where the original buildings stood. We see a large one there that is now a museum. Were there others?"

"Jolly good question Sahib. I am knowing a true scholar when I am seeing one. No Tourist Tommy. Yis, that is a large building. The front is 37 meters long and at the highest point is 8 meters high. The twelve steps go up to three doors, the largest is in the middle, which, of course, you may see with your own eyes it is the largest. That door is made of oak and each side of it weighs nothing less than the amount of 180 kilos. I often think of those poor hinges holding that weight for so long. That is why there are five hinges on each side of the door . . ." I started to edge away but our guide pursued us, reciting numbers more rapidly. " . . . four thousand four hundred and twelve pieces of slate on the roof, which is itself 514 square meters in size . . . seventeen major windows and six smaller windows that were perhaps for toilets . . . each major window is one meter high and half a meter . . . "

"Stop," I cried, with more fervor than was prudent. In a more collected tone I asked, almost indifferently, "You mentioned a toilet?"

"If Sahib is wanting to relieve himself I am fearful that the facilities are temporarily closed, but the authorities are promising all repairs finished in March next year."

"Actually, I was wondering about the old toilet the Moghuls built. My wife made some reference to that."

"Why are all the people asking about the old toilets. Yesterday two men want to see the old toilets. This morning a young man asked my friend . . ." he trailed off and looked carefully at Nawaz.

"How interesting," in a tone of feigned nonchalance. "Who could possibly be asking about toilets? More foreigners like myself, no doubt." And I fixed the guide with an inquiring stare to indicate the question wasn't rhetorical.

"Some Indian Johnny. Sikh. Very short man."

Singh. Singh had stood in front of our own toilet as a regular at Tiffany's dinner parties. Ample opportunity to study the writings on the map. What else could Singh know?

"I may actually know the man you describe!" I cried with overdone enthusiasm. "And the man with him?"

"Ah, a large menacing Johnny. Not to my cup of liking at all."

"He and I shall have to get together and discuss our shared interest in toilets, but first you must satisfy my own curiosity. Where was the old Moghul toilet?" Our guide's eyes shifted left and right, avoiding mine. Two possibilities: 1) the information regarding the toilet was super-classified and he feared for his safety should he divulge it, or 2) he knew fuckall. Neither was correct.

"Everyone knows the answer to that. It is exactly the building you see, Sahib. The great Shaista Khan only build one building, the baths, and then he encounter misfortune and return to India. It is beyond any understanding why everyone is asking where the toilet is. That is the toilet." He gestured toward the museum. "That is all there ever was."

What there was was too much. Not in the colloquial sense, but the physical sense. At 37 meters in length, a lot of 'behind the toilet' real estate would have to be excavated to find the treasure, if, in fact it was there. Hoping to limit the search, I asked, "Was the entire building dedicated to toilets?"

"Oh my goodness no. The building was for the baths. The toilet was only a small part of the building."

"Then, not to belabor the question, but where the fuck were the toilets?" Nawaz looked alarmed at this display of impatience. Again our guide looked right and left, avoiding eye contact. I expanded the number of possibilities to three: 1) supersecret info, 2) he knew, again, and was being coy, 3) fuckall.

As it turned out, alternative three was the winner. He tipped his ignorance of the answer, beginning, "Great Khan build baths in 1684 and return to his home one year later, saddened at the death of his beloved daughter, who was only 14 years old at the time, having been born in 1670. If you are asking about the exact whereabouts of the toilets . . ." which, it seemed reasonably clear to any fair-minded observer, I was, ". . . there is some debate on the matter. There are scholars at our own Dhaka University who are studying this and they are disagreeing on the final whereabouts of the toilets of which you are asking."

Stunning news. Not that there was uncertainty, but that someone at DU, my current employer, was engaged in active and potentially relevant research. "Would it be too much to ask the names of these disputatious scholars?"

"By a minor coincidence, one is Professor Choudhuri, and the other is Professor Chowdery. But, of course, in our country it is a name as common as Pacino or DeNiro in yours."

We thanked the guide with a fifty taka note – which he received with an expression of deep disappointment – and thirty minutes later Nawaz and I were wandering the empty halls of the Classical Studies Department.

"You've studied in this department, have you not, Nawaz? What do you know of these two men?"

"Professor Chowdery is not man, Sahib. She come new last year and make upset in department. Old professors say she too much ambitious." I found this hard to believe. DU was unlikely to attract the ambitious; some of the incumbents in named Chairs didn't appear to have a pulse. Nawaz signaled the lady professor's office and, indeed, it was the only room from which emanated signs of activity.

28

In the Land of Beauty
- **P. P. Bilhorn, 1901**

Nawaz should have warned me that Professor Chowdery was attractive. I'd encountered only a few beautiful Bangladeshi women, but when they looked good, they tended to look very good. Taken by surprise as we entered her office, it fell to Nawaz to fill the silence. "Professor Chowdery, I am Nawaz. Maybe you remember I am in your class Introduction to Antiquities last year?"

I immediately empathized with Professor Chowdery. Ex-students were constantly approaching faculty with boisterous greetings that I reserved for the handful of fellow survivors of our squadron in Vietnam. Occasionally a student would want to offer a public testimonial on the contribution you'd made to his or her life; that meant some kind of response was expected. Professor Chowdery clearly had no idea who Nawaz was and was preparing a bland lie when I found my voice. "Professor Chowdery, I'm Max Brown, the Fulbright this year. I've wanted to stop by and meet the people in this department, and Nawaz guided me over finally today. I'm impressed by your diligence. You're the only one here."

"Well, Professor Brown, as the only woman in the department, I find it prudent to work the full six hour day we are all paid for."

Strange that she should start beefing immediately. Most Bangladeshis stuck to gracious and upbeat chitchat in initial encounters; complaining came later.

"I laud your dedication to duty, nonetheless. I'm sure we share some interests. I've long collected antiquarian maps and we just left the Moghul complex where we were informed that you've made that an area of study."

"Study deferred, Professor Brown. I obtained permits to excavate around the site, but the department has blocked the funds that were allocated with the permit." That *would* make a person bitter. "The permits expire in three months and then one of the 'old boys' will use the money I was allocated. He'll scratch around in the dirt, until he finds it too hot, and then he'll spend my small stipend on an air conditioner for his office."

This had possibilities. She probably knew something about the site; she had permits to dig – I hadn't solved the part where Nawaz and I show up at midnight with picks and shovels – and she might be ticked enough to work clandestinely, for a while at least, in order to not attract further attempts to thwart her.

"I have a very small research stipend which I haven't decided how to use (it was $500). I wonder if there's some area where my interest in old maps and yours in the Moghul site might overlap?" She looked up quickly as I struggled to maintain an expression of guilelessness. "It's not much money and I can't promise we'll find a project to collaborate on."

"What are your interests, Professor Brown? I will guess that you are one in a long line of treasure seekers?"

What would be the best tactic here? The immediate inclination was toward denial – which would be unmasked in due course. Perhaps for the novelty of it, I went for candor.

"You are a remarkably perceptive person – for a professor, Professor. In fact I have come into possession of information about the treasure which I believe is unique."

"If you're referring to the old map hanging in your bathroom, the information may be unique, but it's also widely disseminated." Wow! Word had gotten around fast! "And your stubby colleague, the Sikh spook, was here earlier sniffing around."

I was starting to simultaneously like and be annoyed by this brassy woman. "Your direct answers are refreshing, Professor Chowdery. I'll ask another. I may have more information coming in on the whereabouts of the treasure. Do you wish to join me? Or the Sikh spook, as you call him?"

"I have no interest in joining either of you. The evidence that there is a treasure is weak, at best. The likelihood of a university professor unearthing it is so remote as to beggar imagination." She picked up a yellow post-it from her cluttered desk and examined it before resuming.

"I gather that you acquired a map in Bangkok that indicates the treasure is buried behind the toilet. It seems unlikely that a man of Khan Shaista's resources stashed his mad money in the ground as he pulled out, perhaps knowing that it was for good. Here was a man who had more than 30 elephants and unnumbered horses and camels to haul his loot home. Okay, let us grant he was distraught over the death of his daughter. It's still hard for me to believe that he snuck out to the backyard himself and planted the trove. And it seems even less likely that he trusted his lackeys to prepare the site. The Moghuls were not trusting people, and with good reason."

It all sounded plausible. The Khan would've taken his booty with him. He couldn't bury it personally. Would he trust his minions? If he had, wouldn't someone sneak back and dig up the treasure. "Professor Chowdery, you're a real kill joy."

"I'm pleased to hear I still have the touch. But, having said that, what are you offering, Fulbright professor? A percentage of the take? Academic notoriety? Or, the plum of all plums, tenure at Dhaka U!"

"You're also a beautiful and intelligent woman; are you not an adventurous one as well?" She accepted the compliment with a radiant smile, displaying a sparkling array of perfectly aligned teeth between full red lips. Since this had gone down so well, I continued, "I'm just a poor, world-weary savant looking for an exit ramp off this treadmill. A few million in Moghul baubles seems increasingly my due. Will I share? What's your contribution? My informants tell me that you're as confused as everyone else regarding the layout of the baths, which you now know may be the key to unearthing the treasure. And, if I may hazard the question, if you're so convinced that there's no treasure, why do you bother to ask what I'm offering? Idle curiosity?"

"Ah, Professor Brown. You are, indeed, adept at interrogation. You charm, then you challenge." Had she read the same USAF manual on interrogation techniques I had? "Do we have a CIA plant strolling with us through the groves of academe? In fact . . ."

"Wait, wait." I interrupted. "Hit the pause button; freeze the frame. Where's the demure Asian woman?"

"Asian woman? She's as meek and self-sacrificing as ever and lives on in fiction." Professor Chowdery paused. "Let me redirect the conversation down a less confrontational avenue. If you are familiar with the sociology of British universities, stop me. What you are experiencing is what I refer to as Red Brick Bravado. It's the alternative to Red Brick Cringe. In the British academic pecking order there is Oxbridge, there is gray stone, and there is red brick. Red brick universities are totally devoid of tradition; their history barely spans a few inconsequential decades. No one of renown has graduated from them. The faculty at these dreary institutions – and the faculty are the rôle models for the doctoral students we recently were – assume one of two defense mechanisms. The cringe is self-evident. Those who adopt it know and acknowledge that they are at the bottom of the academic heap. Others practice the nose stroking, chin tilted affectations of the Oxbridge crowd. I've labeled this Red Brick Bravado. Outside of Blighty that posture seems less demeaning, don't you think?"

I was really enjoying this. There was something erotic about this exchange and I was prepared for Professor Chowdery to tear my clothes off at any minute. If that happened I'd already decided not to resist. "Professor Chowdery, this is most illuminating. I'm sure there's the kind of publishing possibilities in your observations that would advance any career. But let me drag you back to my earlier proposition: Do you want to cast your lot with the Good Guys – the irresistible Nawaz and your humble servant – or do you wish to go down the dark path and link destinies with the *petit poseur*, Professor Singh? Think carefully before answering."

She beamed again. With a smile like that she could spout any kind of malarkey and I'd agree. "I was so enjoying the discussion that I forgot from whence we'd started. No, I don't wish to cast my lot with either of you. Why? Really very simple. First, I would wager sixteen to one that there's no treasure to be found. In the grand unlikelihood that there is, I would wager fifty to one that none of you will find it. In the Olympian improbability that you do, I would go one hundred to one that you will kill one another off. I believe we have here a Markov chain which I leave to you to multiply out – I get confused on the number of zeroes when I try to do the maths in my head. In sum, joining either team is a low percentage play." Then she leaned forward, exposing a high percentage of her breasts.

Rising above the distraction, I countered, "Another hypothesis is forming: you think you can go it alone. That makes me wonder, do you have the information I expect to get? I doubt it. However, if you're sincere in your belief that the treasure won't be found and enjoyed – 80,000 to one are the odds you're giving – I *can* do the 'maths' in my head – you won't mind sharing with me your own opinion of where the toilets were."

A look of confusion crossed her splendid face. Surprising, as the challenge had seemed predictable.

"No, of course not. The toilets were on the left side of the building as you face it. The smaller door sizes, the lower elevation behind the building for drainage – there can be no other possibility. Choudhuri cites a few descriptions of designs in India that put the toilets to the other side of the baths, but those descriptions are few in number and not consistent among them and certainly no guide for what might be built a thousand kilometers to the east." I expected her to continue, but she returned her attention to the post-it.

"I can see you've arrived at some clear conclusions, Professor Chowdery. May I assume there's more?" She abandoned the post-it and looked up. "Are you going to tell me, or do we have to plow through a dreary guessing game as I try to extract the information?" Why was I growing so snotty and British in my speech? Easy to answer: I'm intimidated by beautiful women, especially the brainier of the species, and intimidation brings out hostility.

"I gather you don't have many friends, Professor Brown?"

"Of course. I apologize for my seeming rudeness." Had to shake the prissy Britishisms. *Max, you live with a beautiful woman. Why was this one derailing you?*

The corners of Professor Chowdery's luscious full lips turned down; she checked her watch, a clear sign she was tiring of the conversation.

"Alright. Cutting to the chase, here's what else I think may be relevant to your game of Moghul hide and seek. First, as I said, the toilets are on the left of the building. The original level of the land may have been about half a meter higher then than now. You can see exposed half a meter of very ugly and low quality stone masonry along the base. One assumes that the great Khan would not want unembroidered masonry welcome him to the loo." She glanced at the post-it for the third time – was the information on it that hard to digest? – then continued. "There were at least two sets of toilets as there were two sexes living on the premises. It's likely that servants were not allowed to deposit their lower caste feces in the royal shitter so there would have been another set of toilets for them. As far as we know, there were twelve people in the royal party and high court officials. Another 100 or so hangers-on and camp-followers. If we assume that a more liberal logic governed back then than determines the design of toilets on today's airliners, there would have been from five to ten facilities for each sex, plus a more regal crapper for the head man – pun intended."

I tried to take this all in. "I assume the reason for your discourse on the number of toilets is to estimate the amount of floor space dedicated?"

"Sharp as a tack, Maxwell, if you will allow me the liberty?" A reasonable request as I wished she would allow me a few liberties as well. "I would hazard that of the total length of 37 meters, the left-most 8 meters of the building housed the toilets."

Still a lot of ground to dig around in as I had no idea how far back the description '. . . buried behind toilet' could extend. Eight meters times infinity is a lot of acreage to excavate.

"And now, Professor Brown, although I would love to continue talking with you, I have a mountain of student papers to mark and an academic reputation to establish. See you around campus." Another megawatt smile, devoid of the slightest hint of sincerity. I did my best to respond in kind.

Nawaz and I backed out, muttering our gratitude for the information.

"Able assistant," I exulted, "what do you think of that?"

The advance in our knowledge failed to excite Nawaz. "Still too much area and we not have permission to dig. Professor Chowdery have permission." Nawaz was fully up to speed on our situation.

"If we had the information Rahman was killed for . . ." and my voice, and thoughts, trailed off with the approach of . . . "Professor Singh! A Singhular pleasure to see you!"

"And the same in many returns, Professor Max. Don't tell me your fascination with the Moghul treasure has you prying information out of our colleagues in the Classical Studies department? I do not wish to be untrue to my own institution, but let me tell you these Johnnies don't know where to go to the toilets themselves, much less where the Moghuls did."

I chuckled indulgently at Singh's wit while wondering why he was talking about the Moghul toilets as he and I had pursued our inquiries independently. He was careless to mention this . . . or naïve and innocent. Which, was answered by the stricken look on his face and the stammered retraction. "Toilets? Did I say toilets? I guess that reveals how little I know about the Moghuls other than the old fairy tale about building only the baths and then leaving." This was followed by a forced laugh. Nothing revealed here to us, but now Singh knew that we knew he was also pursuing the treasure. "Well," he muttered, "must be off. Lots of papers."

Nawaz watched him go and then said to no one in particular, "All professors have assistant to mark papers. Not Mrs. Chowdery, not Mr. Singh mark papers."

These small lies didn't trouble me as much as they seemed to perplex Nawaz. I was more interested in why Singh was in this department, which was far from our office building, and if his presence had anything to do with Professor Chowdery's repeated checking the post-it, her concern for the time, and our abrupt dismissal.

"What do you say we visit Rahman's brother-in-law? We've blundered around enough now so our interest is no longer a secret."

Nawaz reflected on a piece of hanging cuticle suspended from the ring finger of his left hand. I knew he was preparing to remove the offending cuticle and anticipated it would tip his answer. If he tore off the cuticle resolutely, it meant he was in the game. If he took a more deliberate approach, that would mean . . . At this point in my analysis Nawaz resolutely ripped off the hanging flesh and said, "No. I afraid now. I wish you assign different duties. Maybe I mark papers also?"

So much for analysis of Nawaz' body language. I would have to go it alone. Reminded of my other concerns, teaching, I said, "Nawaz, you may teach the entire damned course." Leaving him to work out the implications of that, I gave him a wave of dismissal and trudged back to Home, Hearth, and Harpy.

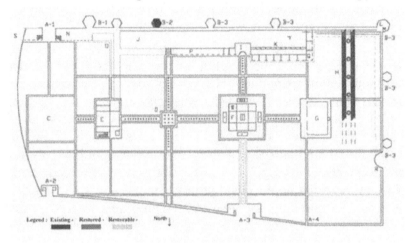

Layout of Lalbagh Fort, from *Banglapedia*.

29

Partners of a Glorious Hope
- C. Wesley, 1873

"Fern tip. I'm ho-ome." A grunt of acknowledgement issued from the balcony where I found Tiffany sipping a gin & tonic and contemplating the vista over the balcony railing – dourly.

"We have to talk," she said, without turning away from the sweeping panorama of heart-breaking poverty. I waited for guidance. And waited. In the fullness of time her head swiveled around; arched eyebrows signaled she was waiting for a response to that open-ended command.

"Right . . . talk. Do you have a preferred topic for us to start with?" This accompanied by a counterfeit smile lest my response be interpreted as sarcastic.

"Relax, Max. I don't want to talk about our relationship. I don't want to talk about leaving this hellhole. I don't want to talk about what you probably want to talk about and that's the notable lack of physical intimacy around here." This was all fine with me. The first two were non-starters and no amount of discussion of the third topic was likely to lead to an improvement.

Tiffany sucked noisily at the ice cube in her now empty G&T glass. "I want to talk about finding the treasure."

God's glottis! There's a conversation stopper for you. Tiffany returned her gaze to the horizon. Time passed. A family of mosquitoes dined leisurely on my forearm. Finding my voice I asked, "Isn't this a turnabout for you?"

More ice cube sucking.

"I realized three things. First, my miserable life could not possibly be made worse by a little wealth. Second, I feel like a little excitement." In point of fact she looked like the near total absence of life, let alone excitement. "Third, I have a lead."

She turned away from the view and studied me. "This is proving to be fun already, Max. If your eyebrows stay in that position much longer they'll merge permanently with your hairline and your academic high brow will be history."

"Tiff, this is wonderful news. Us joining forces. The dynamic duo."

"Can it, buddy. But you might be sincere about my having a lead being wonderful news." Then she resumed her expressionless stare across the balcony wall.

"Is part of the excitement having me beat the information out of you?" This got a small smile.

"Okay. I've been trying to decide whether to tell you all afternoon. It was a close decision and apparently one part of me is still holding out." Holding out was what Tiffany was best at. "Here's the deal. Some guy named Iqbal called right after noon. He said he was related to that dead guy, Rahman, and he wanted to talk to you." Pause for a noisy suck on an ice cube. "I said he could talk freely with me and he said that was fine, but not over the phone."

"It fits. A guy claiming to be Rahman's brother-in-law went looking for Nawaz last night and accused him of being responsible for Rahman's death. Probably the same guy you talked to. If there's treasure involved, this idiot's thrashing around publicly which doesn't seem like a good idea, especially given what was done to his brother-in-law."

"People do strange things when they're panicked. Anyway, he wants to meet just after maghreb prayers by the East Gate."

The call to prayer began to rattle the windows as she finished her sentence. "In that case, Rose Stem, we'd better hoof it. We only have a few minutes."

"Funny. Now I'm getting cold feet. You go alone, Max."

That was fine with me, but after a quick trip to the bathroom I found Tiffany waiting by the door.

We walked toward East Gate in silence until it occurred to me we had no idea whom we were looking for. I raised this problem and Tiffany pointed out, "We won't have to find him. How many Western couples are foolish enough to, a) be in Bangladesh, and b) are cruising around at dusk in this neighborhood?"

We didn't have to wait at the gate. As we approached, a boy, maybe 12 years old, trotted toward us and asked, "Treasure?" We nodded and he trotted away, looking over his left shoulder to make sure we were following.

After a block of trotting, which took the starch out of the Browns, he flagged a Bajaj and climbed in. A Bajaj, or baby taxi, is the Bangladeshi version of the Thai *tuk tuk*. No single part or place looks like it will work. They're all battered, colored green under the grime, and complainingly cart four passengers – although built for two – and their cargo around town.

The three of us crowded together on the bench seat behind the driver and I wondered if these three-wheeled invitations to a gory end were excluded in my life insurance policy; they should be.

Upon close – and we couldn't have been closer – inspection, our youthful guide turned out to be well dressed. No disagreeable aromas arose from him and he seemed alert. "Do you speak English?"

"Not well," he answered confidently, which suggested the opposite of his answer.

"Can you tell us anything about our destination?" asked pleasantly, trying to sound like a tourist attempting to bridge the cultural divide.

"We go to see my father. He has sister, my aunt, married to Rahman." Thus informed, we rode in silence – if you discount the thunderous racket made by the many vibrating parts on the Bajaj and its unmuffled exhaust.

Less than a kilometer further, the boy gave the driver a series of instructions and we twisted through narrow streets until the Bajaj stopped in front of a two-story building. The house was indistinguishable from every other in that part of Dhaka except it appeared to have a pigeon cote on the flat roof. I handed the driver fifteen taka – trying to avoid direct skin contact – and we followed our guide up the two steps and waited in front of a wooden door.

The door opened, without a summoning knock, and we were invited in with a majestic wave by an old woman. She favored Tiffany with a smile that revealed a maximum of five teeth, widely and randomly distributed on her betel stained gums, and Tiffany favored me with a deep shudder. The woman directed us to a settee and scuttled out of the room, not, I hoped, to pre-pare a lethal tea.

Then, a more ominous possibility: had we been lured into a trap? How would our heads be displayed?

It was growing dark but no lights were turned on in the house. Few street lamps operate in Dhaka and the prospects of them ever working are dim – at a minimum, any functioning bulb will be stolen before morning – so little light came from outside. It was becoming more difficult to make out the features of the room and I was concentrating on remaining relaxed when a tall figure appeared at the door. Tiffany emitted a small squeal. Her thoughts may have veered off in the same dark di-rection as mine.

"Please have no fear," said a thickly accented voice. "I am brother who talk to lady this day. If it is not too troublesome for you, I am thinking it best you do not see my face. I am deeply worried and if you see how Rahman die, you also will worry."

In fact, I was one of the charter viewers of the Rahman death scene, but I didn't trouble our host with this intelligence. It did occur to me that Iqbal might not be the sharpest scythe in the paddy. Concealing his face was no protection. We had come to his house and could easily find it again; I planned to memo-rize the route as we returned to the university.

He sat down. "I am talking to you because of this great fear. I hear from Rahman that you are looking for Moghul treasure. Myself I do not believe in this treasure any more. I am thinking with those who say treasure already found many years before now." He paused to light a cigarette and the match illuminated his face. He had a small moustache, thinning hair that featured two inches of gray root before making an abrupt transition to coal black, wire rim glasses, and a bulbous nose. "But there are other men who think the otherwise. They are thinking the treas-ure is still in the ground. They will make every expense to find it and they are not gentle people." I, and probably Iqbal, thought of the late Rahman, head in hands.

"Rahman find information that maybe, many years ago, help find treasure. I am not understanding this information but now the fact of this information is known. Maybe person who give it to Rahman say something. I am thinking Rahman die because of this information." At this point Iqbal stopped and I tried to imagine his facial features. Was he chewing on his lower lip, deliberating whether to continue?

Trying to advance the conversation I asked, "Which raises a question. Why didn't your brother-in-law simply give this information to the people who attacked him? If there's all this doubt about its value, he would've certainly given up the information rather than his life."

"Rahman not have the thing with him and maybe he not understand it either. He give it to his wife, my sister. She is responsible for storing things not in shop. Rahman not know where wife put thing and he not want these men to seek his wife." Poor Rahman was taking on heroic dimensions, giving his own life to spare his wife. "Police say Rahman not tortured. I think he die before they kill him. Rahman have heart attacks before two times. Same like me."

That would explain something that seemed odd about the death scene. No blood. If Rahman was already dead when his head was removed there would be less bleeding. No gushing carotid artery hosing down the room. An image best not developed further. We were losing sight of the purpose of our mission.

"Iqbal, I'm very sorry about Rahman's death and only a little comforted to learn that he didn't suffer greatly. But I need to be clear why you want to give this information to me." I was making a leap here that he did want to hand over – or sell – the information. Would he take Mastercard?

"Ah yes. I am fearful that these same people will come to me for the information. So I am giving it. I am not thinking it is useful. Even if the treasure is still in the ground this will only help a little. If others have this information the people who kill Rahman will not be interested in me."

It took no deep analysis to see the flaw in this line of reasoning: As long as there was any suspicion that Iqbal, the best surviving source of information on the treasure, might have additional information, the bad guys would try to beat it out of him. He continued to unveil his plan for survival. "That is why, when your young friend come this afternoon, I tell him that he also may have information."

Nawaz! That zit-popping schmuck! Told me he was dropping out of the race and then hustled over here. "Did this young assistant pick at sores on his body?" Just to confirm.

"Ah yes. He ate mucous from his nose." No doubt who that was. "Alas I did not have thing from Rahman wife but I tell your assistant I will give it to you. He was not satisfied with this arrangement but I knew you would understand and forgive him for not bringing the information to you himself. In Bangladesh every assistant feels shame if he cannot complete an assignment and that certainly was what vexed the young man."

Forgiveness was not in the cards. "It's much better that this information comes directly to me. Is it a map?"

"No. A letter." Bad luck. I would have to allow Nawaz back in long enough for a translation, or find another traitorous assistant. "Maybe I am not understanding it well because I do not read English perfectly." Oho! Good luck.

"You mean there's a letter in English that provides a clue to the treasure?"

Tiffany, who had been silent since her squeal, broke in, "It's hard to conceive of any other meaning to the man's statement, Max."

"This letter is written by English sergeant who come to East Bengal with first soldiers and he write letter to wife. Letter not sent because he die and his clothes and other things kept by person who maybe kill him. Rahman buy all these things many years ago from another antique man. Rahman sell helmet, sword, and cooking pieces, but still have clothes and papers."

"Is it a long letter?" Not an important question, but to keep the focus.

"Ah no. Here, I have it now," and he held out what, by feel, was a crisp new piece of paper. As if he could see my disappointment, he explained, "This not original. Remember I want to give this to several people so no one want to kill Iqbal. This is photocopy."

"No disrespect, Mr. Iqbal, but could I see the original so that I can determine whether it's truly old, or whether someone has tricked your brother-in-law?"

Iqbal responded with a "Hmmm," and left the room. Presently there were sounds of a photocopy machine working. I counted four passes of the machine's lamp. Iqbal returned and handed me a wrinkled fragile piece of paper. "You take original. You are professor so maybe you can use this for some worthy purpose, not just money."

That seemed to be the end of the interview. "Tiff, do we need to ask Mr. Iqbal anything more?"

Unprepared to be included in the conversation, she shot a "No," and folded her arms.

This was followed by a brief silence as two vehicles passed the house. The fact that I noticed them was a sign of increasing unease. I wanted to ask Iqbal if he was the brother-in-law who'd visited Nawaz the previous night, but didn't want to prolong our stay or alarm him with questions peripheral to the central objective: gaining sole possession of the letter.

"Mr. Iqbal, I hope you can relax now. If you would like I can share your letter with different friends to ensure that no one will be trying to force the information out of you or anyone else. I too am uneasy that only the two of us have this letter right now."

Iqbal left the room again and Tiffany hissed, "Max, what the fuck are you up to? This guy will see right through this cheap trick and take the original back!" Iqbal returned and handed me – I counted them – four pieces of paper. That plus the first photocopy and the original should account for all copies.

"I hope your plan to spread these around protects both of us, Mr. Iqbal."

"I am sure it is the only way," replied Iqbal, and we left him silhouetted in the darkened front door of his home. The roar of an approaching Bajaj redirected our attention; the drivers don't use lights, either to save energy or because the lights don't function. We hailed it and climbed in.

"I can *not* believe that worked, Max. We now have the only copies and that poor simpleton thinks he's bought piece of mind."

"It came cheap for him. He was going to give the letter away. I wish we had some light in this contraption so we could examine it." I held one of the copies up to catch passing lights as we lurched back toward the campus.

"Holy shit!" cried Tiffany. "We're invited to Dean Mosle-huddin's house. We were supposed to be there half an hour ago."

Interesting that social engagements assumed such impor-tance for Tiffany in all situations. Who could worry about a lousy dinner party when millions might be within their grasp? But on the other hand . . . Singh would certainly be there. Would our absence make him increase the pace of the hunt? Could we dissemble and lull him into a sense of false security?

"Don't panic Tiff; we're dressed well enough to go di-rectly," and I pressed my small Bangla vocabulary into service – 'right,' 'left,' and 'straight' – to vector the Bajaj to Dean Mos-lehuddin's apartment building.

30

Oft Our Trust Has Known Betrayal
- R. Slater, 1953

The party was well attended, resulting in insufficient seating which allowed us to remain standing and join – or escape – conversations of our choosing. We quickly located Singh. "Hail, roommate!" Acting talent like that is wasted in the class-room. Singh did a less credible job of displaying enthusiasm at my approach, but, in fairness, he was taken by surprise.

"Ah yis, Professor Max. We were just talking about you," and he gestured toward a woman obscured by a portly history professor I'd met once and avoided since. Who should peer around the historian but the delectable Professor Chowdery of Classical Studies. I sputtered a howdy and extended my hand.

The exquisite Chowdery laughed at my evident surprise and said sotto voce, "We were speaking in only the most compli-mentary terms, Professor Brown. Singh here was telling me of your broad interests. Ancient maps, I believe? And how difficult the teaching environment is in America – calumnious letters following one around the globe! A shame that practitioners of this noble profession should be subjected to such venom."

Singh appeared to enjoy this last. "My dear Max, it was not my good self who raised the topic." The fat history professor reddened and excused himself for more dip.

"Professor Chowdery, you don't know the half of it," I said with forced confidence and what I hoped would be a tone of finality.

"But I would love to hear it someday," and she laughed again, displaying those fabulous teeth and jiggling bosom. She sold the performance by coquettishly brushing her hair back over her ear, which was Tiffany's cue to make an uninvited ap-pearance. Tiffany looked from Chowdery to me and back.

"I see Max has friends he hasn't mentioned."

Bad opening, Tiff.

"Not yet a friend, Tiffany, but an acquaintance as of this af-ternoon. Professor Chowdery works in Classical Studies and I'd hoped for advice from her. Failing to get it, I'm stumped. You know," I said turning to Chowdery and Singh, "it was my budding fancy that years of map collecting would yield more than wall covering. I thought I might unearth a rare Mercator or Ortelius at an estate sale and make a profit. I guess that's the justification one repeats so often for an expensive hobby that it begins to take root."

Tiffany rolled her eyes, twice, since no one seemed to notice the first time. "I've heard this justification. Max has promised again and again that the diligent collector profits over the long term." This came out stiffly, as a rehearsed line.

"But you, Professor Chowdery. What skeletons rattle around in your closet? What hobbies? We didn't really have an opportunity to chat this afternoon."

"Alas, I'm just a shabby don, or donness if there is such a term. A martyr to the cause of higher education. No hobbies, no social life, nothing."

That one of the hottest looking women in South Asia would have no social life seemed improbable. Tiffany glowered. How reassuring that she'd display so much jealousy so openly. And what irony: she'd been immune to my charms for over a decade but feared other women would find me irresistible?

"We must help you find a suitable beau, Ms. Chowdery." Tiffany supported this with a grunt. "Your taste in men runs to . . . ?"

"Wealth, Professor Brown. While I don't consider myself a gold digger, the opportunities for a woman are limited. Our glass ceiling has a high lead content. Contact with it can cause permanent injury. Excessive aspiration can lead to ostracism, or worse. Better to marry success than seek it personally."

Tiffany seemed to like this answer. "Well, it seems old Maxie won't be in the running then. Success has eluded him like a greased pig at the county fair. But of course, he's successfully married."

Her smile brought a wave of alcohol. She'd been hitting the sauce heavily already – plus the earlier G&Ts in our apartment. Not good. Would she start blabbing about the letter? She could. The options were to get her out of there or get her sick – and out of there. Dismal past experience had demonstrated that neither option was likely to work. Only by careful supervision could I abort a public exposition of our evening's treasure hunting.

A crafty look came over Tiff's face. I tensed.

"Oh Professor Singh? We just had the most interesting conversation."

"Good, right, Tiffany . . . No need to bore the good Dr. Singh with the minutiae of our humdrum lives. Would you refresh this for me?"

Tiffany clumsily pushed the glass back at me and bulled on. "We learned that Max's little pal, Nawaz, went to see that antique dealer's cousin, or whatever. I'm *dying* to find out if he learned anything."

Well done, partner. Stop there and it might work. Faint hope. The lady was not for deterring. "Max and I went to see that man too . . ." she paused and looked perplexed, then continued in a lowered voice, "but we didn't learn anything." No statement could have been less convincing.

Singh willed the corners of his mouth down but his eyes danced with glee. "Ah yis. You are now a co-conspirator with your husband in his search for instant wealth, fair madam?" Tiffany was sober enough to realize that she'd overplayed her hand and replied with a hiccup.

"My dear," I said, trying to speak normally – that is, without gnashing my teeth – "perhaps I could get you some water for those hiccups?" When I turned away from her Singh was gone as was the edible Miss Chowdery.

"Tiffany, you do understand what you've done?" I hissed. That purchased a sullen look and the realization that reprimands are wasted on people when they're drunk and on Tiffany in any condition. She pushed past me toward the buffet where the drinks were lined up. Damage control was still needed lest she mount a table and shout that I had on my person, at that very moment, the much sought after key to the treasure of the Moghuls. I spent the next three hours plodding along in her wake, expecting the worst, but she'd done all the damage she intended that evening.

The Search
- J. Morris, 1854

At 11:00 I collected Tiffany and announced to our host that, due to the mountain of student papers awaiting attention, we were forced to prematurely abandon what was easily the high point of the social season. The dean pointed out that since I was not yet teaching my paper marking load could not be too heavy. "True," I replied, "but I learned today this all-purpose and useful excuse to excuse oneself." This, with as much bonhomie as could be mustered and a meaningful sidewise look at my inebriated wife.

The dean followed my glance and nodded understandingly. "You are an adept student of culture, Professor Brown. I anticipate that you will soon master the subtleties of avoiding committee assignments as your colleagues have." We laughed fraternally and I steered Tiffany outside.

No Bajaj awaited so we started slowly toward home. The sheaf of letters – original and copies – bulged in my pocket, calling out to every miscreant and footpad on the subcontinent. The darkened streets were filled with menace and I wondered if the divinity that protects drunks extends the same coverage to their escorts. This led to a search for a metaphor casting the Almighty as an AlAnon organizer – which I immediately aborted. Too much peril abroad to indulge in idle blasphemy.

A Bajaj hove into earshot coincident with sight of our apartment. We waved it past and weaved onward. Breaking the silence Tiffany stated, "I think I threw teeny Singh off the scent." A sniffle.

I was considering my reply. If Tiffany and I were going to be a team it was high time we elected the team captain: A captain whose orders would be followed without complaint or protest. Whose experience in these matters would be respected. Whose knowledge of the dark nature of humanity would provide a guiding light forward. While rehearsing and discarding this and similar claptrap we came within view of the entry to our apartment building. A stocky man burst out of the door – too distant to see clearly – and trotted to the left. A car started and, gravel spewing, accelerated toward the East Gate of the campus. This hurried exit, in a land where personal energy conservation and the absence of hurry were paramount, was remarkable.

"Teammate. I do have some thoughts on your performance this evening which I'd like to share at the appropriate time. But did you notice a man just run out of our digs? I think something's fishy. You wait downstairs while I investigate."

Tiffany, who was sobering up from the long walk home, grabbed my arm in a surprisingly strong grip. "You're not leaving me down here, bucko. Down here is where the wog was last seen, right?"

Okay. With a grip and attitude like that she might be useful. We apprehensively mounted the endless stairs to our *pied* above the *terre*. Peering up and around the last bend in the staircase we saw our apartment door standing open and light issuing from within, but no sound.

"Police, Max. We have to call the police. You're not supposed to go into a house where you think there's a robbery in progress."

"I have it on good authority that the police are the last people one would summon when in trouble. We go in or we leave." No response and no resistance when I resumed the climb. At the top of the stairs we crept along the wall until we got to the door. Still no sound. Keenly aware that a bullet through the eye would end my treasure-hunting career, I leaned past the doorjamb until I had a view of our entry and sitting room. Pulling back, "Fuck!"

"What?"

"The place has been trashed." Annoyance overcame Tiffany's fear and she wheeled around me to take in the devastation personally. Cushions were slit and the copra fillings shaken out on the floor. Drawers overturned. Tables upended. More of the same in the other rooms. The ransackers had been thorough. Even a tube of toothpaste had been cut in half.

Rage built as we went through the sitting room into the kitchen. Dread started to creep in as we assessed the damage in the pantry. It gained ground as we hurriedly checked our bedroom. And terror had taken complete hold before we were finished looking around in the bathroom. With one voice we said, "We've got to get the fuck out of here!"

There wasn't have time for a careful inventory, but it appeared the only thing missing was the Robinson map from the bathroom. We threw sleepwear, a change of clothes, and the remaining undamaged toiletries into an overnight bag and ran down the stairs. "Which way, Max? They could be coming back from any direction."

"The last man out headed toward East Gate. A logical direction from which he might return." We headed north and immediately bumped into, literally, a parked Bajaj. The collision roused the slumbering driver. "Sonargoan hotel," I implored, waving fifty taka under his nose.

The Bajaj sputtered toward the East Gate while Tiff and I shrank into the shadows of the rear seat. No on-coming traffic passed until we left campus. Soon we were pulling up under the massive portico of the Sonargoan. Sanctuary.

Hoping our humble means of conveyance hadn't been noticed by the receptionist, I imperiously demanded a double room for an indefinite period. Was there a quaver in my voice? Tiff was partially concealed behind a plant.

"Your passport, sir?"

"Being processed by the office, I fear." I wrote 'Silver, L. John,' on the registration card. "You know how they promise immediate attention."

The receptionist offered an unconvincing imitation of a sympathetic smile, collected a cash prepayment for two nights, and gave the room key to a porter who had managed to take possession of our small bag. This worthy took us on an extended tour of the room, beseeching us to examine the contents of the mini-bar, the loft in the towels, and the intricacies of controlling the environment.

Five minutes and twenty taka later, we parted company and I firmly shut the door behind him and locked the deadbolt.

"Now let's see what all the excitement's about," and fished the magic letter out of my pocket.

31

My Darling Prudence,

I write with the Sinkinge Feeling that I will not
survive this Inferno and curse the day your
Brother portuned that I should signe the Agreement to come. I have amply described the Condi-
tions here and will not impose upon You further
with Whinging about that which cannot, for the
moment, be changed. The other men are usually
sick and I thank Divine Providence for a Consti-
tution that defies all the ills that the Orient can
send my way. I eat where I will and suffer little
for my disregard of the warnings of our Surgeon,
who himself, is often Under the Weather as he is
wont to say.

I came across some interesting Papers today in
the Cabin of our worthy Captain, himself coincidentally spending the better part of each hour in
the toilet. Whilst he was thus engaged I studied a
Mapp he had left carelessly on his desk that purported to identify the place in which the old
Muguls buried a vaste Treasure of Jewels and
Gold. The Mapp itself was prepared by our Sur-
veyor of some years back, a Captain Robinson
who lacked either the Daring or Cunninge to extract the Prize for Himself. Our Captain had an
indistinct Copy of the Mapp amongst his other
Papers, but the thing that catches the attention is
the Instruction that the Treasure is burried behind the Toilets. The Baths themselves I have seen
many times and they are overgrowne with the Fo-
liage that springs up overnight.

The Mapp is contradicted by writings on a palm leaf by someone claiming to have been the trusted Servant of the grate Mugul. It appears that the Servant's Tongue was cut out to keep him silent but he must have learned to write in later years and passed on his Knowledge that wise. I will loosely translate, Dear Pru, as best as my poor Knowledge of the Language permits.

"As we prepared to depart the grate Khan entrusted me the Taske of leaving a material Treasure in the grounde where his own life's Gratest Treasure, his Daughter, had been laide. Wishing the Khan's Tribute to remain undisturbed, I caste the Box down amongst the stench and filth of the lowest in the Court. My Fealty was rewarded although the Khan took the caution of silencing me."

Who to believe? Our Captain is clearly entranced by the Mistery but is never distant enough from the commode to investigate. He is losing weight visibly.

Enough of this idle gosip. I write to You every week to remind myself that there is a better Life waiting for me elsewhere. My Words echo off the Pages and a chill (unlikely that, what?) overcomes me that I shall not see You and our Home again.

My Love Undying,

Your Maxwell

What a coincidence, the name.

"So, what's he telling us, Max? This reference to 'down amongst the stench and filth of the lowest in the court?'" My namesake seemed perplexed by the same statement.

"When I spoke with Professor Chowdery yesterday, Tiff, she pointed out the obvious: The hoi polloi wouldn't be invited to use the same sanitary facilities as the hoity-toity. The trusted servant was asked to hide the treasure during the last minute arrangements before departure. He improvised and threw the loot into the servants' toilet." Tiffany's brow furrowed and she resumed studying the letter.

It appeared that the Robinson map – our bathroom map – was well known and the inspiration for early exploration, had the 'worthy Captain' been able to venture far enough from the crapper. Why did Robinson write on his map that the treasure was 'behind' the toilet when the servant wrote he had dropped the loot into the servants' toilet? Maybe that was the information Robinson had, or maybe, as Nawaz had observed, there were language errors on Robinson's map and the writer had selected the wrong word. I called the hotel's reception desk.

"A translation question."

"Yes sir?"

"What would the words in Bangla be for beneath and behind?"

"For beneath, Bangla speaker sometimes says 'adhina' and for behind 'taladese'."

"So," not much helped, "very different sounding words."

"Yes sir. But sometimes same word mean both. 'Antarale' mean both behind and under."

Without access to the map I couldn't check which word had been used, but the receptionist's information increased the possibility that Robinson had accurate information, but imprecise translation had misled fortune hunters for centuries.

"Tiff, I think I'm on to something," excited to share this new possibility. Alcohol and emotional exhaustion had caught up with Tiffany. She was sound asleep.

Many Seek for Earthly Treasure
- E. R. Latta, 1887

Where were the servants' toilets? The desire to take this question to Professor Chowdery was based largely on wanting a pretext to luxuriate in her presence. Cold logic dictated that the fewer who had this information, the better.

Where does a professor start any research project? In the library. I slipped out of the hotel room the next morning without disturbing my hung-over co-conspirator and returned to the campus.

———

The Dhaka U library presents a different challenge to the researcher. Given a few uninterrupted weeks you could read every English language volume in the place. It wasn't size that presented a challenge; it was the cataloguing which was chaotic. As examples encountered that morning: Nestled amidst the biology books were two locally published cookbooks, assembled by foreign women's groups as antidotes to boredom. Resting across the meager collection of Shakespeare's work we discover a novel by Isaac Asimov.

There was a card catalogue, of sorts, although the drawers had been replaced randomly. I elected to start with a known reference and see what that led to. The known reference was Professor Hasina Chowdery in the expectation that the university would showcase its own. Or, at the least, faculty vanity would ensure that their own oeuvres were on display. Six card boxes were devoted to Chowderys of various spellings and disciplines and it took fifteen minutes to locate fair Hasina C's three catalogued publications. All were on the layout of the Moghul baths and, upon examination of the indicated shelf space, were absent.

The librarian seemed pleasantly surprised that anyone would address her with a question. "I'll check instantly, sir. Oh dear. Here are the cards and all three have been checked out." I was more surprised by the efficiency with which she located the cards than the news that the books had been checked out.

"Is it possible to recall those items?"

"Of course, sir. We allow two weeks of uninterrupted use, then, if there is another student or faculty member requesting same document, we send a notice demanding return. Please complete this form and I will do the needful."

"Excellent. When might I expect to receive these documents?"

"Well sir," brow furrowed as the math was done, "they were checked out yesterday so we will issue the letter in twelve days and we usually receive the book back within a fortnight."

Not a lot of help there. "Perhaps you might tell me who has these documents – on the off chance it's an acquaintance – and I could read over his or her shoulder, as it were?"

"Alas, our library policy forbids such divulging. For good reason as there would be no end of pestering."

"Certainly." The cards sat on her desk, just beyond reading range. "Would you have a copy of the library's policies that I might read? It seems my unfamiliarity with the norms has me always putting the wrong foot forward."

"Well, there is a file copy I could photocopy, but I would be obliged to ask you to pay the cost of the machine. Another policy." She held up her palms to signal helplessness in the face of remorseless bureaucracy. As soon as she turned her back to fetch the 'file copy' I leaned forward and snatched up the three book cards. All signed out to my chum, Singh.

The librarian returned, looking distraught. "Oh dear! This is upsetting. The file copy is missing!" I assumed a funereal face to signify either condolences or shared indignation, whichever might be expected under the circumstances. I had my own reasons for disappointment. I wouldn't be reading Chowdery's manuscripts over Singh's shoulder.

"Ah well, ma'am, these documents grow legs of their own when unattended for long. But I've had another thought. Do the academic departments maintain specialized libraries for their students and faculty?"

She focused on my question with difficulty. "I suppose . . . of course . . . I imagine some of them do."

Thanking her I hied to the Classical Studies building and selected an entrance that seemed remote from Chowdery's office. It was locked. Another door. Locked. A third tried with the same result. The irony of a learning center that locked out the learners was less entertaining than it might have been a month earlier. I finally resorted to the main entrance and worked the door as quietly as I could. The department secretary's office was a few quick steps away and I closed the door behind me as I entered her domain. The secretary looked up in alarm. A strange pale-faced and overheated man was locking her in with him.

Counterfeiting a disarming smile, "Pardon, I'm the new professor from England (I'd been warned that an American is perceived to be so close to his savage frontier past that rape is never completely out of the question) and I'm looking for the collection of books and manuscripts written by members of this department." The secretary examined me intently, taking testosterone readings and checking for extra Y chromosomes.

At length, and with deep suspicion in her voice, "I can't stop you from reading if you are a professor. Everything we have is in the faculty lounge," and she took this opportunity to escape from behind her desk into the hall where she signaled a door further along.

I thanked her with a nod and smile so as not to make my presence audibly known should Professor Chowdery be in her office two doors back.

The department's 'library' consisted of old newspapers, a few popular magazines of great age but no value, and coverless manuscripts. By methodically combing through the disorderly heaps of paper I unearthed two manuscripts by Chowdery. The second contained a simple map of the Moghul site.

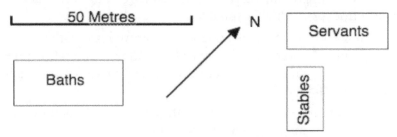

From this, the ex-pilot was able to determine that the servant's facilities were 41 meters from the northeast corner of the surviving building on a bearing of 020°.

I folded the thin manuscript and shoved it into my pocket and turned to find all of Hasina Chowdery's teeth grinning at me from the doorway where she leaned against the jamb. She'd been there a while.

"My good Professor Brown. I had always hoped to produce a bestseller. Now my ardent fans are stealing copies of early editions."

No bluffing my way out of this.

"Caught in the act. Ah well, Ms. Chowdery. Since you denied me your direct assistance I've had to seek out that intelligence of yours that's entered the public domain."

"Can you be confident that my earlier scholarship was accurate?" Thank you for answering one question: you think this is still good stuff or you wouldn't try to raise doubts. "And I'm curious what there is in that paper that would help you, other than general information on the layout of the place." And another question is answered: I'm a lot farther along than you suspect if you don't understand the significance of this paper.

"Leave no stone unturned: my motto. I'll strike the mother lode somewhere." She stretched her arms behind her, projecting those magnificent breasts another three inches in my direction. Redirecting my stare I mumbled on, "Seek and ye shall find. The longest journey begins with a single stumble. And so on and so forth."

"I said it before, Professor Brown, and I know you don't take me seriously. But, in the titanic unlikelihood that you do stumble on something of even the smallest value, I fear for your life. Perhaps it's due to the great poverty in this nation; wealth or the prospect of wealth washes out reason. It's not – as Westerners are fond of sneering as they peer down their long noses – that life is cheap among the disenfranchised. It's that money is dear."

"I'm touched by your concern. Be reassured that beneath this façade, this mild mannered pedant has powers that are best kept under wraps for the time being. But I'll watch my step."

"I trust marksmanship is one of them. With apologies to your Mae West, I assume that bulge in your pants pocket is not owed to your delight at seeing me." She stepped out of the doorway, signaling the conversation was over and I was now free to slink away with the purloined manuscript bulging in my jacket pocket. I needed to find a less conspicuous place to carry the pistol.

In the Bajaj back to the hotel I tried to read – interspersed with long looks at the passing street scenes to keep the nausea at a manageable level – and learned that:

• The Great Khan had 27 wives, none of whom accompanied him on this trip. He may have acquired one or two more in East Bengal.

• The grounds had been extensively excavated, yielding little of historical significance; the foundations of the servants' building had been built of mud and only fragments survived.

• The horses enjoyed more lavish and durable housing than the servants as a stone foundation had been topped by a wooden structure, parts of which survived into the 20th century – barely – and been photographed.

• The author concluded that the servants' building was primarily for their cooking, laundry and baths – including toilets? – as they resided elsewhere in bamboo huts.

These findings were presented in this order, with little analysis, and accorded equal weight. Miss Chowdery may be one first-class dish and all-around hot shit, but she was a lousy writer.

Two heads are better

When I returned to the hotel room Tiffany was gone, leaving no note. Ah well, I hadn't either. The *Bangladesh Observer* was lying undisturbed on the dresser. I hid the pistol in the top dresser drawer under my one spare pair of shorts and leafed through the *BO*. The second page featured a small photo guaranteed to catch the reader's attention. There in grainy solemnity sat the late Mr. Rahman, his head again cradled in his hands.

> Police discovered the beheaded corpse of S.I. Rahman, an antique dealer in the Gulshan area. Rahman was a trusted merchant who is survived by a wife and five children. When asked if they thought foul play were involved a police spokesman said they were inclined to rule out suicide at the present.

With brilliant detective work like that the perpetrator would be in custody in no time, assuming the no-suicide hypothesis held up.

> In a similar grisly occurrence police were called to the store of Mr. Rahman's brother-in-law, Iqbal Khan, who, reportedly, was also found headless by his now widow. The coincidence of the two related men meeting their untimely demise in such a same manner gives rise, according to the police spokesman, that there may be a connection.

Poor Iqbal. Recalling his comment that he too had suffered a pair of heart attacks, I hoped he'd checked out via that exit before the torture began. Then the personal implications dawned: I was on the same short list as these guys, and toward the top. Whether Iqbal had blabbed or not, my interest and activities were public enough to invite close questioning by men with limited patience and a flair for the dramatic and final in their work.

A key working the door lock interrupted these thoughts and I dove behind the window curtain, scooping up a fruit knife as I went. As well as an apple, for what purpose I was still trying to discover as the door opened and I heard the hysterical voice of Tiffany and a lowered male voice. Gripping the handle of the comically small fruit knife – it was sharp, however – I crouched in order to spring on the intruder who held Tiffany captive.

One, of many, liabilities of the academic life is a tendency to over-analyze every situation. Should I jump out screaming and paralyze my adversary with fright? Or should I attack as silently as possible to reduce his opportunities to respond?

Neither. Tiffany was saying, "We've got to find Max and warn him before the same happens to him. Ohmigawd!!!" Then more wailing. The lowered voice belonged to our good dean.

Stepping from behind the curtain, "Warn me of what, Buttercup?"

"Oh, Max, you're alive! Dean Moslehuddin has just given us the worst possible news." Wailing again.

I looked to Mosleh for the next installment.

"It appears there has been another incident like that which occurred to the antique dealer. I was apprised of this by the police early this morning. I had trouble finding you. The sight presented by your flat did this old heart no good, I can tell you that."

Not to knock a bad heart in these troubled times. A faulty ticker might spare one an unpleasant crossing.

"Yes, Rahman was the first we know of. I was just assessing our own danger and the prognosis isn't good. The only dark consolation is that perhaps neither victim suffered."

"How can you say that professor? He was skinned alive!"

The *BO* hadn't added that detail. "God's ganglia! And then they chopped off his head?"

"No. The police did not mention any removal of the head. Only the skinning. I am trying not to visualize the final moments of that poor boy's life."

Something was amiss.

"Boy? He looked fifty."

Tiffany came out of her delirium to enter the conversation. "Don't you get it? They skinned Nawaz. The guy who was always picking at his skin. Macabre." I could have laughed had I not felt I might vomit. Dean Moslehuddin clucked sympathetically as I made a precautionary trip to the bathroom.

When I returned Tiffany and the Dean were studying page 2 of the *Observer*.

When Two Who Once Were Joined As One
- M. Bittner, 2004

"We've got to get out of here, Max. There're flights to somewhere every evening, maybe Bangkok. Dean Mosleh has offered to take our check to the bank to get us the cash."

"Mrs. Brown tells me your passports are still being processed. Unusually long. That could be a sticking point."

"No way," reasoned Tiffany. "We just tell them at the airport we're fleeing for our lives and show them the newspaper story."

"I'm no expert in criminal science, pet, but those are actual policemen at the airport and I'm not sure they'll open the exit gate to someone who tells them that they're involved in three murders."

"I fear I must agree with your good husband. The passports are essential. Explanations for your departure must be avoided."

This produced some splendid histrionics from Tiffany. Much as I wanted to enjoy an extended run of her performance, time was pressing.

"Khan notified me just the other day (two weeks ago) that he has the passports back and was intending to keep them in the office safe until I collected them."

"Splendid," cried the Dean. "I too know the combination and I can return with both your money and your passports in an hour or two. You can be packed by then?" Highly likely as all we had with us had been brought in an overnight bag.

The Dean departed and Tiffany slumped in a chair. "We're getting out of here! I prayed for this moment, but I sure never pictured it this way."

For more years than I cared to recall, Tiffany and I'd stayed together out of perversity, habit, inertia, and a desire to get in the last lick. "Not 'we', Pansy Pistil. I'm staying."

Tiffany didn't look at me. "It's the Chowdery floozy, isn't it? You're so eager to cock her you'll stick around despite the guarantee that your head'll be a hood ornament. I saw how you ogled her tits at the party last night."

How I loved it. Despite years of mutual animosity Tiffany could still be jealous.

"Not a woman. I'm infatuated with wealth. You read that old Limey's letter. The treasure was dumped in the servants' crapper. I have a map of where the servants' shed was, including their toilets. What's the likelihood anyone mucked around there thinking they'd find treasure?"

"Certifiable! I'm sticking with the Chowdery theory." After chewing on her lower lip she brightened, "I'll tell you what Max. You stay here and delve into the crapper or the faculty queen, whatever. The money isn't worth it. I didn't really think we'd find anything and just took it on as a game. These people are playing for keeps and I'm ready to fold, take my ball home, cash my chips, whatever. Three really ugly murders – and us front and center for the next one – are three ugly murders too many."

Before she could say 'whatever' again I broke in, "Look, Tiff, the people who've been murdered took no precautions. In fact poor Iqbal seemed to be wearing a sandwich board asking to be killed. If these were cunning killers, not just brutal ones, that'd be different."

What the hell was I saying? These *were* cunning bastards. Three murders in a congested part of the most crowded country on the planet and not a single eyewitness? Pretty good. But I blathered on. "I can feel the money. I'm close. And, if you think these guys are so good, what makes you think they won't follow you?" That question got Tiffany's attention. She didn't need any more threatening news.

"Goddammit, Max. You got me into this mess."

Predictable Tiff. When in doubt, blame your spouse. When angry, ditto. When scared, same again.

"Is 'you got me into this' supposed to mean I'm to get you out by whisking you to safety? I thought you might welcome my staying here to draw their fire." That possibility interested her. Irate that my affections might stray one moment, ready to leave me behind as bait the next.

Her mind made up that this might be the best deal available, she declared, "Okay, genius. If that's the way you want it. We've always done what you wanted. Why change now?" This, accompanied by a flip of the hand to signal she'd given up on me. "I hope you find your money. I don't expect any (did she really mean that?) and I hope you survive (she might mean that). I'm on the next flight. Happy treasure hunting."

"I'm with you in spirit all the way, Tiff. I'll understand if you don't try to contact me for a while so you can't be traced."

How could this be so matter of fact? This frigging relationship had staggered along for over a decade as if there were no alternative – despite the high mortality rate among the marriages of our friends and acquaintances – and now, without breaking crockery or hurled epithets, we were calling it quits? I sure didn't expect we'd get together again, especially if I found the swag.

She went into the bathroom to collect her handful of toiletries and I went down to the lobby shops. There was a lot to do. I'd just dissolved my marriage and the day was still young.

32

There Is a Safe Retreat From Every Evil
- C. H. Gabriel, 1905

The hotel shopping arcade featured a store specializing in 'personal care' items. I hadn't settled on a disguise but wanted something convincing, yet not too hot to wear for extended periods outside.

Many preparations were available to make one look younger; none to look older. Too bad. Perhaps a white haired ancient might have fooled them, even if still a foreigner.

I checked out the possibilities to pass as a woman. No wigs.

Too big to be a child. And too lined. And not spry enough.

Nothing available to go as an eccentric: no monocle, walking stick, or pith helmet.

I wasn't getting anywhere and the gift shop seemed even less promising. With no regard for seasonal demand, everything acquired over the years that could be fit onto the shelves was on display. Christmas cards sat near a witch's hat, which was not far from a stuffed rabbit sporting a valentine heart on its grimy chest. With fading expectations I pawed through the plastic toys and dusty toiletries, settling finally on black hair dye, a lungi, sandals and a polyester long sleeved shirt.

Tiffany thought the disguise pointless. "For starters, you're taller than most Bangladeshi men. Second, your skin is far too pale. And third, your posture is still standard issue US military – not the national slouch. Can I propose as better concealment an orange hunting vest, a propeller beanie with flashing light on top, and a Groucho Marx glasses, nose and moustache combo?"

She was right. I wasn't thinking this through. Where was I going to go with the disguise anyway? My erstwhile ally, Nawaz, had checked out, paying dearly for his perfidy, and leaving me short-handed for any outdoor work involving digging, talking to locals, or even finding my way around town. At this juncture Dean Moslehuddin knocked on the hotel room door.

"That was fast!"

"The situation is more dire than perhaps we had expected," he blurted. "A stranger was in your office when I passed the door and I did not recognize two other men waiting down the hall. They seemed, in the vernacular of your television, 'serious men.' I fear that you are a hunted man, Professor Brown."

"And the good news?" I asked through a constricted throat.

"Ah yis. I was able to retrieve the passports without, I believe, attracting suspicious notice. The bank negotiated your check without problem although I did have to talk to the manager and explain that I was your dean and you were incapacitated and in need of the money for medical expenses." He handed over two envelopes.

"Dean Mosleh. You are indeed and literally a life-saver. Assuming, that is, that we survive the next few hours. I want to check with the travel people in the lobby about flights." Tiffany stood to accompany me.

"I do not wish to be seen as too much the nervous Nelson, but allow me to go down and make inquiries. I fear that we are dealing with professionals who may have deduced you would take refuge here."

Dean Mosleh – God love the man – departed for the lobby while Tiffany and I sat in silence. No doubt this was the time for final words, but thoughts of beheadings and skinnings crowded out sentimentality, final jabs, soliloquies on the death of love and other suddenly lower-order concerns. Tiffany broke the silence by turning on the television where Jane Fonda, in leotard and flanked by other buff exercisers, was encouraging us to 'make it burn.'

Mosleh returned within ten minutes. "I was able to book seats on the Thai Airways flight this evening. Regrettably only business class seats were still available. But, of greater import, I believe one of the men I saw in the corridor back at the office is in the lobby, pretending to read a newspaper. We will have to think very carefully how to extricate you."

I'd not been clear about how many seats to book, but the cascade of frightening news was undermining the resolve to continue as a fortune hunter. Khan's warnings about RAW came back and I asked Dean Mosleh his opinion.

"Ah, RAW. A deliberately fear-inducing acronym for an innocuous sounding title, Research and Analysis Wing. Anything is possible, Professor. As you know, when we were fighting to obtain our independence from West Pakistan in 1971 – and doing poorly I must confess – it was the Indian Army that marched in and settled the issue. There has always been, at the highest levels, an unspoken debt of gratitude and India has been allowed more freedom within our borders than perhaps is healthy. That beggars the question, would an official Indian agency such as RAW commit murders in the pursuit of jewels? And what would they do should they find such? Take them back to India for a museum? Or are these Johnnies 'off the clock' – as you would say in your country – by which I mean are they operating in some unofficial capacity for their personal benefit? I believe we should assume that RAW is a professional organization and these men have no current connection with the Indian government."

I was too distracted by my own problems to break this flow. Ask an academician for a simple answer and you get a lecture. Mosleh had started to catalogue previous incidents where RAW involvement had been whispered when I finally interrupted, "By this, I gather you're suggesting extreme caution and, perhaps subterfuge, if we're to gain the airport. Our pursuers are numerous and skilled. And, does their presence in the lobby indicate that you were followed here which now puts you in jeopardy as an accomplice?"

Mosleh jerked upright in his chair; it hadn't occurred to him that his assistance would place him in peril.

"Professor, may I use your telephone?" A woman eventually answered his call. The conversation, in Bangla, was characterized by rising pitch until it reached a crescendo of arm waving and shouting; then suddenly the tone dropped back to almost whispers. The dean was perspiring when he hung up. "Wretched woman. She fails to understand what must be done in such circumstances. We shelter our women from the world and when the world intrudes they are unprepared to respond in an appropriate manner."

"Will she go to ground?" I asked, now deeply concerned that the body count, caused by my naïve and reckless inquiries about buried treasure, was going to mount further.

"Yes, as the smallest possible side-benefit of our chaotic and dangerous history, we have contingency plans to find safety when needed. She is on her way . . ." I held up my hand.

"Mosleh, dear man. Don't tell me anything that you wouldn't want my torturers to discover." Wow! The words filled me with antithetical feelings of heroic purpose and an urgent churning in my bowels. Shifting gears quickly, "Let's focus on getting Tiffany and myself to the airport while disassociating you from all this."

This brought nods of agreement and a grunt from Tiffany who'd been uncharacteristically silent. Was she mulling the implications of suddenly being single?

"My first thought is safety in numbers. Is there a small bus that ferries guests to the airport?"

"I doubt very sincerely, Professor, that these men would hesitate to stop the bus and remove your good self and your wife from the bus. I would also counsel against asking the police to escort you. They are as much to be feared. A few takas would buy their cooperation. I believe the solution here is to leave the hotel without detection. Perhaps there is an exit that is difficult to observe."

On our first stay at the Sonargoan we'd noticed that the employee bus entered and left through a chain-link gate in back. A few service vehicles used the same access point. A ten-foot high hedge obscured the view of anyone getting into or out of these vehicles. I proposed this route to Mosleh, who, despite my avowed intention to get him out of our affairs, was implicitly being asked to aid us further.

"Who can we trust?" he asked. "It is a simple matter for a man of my standing to request this access to the hotel from the manager. But will he share the request with the wrong people? I can also arrange for a service van from any number of sources to collect you and Mrs. Brown and convey you to the airport. About this I feel more secure. But the hotel management, I am not so sure. Perhaps we can accomplish this with a minimum of parties involved."

Another phone call, and he announced that a food service van that made routine deliveries to the hotel would arrive two hours before flight departure and we should be prepared.

Still holding the phone, Mosleh dialed an internal number. After a conversation in Bangla, punctuated by long pauses, he disconnected. "I fear these are practiced men. The travel agent in the lobby informs me that there have been two inquiries about your plans. I regret that one of the men described seems to be none other than our own Professor Singh. I further fear from her hesitation when I put the question to her that she has divulged all. Alas."

Alas, in fucking deed! But wait. Why two different inquiries? Was there a breakdown within RAW, or whoever the opposition was? A small advantage. Or were two different groups chasing us? Not an improvement. Or just double-checking? At this point we were on autopilot, going forward with a flawed plan because we had no other.

If a plan didn't spring to mind, a cliché did: sow confusion.

The daily flight departures from Dhaka International were locked in memory; I'd checked them wistfully in the *Bangladesh Observer* every morning over coffee. "Mosleh, there are two flights leaving at about the same time: Thai Airways to Bangkok and Singapore Airlines to Singapore. You believe that the goons know about our booking to Bangkok. Do you think we could change one of those to the Singapore flight?"

"Perhaps. The travel woman must understand that she has violated a confidence and may be experiencing some feelings of remorse for which we could offer atonement. Let me call her now." Another Bangla phone conversation to the lobby, some of it conducted in threatening tones, at the conclusion of which a smiling Mosleh turned to us.

"The matter is resolved then. I have placed Mrs. Brown on the flight to Singapore. Forgive the male chauvinism, but it is safer in Singapore where they whip one should that unfortunate chew gum or spit on the sidewalk. I believe the fair lady will feel more secure there while you sort out your next moves."

True, provided she's careful about the gum and spitting. "The new ticket will be brought up shortly and the travel woman has vowed most urgently that wild donkeys could not extract this information from her."

Within minutes the agent delivered the revised ticket. She confirmed that her interrogator was still lolling around the lobby and we asked her to remain with us in the room and leave only after the two flights were in the air. She looked around at the luxurious appointments, her eye settling on the television where Jane and her colleagues were cooling down with stretches. Mosleh used the remote to locate a Bangla soap opera that might hold the woman's attention and turned up the sound.

The Righteous Souls that Take their Flight
- George W.A.H. Drummond, 1790

As the sun was setting over the vast misery that's one of the world's poorest and saddest countries, Tiffany, Moslehuddin and I took the service elevator down to the loading area where we pressed ourselves back into the shadows, dislodging two disgruntled pigeons, and waited for the delivery van.

"It's here," whispered Mosleh. A comparatively new Mercedes panel van, its diesel engine clattering, stopped at the loading dock and the side door slid open.

"I'll go first," fully expecting rough hands to grab me as I climbed inside. With head down I walked as nonchalantly as possible the fifteen feet to the van and leaped through the door. Smack into a hanging skinned goat. The van was filled with the corpses of the animals, all swaying gently, each a reminder of Nawaz's fate. "It's okay," I called back, "but the thing is full of dead animals. On the positive side, it lends verisimilitude."

Tiffany followed me, crouching as she came across the drive. She gave the goats a quick look, but made no comment. I'd expected her to refuse to board, followed by an argument which I would eventually win by pointing out that our options were down to this one and we couldn't be picky.

The woman has a great sense of irony. Now that we were splitting, she was behaving like an adult.

I was surprised when Mosleh also boarded. "I'll get out along the way. Given the presence of that man in the lobby I feel safer using this exit and then I can go to my wife and children."

The van left the hotel grounds and joined the crush of bicycle rickshaws, taxis, buses, cars, trucks and limousines inching along in rush hour traffic. Thanks to the high level of petty crime in the country, the doors on the van had serviceable locks which we latched. Tiffany took up a vigil at the back windows to see if she could detect any pursuers, a task complicated by the hundreds of vehicles following us slowly up the airport road.

At an intersection Mosleh suddenly slipped out the side door – we didn't even have a chance to thank him – and disappeared into the throng. I elbowed my way through the goats to the back windows of the van to see if there was any reaction among the vehicles behind us. It seemed not. "Tiff, that's one first class guy." We started to inch forward again, the corpses swaying in unison as we bumped along the uneven road.

"I'm confused, Max. A few hours ago you vowed to pursue the Sultan's booty until the flesh was stripped from your body and your head was displayed in a jar. Now I didn't hear you countermanding any of Dean Mosleh's efforts to spirit us both away. What gives?"

"Second thoughts. The competition is better than I expected. There seem to be a lot of these guys and they're not amateurs. I thought I was just dealing with that fop, Singh. Money isn't everything, right?"

"Okaaay." She scowled. "Then I may be confused on a second point. We seemed to have finally agreed to drive a stake into the heart of our walking dead marriage. What are your current thoughts on that, pray?"

"Ah, Tiff. This is a difficult day. It's hard to focus on relationships and survival at the same time. You know I've envisioned, many times, our departure from Dhaka. Not one of those visions included dead goats or the real prospect of torture and decapitation."

Silence. The goats continued their gentle swaying. Tiffany must have some parting shot she'd been saving for this occasion.

"Okay Max, here's the deal. You go to Bangkok or stay here. Pretty much the same to me. We've beaten up on each other for several years. I don't know what went wrong. Maybe it was wrong from the start (my guess, but this was not the time to conduct an autopsy on our marriage). I was only five courses away from a degree when we left the US. The smart thing would be to clean that up. I'd ask you to send money but I know the state of our finances better than you. We can split up what's in that envelope and both get back to the States."

A blue light flashed several cars back. Corrupt police? Then the flashing stopped. We scanned the traffic; nothing appeared to have changed.

"If I get back to the apartment first, I'll box up your clothes and maps and send them to your parents. Keep in touch, or don't. I suppose I'll always be a little curious about how you land." She chewed on the inside of her cheek. "I assume an American murdered on foreign soil would make the news, should that happen."

We started to turn toward one another, but abruptly shifted our gazes to our traveling companions, the sightless eyes of dead farm animals being easier to look into than each others'.

Dhaka International Airport requires alertness and full attention to navigate; the emotions of the ride evaporated as the van rolled to a stop at the departures terminal. Glancing anxiously in all directions, we went to our separate check-in counters and then passed through immigration together. Again, the immigration agent spent undue time perusing our passports as I expected to be hauled away by a bribed official at any minute.

Despite the feeling of constant menace, I was still considering doubling back down through customs and slipping into the city. But the money for the ticket was gone and I had no plan for what I would do after I left the airport. As we exited the immigration area an agitated man appeared at the far entrance and seemed to be scanning the people in the lines to the immigration booths. Looking for a family member or friend? Not my guess. That clinched it. Pulse pounding in my ears, I opted to get on the flight – if not intercepted first.

"Okay Tiff, hate to rush, but I think company's coming. Your gate's that way, mine the other." We stood in the poorly lit concourse, facing each other for the first time in what seemed like years. Reflexively, I stepped forward and enveloped beautiful Tiffany in my arms. I could feel her convulsing against me.

"Max, please don't misread this. I'm just exhausted . . . spent." Then she pulled away, turned, and walked unsteadily down the dingy concourse. The flickering fluorescent lights played on her, suggesting poetic imagery, although I couldn't put it into words. Other words did come to mind:

Damn! What have I done? That is a fabulous looking woman!

The feeling didn't last. Somewhere in the terminal a RAW thug, with mayhem in mind, was looking for us. I ran to the departure gate and asked to board immediately. My arrival and request were met with indignant glares from the small knot of passengers at the counter, clutching their economy class boarding passes and nursing the wan hope they'd be granted an upgrade.

Thai Airways tries to meet every request, no matter how unjustified or inconvenient – from a business class ticket holder, anyway – and I was ushered on board as the cleaning crew vacuumed and restocked magazines, pillows and blankets. The pretty Thai stewardess offered orange juice and champagne.

When the other passengers began to trickle in she turned her attention to seating them. With my heart still pounding from the dash to the gate I fought the urge to turn and examine every person who boarded, then discovered the little TV screen in the seatback could be tilted to provide a hazy mirrored view of the door.

Question: Does this new lifestyle that keeps one's heart beating at or above its target rate contribute to cardiovascular health? Ah, the irony at the post mortem: "His ticker could go on forever. Too bad he has no head or skin."

When it looked like the last passenger had enplaned, and I resumed breathing normally, the man we'd seen at immigration suddenly appeared at the plane's door, pursued by two shouting ticket agents. There was shoving and tugging as the ticket agents pulled at the man's arms. Three uniformed security guards joined the ticket agents and the thug, now shouting "American assassins" was pulled back into the loading gangway and the flight attendant closed the door, throwing the large lever over into the locked position with reassuring finality. Those in neighboring seats cast uneasy glances my way. Not many Americans on board; which one is the assassin? I concentrated on trying to breathe normally for the next several minutes, with limited success, until the engines had started and the plane pushed back.

As we taxied out Tiffany's flight rolled down the runway. Good. In a surge of affection and concern that had been absent for years, I watched the plane's lights retreat up into the night sky. She'd made it; the thug's use of the plural for assassins meant they still thought Tiff and I were traveling together.

Meanwhile my own Airbus trundled along the taxiway as if the plane was undecided about making the trip. How much time did the thug need to get to the tower and persuade or bribe the controller to order the plane back to the gate? He could be pounding up the steps to the glass-walled control tower already.

Why do these big buses taxi so damnably slow? I knew how fast a plane could taxi. Mentally urging the pilots to step on it – rocking forward and backward in my seat to impart momentum to the plane – I tried to recall the terminal's layout should I be able to break away from my captors when, as seemed increasingly a certainty, the plane turned back to the gate and I was handed over to men with skinning and beheading in mind.

The end of the runway was approaching. The taxiway made a right turn; the familiar double yellow lines that indicated the hold line were just ahead. Engine power came up . . . we were about to enter the runway. And then the plane jerked to a stop as the brakes were abruptly applied. *Unless this is a clearance hold, I'm fucked.* I looked around frantically. Were there sharp knives in the galley I could arm myself with? Would the stewardess give me one? Another mental review of the layout of the terminal; there were emergency exit signs. Where did those lead to?

The engine power came up again and the plane swung out onto the runway.

The flight left Dhaka behind on time, but the accumulated anxieties of the past 24 hours stayed on board. Every bank or change of engine sound was immediately interpreted as a return to face unspeakable horrors. Only when clear of Bangladeshi airspace did my shoulders start to drop back to their normal position and I partook liberally of the complementary drinks on the justification that, at this point, relaxation came ahead of vigilance.

33

I Met Jesus at the Crossroads
- **R. P. Overholtzer (ed.), 1951**

You don't appreciate how anonymous a person feels in Bang-kok until it's important to you. The long immigration lines, throngs milling around baggage turnstiles, queues at the cur-rency exchange counters, the steady flow of impatient passen-gers into taxis. Justified or not, all of this contributes to a sense that one is subsumed by this mass of moving humanity and safe from easy discovery. No doubt that feeling of anonymity is a good thing for the sex tourism trade. Did the Thais plan it?

Installed at a modest ($32/night) hotel, a weepy moment ambushed me. Tiffany. The tears had to be from emotional ex-haustion, right? How could anyone regret the departure of someone who'd made their life miserable for over a decade? Recovering from this embarrassing descent, I located the in-house 'massage' parlor, where, through persistent redirections of the masseuse's efforts, I was able to get her to massage neck and shoulder muscles that had been tensed for 24 hours. Given how unsatisfactory it was you had to wonder whether the woman had ever been called upon to provide an actual massage.

But, what next? I found Terd's phone number and set up a meeting with him the next morning at TIT.

"Max! You look . . . different."

"Ah, just more of the usual. I've accepted it as my lot to be rectally abused by all manner of men. But I haven't been sleep-ing well and find myself at a crossroads."

"A strange coincidence. I too find myself choosing among paths. Our mutual acquaintance, Leung, has invited me to join his enterprise. TIT is less rewarding every day – and no one is here for the money – but you understand that Mr. Leung is not an ordinary businessman and one casts his lot with misgivings."

A strange coincidence indeed. I'd considered approaching Leung but had no idea what to ask or propose. "I understand completely. While I hold a certain admiration for Leung, one does wonder what tasks might be assigned. That aside, I would like to say hello to the gentleman."

Terd dialed his phone and spoke in Thai to a series of intermediaries before the conversation changed from imperious to obsequious. Hanging up, "Leung welcomes you to join us at dinner this evening. I believe it will be just the three of us but do not be surprised if there are others."

Dodging his questions about where I was staying, we set up our rendezvous and I went into the street looking for a change of clothes. Street vendors up and down Sukhumvit hawked two dollar polo shirts and five dollar pants. For under thirty dollars I was provisioned with a dress shirt, pants and sports coat. Then I lay by the hotel's tiny rooftop pool and tried to organize my thoughts.

• My pursuers had shown themselves to be committed and skilled men, despite my limited regard for Singh.

• Let's assume that they didn't behead and torture for sport; therefore it seemed inescapable they believed they were on the trail of something big. That meant I also was on the trail of something big.

• They'd committed resources to finding out what I knew – the ransacked apartment and pursuit – and their continued interest indicated they believed I had valuable information.

• But what did I know? The fair Professor Chowdery made a persuasive case that the Khan wouldn't simply abandon a treasure since he'd made an orderly departure from the country and he had the capacity to haul any number of fortunes back to Shahjahanabad. Then again, Hasina, despite her disavowals, had made slips that suggested she hadn't abandoned the hope that something valuable was still interred at Lalbagh Fort.

• What I knew that others might not, was: a) there was a further testimonial that the Khan had left 'a material treasure' to commemorate his daughter's death; b) an area beneath or behind the servants' building had been cited by two sources as the location of the treasure; and

c) thanks to Hasina's scholarship, I had a pretty good idea where that building had stood.

A second Singha beer and I was asleep by the pool.

The searing pain of a sunburned back awoke me in time to dress – very carefully – for the meeting with Leung and Terd. Cursing the carelessness that leads to self-inflicted harm I arrived at the great outdoor restaurant and scanned the crowd for a slight ethnic Thai professor and a corpulent Chinese 'business' man. A firm hand on a flaming shoulder caused me to jump and cry out. "Please, this way," said a grave-looking heavy who nodded toward the far side of the restaurant. If this wasn't one of Leung's bodyguards, would a sunburn make skinning more or less painful? The chill this thought provoked brought momentary relief from the sunburn.

"Professor Brown. A delightful surprise to find you back amongst us. I hope the trip was not owed to misfortune? So many foreigners residing in Dhaka are rushed here for medical treatment. This trip was not for your health, I hope?"

Making a decision I'd debated for the past 24 hours, "In a very direct way, yes, my departure from Dhaka was prompted by concerns for my health. We can get to that later. But tell me about yourself."

Leung wasn't one to divulge anything useful about himself so the conversation turned to Thai politics – always on the verge of spinning out of control – the state of the economy, the corruption of the current government, speculation on when His Majesty might intervene, and the most recent futile plan to address the city's legendary traffic problems. Terd excused himself, perhaps on a signal, and Leung leaned in toward me, "Now, Professor, you mentioned a health concern?"

"Sir, you are perhaps the only person I feel safe speaking with. Some skillful thugs – perhaps former elements of RAW led by a Sikh named G.I. Singh – have decided I have information that would be useful to them. Three innocent men are dead and I believe I was next on the list."

"And the nature of this information?"

"The whereabouts of the Khan Shaista treasure."

"Most diverting, Professor. We have many such stories in the region. The Lalbagh jewels is one of the most enduring." He chewed his lower lip. "Let me guess. The fact that you are not on your way back to the US and are sharing this with me indicates you have not given up your own quest for the jewels?"

"Undecided. One part thinking out loud; one part hoping you might provide counsel that would help me decide."

"I am flattered, Professor. However I would never advise a man when the stakes are so high, in this case your own dear life. I am also assuming that you are unable to call upon the resources of whomever it is that employs you," knowing smile, "and are operating on your own."

I'd forgotten that Leung believed I worked for an intelligence agency, but no point in disabusing him as his mistake might increase my own capital. "I could not possibly be any more on my own."

"What could a simple businessman do for someone engaged in such pursuits?"

"I'm unsure. Mainly because I haven't decided on a course of action. My one associate was tortured to death although he had little information to offer. I don't see myself recruiting allies in Bangladesh to aid me. The few people I trust, I care about."

"Well, Professor. Some pointers on the practicalities of the situation. Should you return to Dhaka, airport immigration will have been bribed to notify the competition of your arrival. I doubt you would have more than an hour's head start, assuming you are not detained at the airport for collection by the other side. Your options are to arrive overland or by air under another identity. The latter is the more practical, although slightly more hazardous if your picture has been shown around the airport. If you do not already have documents for alternate identities, there are two shops on Soi 55 that do a decent job that would fool Bangladeshi immigration.

"Regarding manpower, there is a man I have worked with before who lives in Chittagong. Typically he works on commission and I would not allow him too much time to think about his own options; he may choose to take all rather than the agreed upon percentage. Perhaps he will value my continued business over the quick kill – sorry, poor choice of words."

Terd approached and our earlier conversation resumed as if there had been no interruption. As we broke up two hours later Leung clasped my hand, "My card. Not a direct line, of course, but if the person who answers is persuaded you can speak openly he will connect us." The card purported to advertise for a car rental agency. Leung limited his exposure.

I Will Change Your Name
- D. J. Butler, 1987

There were several shops on Soi 55 that immodestly professed to no less than absolute wizardry when it came to producing printed documents. After going into several that appeared to specialize in T-shirts and office supplies, I entered a shop that displayed few products. The passage between the front and back of the shop was a solid-looking closed door with two deadbolts, unlike the cloth curtains that separated the two rooms else-where. "May I be of assistance?" from a disembodied voice, which ultimately took form as an old man rose from a mat on the floor behind the counter.

"Perhaps. I've suffered an inconvenient loss. My documents were destroyed in a minor accident – the result of smoking while drowsy. I'm told that it will require considerable time to replace them and I was hoping to resume travel immediately."

The old man studied me for a moment, and then asked, "Is sir perhaps Canadian? At present we are only able to facilitate replacement travel documents for men from that country."

Some poor Canuck was, at that moment, patting down his pockets and beginning a panicked search for his passport.

"What marvelous luck! Yes, a proud denizen of Vancouver, the pearl of the Pacific." *Steady, Max. No need to oversell this guy.* "What would be the price and how soon could you de-liver?"

"Owing to ever-rising costs, we are currently obliged to charge four hundred US dollars. In advance." Noting my alarm, he continued, "Sir can weigh that against the inconvenience of waiting while the official wheels slowly turn. I must also advise sir that there will be minor changes in sir's name and personal details." Would I wind up with the passport of an eighty year old named Rama Lama Dingdong? Pleading that I had only half the amount with me, the forger accepted the cash, took my picture, and promised delivery within 24 hours.

———————

To my pleasant surprise, upon presentation of another two hundred dollars, I received a well-used Canadian passport issued to Randall S. Goodwell, a sojourner five years my elder and currently absent from his home in Ottawa. Presumably the name had been altered should the passport be on a watch list and the five years were no problem. Whose appearance doesn't age at least that much on international flights?

When I returned to the hotel, reception produced an envelope containing a name and phone number which I recognized as a Chittagong exchange. Leung had tracked me down. Impressive, and unnerving.

So much for relaxing in anonymity. Was Leung, in using this method of communicating with me, sending notice of how vulnerable I was? Of course he was. Without further analysis of the options, I booked on the early evening flight back to Dhaka.

34

I was reconsidering those options as the plane began its descent. Daniel's situation in the lions' den seemed far better than mine. No plan; no support aside from an unreliable crook in Chittagong; an unknown number of professional adversaries; and, unlike Daniel, no expectation that the Almighty would overlook a lifetime of taunts and blasphemy and pull my chestnuts out of the fire at the critical moment.

Aside from mounting panic, the sight and smell of Dhaka brought back the same emotions as before and I was acutely conscious of Tiffany's absence as I went through immigration and customs. Add depressed to scared shitless.

I directed the taxi driver back to our old apartment on the thin logic that this would be unanticipated by the opposition. And it was cheaper; money was running low. The building seemed even darker and grimmer than before and, leaving the lights off, I negotiated the uneven steps with difficulty. I'd taken the pistol out of the checked bag – why had I not bought more ammo in Bangkok? – and pushed the door open. No evidence of a surprise party or further examination of our humble belongings. I wedged those pieces of furniture I was able to move in front of the door and took stock.

The ransackers had been thoughtful enough to close the refrigerator door, and, blocking its small light as best I could, I extracted a beer and cold cuts. After an unsatisfying meal, I called Leung's contact in Chittagong who said he would take the night train to Dhaka and we could meet at 6 AM in the station's cafeteria. He would wear a bright red shirt.

The mattress required multiple sheets to cover the slashes made by our night visitors, and two pillow cases held a pillow together. The night passed slowly. Tiffany's scent was all over the bed. Sinking lower, I sniffled into the pillow. Missing her? Or scared shitless?

––––––

Even in the pre-dawn hours, the train station was packed and the cafeteria unapproachable. Just as well; best not to be tempted by any of the toxic foodstuffs available. I was trying to make myself invisible by crouching below the shifting sea of humanity when raw nerves and a raw back caused me to jump as a hand was placed on my shoulder. A thick voice asked, "Mr. Randall? Friend of Leung?" Expecting serious muscle, it was a surprise to find my new collaborator was short, bald and long past his fighting prime. "I am Kamal."

Waving an ID card at guards, Kamal secured the use of a small room in the station. "Best to get out of sight. You are be-having in a very suspicious way. Someone, maybe police, per-haps will notice and make inquiry." Further evidence, should any be required, that I was ill-suited to cloak and dagger work. "Please tell me what services I may provide your good self?"

Deciding that Kamal's loyalty might be strengthened if he believed Leung and I were partners, I explained that we had in-formation on the whereabouts of something of value, but that it needed to be dug out of the ground and the digging had to be performed clandestinely. While my motives were driven purely by academic scholarship – the artifact would be spirited away to a museum in Canada for display to the general public – our management was well aware of the obstacles that could be erected should government officials become involved.

"If you are knowing the precise location we should dig dur-ing the daytime as I can convince whatever minor official is present to leave us in peace for a few hours. Longer than that . . . ?"

"I wish I could be precise, Kamal, but the area is at least 20 square meters and the depth of the artifact is unknown." I had guessed a cesspit might be 1 – 2 meters in depth, but had no idea whether the ground had subsided over the centuries, or been built up. "It could be buried anywhere between one and three meters deep."

Kamal reflected on this information and, applying his knowledge of local soil and the rate at which a Bangladeshi la-borer could dig, announced, "If two meters below ground, we want five men for six hours." This seemed an unsatisfactory solution and he thought some more. "Is the object you seek made of metal? I can procure a metal detector which would ac-celerate our work?"

I began to see Kamal in a new light. "An interesting idea. I do understand, however, that the range of these devices is limited."

"I am unfamiliar with the technical specifications, but, as you are saying, such instruments will not find objects that are buried deeply. I can report, however, that I witnessed the use of such an instrument on a Chittagong beach and it located many pieces of metal buried under the sand. I have access to that instrument and I believe my son could bring it to us this very evening."

"An excellent suggestion. An important detail, sir. We should establish your expectations regarding remuneration. Mr. Leung led me to believe that you prefer to work on a percentage of the take."

"I do, but I am unsure what the 'take' would be, as you say your objective is scientific and not for money. Not to be whimsical, but I would not want to be paid in museum passes. I am confident, however, that your partner will compensate me fairly." I assumed Kamal saw through the 'academic scholarship' bullshit simply on the strength of Leung's participation. Whatever fine qualities Leung might possess, it seemed unlikely he was a patron of Canadian museums. "While we are waiting for my son, perhaps we should examine the area?"

We Are Here to Gather Jewels
- T. C. Neal, 1898

Kamal made a phone call to his son, then found a taxi with heavily tinted windows. When I told him our destination was Lalbagh Fort he was visibly dismayed, his confidence in our prospects diminished. When we got to the fort *I* was dismayed to see mounds of fresh dirt that signaled recent excavation. Crowning this unwelcome news, two director's chairs were placed by the dig under a large umbrella. In the chairs, supervising the work, lounged my old colleagues, Singh and the ravishing Dr. Chowdery.

"Your expression tells me there is a problem, Mr. Randall. Does the presence of the other diggers signify that we have been pipped?"

"No, Kamal, it does not. They're digging in the wrong place. However, their presence does create access problems." That goddamned Chowdery! Why are the most beautiful women always the most trouble?

"We will wait for an opportunity, then, Mr. Randall. Have faith in Allah." We watched the excavation from the distant taxi. Five men, one of whom looked familiar although I couldn't place him – the airport? – rotated use of three spades. A cry of discovery would alarm us and Singh and Chowdery would rush to examine the find. Then our spirits would recover when our two competitors plodded back to their chairs. Kamal kept us supplied with water and food; I tried unsuccessfully to nap in the sweltering backseat of the taxi to stem the encroaching fatigue.

———————

Nightfall brought a suspension of digging, but it also brought a guard; one of the five diggers remained when Chowdery and Singh departed.

Kamal's son, Hamad, arrived with a spade and a well-used metal detector which he tested with coins scattered on the ground. The apparatus emitted a small shriek when within two meters of a coin. Then we returned to the taxi; the driver seemed content to run up the clock indefinitely. Two hours after sunset the guard abruptly left his station, perhaps in search of food, and, after waiting a few minutes we tumbled out of the cab. I paced off the 41 meters in a north-northeast direction and waved my hand over the area of interest. Hamad instantly and silently went to work, methodically moving back and forth over the area. The machine would chirp and Hamad would take the shovel and unearth a can or trinket while his father took over the scanning duties.

We'd covered no more than half the area when Kamal pulled on my sleeve; the guard was returning. We fell back toward a ramshackle building and I worried whether we'd done an adequate job covering up the few holes we'd dug. The guard settled into one of the director's chairs and, tired after digging in the heat all day, his head began to nod, then sank forward onto his chest.

Hamad wrapped a handkerchief around the handle of the metal detector to muffle the alerts, and cautiously resumed the scan. After an hour he stopped and worked the detector back and forth over one spot. Placing the machine on the ground to mark the location, he summoned us. "Weak signal. Maybe little piece or maybe big piece down deep."

I took the first turn with the shovel. The signs were good. The deeper we dug, the louder the machine chirped when we checked our progress. These tests were conducted with 'bated breath. At the squawk of the detector we would all turn toward the dozing guard. At one meter down we suspended further testing and dug on, sweat pouring off us. Hamad was the hardiest, but he needed to be spelled. Kamal was ineffective with the shovel and I resented that he insisted on digging as he seemed to spill as much dirt back into the hole as he removed – and used up our limited remaining allotment of darkness.

It was Hamad who struck pay dirt with a clank that sent our heads swiveling toward the guard. Kamal pulled out a penlight and ran its small beam over the bottom of the pit. Hamad scratched away with his hands and pulled up two metal bands that could easily have been on a strong box. There would be no intact strong box, I realized; buried wood could not have survived three centuries.

"Wait," said Kamal to his son. "Allow the representative from the museum to be the finder of that which he seeks." Hamad, reluctantly it seemed, came out of the hole and I slid down the side into it. I should drop onto my knees and scrabble at the dirt, but I wondered whether Kamal's invitation was a prelude to braining me with the shovel while I was distracted. Add buried alive to skinned alive among my mortal concerns. Would the 'quick kill' Leung had mentioned actually be a slow one?

Accepting Kamal's earlier advice, I placed my fate in the hands of Allah and dug tentatively, holding the penlight in my teeth, although alert to any unusual movement above. Another metal band. More dirt. And then a coin. And another. And several smooth polished stones, each with multiple flat surfaces, that – if I allowed my hopes full scope – were jewels. Shoving these into my pockets I continued scratching, finding more coins and polished stones. I was digging feverishly when the shovel tapped my shoulder and Kamal whispered, "Guard moving. Maybe waking up." I was tempted to take on the guard in order to complete the search. I had three bullets. What did he have? Probably a lot more, plus the unfair advantage of being able to aim accurately. And any commotion, much less gunfire, would attract spectators. I climbed out of the hole and the three of us retreated to the taxi.

"We should fill the hole or our work will be discovered in the morning." My two companions looked at me as if I'd lost my marbles. Take the money and run was their credo.

"If it is important to keep the finding a secret, we will wait to see if the guard sleeps again." As bad luck would have it – and, in fairness, our luck had been pretty good to that point – the guard was fully refreshed by his nap and remained alert, occasionally patrolling the area and stopping once to examine our excavation. The call to fajr prayer signaled it would soon be light and Kamal asked to be taken back to the train station.

As we drove, we examined our haul with growing excitement. These were large red, green and clear jewels. Seven red, two green and six clear.

"It appears that the great Khan left rubies, emeralds and diamonds," announced Kamal.

The four small gold coins had rudimentary engravings stamped on them. "No faces?" I wondered aloud.

"It was long a violation of Muslim laws to depict the human form." Turning to the practical, "And where will you be going Mr. Randall, now that your mission is accomplished?"

"To Bangkok to celebrate with Leung, of course."

Sanctuary
- J. B. Dykes, 1871

Traffic, never fast, was almost at a standstill and it took over an hour to deliver Kamal and Hamad to the train station. Where to for me? I had one gun, two passports, three bullets, four gold coins, and fifteen gems. There were no flights for several hours and I needed to stay out of sight so I asked the groggy driver to take me back to my apartment.

I also needed to lie down. Euphoria competed with exhaustion and fear; alertness was a distant fourth. Despite that, a self-preserving instinct kicked in at the last minute and I instructed the driver to pull into a driveway 200 meters from the building Tiff and I had despairingly called home. A car was sitting in front of the building – a first, as best as I could recall – and a trail of exhaust indicated the motor was running. "I'm blown," I announced with resignation to the disinterested driver. Chowdery and Singh had discovered our night's work and alarms were going off. Where to find sanctuary? "Drive," I instructed. A moving target is harder to hit? It wasn't reassuring that my tactical decisions were based on clichés and aphorisms.

The driver, who'd been on duty for almost thirty hours, was becoming increasingly erratic. We rolled through an intersection to the accompaniment of blaring horns as a truck and bus swerved to miss us.

I had to wonder about my own state. Eyes bright with pain in the harsh mid-morning light, I stared uncomprehendingly at the forest of signs in Bangla. In the distance a blue and white sign announced the presence of a UNFPA Godown to the left. Any port in a storm. Another cliché substituting for thought. In the unlikelihood that Singh's goons would be checking the UN's family planning warehouses, I directed the driver down the alley until we came to a gate and guard house.

"Your business?" asked the guard.

"Yes. Mr. Goodwell of the Canadian Embassy. Just a quick look around, if I may?" Unshaven and covered in dirt, I was no credit to Canada and the guard looked unconvinced.

"I call godown manager." And he retreated into the hut to seek guidance from his superior. At length he emerged. "You talk Mr. Hasan building 1." The taxi driver put the car in gear. "Taxi wallah not go." The driver didn't object to this. I got out and handed him 800 takas, more than Kamal had negotiated, and my conveyance retreated up the narrow alley.

Mr. Hasan was a well-presented UN local employee. He eyed me with clear misgivings.

"Sorry to look so rough. Been conducting site visits of our agricultural projects and thought I would try to cross one more off the list before returning to the Embassy. I know the Yanks put up most of the wherewithal for the products here, but we Canadians do chip in a few of our under-valued dollars, you know." Big smile, which apparently didn't sell the act.

Looking again at my dirt encrusted trousers, he finally decided he had little to risk by playing along, "What would you like to see Mr. Goodwell? Only contraceptives here and that can't be too exciting."

"I suppose so. Ah, but I don't mean to demean. Worth a look-see, don't you think? The Canadian taxpayer can be assured his money is well-invested and well-protected?" With a shrug, Hasan lifted a ring of keys off a hook and led me toward the large modern warehouse that was out of place in the neighborhood.

"Please advise your taxpayers that our security arrangements are light. Contraceptives have low commercial value as the government hands them out for free and the private sector products are so heavily subsidized that it comes to almost the same thing. I suppose it would be a good thing if the criminals were to steal contraceptives. Those are the people we most hope will not reproduce, don't you agree Mr. Goodwell?" I was slow to realize this was family-planning humor and forced a belated chuckle.

Wresting the door open he admitted us to a spotless warehouse 60 feet long, 30 feet wide and a roof at least 20 feet above us. He threw a switch next to the door and the building was flooded with light. "As you can see, the products are neatly arranged. The most recently arrived products are placed at the back of the shelves to reduce the likelihood that something might not be distributed before it passes its expiration date. We call that first-in, first-out, or FIFO." He then launched into a discussion of the expiration dates of different contraceptive pills, the injectable, "even the lowly rubber is not immortal," he confided. Before I could coax a cogent interjection from my tired mind, he picked up again, this time on temperature and humidity control.

I finally rallied to blurt during one of the infrequent pauses, "I gather you don't receive many visitors here then, Mr. Hasan." Stupid. He reddened with embarrassment.

"My mistake, Mr. Goodwell. I should have understood you did not want to get into so much depth. Assure your Embassy we are taking good care of the contraceptives and UNFPA is grateful for every Canadian loonie we receive."

Had my behavior been that bizarre? I shot him a sharp look, considered protesting the insult, but his statement was clearly a farewell and I had nowhere to go. "Mr. Hasan, I'd no intention of being flippant and you've been most generous with your time and information. In my defense I've been traveling all night from the rural areas and am not myself. Could I impose upon you to use your phone, perhaps sit in your office and cool down?"

"Of course, Mr. Goodwell. You may wish to wash up, as well." After a wash, cold drink, and two of Hasan's proffered biscuits, I sank into an over-stuffed chair in his office. He excused himself to run a short errand. I dialed Thai Airways without success and, replacing the phone in its cradle, was immediately asleep.

———————

The last rays of sunshine were slanting through the windows as I awoke with difficulty and checked the clock on Hasan's desk; at least five hours had passed. The office was empty, but there was movement outside. A quick inventory of my pockets confirmed the gun, passports and gems were still there. Groggy, I was preparing excuses for over-staying my welcome as I opened the door and found Hasan talking with a large man who looked vaguely familiar. If I couldn't place his face, I was certain of his disposition: terminally unfriendly.

35

USAF Small Arms Expert Marksmanship Ribbon

"Mr. Goodwell, if that is your name, you are an imposter, unless you can prove me wrong." I was framing a protest when Hasan continued. "My suspicions were aroused when you failed to recognize that loonie is the popular term for the newly released Canadian dollar coin. I was disposed to put that aside, but I was concerned for your state – since I could not wake you – and I called the Canadian Embassy. They have no knowledge of a Mr. Goodwell on their staff. I did find an identity card in your wallet for Dhaka University and I called the indicated department to see if they could identify a Mr. Brown. They dispatched this gentleman who will take responsibility for you now." In the midst of a king-sized catastrophe, a very small blessing: apparently Hasan had begun and ended his search with my wallet.

The unfriendly gentleman motioned me back into the office. "You make much trouble," as he scanned me with an appraising look. I had to guess he was surprised that anyone so unthreatening could cause so much inconvenience.

Hasan followed us into the office, where, fatally, his UN bureaucratic tendencies kicked in. "Before you depart with Mr. Goodwell – or Brown – could I ask to see identification? You know, insofar as there seems to be some uncertainty about who he is, to protect myself I need to know who's taking responsibility for him."

The thug, who'd been holding my arm in a tight grip, responded to Hasan's request by grabbing the UN official around the neck, either to strangle the man or break his neck. In the struggle they fell into the office and I ran through the door, slamming it shut behind me. The exit gate, thirty meters away, appeared locked and there was a car approaching. The warehouse looked like the safest bet – a warren of narrow aisles, shelves and packing crates. The door was unlocked and I slipped in, latching the insubstantial catch behind me. The best concealment seemed to be on a bottom shelf behind cases of

Depoprovera, which, the label promised, provided 90 days of worry-free protection against unwanted pregnancy.

Conflicting thoughts. I had a gun. I could have shot the thug who apparently had decided to silence a witness – probably not for the first time. But I was still waking up, groggy, and taken by surprise. And Hasan had sold me out. But, a logical thing for him to do, given the circumstances. And why was nothing happening? It was getting darker and, aside from a murmured conversation a while back, nothing. No pursuit, no breaking down the door. Were they waiting for cover of darkness? Reinforcements? An order from the top? Should I bolt? With whom would the gate guard side? If he was still alive. I hadn't seen a weapon on him.

Be Thou My Vision
- M. E. Byrne, E. Hull, 1912

Night arrives abruptly in the tropics and it was soon dark; skylights admitted only enough light to make out the aisles. My legs were starting to ache from the balled up position I'd assumed behind the cartons – who would have expected the pursuers to wait so long? – and I was crawling out of my hiding place when the warehouse door crashed inward. Silhouetted against the yard lights the thug peered into the warehouse. A perfect opportunity to shoot him but the pistol was inaccessible, deep in a pants pocket. He stepped into the shadows as I crawled backward toward my lair.

Behind the 90 day injectable contraceptives again, I eased the gun from my pocket and wondered if one of the three bullets was chambered to shoot. Opening and closing the cylinder to check would be audible in the echoing warehouse.

Footsteps approached, and then retreated. It sounded like the thug was methodically going up and down the aisles. After every few steps, boxes could be heard tumbling out onto the floor. It was a matter of time. When the footsteps seemed to have reached the far end of the warehouse I crept forward again and moved noiselessly to the door. Picking up a small carton, I threw it toward the far ceiling. As it clattered about among the rafters I shielded my eyes and threw the light switch. Even through closed and covered eyes the light was intense. I turned the switch off and determined to track down my blinded quarry.

Beside me a carton of condoms exploded, the impact followed by the spit of a silencer.

Revised plan: Maybe I should let him come to me. Although his night vision wouldn't return for several minutes, this seemed to be a person who took the initiative, whether he could see what he was doing or not. Too bad about the silencer. Unmuffled gunshots might have brought help.

Falling to all fours I crept away from the door. Almost immediately there were footsteps coming my way but they seemed to be in the next aisle over. The steps stopped. Lying on my side and peering under the bottom shelf I could make out legs which stood opposite me. If I could take out his ankles, that would be a good start, but they weren't a large target.

Stabilizing the pistol by resting my hand on the floor I slowly applied pressure to the trigger. Even with the back of my hand against the floor, the more I tried to steady the gun the more the barrel danced. *Don't jerk the trigger, Max . . . just maintain steady pressure . . . a little more pressure . . . don't jerk the trigger . . . don't anticipate recoil . . . keep squeezing . . . keep squeezing . . .*

Click. An empty fucking chamber! All around glass shards cascaded down as the thug fired twice in the general direction of the small sound. Apparently some contraceptive is kept in glass vials. And, apparently, the goon hadn't recognized the click for what it was as his legs hadn't moved. I could hear him breathing. Could he hear me?

Second chance. *Hold breath . . . aim carefully . . . try to keep hand steady . . . banish thoughts about what a terrible marksman I am. I squeezed again. Slowly . . . don't jerk the trigger . . . don't anticipate the kick . . . maintain that steady pressure . . . Click.*

Sonuvabitch, God! How about a little cooperation here? Another shot from the goon's gun and more raining glass. How much contraceptive drug was I coated with? Would I ever get another erection?

The fireworks had accomplished one thing; there was an unobstructed view of my adversary's torso through the shelves. At two meters, even I could hit the bullseye. Aim . . . squeeze . . . the blast reverberated off the metal walls of the warehouse. The thug flew backward and collapsed on the boxes behind him.

No time for celebrations. Crouching low I slid out the door, pistol held in two hands at eye level, TV cop style. Should I check on Hasan? Hell no. He was dead and I hoped to remain alive.

From the door of the warehouse I moved around the perimeter of the loading area to stay in shadow. Stealthily across the crunching gravel to the gate.

Guard? No guard . . .

Pull at the gate here. Doesn't move . . .

Is it locked? Can't see a lock . . .

Stuck? Pull it there. No . . .

Search for a latch. Ah, here it is . . .

Raise the latch, push the gate. No, it opens inward . . .

Pull the gate. Slip out into the alley.

Take a breath. Relax.

"Good evening, Professor Brown."

Ah fuck! Singh.

36

"I must say, Maxwell. You are a most tiresome person. And now you seem to have shot one of my lieutenants." His face betrayed no emotion. "We have business to conduct. First, however, will you do the courtesy of dropping your weapon." Singh held an intimidating automatic, leveled at my chest. Apparently I gave no sign of recognition. "Your gun. The metal thing dangling limply from your right hand?" I dropped the revolver. "Back to the warehouse, please. Perhaps your shot was not fatal." Singh picked up the pistol and prodded me with his own gun back across the gravel to the warehouse door.

"Patel. It's me, G.I. Don't shoot." He threw the light switch. Patel's dead eyes were fixed on the wall above our heads, the wound in his chest visible from the doorway. Again, Singh's expression didn't change. "A tragic loss. My colleague knew the risks in our profession; nevertheless I cannot help but hold you accountable for his death. I will mourn later; for now I propose we take a ride together. We have many things to discuss."

Mourn? He seemed to be enjoying himself.

Nearer My God to Thee
- S. F. Adams, 1841

There was no car by the gate; Singh must have read my thoughts. "I sent my car back. It would be too easy to recognize and now that there are two bodies here, one, inconveniently, a UN official, there will certainly be inquiries. You will note, however, that the UN has several vehicles over there and I brought the keys from the office." He shepherded me back through the door. "At some point even Dhaka's lackadaisical police will respond to a report of gunfire. Shall we go?" Three new Land Cruisers were parked in the yard, white with the large blue UN on the sides, tailgate and roof. Where would the Toyota company be today were it not for UN agencies? Singh tried the keys and found they unlocked the second car.

"Ah, Professor, I was wondering about this. I shall have to ask you to drive. I note the vehicle has a manual transmission with which I am less familiar and I don't have material to secure you. I will be more comfortable sitting beside you with the gun trained at your ear hole. All aboard?"

Singh let himself in the passenger side and then handed me the keys. I reflexively clicked the seat belt and shoulder harness and noticed that Singh did not. His face was just visible in the left corner of the rearview mirror; he didn't seem to notice that I could watch him.

The big diesel started noisily and we inched out into the alley. No desire to hurry.

"I will direct you. Please turn right at the intersection." Singh sat back without lowering the gun. "Now, let us share our stories. Me first, although you should feel free to jump in when you have something important to add.

"We uncovered the evidence of your night's enterprises and are dying to know what you discovered. Before I left in search of you our diggers had uncovered a gold coin and three rubies which I will show to you when we reach our destination. At the very least I owe you a view of that which is costing you so dearly." He stopped to see how I would interpret his statement. Not well.

"Ms. Chowdery phoned me later at the University to say they had uncovered another gold coin but that seems to be the sum of it at that location. Tell me, Maxwell, did you fare better? I believe a wealthy khan would not bury so little. What's the point? But I am rambling on. What concerns you, dear Max? I will wager your thoughts are much occupied with your eventual fate this evening, are they not?"

The miserable fucker really was enjoying this. Of course I was preoccupied with my 'eventual fate.' I cast him a sidelong glance. "Well, I will dispel what uncertainty that I can, but I confess I do not know completely how things will play out. I should tell you, however, that we will soon meet with the brother of the man you killed in the godown. The two men were very close, I'm told."

Singh sat back to allow this to sink in. Sink in it did and I clenched the steering wheel tighter to conceal the tremble in my hands. Meanwhile we moved along slowly toward the north. If we got to an open road and picked up speed, I might try crashing the car in the hope that I would fare better than my passenger.

Singh apparently felt he'd allowed enough time for me to digest the latest information. "Yes, Max. A quiet location where we can have a good chin wag. Two scholars, discussing archeology. That's what I have in mind. If your memory fails, my research assistants, as I like to call them, can assist you in recalling the most minute details. I look forward to a long and informative discussion. I can hardly wait to get started. Same for you?"

I realized what he was doing. I'd assumed he was prattling on because he was a miserable pompous little fuck. Maybe he was, but he was also artfully undermining my resistance. Without talking directly about skinning or beheading he allowed me to fill in the blanks about the immediate prospect of a prolonged and unpleasant end to my life, and he'd done it in a way that was more compelling than if he'd made threats that I would have defiantly closed off. A shudder rippled through me which Singh could not have missed. Traffic came to a halt. Could I get out the door and into the crowd before he fired? I regretted fastening the seatbelt. We inched forward again.

One of the less agreeable experiences the Air Force serves up to pilots is Survival School. I had the pleasure of attending one of the final sessions conducted at Stead AFB near Reno. It started with survival training. The instructors dropped you and your group off in the Sierra Nevadas with a live rabbit – we let ours go – and then tried to catch you. After hide-and-seek was over the real business began: resistance training. The motto of the 336th Training Group, which ran the show, was 'Return with Honor.' With sights firmly set on the last war (Korea), the Air Force didn't want to see any more GIs confessing to US atrocities on videotape. Apparently the purpose of the training – which included being locked up in small boxes, sleep deprivation, stress positions – was to inoculate us against brainwashing by giving us a diluted taste of what to expect once in the enemy's hands. For me it was pointless; I'd decided much earlier that honor was a distant runner-up to prolonging life and avoiding serious discomfort. (*Remember What's Important.*) I was going to tell Singh anything he wanted to know.

If there were any vanity in Singh – and the evidence all pointed to there being lots of it – it might be possible to change the course of the discussion. "Singh, if I might have the floor briefly?" He beamed and nodded acknowledgement. "There's been talk in the University of your possible association with RAW, mostly encouraged by hints that you yourself had dropped. These were discounted by our colleagues – and I mean no disrespect here as you know my hand is not a strong one – they felt . . . how to put this delicately . . . that a RAW agent would be more discreet and perhaps . . . more intelligent?"

If he's going to shoot me, this would be a good time.

The reaction was volcanic. "What the deuce are you telling? What is it that you are telling?" The questions shouted. "You will not inform anything, that is certain, but you will understand that I was one of RAW's most promising agents in East Bengal." He started waving the pistol menacingly to punctuate his statements; not an escape opportunity since it remained pointed at my head. "I was destined to be Head of Station when a misguided decision in Delhi decommissioned the office here and six of us were suddenly without regular work." He paused for breath. "So, who are these colleagues who deny my intelligence? Not that idiot Moslehuddin! Not Yunus who drools when he talks. You are baiting me Brown. There is no one. I am the one with the jewels and the gold coin and if there is more treasure I believe you will be only too willing to tell me where it is located."

"In my defense," trying to sound as if I were reluctantly yielding to a superior argument, "I wasn't persuaded by that talk, and to give you full due, you got me to witness Rahman's death and read the threatening note; you tracked us to the hotel; you found me at the UN godown; and you have recovered the treasure (the negligible leavings not in my pocket). As a layman, I'm impressed." Singh appeared to be collecting himself; he stroked his beard.

I paused to signify a redirection of the conversation, "How long has it been since you and your friends worked for RAW?" I asked as if this were no more than cocktail party chitchat. Singh fell in and answered.

"Twelve years, 1974. Delhi instructed me to obtain a copy of the Defense Ministry's annual budget. Can you imagine a more trivial assignment? A five year old could do as much, with all the leaks. And why bother? Dhaka had no defense. We in India were still footing the bill so what was the mystery? That assignment was an insult, I tell you truthfully. We resigned and we have never had contact with them, although I think one of the boys may have done a small job later."

Okay. We'd gotten away from veiled threats of unspeakable torture; how to maintain that? "You seem to miss it Singh; was it that rewarding?"

"Of course. But you're a sociologist, so you will be expecting a treatise on the lonely and noble calling of a spy who, without public recognition, defends his country against threats that the public chooses not to know about. It's like any job, so-ciologist Max. Mostly dull. But there was a bond I miss. It was like an international fraternity. We competed with the other national agencies, but we also traded favors. The Americans, of course, but also the British and French. There was even a bloke in Pakistan's ISI with whom I would barter small bits of information. A strange world, isn't it Maxwell, where he would rather come to me, an Indian, for help than to his fellow Paks in the FIA?" Singh's voice had become soft.

"I still keep in touch with some of the men back in Delhi. They do me the odd favor when I need information. But the higher-ups? Men of no vision other than their own ascendance within the organization. They believe themselves Brahmins but I tell you earnestly, I would rather be a Dalit than a Brahmin of that stripe!"

His eyes lost focus and I debated whether this was an opportunity – the last – to grab for the gun. Thought about it too long; Singh snapped back to full alertness and sighted down the barrel the short eighteen inches to my left temple; he was back on the job.

"Could you give me a general idea of where we're going? It's difficult to change lanes in this traffic and I confess my driving skills are both rusty and unaccustomed to driving on the wrong side of the road, as they say in America."

"Out past the airport. Just watch for the signs. One of the vestiges of our RAW days is a safe-house. Strangely, it is now visited mostly by foreigners who picnic there on Fridays. I believe that is because the locals stay away from the place and leave the foreigners alone. The house still has a bit of a reputation among the folk in that area.

"But yis. Going back to your earlier remark, thank you for acknowledging what is obvious. We have not lost the touch. For example, perhaps you did not know that we are aware that your pretty wife went to Singapore while you went to Bangkok." My hands tensed on the steering wheel.

"No, Maxwell, I have no intention of harming her. Firstly, it is our code – rarely violated – to leave family members out of it. Secondly, Singapore presents special challenges so one must weigh the potential benefits against the costs. And thirdly, she would know nothing that you do not know. And you are here." Back to the specter of torture.

Traffic opened up slightly and our speed increased to 30 kph, not enough for a crash to have any effect on the car's occupants. I focused on controlling the shudders and trembling that increasingly threatened to overcome me. "Tell me, Singh, since we're sharing confidences, at what point did you enlist the lovely Dr. Chowdery?"

"Never. She is but a pawn. She had some small information about the archeological site but that was known to me several days ago. I believed her presence was important when we started digging. Officials at Lalbagh Fort will find a classical history professor more credible when it comes to permits, and when she leans forward they will be convinced." I joined Singh in a smile at the thought of Hasina favoring the officials with a glimpse of her cavernous cleavage. "She is a practical woman, Brown. She talks aggressively, but she understands the realities of the world. For a very small percentage, and guarantee of her safety, she will make no claims on any treasure, and forget it was ever found."

Singh was a pro in at least some regards. He never lowered the pistol, and after the one wistful moment when recalling his salad days as a spy, he didn't allow himself to be distracted. But the pistol looked heavy. At some point would he want to change hands? Perhaps a second opportunity, and there would be few more of those.

"Could you tell me who betrayed me at the Department?"

"Why, no one betrayed you, Maxwell. When the UN facto-tum called, Mr. Khan took the message. You had disappeared for four days and he was concerned. News of a disheveled and confused man answering to your description and with your cre-dentials was a source of relief, and may I say joy, to the good Mr. Khan. Only with difficulty was I able to convince him that I should investigate whilst he stayed by the telephone."

"Not to advise you on your business, Singh, but doesn't it concern you that several people know that you went to pick me up?"

"Ah, Maxwell, Maxwell. You underestimate our attention to detail. Patel arrived before me and had already killed the UN person and you were hiding somewhere – we thought probably in the godown. When I arrived I simply called back to the uni-versity to report that things seemed normal, there was no sign of you, and I was going home. Khan was disappointed to hear this, of course. Now, even as we speak, one of my colleagues is tidy-ing things up at the godown. Perhaps he will concoct a montage that indicates the UN official surprised someone in the act of thievery and both died."

From what I'd heard of the crime-solving prowess of the po-lice, this simple story would suffice and my disappearance would never be explained or pinned on Singh.

"It would be convenient to leave your body at the site as well, but unfortunately I doubt we will be finished with you in time to place it before the crimes are discovered. Unless you want to move things along, Brown? It would be a help to me."

A smug grin accompanied the last. Did this guy actually hate me?

"Now, as far as any connection between you and me? There might be surmising, but this is a country that thrives on conspir-acy talk. There is, I believe, no evidence that you are in Bangla-desh aside from a report from a now deceased UN official that a man with two identities was in his office. No body will be found. At least not a recognizable one." He paused, perhaps relishing the image?

"How did you return undetected, Brown? Not through the airport, if my contacts there are to be trusted." I swerved the Land Cruiser to miss a Bajaj that had abruptly switched lanes in front of us.

"Slight of hand, Singh. Now you see me; now you don't." That only served to make him clench the pistol more securely. Further taunts might not be a good idea. "Yes, through the airport, under that second identity."

"Perhaps we missed you because – and I tell you truthfully – no one seriously expected you to come back. Three corpses would persuade most men to abandon the search, would it not? Especially that of your assistant, Nawaz. Did you see him after Patel cured him of his skin problems? No, how could you have."

Singh lapsed into thought. What the hell could he have to think about that rivaled my concerns?

"I won't say that Patel was creative in his work, but he did have a sense of irony. What would be appropriate for you I wonder? Given your sharp tongue and arrogant speech, perhaps your mouth would be a good place to start." He stopped to consider this possibility before discarding it. "No, that would impede your ability to communicate, and we do want to be able to converse as long as necessary." He stroked his beard, then brightened. "Of course! There is your history of sexual impropriety. That would suggest focus on another part of the body. We will have to discuss it, the boys and I, but there is no pressure. You might say that we have time to kill." I was trying not to listen. "Get it Brown, 'time to kill'? Oh dear. I fear you've lost your sense of humor."

On the positive side – which had become vanishingly small – Singh had convinced me I had nothing to lose from even the riskiest attempt to escape. If the attempt failed I might at least pass over into the next world with less unpleasantness. What awaited on the other side? Would I find Debbie? Were my questions about the nature of God about to be answered? No rush, God. I can live with the uncertainty a while longer.

"Tell, me, Singh, is there any room for negotiation here?"

"Little, I fear. What you have I am confident my associates can extract at no cost to us. Your continued presence on this earth would be a liability, and so . . . You would perhaps like me to give you false hope, but I can not."

And so we remained stuck in the softening-up mode. Strip the victim of any reason for resistance.

"But, listen to me. Here I am talking gloom and doom when we have at least another 15 minutes to our destination." Singh was good; when he wasn't telling me what his 'associates' were going to do to me, he was telling me how soon they would start. Samuel Johnson had it right: it does concentrate the mind.

Perhaps he has a better nature?

"Since we're killing time, Singh – as you pointedly put it – I'm surprised by your involvement. I'd concluded you have no stomach for blood. You were visibly upset at the sight of the headless antique seller."

Singh laughed softly. "Ah, Maxwell, Maxwell. One does acquire a few acting skills in this line of work." Another self-satisfied chuckle. Proud of his performance.

"Still, you're a learned man. And presumably you didn't escape religious instruction as a child. How do you square your participation in murder and torture with your sense of morality?" A huge leap; Singh has a sense of morality?

"Ooh, very good, Brown. Trying to undermine my resolve. I like that." That's as far as he'd take it.

Another shot. "Seriously, G.I., you can't be indifferent to the suffering you cause. No agonizing? No sleepless nights? No doubts?" This did appear to hit a nerve. I watched in the mirror as his features tightened.

"If you think this conversation is going to change the outcome, Brown, let me assure you, it will not. Nor will I favor you with a rationale or rationalization." Then, after a long silent moment, he did just that. "Spies are asked to operate against their basic nature. Like everyone else we're social animals, but we're isolated from most normal social interaction. My own wife has no idea what I do when I'm not involved in academic activities. I think that isolation makes our few work contacts more precious. The boys and I are a team – maybe closer to a family. We share things that only we can know about. Some of us are less troubled by the hardship we inflict than others, but we arrive at a happy medium." Again, his eyes lost focus. A chance? No. The gun never wavered.

"Were you always this savage?" Let's call a spade for what it is.

"Savage, Brown? My, my. How judgmental. But yes, we have always been this 'savage.' The objectives have changed over the years. No longer in the service of India, of course, our glorious homeland. It only took a few assignments before we realized that our 'savagery' – to stay with your description – was often in the pursuit of very trivial objectives. We were expected to kill to obtain a document that probably already languished in the desk of a RAW bureaucrat. In light of those experiences, it seems almost more principled to commit the same acts for money that can be used to send our children to good schools. But, you're probably one of those uptight Christians who shrinks from means-ends calculations."

This was going nowhere. He'd rationalized the transition from torturing for the nation's good to torturing for personal gain. "Sorry I asked, Singh. I can see we operate on different moral planes." Would insulting him result in harsher treatment? Only if there were room for clemency, which seemed unlikely.

We passed the airport off to the left, Singh sulking after his treatise had been cut short. *The airport: that's where I should be heading. How had it gone so wrong?* Traffic was thinning out but I didn't speed up. Crowded buses overtook us.

"Are you delaying the inevitable with this slow pace, Brown? It makes no difference to me. The night air is refreshing don't you find? Good to get away from the city."

I maintained 40 kph, far too slow to produce a crash of any consequence. And it was clear; I was stalling when I should be taking the initiative.

I said it before. I've never been a 'rip the bandage off' kind of guy. It was reminiscent of those terrible hung-over mornings when relief could be accelerated by purging the stomach, but I would lie in prolonged misery, hoping some less unpleasant way forward would present itself. None ever did and any rational person would conclude that, in the present case, my goose was incontestably, incontrovertibly cooked. I just didn't want to accept it. *These things don't happen to people like me. Life isn't snatched from us by brutal men with no sense of humanity. We grow old and querulous, clinging stubbornly to life well after it's ceased to be rewarding.*

It was time to get out of these unhelpful ruminations; probably focusing on them to keep my mind off the unpleasantness that was fifteen minutes off. Where's the swaggering combat pilot?

Time to hatch a plan. Maybe a distraction followed by a lunge for his gun? How about vomiting on Singh? A Technicolor visualization of the flaying process might produce an eruption from one end or the other, or both. Would he recoil, hands rising, which might provide an opportunity to go for the gun? It was easy to imagine him recoiling in disgust, but equally easy to see that I would be too busy heaving up Hasan's biscuits to carry out part two of the plan.

Stupid idea. Back to plan A: crash the car. But past experience on this road had shown – reconfirmed by our current pace – that we wouldn't attain enough speed to make a crash effective.

On both sides of the two-lane road an irrigation ditch ran at least two meters below road level. That was good, but it was also possible that the muddy bank of the ditch would absorb much of the impact. And there was a steady stream of walkers on both sides. I needed to accelerate to at least 90 kph without arousing suspicion, and then swerve off the road into something solid without killing anyone other than Singh. I didn't doubt that Singh would fire if he thought something amiss and then grab the steering wheel. But would he shoot to kill? If he wanted me alive for interrogation he'd have to re-aim before pulling the trigger. We came up behind a bus that was lumbering along. I tailgated, our car enveloped in swirling black diesel exhaust. After a minute Singh became impatient, "Go around." The speedometer read 55 kph.

I eased out from behind the bus across the centerline and saw headlights, high and wide apart indicating a large vehicle, coming toward us. Not a good passing situation. "Is the road clear, Singh?" a pointless question as I had the better view forward. Singh – his second mistake of the evening – extended his head out the passenger's window to check the road ahead. "Alright," I announced and shifted down for better acceleration, floored the pedal, and swung out to pass.

"You fool, don't!" cried Singh. Keeping the accelerator to the floor, the Land Cruiser shot forward along the side of the bus as the approaching headlights flooded our windscreen. A loud horn filled the car and Singh's hands were reflexively extended in front of him. Just before impact I threw the steering wheel to the right and we started to tip over when the onrushing truck nicked our side and righted the Land Cruiser as it flew off the road. Darkness.

> The Air Force conducted tests of seat restraints, presumably to inform the design of belt and harness systems for planes. To encourage seatbelt use in our personal cars, we were shown films of a volunteer strapped into a rocket-propelled sled that would race down a track and then abruptly stop. This demonstration answered one question: how effective were the restraints? But raised another: how stupid was the volunteer? The sled would slam to a stop from 60 mph in three feet with almost no damage to the idiot strapped in it. Seat belts, especially those with a shoulder harness, improve your odds in a crash.

I regained awareness in a panic. How long had I been out? Debbie. Where was Debbie? The front of the car was buried in dirt; water ran slowly by below window level. Debbie wasn't there. Dad wasn't screaming. Mom wasn't slumped unconscious halfway under the dash. I wasn't on US 6. I was on my way to being tortured to death.

The world came into focus. Singh's legs and feet were beside me. His upper body had been thrust through the windscreen and was resting on the hood, crumbs of glass scattered around him. I inventoried myself and found blood on my forehead at a tender site above the left eye. That would explain the brief period of unconsciousness. Was that it? Arms worked. Legs worked, but the knees felt like hell. They must have bounced off something below the dashboard.

Probably little time had passed but a crowd was already gathering at the top of the ditch, peering down at the steaming wreckage. Notify Toyota the UN needs a replacement. I released the blessed seatbelt, a short nondenominational prayer of thanks to the designer rising, and with difficulty pulled Singh back into the car to see if he was dead. If not, what? One thing to shoot back in self-defense; another to kill a helpless man. The body was lifeless – that seemed good enough. I rifled his pockets until I located a small cloth sack that held the coin and jewels. Next I found my pistol and pocketed that; I was becoming attached to it.

Responding to my gestures for help, five men descended the bank and pulled me through the window. My legs wouldn't hold so they dragged me to the top of the bank where I resumed examination of my knees. Very sore, but functional. With assistance I tried to stand again and was able to maintain a wobbly, if painful, shuffle.

"English?" Asked hopefully. No response. Traffic was stopped and backing up in both directions. Seeing an empty Bajaj, I shuffled over, followed by my small retinue of rescuers, and asked the driver, "Airport?" He looked uncertain, probably not about the name of the destination, but whether he should abandon the party. Then again, I was one of the star attractions, so he motioned me into the Bajaj.

We wove through the cars, trucks and buses that had stopped to view the accident and were soon chugging back toward the airport. As we approached the terminal I noticed a row of small shops and directed the driver to stop there. The offerings were the same at each shop. Is this where corrupt customs officials disposed of the goods they'd confiscated from powerless travelers? Shoes, clothing, watches, bags, and similar items that I'd seen entrepreneurs bringing into the country for resale were on display. I bought clean pants, shirt and jacket, a small suitcase, and a lead-lined film pouch. Using the shop's back room to change, I put the coins and pistol into the lead-lined pouch, and that with my dirty clothes into the suitcase. Resplendent in polyester, but still filthy and bloody, I shuffled the

remaining 200 meters to the airport to wash up before present-
ing myself at the Thai Airways counter.

DHAKA CITY

37

"The flight is full."

"Business or first class?" Negative head shake. "This is a matter of some urgency (bad people are trying to fucking kill me!). Could I speak with a supervisor?" The counter agent looked displeased, but retreated through a door. At length a paunchy man emerged with her and approached with an air of resignation. "Could we speak privately?" I asked. With even deeper resignation, he led the way back through the door. "I'm sorry to make special requests, but it's quite urgent that I travel tonight. I've been informed that my wife has been seriously injured and is now at the emergency room of Samitivej Hospital."

"I am sorrowful by your loss, but there is nothing I can do. Every seat is occupied. There is a physical limit to what is possible. Again, I am regretful." He didn't look regretful. He looked annoyed as he checked his watch and directed his eyes around the room and away from me.

Departure was still 90 minutes away so it seemed likely that some passengers hadn't checked in. "I fully understand. I'd thought of approaching other passengers to beg for their mercy and assistance, but my state of mind is such that I can barely focus to speak with you sir. Perhaps another passenger – someone with a family and beloved wife such as my own – would release his seat for compensation?" Before he could shoot that down I rushed on. "The thing of greatest value that I could find as I hurried from our house was an ancient coin, which I'm told is of great value." The man looked skeptical as I fished around in the little suitcase for the booty. Hoping to find a clean specimen I rejected the first coins I touched which felt gritty. Retrieving the cleanest of the lot, I placed it, with reverent care, in the man's hand and studied his reaction. No inscrutable Sphinx, this guy. He looked like he might wet himself. The weight and color instantly convinced him that this was the genuine article, the value of the gold alone being well above the price of any ticket he might liberate.

"Well," he allowed, "I will try to work something." Pocketing the gleaming coin, he went back out to the check-in counters. At first I was relieved to be closed in a back room where

Singh's goons – if they'd heard of the accident and someone at the scene had told them of my request to go to the airport – couldn't spot me. On the other hand, I was trapped. If the supervisor revealed my presence, escape was impossible.

I cracked the door open. At the first class check-in an irate passenger was waving his arms and shouting in an unintelligible language. The supervisor's repeated response was an exaggerated shrug. After this had played for several minutes, the supervisor checked his watch – this seemed to be his standard response to tiresome exchanges – and turned his attention to the passenger waiting in line behind the irate man, motioning the next passenger forward. The un-seated man stood his ground for a minute, then backed away, still shouting and gesturing.

"At some personal cost to my career – if I may speak plainly – I have found a seat in the first class cabin. You may purchase your ticket at the end counter." After thanking the supervisor effusively, I bought the ticket with half of my remaining cash and made my way through immigration as Randall Goodwell. Again, heart palpitations reached a crescendo as the immigration official studied my passport, consulted various documents on his counter, studied the passport again, and, at length, smacked a stamp in it.

Thou Art My Protector
- Fanny J. Crosby, 1896

Ah, Bangkok. Who would expect to develop such strong and positive feelings for a city that was famous for infamous behavior? I took in lungs' full of the warm polluted night air and contentedly patted the gems in my pocket. Everything was going my way. The little suitcase containing the roscoe and coins was spit out onto the revolving conveyor belt and I passed unchallenged through the green line of 'nothing to declare.' Where to stay? From the terminal I called the number Leung had given me and his intermediary picked up on the third ring. "Leung gave me this number. I would like to meet with him and I also need his recommendation regarding where I could stay while preserving my anonymity." The intermediary fielded the second request first and provided the name of a hotel in the center of the city. Regarding the first request, he said that Mr. Leung was away for a few days but that we might confidently expect to meet in less than a week. Funds were running low but there was little that could be done about that. Perhaps the hotel wasn't expensive.

Not to worry. The Get-Your-Rocks-Off Hotel/Cat House was definitely downscale and the only other guests were 50 horny middle-aged Japanese men. The thumping from loudspeakers in the basement nightclub resonated throughout the building and insured no one would sleep before 3:00 AM. After 3:00, squeals and laughter from the corridors kept those of us with frayed nerves and a super-sized helping of paranoia awake until dawn.

Hoping that exercise might help me sleep through the racket the next night, after breakfast I tested how far my sore knees might carry me and stepped into the street, booty in one pocket and the roscoe in the other. As I was shuffling gingerly along through the heat and choking exhaust, I noticed another walker, a consistent fifteen meters behind, who was either similarly disabled or tailing me. *Ah shit! When will it end? C'mon, God. Isn't there someone else You'd like to be messing with?*

Trained in these matters by American TV, I turned the corner of a building and waited. Almost immediately my pursuer sped around the corner. I tripped him – at great cost to the right knee – and as he lay on the sidewalk I placed the howling knee in his back and the pistol to his neck. "I don't know how the fuck you bastards keep finding me, but this shit has to stop," and I pulled back the hammer on the revolver.

"Mr. Leung tell me where find you. I security. Mr. Leung want you safe person." The man made no effort to wriggle loose or attack as I rose off him. His story was more plausible than the ex-RAW goons having caught up.

My 'security' rose to his feet and inclined his head in respect.

"Would you like to walk with me?" Perhaps he could double as bodyguard and tourist guide.

"No. Better not close. If bad men know I security, they kill me first, then kidnap you. I not useful to you close." This also had a ring of plausibility so I set off shuffling again, planning to circumnavigate the block on this trial outing.

Bangkok is not pedestrian friendly. The blocks can be enormous. Side streets dead-end. Gentle bends in streets cause you to lose your bearings, and amidst the tall buildings you instantly lose sight of familiar landmarks. After thirty minutes I turned back to my 'security' and asked that he lead me home.

I passed the time washing my few clothes and watching incomprehensible TV. The second evening the room phone rang. Mr. Leung looked forward to having breakfast together next morning in the coffee shop of the Hilton. Please bring anything I might want to show him.

In the loupe

"My excellent Professor! News has trickled through that you have had several very full days. Don't be alarmed. This is based on a report from our mutual acquaintance in Chittagong who sends his best regards." Leung had risen from a corner table to greet me. With newly heightened sensitivities, I noticed that the tables next to his were vacant despite a crowded room. He followed my gaze and clarified, "One is often least conspicuous in the most public places, although one does want some privacy. But please, fill me in." He signaled a chair. "I don't mean to rush you, but my absence from the city means that things have piled up for my attention, and I assume you would like to remain on the move."

Unsettling. Did I need to remain on the move?

I launched into my briefing, starting at the Dhaka train terminal, Leung interjecting from time to time to speed the narrative past events of less interest to him. After I covered the successful bribery at the airport and my departure, Leung sat thoughtfully for a while.

"Well, we have three things ahead of us. First, we must convert the jewels and gold – that which you do not want to keep as souvenirs of your adventures in the orient – into cash and, second, agree on how to channel your share – the lion's share, I assure you – to a haven that is free of burdensome taxes and nosy officials. Those are routine matters which we can get underway today. Third, and I am sorry to tell you this, your problems are not quite over. Singh survived. Ironically, he was brought to Bangkok yesterday for treatment."

Irony? How about two identical accidents. Debbie dies; Singh survives. As Debbie would have said, "It's not fair."

"He was accompanied by two others who do not share Singh's family name so we may assume . . . well, we may assume the obvious. I will try to discover his prognosis but he is just one of several interested men. The others can operate without him."

"There are a maximum of four, plus Singh, I believe."

"Very well. And their motives have moved from pecuniary to personal. Even when the treasure is converted to cash and placed beyond their easy access, they may retain an interest in you. That is the reputation that RAW has carefully cultivated over the years: they never let up. Part of the mystique, I suppose. I have never understood what drives these ex-spies. More your field. Anyway, let us do what we can at present."

Leung nodded at a nearby table; a sallow man with a briefcase and wearing a suit two sizes too large came over. He withdrew a jeweler's loupe from his vest pocket which clarified what was expected of me. As inconspicuously as I could manage, I passed each jewel in turn to the appraiser who, his back to the rest of the room, studied it for longer than seemed necessary, then wrote on a pad. After he'd examined the last jewel and coin, he went to work on the pad. My palms were damp; Leung looked like he'd never been more at ease as he sipped his tea and contentedly surveyed the room.

At length the appraiser looked up and began to speak in Thai. Leung held up a hand, nodded at me, and the man started over in measured English. "The quality is uneven as one might expect from old stones which the powerful collected without regard for their purity. The gold, on the other hand, is very fine. Melted down each coin would fetch over three thousand dollars. As antiques on the auction market, I will guess they will fetch ten times that much.

"But the real value is in the gems. I have totaled up my best estimates and, if these are sold on the international market, will bring the seller no less than four and a half million dollars." Noticing my raised eyebrows, he explained, "The diamonds are very large, although two lack the clarity one expects in the best gems these days. Of course I understand that you are thinking of another market where the provenance of the stones would not be questioned. There the pricing is not as certain. Mr. Leung will be a better guide."

Mr. Leung looked like he hadn't expected to weigh in on value and glanced sharply at the appraiser, who excused himself and returned to his table.

"I am not a good guide, I fear. Gold? Yes. That is what I usually deal in. But gems . . . I would have to research. If you will trust me, Professor, I will show these to an acquaintance. Since he and I will be negotiating almost from the first moment, could you tell me what your bottom price would be?"

I also hadn't expected to weigh in on value. "I haven't formed a clear idea. An hour ago I'd hoped to take away a nest egg that would allow a comfortable, but not extravagant lifestyle. On the basis of your remarks, however, I now wonder if I won't have security expenses to cover. At the least, I'd want enough money to remain inconspicuous until the other side loses interest in the game."

"Very well," said Leung. "I have the appraised value. I will negotiate as aggressively as seems prudent. I must say, however, that it would be in your interest that this is concluded rapidly so that you may move on to a more secure location."

I handed Leung the cloth sack – not without misgivings – and then remembered to ask, "Thinking of that future, your second point?"

"Of course; my mind was fixed on the immediate problems. The options you have certainly read about. The Swiss never turn away large sums of money and it is possible to invest those funds so that you may live off the proceeds anywhere you wish. There are also Caribbean islands that are competing for the same business. The Caymans for example, or Panama. A business associate told me he bounces his wealth through Switzerland where it loses its identity as his, then on to the Caymans where an anonymous account invests in a conservative portfolio of stocks, bonds, commodity futures and currencies, and sends the proceeds to bank accounts in different US states." He rose,

"I do deeply apologize. I must run. Given what we have learned of Singh, I had a reservation made for you in another hotel under the name of Ludwig Schultz. They are expecting you and the bill has been satisfied. They will not ask for identification. I think you might want to remain out of sight and I am confident of your security at this hotel. I shall contact you tomorrow afternoon, I believe, if I can meet with this gem merchant." He handed me the hotel's card and, smiling graciously, left. Two athletic looking men at tables in different corners of the room rose and followed him out.

This is how hardball is played, Max, and you don't belong in this league.

When Doubt and Fear Assail Me
- C. A. Miles, 1906

If nothing else concrete was accomplished, the day produced a major upgrade in living accommodations. Leung's recommended hotel boasted four honest stars. The pity was, I'd been instructed to lie low by which I interpreted: stay in the room and away from the pool, fancy restaurants, and bars. In small compensation, the televised fare was better than in the last hotel.

Room service brought in the meals, each knock on the door generating images from old movies in which the bad guys gain access by posing as waiters. I over-tipped on the hope that room service staff would be less likely to sell out someone who gave them 25 percent as opposed to 15 percent.

I also experimented with different hiding places for the gun – under the bed pillow, concealed beneath an open book on the nightstand, tucked behind me in my waist band – changing its location as I envisioned different abduction scenarios. Would it be fake waiters? Or an agile abductor who could creep along the outside ledge and burst through the window? Would the door come crashing down in the middle of the night? Maybe the food itself might be laced with a powerful sedative. Plenty to think about.

One constant: one of the two remaining hollow point bullets was always chambered.

The next afternoon passed without news from Leung. There were logical explanations, but also the growing fear that I'd almost lost my life – and still might – only to hand over the treasure to a smiling Chinaman, never to see it again. Couldn't call the number. That would look like I didn't trust him. Besides, if he'd cheated me a phone call wasn't going to change anything. I waited.

Another day passed. I donned dark glasses and slipped down to reception to ask if any messages had been left for Mr. Schultz. No. Then a dispiriting thought occurred: If Leung had absconded with the booty, might it also not be to his advantage to have me removed? An efficient solution would be to alert Singh's heavies to my whereabouts. I went without room service that night, supping instead on nuts, chips and Toblerone chocolate from the mini-bar.

The room phone rang early the next morning. "Professor! Apologies for the delay. I hope you weren't concerned. The news is generally positive; perhaps I could join you for lunch at your hotel?"

At noon I waited in the most secluded and unoccupied corner of the restaurant. Thirty minutes late, Leung strode into the room. "Dear sir. It is a glorious day. Come let us sit by the window so that we may rest our weary eyes on the bikini-ed lovelies tanning themselves by the pool outside." Noting the table I'd selected, he laughed. "We won't be passing jewels around today."

Seated, he gazed appreciatively at the sun-bronzed nymphs and asked, "There is, as always, good news and bad news. Where do you want me to start?"

"I would guess that the bad news concerns Singh."

"Always perceptive, Professor. The result of your excellent training. Yes, Singh will recover, although his movements will be restricted. The well-meaning souls who extracted him from the car – did you know it burned? – caused him considerable damage so he is without a lung and is unlikely to regain use of his left arm. Convalescence? Six weeks to three months. Both of his attendants have disappeared although we may deduce they are not inactive."

"And the good news concerns the whopping great deal you got for the treasure?"

"Not whopping, but respectable. I have sent ten thousand dollars to Kamal and his son, retained one hundred thousand for my estimable services, and 3.2 million sits in my account awaiting your instructions."

Yowser! A larger number than I had dared consider. We had a fine lunch. I watched the young women and thought of Sally. Why not Tiffany? At the conclusion, Leung shook my hand vigorously and I had the feeling this was goodbye.

O The Blessings, Rich and Many
- N. H. Caterbury, 1892

My 'security' stayed with me to the local Credit Suisse office where I filled out papers and was finger printed and photographed from a variety of angles. A passbook was presented – Gutenberg Bibles are handled less reverently – with stern, and repeated, instructions that the contents *must* be committed to memory. Until the extent of your wealth is established, you can expect that a Swiss banker will look down on you. Ah well.

I called Leung's number to ask for the funds transfer. The intermediary said he'd been told to make the arrangements, took the account information, and rang off.

"When," I asked the stuffy branch manager, "will my funds be available? A transfer is in-coming from an associate."

The banker seemed pleased by the question. Assuming a military stance, he launched into a well-rehearsed sermonette.

"For us at Credit Suisse, security and privacy are paramount. We place them ahead of speed at every turn. Our more prudent clients (not me, apparently) understand these priorities." He took a moment to appraise me in my cheap street-vendor-purchased clothing.

"One must be patient, Mr. Brown," he admonished. "One must plan for the future and not expect the banking system to respond to every whim, nor to every temptation to throw away money on impulse." What a fuck-nut. He was about to resume when a subaltern crept into the room, handed the banker a piece of paper, and nodded in my direction.

"Ah, Professor." Much friendlier now. "I am informed that the transfer was internal – within our walls – and has been accomplished. Your balance is now US$3,201,020. What are your instructions?"

I asked for ten grand in cash and informed the suddenly unctuous shit that the Montreux branch would be my primary place of business for a while. This was received with a thin smile and I was handed a portfolio fat with brochures and instructions.

Ten grand is 100 C-notes which I distributed among different pockets, leaving one pocket free for Roscoe – extended familiarity had put the revolver and myself on a first name basis – and emerged into the late afternoon rush hour traffic. My former 'security' was nowhere in evidence, signaling the partnership with Leung was over. This was underscored back at the hotel where the receptionist inquired if "sir will be checking out soon?" No hard feelings. Leung had to be concerned about the negative attention I was attracting.

A telephone call to Swissair secured an economy class ticket on the midnight flight to Zurich. One last trip for Mr. Goodwell. I asked the front desk for a limousine to the domestic airport, then caught a cab at the taxi stand to the international airport and said goodbye to Southeast Asia.

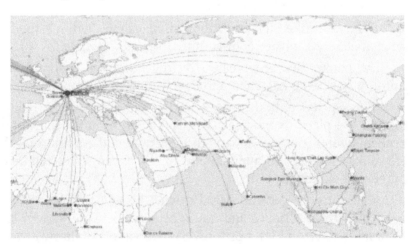

Swissair routes.

Section V
How I found love.

The Kingdom of Love. Tristan l'Hermite and Jean Sadeler, 1659.

38

My Hiding Place
- R. Hutchinson, 1871

Why Montreux? 'Because,' I answered, when repeating the question on an hourly basis, 'it seemed like such a good idea at the time.' I had some memory of Montreux being a hangout for Freddie Mercury and Vladimir Nabokov, both of whom I admired, and it wasn't an obvious haven for tax dodgers as were Zurich, Lausanne or Geneva.

Or so you might expect. In fact, of the small town of less than twenty thousand, almost half were 'foreign national residents,' a point of inexplicable pride to the local tourism bureau. These were people like me, although a lot older. From the balcony of the apartment in the rambling Fairmont Palace I watched elderly coupon clippers pass their days on the lakeside benches. No sign of Freddie or Vladimir.

Some facts.

• Montreux is justifiably famous for spectacular vistas in any direction. Over the lake, back up to the towering alps, to the south across rising foothills and vineyards – anywhere you looked. I'd like to say that the majesty of the landscape brought a gasp of wonder each time I beheld it. Not after a few weeks.

• Some interesting architecture, including the Chateau of Chillon, made famous by Lord Byron in his poem, *The Prisoner of Chillon*. Have you read it? Don't. Narrated by the last survivor of seven dungeon dwellers, it's a dreary account of how the first six expired and the seventh isn't doing very well. I purchased the poem in the gift store and read it before taking the tour. I'm not sure whether the news, imparted during the tour, that the story was fabricated out of whole cloth cheered or depressed me further.

• A recording center of some note. Not only Queen recorded there – they liked it so much they bought the studio – but Frank Zappa, Deep Purple, and other notables came to town to lay down tracks. The half of the town's residents who were locals may have had mixed feelings about the steady traffic in rock groups. A fan of Frank Zappa fired a flare gun *inside* the Montreux Casino, burning the landmark to the ground. Deep Purple memorialized the event in the song *Smoke on the Water*.

• The weather was said to be better than in Geneva. The comparison would only matter to the Swiss, but it mattered deeply. Given half an opportunity a resident would tell you that the clouds all piled up at the west end of Lake Leman, keeping Geneva shrouded in gloom, while Montreux basked in an almost weekly outburst of sunshine.

• The International Federation for Rolling Skating was founded in Montreux. It can't get any more exciting than that.

That's pretty much it. Grey, leaden skies much of the time; the same two adjectives could describe the disposition of my national hosts; few diversions aside from the occasional blockbuster concert; and a service industry oriented to the needs and interests of the elderly. Did I feel like I belonged in Montreux? You know the answer.

I tried. For weeks I endeavored to become one with the idle rich, but without descending to foppishness. Every morning I purchased a copy of the *Herald Tribune* which I stashed under my arm while I strode to a nearby café. Once the order for a café au lait had been placed, I went about the important business of reading the paper.

How to read a newspaper

It appears that few people (you?) know how to read a newspaper. And it may get worse. I recently saw a television report where a person was reading the news from a computer. Hunched over, squinting, drumming his fingers as the machine laboriously brought the material to the screen, the very picture of uncool. A person can read a newspaper with flair and a sense of grace. A computer screen? Never.

Here are some suggestions from a trained sociologist:

First you must take control of the paper, opening it with authority, flexing the creases so that the article you want is displayed flatly and neatly in front of you. Practice this at home so you don't struggle to flatten the paper or need to smack a fold a second time – the mark of an amateur.

Second, allow yourself only the subtlest changes of expression as you read. Never – this is important – never nod vigorously in agreement. Remember that you are an independent thinker and not a person who takes his intellectual lead from some hack journalist.

The information in the paper is already known to you; you're only checking how widely it's disseminated and how accurate the reporting is. You can, however, tear out an article for later reference or checking. Do this quickly without regard for neatness and stuff the article into your jacket pocket.

It's okay to read the comics, provided you smile indulgently to signify that at least some of the strips rise to a primitive level of amusement. However, do not, under any circumstances, take out a pen and start working on the games or crossword in public. Only a man with no other challenges in his life has the time or interest for such trifles.

If available, bring more than one newspaper with you. This, obviously, identifies you as a person who is either open to alternative views, or needs to be alert to those views to defend your vast interests. This extends your reading time, but it's worth it in terms of the perceptions of the other patrons, your audience. Order another coffee.

When done, leave the newspapers behind. You've extracted everything of value from them.

Early into the third week I realized I was only reading the *Trib* for Art Buchwald's humor column. I abandoned the rôle of international mover and shaker for that of intellectual, and toted to the café a fat volume of Proust (*Remembrance of Things Past* – God, it's awful) which I would open to a random page and pretend to read as I sipped coffee.

By the fourth week I gave that up as well and watched the girls go by.

Purify My Heart
- J. Nelson, 1993

A lamentable habit *Tiffany* and I had fallen into was eating dinner in front of the TV. There was rarely anything on that we wanted to watch, but it spared us the burden of making conversation and minimized the risk of a conversation going off the rails.

Alone in Montreux, the television set again became my evening dining companion. That's not so bad is it, when you're alone? To further justify the practice, I tried to find 'educational' programming. That's how the trouble started.

A local channel had picked up a series called *First Tuesday* produced by Yorkshire TV, with French subtitles added. I tuned in a few minutes late one evening – busy perfecting a 'heat and serve' packaged meal I'd picked up at Aldi, while getting a head start on the wine – and missed the title of the episode, *Four Hours in My Lai*. You know where this is going, right? I was about to be blind-sided.

Within ten minutes I was blubbering uncontrollably. At around minute 15 I smashed the two plates and wine glass. A minute or two later the wooden chair had been reduced to half a dozen splintered pieces. And the TV droned on. I could not turn the goddamned thing off.

Do *you* know what happened in the village of My Lai? You should. Good decent American boys went nuts. There wasn't an ounce of humanity in them.

At 20 minutes into the program PFC Michael Bernhardt was being quoted,

> "I walked up and saw these guys doing strange things...Setting fire to the hooches and huts and waiting for people to come out and then shooting them...going into the hooches and shooting them up...gathering people in groups and shooting them... As I walked in you could see piles of people all through the village... all over. They were gathered up into large groups. I saw

them shoot an M79 (grenade launcher) into a group of people who were still alive. But it was mostly done with a machine gun. They were shooting women and children just like anybody else."

Those were fatal words for the little TV. I kicked the screen hard. It imploded with a loud pop, but in a belated and futile act of self-defense shot glass shards into my ankle. I looked around the suddenly silent room for more things to break, then fled down the stairs and out onto the quay. A light fog blanketed the lake: a fittingly indifferent listener.

"Jesus Fucking H. Christ! What have we done? What, oh what, oh what the fuck have we done?" A scavenging pigeon waddled away. I raised my voice another notch. "How could we do this? Aren't we the good guys?" The lake had no comment.

Grasping for a scapegoat, I cried "C'mon God. How can it happen? We're made in *your* image? You sick mother-fucking son of a bitch!" I threw an arcing punch at the sky, almost losing my balance. Grief was veering toward burlesque. The pigeon increased its distance and disappeared into the dark.

A policeman approached. "Sir, I must demand you are quiet. You disturb others." I turned toward him and he saw my tear-covered face and bloody foot. His tone changed. "You are disturbed. Perhaps you talk with someone. Perhaps you may tell me what is your problem."

"My problem? My problem? I'm alive, officer! I'm fucking alive!"

"That is a good thing. Is it not? But I see your foot is injured. Do you wish transport to hospital?"

"There's no reason for me to be alive. No reason. Better men than me are dead. Better men than me went insane and did things they'll never forgive themselves for. That's my problem officer. I don't belong here any more than . . ." I couldn't say their names: Tom, Chuck, Bill. I can hardly write them.

I'll spare you the rest of the melodrama. Somewhere in the tirade I shouted "Viet-fucking-nam," and looked imploringly at the cop, my hands stretched toward him, shoulders shaking as I sobbed. He seemed to understand. I wasn't the first head case to come to town.

A police car provided transport to an infirmary where a sour-looking nurse tweezered the glass from my ankle. Cleaned up by nine o'clock, I wasn't ready to go back to the apartment and was granted permission to spend the night in the infirmary's waiting room.

Fifty-eight thousand. And that's a pittance compared to the number of Vietnamese, Laotians and Cambodians who died. Please care.

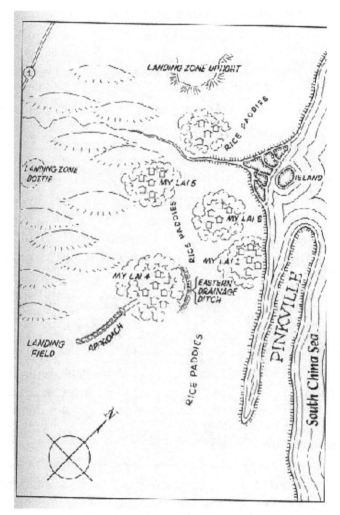

My Lai, Quang Ngai Province
Map of 16 March 1968 assault

39

Did I say at the beginning that money is important? It is, but money, by itself, doesn't entertain you. I was spending a lot of time on the balcony – my most reliable companion a molting pigeon with a crippled leg – watching bald pates and blue rinses totter slowly beneath or doze on the benches. I felt sorry for the older people who were single, almost all of them women, but that sympathy evaporated whenever snatches of conversation drifted up. The scolding tone came through, irrespective of language.

Will the Real God Please Stand Up

This observation gave rise to a new and depressing image of God: There was a Mrs. God, an accomplished contrarian, challenging God's every move and utterance. "So, I see you put that comet on a collision course with an inhabited star system. Interesting."

How do women do that? Every comment becomes a challenge that demands a response. Will God try to defend why He sent the comet in that direction? Or, has the relationship so soured that He'll simply fix his gaze off into space and ignore Her?

I was living proof that this constant rain of criticism – direct and indirect – would undermine a man's self-confidence to the point where the criticisms become increasingly self-fulfilling. God may have held it together for a few billion years, but the steady fault-finding and belittling had reduced Him to a henpecked fuck up. When He acts it's in anticipation that He'll hear that sharp voice, second-guessing Him. It's hard to keep your eye on the ball under those circumstances.

Coming full circle, just as at age ten I'd again created God in my own image.

Even without a Mrs. God, consider what time will do to a man, or a deity. The universe is approaching 14 billion years old. A guy can grow forgetful, inattentive. He shouldn't drive at night. He makes inappropriate comments to younger women.

But I was too bored to play the game with the same commitment as before. Tiffany had beaten it out of me with, admittedly, some telling observations. Did I still care who God was? As much as ever, but the search for God through experience-based metaphors hadn't been productive, and Bangladesh was confusing. The country was home to over 100 million Muslims who believed that Allah's will drives everything, and most of them live in heart-breaking misery. Yet they cling to the image of a great and merciful supreme being. How? Christianity had been a bust, Islam no better. It seemed unlikely any of the other 'great' religions were going to pull back the veil.

Was the problem monotheism? Too many contradictory elements for one deity to encompass? The ancient Greeks, Hindus, and Assyrians had handled this by assigning different characteristics to a colorful panoply of deities. With little expectation that I was headed in the right direction, I checked out a book on ancient religions from the Montreux library. This served mostly as light entertainment, not enlightenment, although you had to be impressed by the Assyrians' Ishtar; she was the goddess of love and war, and in some accounts, also of prostitution. An intriguing combination of responsibilities. Makes you wonder what the Assyrians were up to.

How to deal with boredom

One way to keep boredom at arm's length is to nurture a state of incipient alarm. Legitimately so, if Leung's assessment was correct that Singh and his boys now had a score to settle. It was largely because of its fortress-like appearance I chose the Fairmont. That, plus the labyrinthine internal layout which added another layer of protection.

At first I kept a weather eye out for men of a sub-continental cast. Easy to spot in Montreux. Then the obvious dawned: Singh could outsource the work. Contract killers could be any nationality. I needed to up my game.

On two occasions when I returned from trips, the apartment looked different. A chair not where it had been left. Papers in a drawer that seemed to be in a different order. There was a weekly maid service, but the Czech woman didn't appear enterprising enough to go through personal papers. It seemed unlikely that Singh or his goons would inspect the apartment. They would come only to kill . . . unless they thought they might find some of the treasure, or a lead to the treasure. Could be Singh and Co. after all. Not a bad idea to spend more time on the road. Roscoe became my constant companion. I also left subtle markers in the apartment that would signal if something had been disturbed, but these revealed nothing that couldn't be explained by the normal cleaning activities of the maid. A more active approach was needed. Harden the target.

The evasion tactics were drawn directly from movies: frequent changes of transport, ducking in and out of shops to see if anyone was following at a consistent distance, lurking around a suddenly-turned corner where I awaited an imagined pursuer, laboriously retying a shoelace while watching to see if someone had taken an interest in a store window.

One needed to be alert not only to stalkers, but to motorized assassins; the attack might come from a passing vehicle. Consequently, I always walked facing on-coming traffic, the better to spot suspicious activity in approaching cars, and I never took the same route two days in a row.

After a few days of this cops and robbers game, vigilance fell off, only occasionally jerking myself to the frightened realization that my guard was, most of the time, down. I'd get back into spy-vs-spy mode for a few hours, then boredom would take over again.

How do the idle rich pass the time?

Financial management seems an obvious use of excess hours. I met weekly with my financial advisor, infelicitously named Herr Swindel, at Credit Suisse to track how the portfolio was performing. Swindel appeared to have few other clients, probably because of his name which secured my sympathy. Those of us with unfortunate names need to stick together.

"Zo, as zees graphs vill show most clearly, you haf been a most vise investor, Dr. Brown." The wisdom to which Herr Swindel referred was my unquestioning acceptance of every proposal he'd made.

"I must demur, Herr Swindel. The portfolio's performance is due entirely to your enlightened stewardship." Swindel would smile contentedly and sit back in his chair, signaling that I should inspect the graphs and tables spread out on his desk one more time. He would congratulate me again and I would have used up less than an hour of my idle time.

A parody of 'bankers' hours,' the Montreux branch of Credit Suisse only opened on Wednesday.

Dating. There's a sure-fire distraction; get back on the horse that threw you. The options were two: 1) Young back-packers, usually German fräuleins, some of whom displayed a frightening tendency to nymphomania, and 2) middle-aged American and British women taking the European tour they'd been saving up for lo these many years.

The young: "Zo, I see you look in my direction. Are you thinking maybe ve hook up?" The speaker is an early 20's blonde who had crossed the nightclub dance floor after an apparent rebuff from an older gentleman seated at a table with two male companions. She wasn't bad looking.

"Hook up?"

"Ya. Ficksen, bumsen, vögeln. Zay all mean same. You take off your clothes. I take off my clothes. Zen you put in your penis in mein Muschi. Is dis not clear?"

"Blindingly."

Romance is not what it once was.

The no-longer-young: Many of the second group, the sojourning 40-somethings from Liverpool and Des Moines, were grimly determined to cap their trip with a whirlwind romance, a romance they could tell their friends about for years (and years and years). I wasn't the dashing Latin lover they'd had in mind during the planning stages, but by the time their tour group arrived in Montreux, expectations had been ratcheted down.

"Do you mind if I ask you a question?" Here the speaker's a semi-attractive brunette with streaks of grey at the temples who'd been sitting on the adjacent barstool for ten minutes, fidgeting with the tiny straw in her cocktail.

"Shoot."

"You're not Swiss, are you."

How difficult for this woman. She was part of a group and three of her co-travelers, seated at a table nearby, had been sending her hand signals of encouragement. I'd seen a T-shirt in Bangkok, *I'm your last chance* printed across the front. Should I be wearing something like that? Apparently it would have been redundant. I was broadcasting that message already.

I confess I took advantage of one woman from each group – or did they take advantage of me? – only to nervously examine myself for signs of infection for days after the encounters. You can trust condoms only so far. After hungering for sex for years, this was it? Dating (aka one night stands) wasn't working.

Travel. That's the answer, and it would make me harder to track down. I started locally, hiking up toward the Rochers-de-Naye, planting my alpenstück purposively with each step, responding to the salutations of on-coming hikers in their own language.

But my ability to accurately assess danger was unreliable.

I skipped a Wednesday meeting with Herr Swindel in order to take advantage of good weather and hike from Gstaad to L'Etivaz along the famous knife-edge mountain path. Roscoe was not invited; who needs the extra weight when laboring up Alpine paths?

After changing trains in Saanen I noticed a darker hued man in the same car, reading a Hindi-language newspaper. I tried to catch his eye but he avoided looking at me.

Arriving in Gstaad, I walked quickly to the cable car station. The man followed, 20 meters back. Where does coincidence end and malevolent intent begin? With relief I was the last person admitted to a gondola. At least now he couldn't force open the door and throw me out halfway up. He caught the next car.

Bounding out of the cable car at the top, I set a strong pace along the narrow path to put distance between me and my subcontinental pursuer.

His gondola arrived at the top and, alarmingly, seconds after he stepped onto the platform, he called out and started walking rapidly to catch up. I quickened my step, maintaining 100 meters between us until I came upon a family of day-hikers resting in one of the lightning shelters. Joining them, it belatedly occurred to me there might be no safety in numbers. The killer could just shoot all of us, then roll our bodies over the edge of the ridge into a gorge where we wouldn't be found for months.

I looked into the faces of the family sitting on a low bench, sharing a package of crackers. Four innocent men had already lost their lives thanks to my clumsy pursuit of wealth. Was I about to add two children and their parents?

Too late to take off again. My pursuer was now within easy shooting distance. I leapt to my feet and ran toward him, zig-zagging as much as the narrow trail permitted. A last and long overdue act of courage from Max Brown.

Take me, you bastard. But leave these poor people alone!

The man halted and reached inside his jacket – I froze – and he pulled out . . . a small piece of paper. "Votre billet de retour, monsieur," he panted, hands on his knees. I'd dropped the re-turn portion of my train ticket when I'd pulled out a handker-chief back at the lift station. Poor guy.

He plopped down on a rock, wheezing. I offered him some gorp which he declined. His turn to be suspicious.

Perhaps traveling with a group would reduce the likelihood of embarrassing blunders. I joined a coach tour of regional winer-ies. A mistake, as I was the youngest tour member by half and was hit on by three sexagenarians – extending a generous bene-fit re their ages – who were vacationing from New Jersey. To spare their feelings I intimated I preferred my own gender. A gay gentleman in the group picked up on this and – trapped in my lie – he pursued me for the remainder of the tour.

Going further afield – solo again – I did Geneva. Then Ven-ice. Then Rome. Every bit as impressive as the guidebooks promised, but it's not that much fun, seeing these places alone. If I find my own company that unrewarding, what must others think? Even the presence of an indefatigable critic like Tiffany seemed better than nothing. The melancholy realization settled on me that I was one of those pathetic men who could not live alone.[*]

---

[*] Sartre said that if you're lonely when you're alone, you're in bad company. Then again, he's famous for complaining that "hell is other people." Maybe not the right guy to look to for advice on rela-tionships.

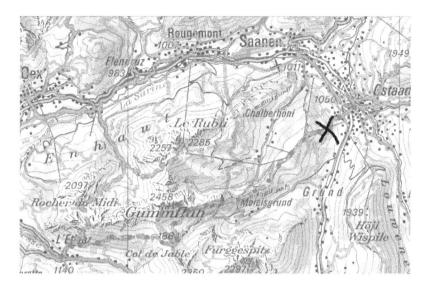

Hiking route, Gstaad to L'Etivaz

40

Dear Sally,

You are probably as surprised to receive this as I am to find myself writing it. There has been some unpleasantness between us, but I can't help remembering how impressed I was with your intelligence and charm. This is not a stuffy old professor commenting on your class participation. I would love to hear how you are doing? Did you finish the MBA? Are you still working? I understand that you traveled in Europe. Does that mean time off and you have some money? All questions of interest to me.

My own life has been unusual: long stretches of boredom punctuated by brief episodes of more drama than I am equipped to deal with. Please write. For the next few weeks I will be collecting my mail at Poste Restante, Geneva, Switzerland.

Best regards,

Max Brown

The fact that I was impatiently counting down the days until I could reasonably expect a reply confirmed the worst: I had, maybe, a tiny crush on the girl.

♡

The Swiss post office keeps a general delivery letter for 15 days. Our letters might take two weeks to make the round trip, so I waited three weeks before boarding one of the lake steamers for a leisurely, four-plus hour trip down Lake Leman to Geneva. The train required one-third the time, but I had time to kill.

The Poste Restante window was clearly marked where an officious clerk took my passport and began working through the letters in a box marked B. With no visible show of elation – I thought he might be pleased at my good fortune – he withdrew one and delivered it with my passport. I rushed down to the pier to catch the last boat to Montreux and nervously opened the envelope.

Asswipe, (not the salutation one hopes for)

What nerve! All the shit you've done to me, and now you want to be penpals? Holy Sweet Mother of God! You are either fucking with my head, or the most pathetic person in the northern hemisphere. (I'd go with the second option)

Yes, although no thanks to you, I will get that degree in a few weeks. No, I am not employed and rich. Yes, I did go to Europe with a man who talked of our life together but, in the end, just wanted to stick it in my end. And speaking of that, are you the little deviant who arranged the welcoming party when I got home? Full cavity search is pretty descriptive. When I think of you at all, I am administering that kind of search to you. With prejudice.

I heard around the management department that your wife dumped you. She's taking some classes and is telling anyone who will listen that you were a lousy fuck and a mean SOB. I say, go girl!

Have a nice day,

Sally Taylor

It could have been worse, right? She had written back. Two days later . . .

Dear Sally,

I received your letter. A little hot under the collar? Think back, Sally. You came on to me. You couldn't have known, but you also caught me at a vulnerable time. You pretty much wrecked my academic career in the US and then tried to do the same with Fulbright and Dhaka University. How about acknowledging a little responsibility here?

I'm not looking for a penpal. Sounds like
you have no commitments in the US. I'll send
you a prepaid ticket, round trip. If we get
past the first few hours, we can travel
around. Nice sights, but I'd rather see them
with company. Seems nutty? Absolutely!
Here's the nutty logic: Mrs. Brown and I
started out with unsustainably high expectations of each other. There was only one direction: down. And we didn't seem to be able
to pull out of the spiral. Inverting that,
you and I can sink no lower. Better to start
a relationship that has nowhere to go but
up. And, to repeat, I do find things in you
that I admire, despite all of the crap you
have sent my way.

Best regards,

Max Brown

p.s. If you reply, please send to my name at
the following as I have been thinking of
heading up to London to take in some plays.

POSTE RESTANTE
Islington Post Office
116 Upper Street
London N1 1AE, United Kingdom

Max, you dreadful man! Dangling your wealth in front of an
unemployed woman! My thoughts of Sally increasingly involved dangling something else in front of her. Then, waiting
again.

After two weeks of finger drumming I headed northwest-
ward. Two unrewarding days in Paris, then on to London.

———————

Now with a little money for the first time in my life, I headed to
a destination I'd known only from antiquarian catalogues: Cecil
Court. It's pedestrian only, less than 100 meters long, but it's
lined with antiquarian shops, the majority offering ancient
maps.

It was a fine crisp early spring day; a day when it's easy to be optimistic about your prospects. The nearest tube stop is Leicester Square where a coterie of mooching pigeons attached themselves and provided escort. I purchased a bag of birdseed to feed my retinue – perhaps they could be wooed to my side, pigeons seemed to presage momentous events – and regretted the gesture when they became so aggressive I threw the bag at them and fled.

Below is the most expensive map purchased, a 1572 topographical rendering of London taken from an atlas, *Civitate Orbis Terrarum* (Cities of the World).

Note the four figures at the bottom of the map. One of the collaborators on the atlas, Georg Braun, added pictures of people in local dress to reduce the military liability the collection might create for the 300 cities that were included in the six volume set. It was Braun's conviction, stated in the Forward, that the dreaded Turk wouldn't be able to study the maps for military purposes because, he argued, Muslims were prohibited from looking on representations of human forms.

Other maps purchased on the same spree are sprinkled throughout this book. My second favorite is the map of the Moghul empire on the cover and title page, published in the early 1600's by Henricus Hondius, a Dutch cartographer. There are quite a few copies of this map in circulation. The 1850 map of Dhaka (chapter 27), although not distinguished in any regard, was to replace the Robinson map Singh's ransackers had taken.

The following day, I went to the Islington Post Office, mailed the maps back to Montreux, and presented myself at Post Restante. There was a letter.

```
Shithead,

I don't buy the 'nowhere but up' bullshit
for a second. Here's the deal: you can send
me the ticket and I will think about whether
I want to use it. Your low opinion of me
notwithstanding, I will not use it unless I
am coming to check out how things might go.
I did once see something of value in you —
 God knows what.

Be clear on separate bedrooms, no groping,
and all the other reasonable no-noes that
you lechers have trouble remembering when
your nuts override your tiny brains.
```

Sally Taylor

Most excellent! At the British Airways office in Islington I ponied up for an open business class – harder to turn down – round trip ticket to London.

"Ms. Taylor will be informed of the PTA today, if our agent can contact her. Will you be wanting to know her schedule when she books?"

Hell yes!

"That would be useful. I could meet her at the airport. Friendly face, and all that. I can be notified at the Fielding Hotel near Covent Garden."

Sally had already considered her decision long enough and the following day I received a call that Ms. Taylor would be arriving at Gatwick, "two days hence."

I hadn't thought beyond what seemed an unlikely outcome: that she'd say yes. I was mostly just filling time. What did her quick assent mean? Probably she's looking for a chance to dress me down personally. I had to be ready for contumely on a cosmic scale. Excited and anxious, I spent the hours between 4:00 and 6:00 AM rehearsing arguments, parrying accusations, scoring debating points.

Throttling these unproductive thoughts, I moved on to more proactive issues: how to entertain her and derail the anticipated barrage of vituperation. I knew nothing about the woman. Plays, musicals, museums, dank cathedrals? The brochures in the hotel's tiny lobby were little help except for one that entreated the traveler to sample the castle-hotels of the rural countryside. Why not? I dialed the number and a prissy voice guided me through car hire and selection of two castle-hotels in the west country, one near Stonehenge, the other in Tintagel which lays claim to King Arthur's Camelot. Separate rooms.

Then I scouted the immediate neighborhood for pubs and restaurants that might impress.

Sure that my luck had taken a turn for the better, I decided to stick my head up. A telex to Fulbright:

```
Assume you informed by Dhaka U of my need
for hasty departure. Also assume in light
of loss of life and ongoing peril, have
no further contractual obligations.
Regards,
```

I wasn't sure Mosleh had informed Fulbright because I wasn't sure Mosleh was still alive. Although the telex was a risk, it seemed the responsible thing to do.

```
Dr. Brown, Good to hear from you. Yes,
Dean at Dhaka U did inform us you left
under duress. Hope things are calmer now.
A colleague from DU, Dr. Singh, has
called asking for contact information.
Shall we supply him with the London hotel
from which your telex arrived? He says he
has urgent business to conclude. Mean-
while, seeking appointment so you may
complete award.
```

That persistent little fuck! As for the Half-bright people:

```
Singh is the man who killed three others
and tried to kill me. I only escaped by
```

```
wounding him. He seeks my whereabouts to
finish the job. Please destroy any corre-
spondence that would place me in Europe.
He has connections everywhere and was
once in Indian Intelligence before being
cashiered. If Singh inquires again, put
him off the scent with a general address
in Mongolia or Bolivia. Re new appoint-
ment, sorry, I am obliged to remain un-
derground. Apologies for the drama. Trust
other Scholars have smoother time.
```

I had zero confidence that the idiot secretary at Fulbright wouldn't do the opposite of that instructed, if she hadn't already. I needed Sally to arrive to get my mind off Singh and his boys.

41

Grand Tour

Travelers unaccustomed to business class are invariably eager to take advantage of everything on offer: food, the slippers, better headphones, funny little sleep mask, and, most copiously, the free grog. Jostling as genteelly as possible with the other greeters at Gatwick arrivals, I was bracing myself for Sally's initial onslaught when I caught sight of her dragging her roll-on suitcase out of the customs area, and rolling slightly from side to side herself. Three hours of pounding down cocktails, wine, cognac, and God knows what else, followed by a few hours of fitful sleep, she was the embodiment of what a friend called lagover: jetlag plus hangover.

I ducked under the restraining rope and ran up to her before the inattentive guard could react. She looked up sheepishly. "I'm not a very good traveler," followed by a slight gagging sound.

How about that? A business class dividend. It looked like I'd be spared any grief from Sally, at least for the day.

"C'mon. Let's sit you down for a few minutes in a café. Some coffee. Then I'll take you to a relaxing place where you can catch up on sleep." This was acknowledged by a slight inclination of her head which seemed to signal assent.

Most of the flights from Gatwick are on low-cost airlines and charters to destinations in Europe. The backpack-toting passengers are long on facial – or underarm/leg – hair, short on personal hygiene, and famously reluctant to part with cash. Tony restaurants are few but we found refuge in the Hilton's coffee shop where Sally sipped at a cup of coffee while I plied her with the customary questions about her flight. Seeing that the conversation was pointless and a drain on her dwindling resources, I announced. "Plenty of time for talk later. When you're ready we can head out. It's about a 90 minute drive, if we don't get lost." She looked stricken, reckoning I suppose, that 90 minutes was at the outer limit of her reserves. "We won't get lost."

Of course we did. Why can't the British come up with a decent roster of town names? They just repackage the same ones. There was a Middle Wallop, a Nether Wallop, and an Over Wallop, all within a two-mile radius. Further afield lies Fairleigh Wallop. But we couldn't locate plain old un-prefixed Wallop.

It was only a few minutes delay before we found someone who could direct us to our castle-hotel, but it was evident the uncertainty was undermining Sally's enthusiasm.

Compounding her malaise, I'd selected what, logically, should be a fun, quintessentially British car, a Mini, and had pointed it's tiny bonnet westward, timorously negotiating roundabouts and narrow hedgerow-enclosed lanes. Sally discovered the seat wouldn't recline and the noisiness and stiff ride were further eroding her expectations for a Grand Tour.

As we pulled up the blue-graveled drive to our destination the day was saved by the arrival of a sleek helicopter which set down on the lawn and deposited a young couple swaddled in furs and reeking of new money.

Sally took in the castle with renewed interest. Not Buckingham, but still pretty good. Her enthusiasm was further stoked by the large wood-paneled room, a four-poster bed, and long views of green fields. "Okay. So far, I'm impressed." She gazed out the leaded glass window. "But still, no hanky-panky."

The way she put that – 'still' – encouraged the hope that we simply had to pass a probationary period. It also seemed logical that since she'd given herself so cheaply the first time, she now wanted to be seen as a decorous, if not chaste, woman.

"You certainly need rest. I'll be in the next room or downstairs should you want to go out for dinner. If you crash and I don't hear from you by 7:00, I'll assume you're asleep and see you in the morning." I hoped these declarations would indicate I was setting the agenda, although I'm not sure why that was important.

Four hours later there was a knock on the door. "I'm famished."

"Grab your warmest clothes. There's something I've always wanted to do. Yes, it involves food." Two minutes later she returned, bundled in a sweater and coat, a knit hat struggling to contain her red hair. I snuck one of the extra blankets out of the hotel room closet and we went out to the Mini.

Give Me That Ol' Time Religion
- C. D. Tillman, 1873

While I'd not *actually* always wanted to do this, pictures of Stonehenge in the moonlight exerted a strong pull. I'd purchased a picnic hamper at Fortnum and Mason – contents of the basket a mystery other than it was priced in the middle of the range – and, with the hotel's blanket as ground cloth, anticipated a memorable, perhaps even romantic, tête-à-tête on a hilltop overlooking the ancient Druid monument.

The plan went well. Found Stonehenge. Spotted a hilltop across the road. Parked. Lugged the basket and blanket up the hill. And met the howling Salisbury Plains wind, smack in the teeth.

Sally, bless her, remained game and while I futilely tried to improvise a shelter against the gale, she unpacked the hamper, examining each item with pleasure or curiosity and set them out on that portion of the blanket I wasn't trying to stake upright. So many elements were right: As the sky darkened, a gibbous moon illuminated the monument. Sally was festive, although she was increasingly drawing into her coat to escape the wind. The meal looked good and there were two bottles of wine. So close! But I was freezing my nuts off and on the verge of retreating to the Mini when the wind began to subside. Of course; forgotten from an Air Force meteorology course, surface winds usually abate at night.

Sally snuggled against me. "Cold. Don't make a big deal of it," as I wrested the cork out of a bottle of Châteauneuf-du-Pape and poured two glasses. The mesmerizing view made conversation unnecessary, if not sacrilegious.

We wordlessly made our way through the pâtés and cheeses, Sally close to me. The monument gleamed dully, its shapes morphing as clouds scudded over and the moon rose higher. Sally's head fell gently onto my shoulder and almost immediately she was asleep. So *this* is happiness. About fucking time!

We said goodnight at the door to her room. I think I could have kissed her, maybe gotten something started, but elected to give her my most grateful smile with a reminder of the breakfast hours. If she wanted to be seen as a lady who bestowed her favors parsimoniously, I was willing to go along. Up to a point.

In the morning we took the Stonehenge tour. Anti-climactic. I struck up a conversation with one of the volunteer guides, less for the information than to demonstrate to Sally that I was a man at home anywhere in the world. The volunteer recommended a pub in Salisbury where we had a ploughman's lunch, then we headed west to Tintagel under overcast skies.

Sally produced her guidebooks and began reading excerpts aloud about Tintagel and Camelot. The woman had come prepared and reading as we bent along country lanes didn't make her car sick. A sample of the running commentary:

"Wow, all you need for an endless series of romance novels is just Guinevere. I can find at least three . . . no wait, five different women here. None of the early legends has her the same way. The feckless romantic who couldn't keep Lancelot out of her head – or her undies – came later. In Wales they had a ditty about her: 'Gwenhwyfar, daughter of Ogrfan Gawr. Bad when little, worse when great.' It looks like it might rhyme in Welsh, which I won't attempt.

"Here's another one where she was, and I quote, 'an opportunistic traitor who abandons her husband in his hour of peril'."

Coincidence. I knew a woman like that once; the recollection reaffirmed the hope that things would go well with Sally, who moved her research on to Arthur.

"Arthur seems to be portrayed more consistently. He was a sap for a beautiful woman and endured Guinevere's hanky-panky until it was out of hand."

Another parallel – the sap part anyway – as I never had reason to believe Tiff was fooling around behind my back. Why would she? She had me.

Who am I kidding? The real reason I felt secure was that Tiffany was so intimidatingly beautiful few men would have the balls to approach her. As you may recall, it was the exceptional circumstances of the Great Bar Fight that gave me the courage to speak to her. All that aside, now that the similarities between King Arthur's weakness for a beautiful woman and my own had been established, the ancient site felt like familiar ground.

The accommodations were more English Country-Inn than the advertised castle, but the town is dramatic, sloping steeply down to the sea, and the reputed site of Camelot, set out in the Celtic Sea on a high point, is breath-taking. We walked all afternoon, eschewing the donkeys that transported simpering hausfraus up the steep hills in the town. Politely sending Sally up narrow trails and staircases ahead of me, every curve and fold in her tight jeans was indelibly etched into my cerebral cortex before the day's sightseeing was concluded. *

By evening, jetlag was catching up with Sally and conversation over dinner was sparse, mostly disconnected comments on the sights seen during the day. Delivering Sally to her room, I gripped her hand and said with conviction, "I've never had a traveling companion as enjoyable as you." She blushed. Before she could rally and warn me off again, I rushed on, "Breakfast at 8:00 alright with you?"

Returning to my own monastic cell, I stared at the door connecting our rooms. *Would a credit card defeat the lock?* God, she was good looking and she was right: a man's nuts can override his tiny brain. Before something irrevocably stupid occurred, I retreated into the bathroom but decided against a cold shower – when has that ever worked? – settling for a soapy pull to cool my ardor.

The next day we returned to London. Sally wanted to experience driving on the wrong side, a nerve rattling experience for us both, made worse by a gusting wind that buffeted the Mini as we careened down the motorway.

As we drove I learned that she was a late and only child; both parents had died within the past few years. She'd been briefly married when she was in the Army (surprise) to another soldier. She opined she'd married the guy as much to stem the constant barrage of sexual harassment from the meatballs she worked with as any romantic interest. She'd spent most of her short military career working at the base firing range, site of my

---

* I know; who would have expected that level of interest?

annual humiliation as I drilled .38 caliber slugs through every-thing but the paper target. After discharge she worked a variety of jobs, mostly food service because patrons found her 'easy on the eyes' and the schedule allowed her to attend classes. GI bill benefits had helped her through school. She had no long-term goals or expectations. She hoped to be able to take care of her-self and have a little money for travel. "This trip is a dream come true, but not the way I thought it would happen." When asked if she wanted to drift around the countryside, or do Lon-don, she opted for the latter, while not ruling out the former.

Should I read that as a decision to stay with me for a while? Welcome news, and although Herr Swindel had put me on a generous allowance, I was out-spending it at the moment when you throw in the business class ticket.

Acquaint thee, young spirit, acquaint thee
- William Knox, 1886

Sally and I chatted and bantered constantly, but the topics were always in the present. Perhaps that's to be expected when you're sightseeing. Discussion of our shared past was a mine-field neither of us seemed ready to enter. Presumably, however, it was safe to talk about our lives before we'd met each other, and over dinner at a crowded wine bar in Covent Garden I asked Sally to expand on the brief sketch she'd provided in the car. It had seemed unwise to distract her with follow up ques-tions while she was driving (terribly).

"Only too happy to oblige," with a wide smile that made me nearly groan with desire. "I was an only child and not sure what my parents wanted for me. It seems that a lot of middle-class kids get all kinds of signals from their parents that they can ei-ther follow or rebel against. I didn't pick up any of those sig-nals. Without that motivation to comply or rebel I wasn't com-mitted strongly to anything. I went to the junior college for two years, but then began to feel self-conscious about living at home." She tossed her head back and forth as she spoke, great mop of red hair following the movement. "A couple of things fell through – move to a four-year college, better job – nothing seemed to be working – and one day, completely, utterly, totally impulsively . . ." long pause to signal wonder at her impulsiveness, "I stopped to talk to an Army recruiter in a booth at the mall. I don't know if all those guys are that slick, but this guy was incredible. I left believing that I really did need to take two bathing suits to boot camp in case I wanted to go into the pool again the same day, and, as he put it, 'not have to wrestle with a cold wet suit.' I also left his booth with my signature on an enlistment form.

"Nam had been over for two years but there was still a lot of shuffling people around as the draftees either left the Army or cashed in their combat points to get good assignments. I wound up in Kansas on the firing range, narrowly escaping the typing pool." She paused to sip some wine and examine the legs it made on the side of the glass. Small decisions were being made, perhaps on how much to reveal?

"The Army helps you develop realistic expectations. If I didn't get groped, it was a good day. It was hand-to-hand combat around the clock. After a few weeks on the range I could spot the signs and take precautions. If a grunt did well – maybe earn his marksman ribbon – you could guarantee he'd be feeling frisky or entitled or God knows what. Anyway, I learned to keep some kind of a barricade between myself and jerks like that. That didn't stop the talk, of course. Like I said in the car, that was probably much of the reason why I married Arnold, thinking – naively – that a married woman would be treated with respect. He was six years older, a staff sergeant, and he expected good things from the Army. I was expecting full time sexual molestation and after 18 months when he came up for reassignment I told him I'd had enough of the military and was applying for separation – from the Army, that is." Another pause while she considered how much I was entitled to know of her and her life.

"He couldn't leave the Army; I don't know exactly why. Maybe he thought he'd made too much of an investment to turn his back on it? Maybe he didn't think he'd make it on the outside? Maybe he'd never even considered a different future for himself? Accompanied postings were possible, but not common. I was looking forward to a lifetime of gossiping with – sorry, mutually supporting – other Army wives while our husbands were overseas. The divorce rate was sky high so that was probably in my future too. I know I said earlier I'm not terribly ambitious, but that seemed a little too bleak, even for me. My parents weren't well, so Arnold and I split. Not his idea, and I still feel guilty when I think of the dear slob, standing in the doorway, blubbering. All dressed up in his fatigues. Not a great recruiting poster, but a strong mental image. Funny. I received one postcard from him three months after the divorce. He was engaged to his high school sweetheart. And that was it." She was playing with the ring finger of her left hand, as if she were twisting a wedding band. Catching herself, she looked up.

"You're a good listener, Professor, or a good fake. Well-timed nods, good eye contact, although I did notice your gaze drift southward when I mentioned the groping. Power of suggestion?" *She doesn't miss anything, does she? Dear Lord, don't let her be privy to my lust-filled thoughts.*

"Let me know when you need a rest break. I find the story pretty tedious myself." To emphasize how boring she thought it was, she stretched her arms back, her breasts . . . you know what her breasts were doing. Not fair. How's a guy not to ogle?

"Well, mom and dad died – within six months of one another – and I felt like I had no moorings at all. I got a job as a cocktail waitress which lasted two nights. Why didn't it occur to me it would be like the Army times ten? Someone mentioned I had GI bill benefits and that's what got me back in school and that's pretty much the situation you found me in three years later. Waiting tables and taking classes. I took an extra load of classes and was accepted into the MBA program, without completing the BA, because I had 'relevant life experiences.' Who knew that getting felt up by Neanderthals qualified you for advanced academic placement?" Her smile faded; she folded her napkin and parked the eating utensils at four o'clock on her plate.

"That's it?" I'd expected more drama.

"Aha. The man wants to know about other men." That wasn't what I'd been angling for, but was interested, nevertheless. "Sure. I even slept with a few of them. But, you know, there was this transactional quality to the whole thing." I must have looked unsure. "Transactional – a euphemism for paid sex which is, itself, a nicer way of saying prostitution. Like that guy

I went to Denmark with, or, on a smaller scale, a guy takes you out a few times, he's expecting a payoff. Maybe I should have gone out to Berkeley where everybody was screwing everybody else just for fun. No accounting ledgers. No debts to clear." She took a sip of wine as her brow furrowed. "And now here I am again. Gloriosky! Accepting a trip with a man who has . . . what expectations for repayment?"

Whoops! Tables turned. Could I treat her question as rhetorical? No, she was looking directly at me, right eyebrow arched. A hard question to answer since I didn't know what expectations I did have. I chewed my lower lip, nodded thoughtfully, and tried to buy time until I ran out of facial exercises which might signify I was giving her question the benefit of my full mental faculties. Raising my head and looking her in the eyes, "I'm taking it at face value that you took this trip on the clear agreement that sex wouldn't be part of the deal. Don't think for a minute I've turned gay or lost interest in sex. I guess I went so long without any kind of affection that I've almost learned to do without it."

A brief pause to indicate these were not easy words to speak. And, in truth, they weren't because there wasn't a whole lot of truth in them; I really wanted to get into her pants.

"I said it before – perhaps you picked up the amazement in my voice – I'm having a good time seeing the sights with someone who's genuine, positive, agreeable, spontaneous and basically nice. This is a new experience for me and one I thought I might never have again. You just keep on the way you have been, and we'll call the account squared. Okay?"

"Can I get cranky once in awhile?"

"No."

This got me thinking about what I said at the start – about men wanting sex. Well, of course we do, but there I was, happier than I'd been in years, thanks to an affable, uncomplicated traveling companion. That's not to dismiss the fact that I also really, really wanted to bonk her.

————

Our fourth day back in London, having roared through five museums and galleries and taken in one musical, one comedy, and, inevitably, Shakespeare (*Midsummer's Night Dream* – not the worst), the receptionist at the Fielding Hotel informed me that someone with a foreign accent had telephoned asking if a Professor Brown was registered; the caller hadn't left his name.

"What did you tell him?" I croaked. Good old Fulbright. Founded on principles of openness and honesty.

"Nothing."

Thank God for at least that.

Stonehenge by John Speed, c 1600.

42

Alas What Hourly Dangers Rise
- Anne Steele, 1760

"Sally, we've been evicted. I only booked our reservations through today – not knowing our plans – and I didn't expect the hotel would fill up. Not to worry; fortunately the Savoy, just down the street, has a suite we can take." Holding up a finger to request forbearance, I added, "A suite with separate bedrooms." While she packed I went down to settle the bill and tell the receptionist we were bound for the Lake District.

Dilemma. Should Roscoe come out of the suitcase and permanently into my pocket? Weighing only the negatives, an inaccessible gun is of little value when surprised by an assassin. But a gun constantly in the pocket invites discovery at awkward times: unanticipated metal detectors, or, in a much anticipated clinch with Sally. I doubted she'd hang around long with a man marked for death. But, I didn't know that for sure. Better safe than sorry (*Remember What's Important*), and I pocketed the pistol.

Sally, the diligent tourist, had read up on the catastrophically expensive Savoy by the time we departed the relatively cheap Fielding. She was thrilled. I was picturing Herr Swindel slicing off my balls with his Victorinox knife; he would use the serrated blade. Keeping that 3.2 million intact seemed more important to him than to me.

"This was the first real luxury hotel in Britain," she enthused, "although it was a house of ill repute for a while."

"Did you know that the guy who built it, Carte, financed the whole thing with profits from Gilbert and Sullivan productions?" I didn't. "Max, you've been so generous I hate to even suggest this. Do you think we might find tickets for Gilbert and Sullivan tonight?"

Thank providence for overdone productions. *The Mikado* was playing close at hand at fire-sale prices. Sally was ecstatic. Slouching low in my seat to avoid notice by possible assassins, I dozed from 'Three little maids from school are we' to the end of the first act.

———

After the sub-continent, the second highest concentration of Indians, Pakistanis and Bangladeshis has to be in England. Potential assailants lurked in every alley, waited on our table, and followed us through museums. I gravitated toward pink-faced men in bowlers – few in number – using them as a shield against the sea of darker-pigmented individuals. Sally noticed that I seemed to be scurrying from one knot of people to another, like a man seeking shade on a scorching day. We were taking a breather on a padded bench in the Tate, facing Picasso's *Nude Woman with Necklace* and sharing our incredulity at its popularity, when Sally asked, "Why do we always seem to find ourselves in the most crowded areas?"

"How do you mean?" I knew what she meant.

"I don't know. Like, if we're in a museum, it just seems that you head for pictures and statues that have the most people grouped around."

I started to explain the patently obvious: the greatest art or most interesting exhibits attract the largest audiences. "No. I'd better tell you." Pause, for dramatic effect, and to reconsider my decision.

"I stumbled onto something of value in Dhaka that earned me the prejudicial interest of six unpleasant men. I was pursued and eventually fled the country. That's why I'm in Europe and not in Bangladesh. The experience was intense enough that I've developed an instinctive reaction to men from the sub-continent, especially India. I assume it'll subside over time."

"And your pursuers are . . . ?"

"I understand that one was killed, one was seriously wounded and four are unaccounted for."

"Hmmm." Head down in thought, one eyebrow arched up toward me. "Does this explain your wife's unaccompanied return to the US?"

"The long overdue straw."

"And why you pay cash for everything?"

"Yep, unless I'm leaving a place and then I'll use plastic."

More reflection. "I guess the good news is that you have enough independent wealth to go on the lam for a while." She stood and stretched. "I'm hungry. Maybe not Indian food, though," she laughed. "How about that tea room on the top floor of the Portrait Gallery? I read that the view over the roof-tops is great."

That was a fast turnaround. Her next question should have been about the extent of our peril, not choice of eatery. Independent wealth? Of course. I'd encouraged that perception. What I don't understand is why she trusted me to have told her the full truth.

The rooftop view was underwhelming. Metal domes streaked with pigeon poop – a few of the offenders loitering on the windowsills. *What misfortune do these harbingers portend this time?*

After the tea and pastries had been served, Sally asked, as if it had just occurred to her, "What precautions should we take, just in case these baddies are still after you?"

"My only precautions are to keep a low profile and stay on the move. These are both easy to do since I don't have a profile worthy of notice, and I like to travel, especially now that you're here."

She smiled broadly – fabulous teeth – and kicked me lightly under the table. "Stop it. Y'all 'll turn a young girl's head." I laughed.

"Oh jeez," she moaned, "you're remembering that terrible accent I put on when we, er, you know, met." She slapped clotted cream onto a scone.

"You know," she continued, "I've thought about that a lot. Never faked an accent before. Why then? It just came out of me. Could it be some bizarre psychological thing, like I wanted to be a different person for a while? Maybe, like someone else was selling her body for a lousy grade." The uncooperative cream fell from the scone onto the plate; she scooped it up and smacked it back on the pastry.

The conversation was heading in a dangerous direction. In an effort to get it back on a safer course, "Sally, you continue to amaze me. I don't know; perhaps it's the low expectations I wrote about. Maybe it'll blow up tomorrow, but this has been one really nice week."

Damn. I really truly was developing a king-sized crush on this woman. Loneliness? Horniness? Contrast with the hyper-critical Tiffany? It felt good to experience positive feelings about someone, but vulnerability came with that.

"Okay, enough, or you'll suspect my motives. Let's talk travel plans. I'll need to swing through my new hometown in Switzerland at some point. Aside from that, the world is our oyster." Her shoulders relaxed. The smile returned. No one could have looked happier than Sally Taylor.

"No, wait," smile fading. "There's a hole in the narrative, an elephant in the room . . . I'll leave the metaphors to you. Something we're not talking about."

"Are you sure you want to open this?" Maybe she'd back away.

"Mostly sure. If you drew a timeline of our involvement, 99 percent of it has been unpleasant." No denying that.

"Here's my analysis. Lord knows, I've gone over this enough in my head. Now that I know you a little better, Max, I'm seeing things that I like beyond your appearance and clever speech. I think you're kind, can be warm, but you're surprisingly less sure of yourself than I used to think." Was I that transparent? "Maybe I'm projecting here, but let me go back to what I was saying about how I felt when I sold myself for a C+."

Back to the low grade. Couldn't we move beyond that?

"I felt I was being punished by that grade when I was already punishing myself enough. And it made me mean and vindictive, and childish. There were other things I could've done to make you raise the grade, I suppose, but I mainly wanted someone else, someone who'd been part of the whole stinking thing, to feel some of the same pain."

Despite myself, I felt dampness in my eyes. When the fuck had I become so emotional? Lachrymose Max?

"Oh Sally. What a chord you've struck. Mean, vindictive, childish? That was me, alright. I wanted to strike out at someone, and not think too much about my own rôle." This was really embarrassing. I was going to cry. "The grade changes, cutting off your utilities, the . . ."

"What! You were responsible for me sitting in the dark for ten days, without water or gas to cook with?" That outburst sobered me up. "Okay, what other unpleasant events in my life can be laid at your door? Come on. Give."

We exchanged stories. She figured the grade changes had been my doing and that prompted her letter to Tiffany. Thanks to the university's antediluvian view of computers, the primary sources for student grades were the paper copies which governed whenever a dispute arose; my efforts to get her into academic trouble turned out to be nothing more than a speed bump. And, despite the fiery reaction, she'd been pretty sure I was behind the utility cutoffs.

It's handy to have a devil to explain misfortune. The battery was stolen from her car and she wondered if I'd contracted someone to torment her. Her rent check got lost and suspicion again fell on me. There was little doubt in her mind, however, about who was behind the drug search at JFK.

While this wasn't a bracing exercise, I got the feeling we were burying these incidents as we catalogued them. When we got to the end of the list, we sat silently and played with our teacups. After what felt like the right interval, I said – very uncharacteristically – "I don't want to be that person ever again." And before I could say more or make an emotional spectacle, I excused myself to the men's room.

When I returned Sally was gone. I called for the check and started to worry that she'd left without saying goodbye. Would I find her at the hotel? Was she on her way to the airport? At that point she came back from the women's room and announced, "I'd like to see where you live. Should we head that way, maybe pausing in Paris? I get the feeling you don't feel secure here right now. Something about our hasty departure from the little Hotel Fielding to the Fort Knox Savoy. Besides, England isn't going anywhere."

I took four things from that statement: 1) She was a perceptive lass. 2) Her interest in the domestic part of my life suggested she wasn't excluding a deeper level of involvement. 3) She expected to spend a long time roaming the world with me.

4) She was a person who could let the past stay in the past. Fine on all accounts.

The busboy looked like he was from the subcontinent; I left a generous tip.

Draw Me Closer to Thee
- J. R. Bryant, 1892

The channel ferry is a great place to either feel isolated and in your own world, or toss your cookies over the rail. The weather favored the former, and, as bickering gulls wheeled over the ferry's broad wake, the descending sun painted Dover's white cliffs with slashes of orange. We braved the cold on the aft deck, nursing teas, and, after several false starts I popped the question.

"Tell me about your mother. What was she like? How did she get along with your father?"

Again, the arched eyebrow. "Why, Max the Fourth! What should I read into that question?" she laughed. Then, looking at me with what I desperately hoped was affection, "My mom was old school. Dedicated to the family, always proud of her husband. Dad was a good man, but not a great achiever, which is why I often noticed how mom built him up. He drove a city bus for 34 years before he died, pretty much on the job. She always asked him about work, every night, and he would tell her how he'd dealt with difficult passengers, avoided an accident, given a poor person a free ride. She seemed to hang on every word." Unexpectedly, she kissed me on the cheek. "Is that what you wanted to know?"

Angels were singing in my head. Rainbows arched above my vision. Shooting stars crisscrossed in flight.

"Max, I'm not that good a person." I was ready to believe that she *was* that good a person. "Things are moving faster than either of us expected, maybe, because as you said at the start, neither of us expected much. You're not the insufferable snot and I hope I'm not the emasculating bitch we had each other for. I've made a conscious decision to enjoy each day as it comes along and not think ahead. I'll also be looking over my shoulder for Indian men. Right now, show me a good time in Paris and then we can inspect your digs in Switzerland." Her broad smile slowly changed to concern, then she laughed. "I can't believe it! The Great and Articulate Wizard of Max is speechless!" She kissed me lightly on the lips and went off in search of the loo.

Drifting Apart, Drifting Apart
- K. Shaw, 1877

Paris was a letdown. Maybe we know too much about it. The *Louvre* is long lines, a confusing layout, and a knot of people clustered on tiptoe trying to get a glimpse of *Monalisa*. "It's so small," rises the plaintive chorus. Eiffel tower? We discovered that neither of us is fond of heights. Tomb of the unknown soldier? Snore. The *Orangerie* and *Jeu de Paume,* however, were exceptions. Neither Sally nor I'd seen much impressionist art and we made return trips to both museums.

Our hotel on the île St. Louis was belle époque on anabolic steroids. Charming at first, but when the shortcomings of the heating, plumbing and sound-proofing became evident, the flocked wallpaper, brass beds and open cage elevator lost their appeal.

The 19th century trappings of the hotel must have lulled me into thinking that we'd been transported in time; I registered with my own name, an incautious mistake that's impossible to reverse. But, after another lengthy internal debate, Roscoe, placed in the suitcase for our pass through French immigration and customs, was left there.

Return to dry land seemed to have had a sobering effect. No more gooey exchanges, no flirting. We were content to be together – I especially appreciated that Sally studied up to provide explanations and narrative as we toured the city – and she was entertaining company. Not witty conversation, but she was clever and had a playful outlook. Example:

In the most expensive restaurant we graced in Paris, she announced she'd always wondered what 'made a moue' signified. "Something between a pout and a grimace?" I tried.

"Yeah, I know the definition. But what does it actually look like?" Scanning the 'demoiselles at the other tables for inspiration, she began to work her mouth into a series of progressively sillier expressions that ended only when red wine erupted from my nostrils. We won't be welcomed back.

The laughs were great. I couldn't recall the last time Tiff and I had fun together. But I began to wonder if the magic of the channel crossing was gone for good. Had we somehow time-traveled from first date to old fogeys? Had we leap-frogged over all the good stuff in between, especially the steamy part toward the beginning?

———————

Familiarity breeds content, a bland porridge that sustains, but doesn't fully satisfy. We'd been joined at the hip since Sally's arrival and both came to the same conclusion. Speaking almost simultaneously, "I hope you won't be offended, but I thought we might each do something on our own this afternoon." The jointly expressed thought brought a laugh but it made me worry. I wanted a brief separation to rekindle the channel crossing feelings. Sally probably wanted time off because she was growing weary of me.

"I think I'm going to cruise the antiquarian markets around here. The endless quest for the undervalued map. Objectify some women, of course. Do you have plans?" Maybe I shouldn't have asked. Seems like prying?

"Girl stuff. Shopping. *Galeries Lafayette, Printemps* and points in between."

"In that case, would it be okay if I gave you some money? Since you aren't able to earn any at the moment."

She laughed. "Only if it isn't an insultingly small amount." I fished ten 1,000 franc notes out of my wallet, hoping it wasn't an offensively meager sum. She looked pleased. Later I calculated it was around twelve hundred dollars.

The 'île aux Vaches (upper) and the 'île Notre-Dame (lower) were combined at the end of the 17th century to create the île Saint-Louis where we stayed. Olivier Truschet and Germain Hoyau, 1550.

43

In the Hour of Trial
- J. Montgomery, 1834

How can a person not worry when someone they care about is unaccounted for? Did this start in 'Nam when I'd hung around base ops until every 101 was back on the ground? And sank into dark thoughts when a plane was overdue.

Sally hadn't returned to the hotel by 6:00 when we usually had an apéritif while discussing restaurant options. Still shopping, of course. At 7:00 I checked the guide book to see what time the big stores closed. They were closing. By 8:00 I'd descended into a full-blown funk. The options: a) Desertion. She'd had her fun and would fly back to the US when the money was exhausted. b) She was still trying on clothes at a shop that kept late hours. c) Victim of foul play. d) Run down crossing the street. e) Singh and Co. had caught up with us. And so on.

The concierge said she hadn't come back during the afternoon. At my insistence he checked her room and reported her suitcase and clothes were still there. Of course it wasn't desertion; she would never do that. The concierge was disinclined to further indulge my paranoia and call hospitals.

"She is a beautiful young woman in Paris, monsieur. It would be a tragedy if she did not enjoy herself. N'est ce pas?"

Was that statement supposed to be reassuring? I sat in the small lobby watching the street for Sally's approach. I really hoped this had nothing to do with Singh.

What was happening to Sally was this:

The City of Light has some dark corners. Sally was trying to find the Metro entrance (Chausée d'Antin-La Fayette) and turned down the Rue de Mogador. Burdened by great rustling shopping bags that occupied both hands she failed to hear the footsteps behind her before she was spun around and forced into an entryway and against the wall by a large man with cigarette breath and strong BO. The police later noted that those two identifying features did not appreciably narrow the pool of suspects in Paris.

While this was going on I sat in the hotel lobby and realized my posture looked like I was praying.

———

At 8:40 a black pigeon waddled by the hotel door, pausing briefly to inspect the lobby. Great. This time a _black_ portent of misfortune? The bird took flight as a police car, a blue and white Peugeot, pulled up at the door; a male and female officer got out and entered. My mouth was dry. They conferred with the réceptionniste who nodded toward me.

"Pardon, monsieur. Vous êtes Professeur Brown?"

"Oui. Il y a un problème?" This question produced a volley of French of which two words stood out: 'Taylor' and 'incident', or maybe 'accident', as the first syllable of both seem to be formed high in the same nasal passages.

"Un accident?"

"Non, monsieur. Un _in_cident," clarified the policewoman. Comprehending the full scope of the language barrier she continued, slowly, "Venez avec nous, s'il vous plaît." This request was supplemented by a gentle beckoning motion with her hand. We got into the police car, the woman driving, me in back where a long line of miscreants had ridden, all of them as apprehensive as I was, and proceeded through the streets without flashing lights or siren. Okay, not rushing to the hospital. The morgue? At the risk of provoking another barrage of incomprehensible French I asked,

"Mademoiselle Taylor. Est-ce qu'elle va bien?" The policeman took it upon himself to answer, unfortunately. Again, only a few words stood out. '_Blessé_' was confusing. Blessed? Did that mean good fortune had befallen her? Or did it mean she's gone to her final, and blessed, resting place? Ah shit, no. It came back; _blessé_ means injured. Did he say she was <u>not</u> injured? Or, it seemed there was another person mentioned. Was that person injured? With nothing further to lose I followed up, "Mademoiselle Taylor est blessé?"

The policewoman – the sharper of the duo – said, "Non," and left it at that. The policeman seemed ready to amplify but his partner stopped him. Good.

The police station was filled with characters from Central Casting: drooping moustaches, dangling cigarettes, harried looks, and trench coats draped over chair backs. High counters separated the waiting area from rows of offices, all with frosted glass walls. At the first counter I was asked to provide identification. The officer had no information on Mlle. Taylor. He did not speak English. His job was to laboriously inscribe my name in a large lined book. The task completed, he thrust his chin in the direction of the waiting area.

I took a seat on a bench with a group who were . . . bail bondsmen? lawyers? hookers? pimps? After a few minutes a police officer with rolled up shirtsleeves summoned me from the door of his glass-walled office.

"I regret to bring you here for this situation, monsieur. When someone is seriously injured, as in this case, we have certain procedures that are required of us."

Holy shit!

"May I see Miss Taylor? Will she recover? Is anyone attending to her?"

"You may be assured, monsieur, that Mademoiselle Taylor is well attended. Her needs are met. There are just a few formalities and you may be reunited. First, what is your relationship?"

Well, not sure. In the official environment of a police station, it seemed prudent to offer the most defensible description of our association: "We're close friends, traveling together."

"Ah, then. I may take it that you and the young woman are not married?" He fixed me with a disapproving scowl.

Married? What the fuck! This is France. "No, sir. We aren't married."

"Ah, then. This is a small complication. It is not possible to release her to your cognizance if there is no formal relationship."

"Cognizance? Has she been charged with a crime?"

"There has been a complaint that we must investigate. I am sure everything will be resolved *tout de suite*." Now he was talking down to me.

Sent back to the bench with the other malefactors and their abettors, I watched the doors for any sign of Sally. Time crept. On the pretext of looking for the *toilette*, I walked slowly down the hall, listening through the glass partitions.

"Isn't it clear? The bastard attacked me! Tried to rape me! It was self-defense." Sally's voice! Hearty, healthy, and really pissed off. I opened the door and she leapt up from her chair and ran into my arms. Wow! How good that felt, from every possible angle.

"Monsieur, you must not be in here. Leave at once. We are conducting a criminal investigation." Another officer came in; I assumed he was there to remove me, but he pushed a file folder across the table to the interviewing officer who glanced through it. A forced smile.

"Ah, excellent. You see how these things are resolved when we follow the procedures. You are completely absolved mademoiselle. Your assailant will be charged this very night. Two officers are now en route to the hospital for the arrest."

Sally wasn't through. "How the *merde* – or whatever you say – could you imagine I went out, loaded down with shopping bags, and decided to start roughing up large bad smelling men? Huh?"

"Ah, it was the nature of the incident, mademoiselle. In that area there is the pocket picking and perhaps some youths grab a bag from a shopper, but a physical attack? It is very rare. When the man said you were the *agresseur*, well, what is one to think?" Gallic shrug. "Especially with all the damage that was done to the poor fellow." A second Gallic shrug in case we'd missed the first one.

"Is he, by any chance, Indian or Bangladeshi?" That's me, finding my voice. Something about this attack didn't seem right. Rape in a busy part of Paris? Early evening? But then, although Singh could know about Sally, how would he know where to direct his contractor – if that's who it was – to that part of town?

Feigning a Herculean effort, Sally's interrogator reopened the dossier and scanned the information. "No. I believe not. It says here he is *Bulgare* – you say Bulgarienne? – but his command of the French language is most admirable," dismissive look at me, "despite the condition of his nose," sour look at Sally. "His dossier does suggest he is not a *citoyen modèle*. If you permit us a few minutes we will provide you with a précis of our report, perhaps for your insurance purposes."

––––––––––

The Army grunts dismissively called us zoomies, and we replied from our own larger lexicon of unflattering names, but credit is due: Army training is good for something.

Sally was excited to have an attentive ear. While I was trying to persuade a drunk – via hand-signals – to vacate enough bench space for Sally and me to sit together, she rushed into a recitation of her night's adventures.

"This asshole had me pinned against the wall with one arm across my throat and the other hand was groping my boobs. I got both hands on his groping thumb and bent it 'til I felt it snap."

She illustrated this by bending her own thumb back. I think I maybe winced.

"He took his arm off my throat and I head-butted him straight in the nose. Instant blood. Look at my new blouse!" Her face registered indignation, then excitement again.

Obediently, I checked her blood-stained blouse. Her nipples were clearly outlined through the thin fabric.

"I wondered if another head-butt might not shove the nose cartilage back into his brain and kill him but he turned sideways so I grabbed his wrist and shoved his arm straight up behind him 'til I felt his shoulder go."

"Good God, lady! I think I'm in love with you." What did I just say? She wouldn't take it seriously, if she even heard it.

"Well, it's not like it was the first time I've had to fight someone off. It was, however, the first time I felt free to come back with a 'proportionate response' as the brass liked to say. In the Army a woman's defensive options were pretty much limited to a scowl and a scolding." The recollection brought a frown to Sally's face. "I guess I was making up for all the times I couldn't give some cretin what he deserved.

"Where was I? Oh yeah. Since I was free, I ran back up the street screaming bloody murder. One of Paris' Finest ran up and pretty soon we were surrounded by cop cars. I thought I saw someone pick up my shopping bags and get into a car, but I assumed it must be another cop.

"The asshole was wandering around dazed, but he had the language advantage. I guess he said he was the victim so I wound up here and they took him off in an ambulance."

At this point we were summoned back to the office to receive the précis which was presented with more flourish than you'd expect a police report deserved.

I wanted clarification on a couple of things. "My apologies for taking more of your time." The answering look made it clear that no apology would suffice for the imposition I was about to make on these underappreciated and overworked guardians of public safety. "Does the dossier provide any information about this man that would suggest a motive? I'm impressed by your analysis that this is an unusual crime for the place and time of day."

A little flattery goes a long way. The cop leafed through the dossier more slowly, backing up occasionally; he appeared to be focusing on pagination. He turned to his colleague who had brought the file and who also examined the page numbers. They conferred in lowered voices but the words *Deuxième Bureau* came through once and *Air-Jay* was mentioned several times.

Closing the folder, "Upon further examination, it appears that some information is absent. But we are convinced that there is a satisfactory explanation."

"I apologize for asking further, but there have been recent attempts on my life in another country. The assailants had been members of the national intelligence apparatus. I believe I distinctly heard you say *Deuxième Bureau*, and unless *Air-Jay* refers to the famous author of *Tintin*, I'm guessing that it also stands for a French intelligence service."

"Your instincts do not deceive you, monsieur. *RG* is *Direction Centrale des Renseignements Généraux*, the intelligence arm of the police. It does appear that certain information on your Bulgarienne has been removed from the dossiér. When that happens, we – the working police – first think of our cousins in the *RG*, although I must emphasize there is no direct evidence to support such a theory."

The door flew open and a third cop burst in. This time the conversation was too rapid to pick out more than *Bulgare* (a few times) and *merde* (many times).

"The Bulgarian is missing, right?" That's Sally, fists on hips.

"Ah oui, madame. Je regret que . . ." then, catching himself, "Yes, you are correct. A colleague or accomplice liberated him from the hospital before our agents arrived to place him in custody."

"And, do you have a description of the 'liberator'?" That was one question too many and all three officers donned official faces.

"Rest assured that we will do everything to ensure that justice is done. Our business here tonight is concluded. Except that you must provide a means to contact you should there be developments or the need to appear in court to face the accused." With misgivings I provided the phone number of reception at the Fairmont Palace in Montreux.

While a cop was driving us back to the hotel I beamed at Sally. "I've never been so relieved in my life. God, I was worried. Apparently you know how to take care of yourself."

"Yeah, but I feel awful. All those clothes I bought with your money? Gone. You know, I had a feeling something bad would come from that much self-indulgence."

"Don't think like that. We'll replace them in the morning. I'd like to come with you. Maybe see you in action again?"

"Nah. I don't think I want the stuff anymore. It was more fun buying them than owning them. Not a tragic loss."

Over our delayed apéritif, we rehashed the events of the evening. Sally was undecided who had behaved worse, her assailant or *les flics*. In response to my concern that this might be the long reach of Singh, she didn't recall the Bulgarian saying or doing anything that would be a message. She did wonder about the boob groping. If you're going to rape someone in a public area, wouldn't you bypass foreplay?

I was alarmed. On the evidence of the missing pages in the Bulgarian's dossier it seemed likely he had a connection to French Intelligence – perhaps doing small jobs. If Singh's boasts were accurate that 'contacts must be maintained' and he'd traded favors with the French, there might be a link back to Singh & Co. Did Singh get our hotel information from an old acquaintance in *RG*, and did the same person put him in touch with the Bulgarian, and his accomplice, whose mission was not rape or robbery, but kidnapping? The appearance of the car and second man was consistent with the kidnapping theory. Singh had said they usually kept family out of it, but you couldn't put much stock in his sense of professional ethics. Nothing would get me to fork over the money faster than Sally's kidnapping.

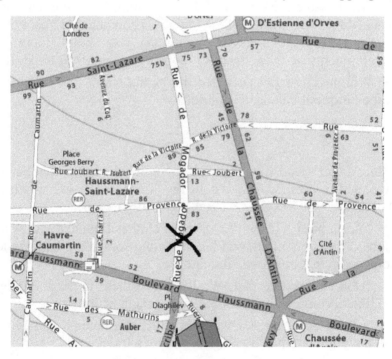

44

Just as I Am
- C. Elliott, 1840

This may not be the best time to bring it up, but over the years I've known the occasional self-doubt (surprising, right?). Sally's arrival stirred those questions about my self-worth. Her basic goodness compared to my basic baseness.

Let's intellectualize – it's the default refuge taken by those with advanced degrees – and ask what sociology can contribute to our understanding. Proceeding deductively:

First premise: We middle-class Americans base our identity and self-regard on what we *do* in society. Father, doctor, hooker, and so on. This premise seems to be pretty much a given nowadays.

Second premise: I'd despised most of what I'd done. Starting with the jobs: Combatant in an immoral war; duty shirker in the same war; a preening, pompous pedagogue who viewed his academic discipline with contempt. And then we turn to my behavior: liar, adulterer, murderer, blasphemer, and other unflattering descriptors I'd earned over the years.

Conclusion: Based on these rôles and failings I should despise myself.

Does this explain why it takes constant effort to maintain a measure of positive self-regard? Is this a common condition? Write and let me know. It's relevant to what follows.

Lord, what a thoughtless wretch was I
- I. Watts, 1750

Sally appeared to have recovered by morning and we went for a bicycle ride through the Bois de Boulogne. Driven into a restaurant by the cold wind and seated across a small table, I had to acknowledge that *I* had not recovered from the night before. I'd come unhinged with worry about this woman, and that meant only one thing: I was becoming more attached than comfort allowed. Struck dumb by this realization, minutes passed before Sally broke the increasingly uncomfortable silence.

"I've told you my life's story. Yours?"

Taken off guard, I sensed we were in danger of Professor Windbag Brown mounting to the lectern; he would drone on for hours, beginning the history in utero and detailing every waking minute up to the present. To forestall that, "Whoa. I need time to make notes. Draw up some charts. Perhaps some overheads to project on the wall." She shook her head no. "I thought I gave a fulsome and self-aggrandizing bio to the class you were in. N'est-ce pas?"

"I must have been absent. Or nodded off soon into your speech." Big grin.

What is it about a woman's smile? I dissolve. "Ah, Sally. I am so under your spell it worries me. That noted – and please don't fuck up the moment with a response – let me give you the abbreviated CV:

"For all intents and purposes, an only child. My childhood behavior – unwaveringly obnoxious – was largely a response to a pretentious name. BA from Boise State. Took flying lessons then went into the Air Force so Uncle Sam could pay for the training. Married in haste. Survived Vietnam by, essentially, shirking my duty. Went to grad school and picked up three legitimate letters to add to the fraudulent Roman numeral. Found myself settling into academe where I despised my colleagues, and became just like them. Went to the orient. Unearthed a small fortune. Killed a man. Tried to kill another man. Fled to Montreux. Wrote to you. Things are looking up."

Sally's large green eyes widened further. Damn! I'd overdone it by mentioning the killing. Was this an attempt to prove that I was in the same league as her when it came to facing down danger? I was trying to figure out how to walk some of this back when she spoke.

"Holy shit. You wrote that there'd been some drama. I can hardly wait for the details. But you seem to be playing it down . . . and your voice sounds sad. You've accomplished so much in your life – pilot, doctorate, professor. What's the big regret?"

A good question. What is the answer? "I guess it's because I keep letting myself down."

Sally looked away and her beautiful eyes grew moist. "Who hasn't?"

Her hand moved toward me and, as I reached for it . . . she picked up some crumbs from the table. Awkward moment. She was lost in her own regrets. Recovering after a minute she asked, "And now the details?" The cold wind was driving large raindrops against the window; we had time to kill.

What to tell her? I'd been parsimonious with the facts to that point. So, I erred in the opposite direction and told her everything, perhaps in the hope she'd become lost in the welter of detail. It took almost twenty minutes, concluding, "I warned you that I needed to prepare. It can get pretty convoluted and boring." This was delivered with a hopeful smile that faded as I watched her expression harden.

"It's easy to follow. You found a clue to a treasure. You went after the treasure. Bad guys went after the same treasure. You killed one of them. Another one captured you, but you cleverly got away and left him badly injured. You cashed in the treasure and sent for me. Then you learned the bad guys knew where you were and they were in hot pursuit. You did *not* trouble me with this information. I was attacked in what looks more and more like a failed kidnapping attempt. Is that about it, Professor?"

"I don't know what to say, Sally. You're right. I didn't tell you and I should have. I gave you partial information which was no help and placed you in danger. I'm so very sorry." Her expression made a slow transition from anger to contempt. "Let's get you packed up and back to the States."

Holy sweet mother of God! Max, you could bring Disney-World to a halt with a dime! Across from me was a wonderful person with whom I was falling in love, and I'd screwed the pooch.

"I need to think." She glared at me, then stared stonily through the window. The rain rattled against the awning and glass. After a minute she stood, put on her coat and hat, and left, stealing an umbrella from the rack as she went out the door.

It took almost an hour to wheel the two bicycles back to the rental kiosk, and another 40 minutes to get to the hotel where I arrived wet, shivering and feeling like the most selfish and worthless piece of shit on the globe. I was prepared for the réceptionniste to tell me that Mlle. Taylor was gone.

Amazing Grace
- J. Newton, 1779

Mlle. Taylor was, in fact, sitting in the breakfast room, warming herself with a cup of tea and wearing an expression that would have petrified a Gorgon. I sat down. She raised her teacup, examined the contents, and put it back down.

"Here's what I've figured out:

"A. You kept information from me because you thought I'd split. A little flattering, but not very, since you assumed I couldn't deal with the truth – or be trusted with it.

"B. I wound up in jeopardy because I wasn't alert to what was going on. Thanks a ton, shithead!

"C. Why oh why oh why do I wind up with such pathetic assholes!?

"D. You haven't figured it out, but I have. I can see you have a thing for me, and I'd developed feelings for you. They're fading fast. That's useful to the other side and they seem to have picked up on it.

"E. They can use that vulnerability whether we're together or not. I'm as easily kidnapped in the US as anywhere else. I'm in constant danger because some dickhead found some jewels and now's pining like a thirteen year old.

"Where am I, G?"

"No, F."

"Okay, F. My options are to split and lie low until the baddies decide I'm no longer a good bargaining chip to get the jewels back, or, I could stay here and duke it out with them. Would you agree?"

"I guess so," I mumbled.

Sally stared at me, arching both eyebrows. "Is that it? Is that all you have to say?"

Jesus, what was there to say? Nothing good came to mind other than to repeat the same apology – which hadn't calmed her. I tried to think of something to add. She was waiting.

"I still have the gun." Is that the best I could do? Damn! Not good.

She continued to stare at me, her expression changing from indignant to stunned. Her mouth opened and closed several times; apparently no words were available to express her emotions. Then she started to laugh.

"You still have a gun? Based on what you told me of your performance in the family planning warehouse, I think my danger level just went *up*." She laughed some more, finally tailing off to giggles.

Then she got serious again. "Okay, here's where I am right now. You seem to put great store in how parents acted toward each other. This is what I saw growing up. My mom and dad didn't keep things from each other. It was never the Strong Man keeping unpleasant realities from the Little Woman. He had chest pains; he told her. Not for sympathy, but so she could be ready if something happened. Another time he thought he might lose his job. He told her. No wailing. Mom just started checking the Help Wanted classifieds. No drama. They just told each other what was going on. Are we getting the picture here? This is how two adults go through life together. If you want to hang out with a woman, Maxie boy, you'd better be prepared to deal with her as an equal. Clear?"

"You're right. One hundred percent right." She didn't look mollified. "I know this will sound like special pleading, but for twelve miserable years, if anything went wrong, I was always, and I mean *always* the cause. Rain on picnic. Max's fault. Economy tanks? Same. She gained two pounds? Ditto. You may find this hard to believe, but that's been my experience with women – or, *a* woman. That history doesn't encourage a person to share bad news. On an intellectual level I understand you're different, but old patterns don't disappear overnight."

She scowled and looked away, chewing on her upper lip, "No, I understand. I know women like that – and men – who're quick to lay the blame for their problems on someone else. But . . . I hope *you* understand. We're in the 1980's, not 1880's. If you like me, you'll adapt. If you don't adapt, you know we won't make it, and, despite how furious I am with you now, I was starting to hope that we would make it. And, remember another thing: last night I learned I could probably beat the shit out of you or almost any other man!" She grinned broadly at the recollection.

"Does that mean you're staying?"

"I guess. Maybe just to watch you try to redeem yourself."

Happiness!

"You won't regret it. I'll be a *citoyen modèle*."

I thought for a minute. I really cared for this woman. Isn't it selfish to want her near, constantly in the crosshairs? "Look Sally, I'm not arguing with your decision, which delights me, but let me describe the risks in clear terms: These guys torture and behead. Their leader may have access to intelligence-service information which makes it easier for them to find us. And I don't mean to take anything away from your great performance last night, but next time they may be better prepared to deal with you. As much as I want you to stay, I also want you to live to a ripe cantankerous old age."

"I thought about those things. The risk goes down only a little if I go it alone. You've been a pathetic selfish asshole, but I see potential. I'm sticking with you a while longer."

I summoned the concierge and asked him to unearth a bottle of Champagne.

"Are you sure this is the time to celebrate?"

"Fucking A! I feel like I just had a near-death experience!"

As we worked through the bottle, me gleeful, Sally wary, the conversation returned to the previous night. Assuming it was Singh, how could he have caught up? Sally told me that, as a lark, she'd applied for a credit card at *Galeries LaFayette* just to see if they'd give her one. They wouldn't, but only after a lot of personal data – including me as a reference – had been typed into a computer terminal. Or the Bulgarian could have staked out the hotel since I'd registered under my own name and someone in *RG* had passed the news on to Singh. Or we could have been identified in London and tailed to Paris. Whatever the means, we'd left a trail.

That led the discussion to the attack. "The guy was pressed hard against me so I should've noticed if he was in a 'state of readiness,' you might say. No hard on. Why the groping? Maybe I read too much into that, thanks to my own history. The forearm across the throat might have been the main play – you know, get me unconscious and then into that car the other guy was in."

We vowed greater caution and started to talk about what we'd seen and which places might be secure and which places not. We quickly concluded the obvious: our current hotel wasn't safe. Was Singh – we seem to have moved to the position that it had been an attempted kidnapping and Singh was behind it – in Paris or had he contracted the Bulgarians from London or Dhaka or wherever he was? No way to know. The Bulgarians might be out of it, but there were plenty of rent-a-thugs looking for work in Paris. The city, so beautiful yesterday, now seemed filled with menace. The discussion had become circular; we kept returning to the same unanswerable questions until Sally finally said, "Spooks and assassins aside, I wonder if I'm tour-isted out? So many beautiful things in Paris that I should be gushing over, but I find myself checking them off and moving on to the next."

"Same feeling. Should we head to my place?"

Coitus Interruptus

That evening we left Paris from the Gare de l'Est. Was booking us together in a sleeperette a violation of the separate bedrooms agreement? Being on my best behavior was more important than ever. But things had changed between us. We'd had a fight. Could that lead to make-up sex?

No. The presence of two young male roommates in the sleeperette scotched any chance of amorous interaction. The two guys, both Swiss, couldn't tear their eyes off Sally and I lay awake on the upper bunk, ready to throw myself down onto the pervert who might try to creep through the curtain around her bunk – probably to save the intruder from dismemberment, given the way Sally dealt with uninvited advances.

Sometime after midnight our car was noisily transferred to another train in Basel and morning brought Montreux, Sally refreshed, me gummy-eyed and grumpy.

As the taxi pulled up to the Fairmont Palace, Sally declared it perfect and was in high spirits as the lift ascended. "There's a second bedroom," I announced, in case she'd missed the 17 prior assurances. "You can have either one you want." Her breast brushed my arm as she got out of the lift.

Our entry was delayed when I had to struggle to make the key work the lock. Had the maid butchered the mechanism trying to enter with the wrong key? She'd made that mistake before. Finally the right combination of angle, pressure and expletives released the lock. "I need a shower. Why don't you explore the place while I scrub off the SNCF? A full tour won't take you long."

"Okay. We have some unfinished business to attend to."

Ominous? I considered the possibilities in the shower. We'd had some pretty heavy discussions the day before. What was left? Relax; probably something mundane: logistics, who pays for what, how we decide where to go – that sort of thing.

When I came out of the bathroom, towel wrapped around my waist, I was met by an arresting sight. Sally, in her exploring, had uncovered the pistol in the side pocket of my suitcase. She turned it over in her hand. "Why Professor. You old desperado you. You really were packing heat all this time. Smith and Wesson Masterpiece. You didn't mention that. A classic. Air Force loyalty?"

"It's loaded."

"I know. First thing I checked. Remember, I was a firing range supervisor. Sixteen months with the lead flying and not a scratch on me. I know how these things work." I couldn't read her. She seemed to be enjoying the situation but debating what to do. What alternatives could she even be thinking about? It was simple: Put the gun down. Take her turn in the shower. Then an early lunch to make up for the leathery Kaiser roll and insipid coffee on the train.

Ah shit! A new thought. Hadn't she written that she looked forward to returning the full body cavity search, 'with preju-

dice'? So this would be payback. Here was a woman who broke
men's thumbs, noses, and arms, and relishes the memory. And
now I'd given her even more reason to be mad at me. The
wench had been playing me all along and, simpleton that I was,
I'd fallen for the act and for her.

"You know what, Maxie? I think it's time for me to take
matters into my own hands. Show some initiative, you know?"
Her expression was playful and she stroked the barrel of the gun
in a way that you couldn't possibly interpret as anything other
than lascivious. "I keep expecting you to jump my bones –
yeah, I know, I told you not to – but," her voice slipping into a
lower register, "a woman's got needs."

She suppressed a giggle and the cloud of doubt and anger
evaporated. I relaxed. Briefly. The barrel came up and pointed
at my crotch. I could feel my penis retracting.

"How about a little rôle play? That's a rhetorical question.
I've got the gun. You don't get to make any decisions. Drop the
towel."

I looked at her to see if she was serious. She pulled back the
hammer; I let go of the towel.

"Good. Glad to see you've kept your figure. Tiny love handles, but we can run those off you before they become permanent fixtures." Then she started removing her own clothes, always keeping an eye on me. Blouse first, then slacks, brassiere,
finally panties. The slanting morning sun cast a beam across
her, making her orange pubic hair glisten. God's great throbbing
prostate! What a fine looking woman!

I must have said that last out loud.

"God's prostate? I think it's yours that's going to be throbbing this morning. Assume the position!"

What position? I raised my hands over my head.

"No, idiot. Get on the bed." Gun still in hand, she climbed
on top, rubbing her Burning Bush up and down my stomach and
willy, her lips parted, fickle Roscoe firmly in her hand. What
happens when she really gets going? She'd moved the hammer
to the half-cocked position. Was I going to wind up the same?
Would Roscoe be a regular participant in our three-ways?

Apparently I was recovering from my earlier fright as Sally eased me into her snug moist vagina. Was there anything not perfect about this woman?[*] She rolled us over, her red hair spreading across the pillow.

Oh Lord, it's always a wonderful surprise to rediscover how good sex feels. That rush of deep contentment to be accepted – no, welcomed – into the body of a caring and warm woman. To know exactly where you belong and want to remain. We moved in unison, slowly, deliberately, wanting to make it last. Then she started to pick up tempo and I could feel the end wasn't far off. Wouldn't it be a great sign if we finished together? I wanted to tell her I was in love with her. I wanted to tell her I needed her by my side. I wanted . . .

That's when she pulled the trigger. Not a metaphor, not a euphemism – she pulled the trigger on the gun. The explosion was deafening as Roscoe discharged by my left ear. Frozen in place above her I felt a warm trickle of blood make its way down my cheek and watched it splash on her nipple, then seep out onto the pale areola. Barely able to hear my own words, I shouted, "Jesus, woman, you shot me."

She was mouthing something. I cocked my right ear toward her.

"Stop staring at my tit and turn around."

Lying in the doorway: Little Singh. His nose had been replaced by a bloody hole. A rare Swiss fly, living up to the industrious standards of its homeland, was already exploring the bonanza. Blood, finding its way along both sides of his handlebar moustache, dripped off the tips and onto the hardwood floor.

Singh? Well, pretty obvious. Dead? Where had he come from? God's gonads! The recalcitrant door lock. I'd missed it.

Remembering that I'd also taken fire, I reluctantly disengaged from Sally – further intercourse seemed unlikely now there was a body on the floor – and went to the mirror where inspection revealed a small part of the lower left earlobe was

---

[*] The answer depends on how you view the gun-wielding thing and her readiness to kill assailants, but I wasn't focusing on those issues.

gone. Ears are prodigious bleeders.

While I was examining this minor damage, Sally, kneeling on the bed, started the refrain, "Oh my God! Oh my God! I shot and killed a man." Joining me at the mirror, she grabbed my shoulders and bounced up and down, her expression alternating between horror and surprise. Her naked breasts bobbed. I pulled my eyes away from her and looked at Singh again while Sally continued her mantra, "Oh my God. I never killed anything in my life!"

"You still haven't." Singh's eyelids fluttered slightly. This produced a resumption of the 'Oh my God's.

"He's alive. He's suffering. I feel sick. I can't stand that he's suffering."

"I can. I told you he killed, or ordered killed, two family men whose greatest crime was to overcharge tourists. He tortured and killed a college kid and he was preparing to do the same to me when I escaped. His agony can't go on long enough." It didn't. A bullet through the nose takes out the brain stem, and maybe chunks of the cerebellum. You don't last long.

Her arm fully outstretched, Sally put two fingers on Singh's neck and shook her head. No pulse. The fly circled impatiently.

The same ugly automatic I'd seen before was clutched in Singh's right hand; this time a silencer had been attached. We noticed the silencer together and came to the same realization: Sally's shot would have been heard throughout the hotel and the Montreux constabulary would come pounding up the stairs any minute. "Get dressed," I commanded, needlessly; Sally was already wriggling into her jeans. "Wait. What happened? We need to have our story straight."

"When you said the door lock seemed to have been jimmied I went looking for the gun – just to be on the safe side. Then I had some fun with it." Grin. "We were pounding away – sorry, I'll come up with a better word – and I noticed this guy in the doorway. He was just watching. I guess he saw my eyes focus on him and he raised his gun . . . he was smiling. So I shot the fucker. Actually," grave face morphing back into the self-satisfied grin, "we were the fuckers."

My girl!

"How about saying you took the gun out of the nightstand when he entered? A less interesting story that won't maintain public interest as long."

Then the significance of Singh's attempted attack sank in. "God, Sally, this is terrible. You're the last person on earth I want dragged into my problems, and it's happening again." Here was a woman I was very fond of – okay, loved – and I'd attracted a murderer to her door, and maybe a kidnapper was stalking her. I moved uncertainly toward her. Encountering no resistance, I took her in my arms, overwhelmed by emotion.

We clung to each other, me trying to hide my sobs when she stiffened slightly. "So, by your count there are four of these dip-shits still alive?" I nodded. "I say we take the fight to them!"

My girl!

45

That's it. I got the money and the girl.

The police noted that Singh had squeezed off a shot and they concluded, to Sally's relief, that it was his bullet that had grazed my ear. The body was spirited away – entering Switzerland on a false passport and attempted homicide (the latter is probably the lesser offense by Swiss standards) – and the story was buried with the corpse. Montreux's economy would tank if the coupon clippers learned that murderers were going door to door.

An epilogue would be premature; still some details to be tied up. Singh's accomplices haven't been heard from, but we keep our guard up and there have been incidents that are difficult to put down to mere chance.

We move around a lot, including a visit to Terd and Leung in Bangkok. They're doing well, but Leung's continuing to put on weight. While there I treated Sally to her own fake passport. You'd have thought it was a Rolex. When we believe it advised, she travels as Ann Hathaway of the UK. Not sure our forger chose a good pseudonym since it tends to spark conversations with the better-read immigration officials who take pride in pointing out the truncated spelling of Mrs. Shakespeare's first name. When you're trying to stay below the radar you don't want to be memorable.

We should probably find jobs; we can't be on vacation forever and there's a management school in Lausanne, IMEDE, that I might look into. But fixed employment makes us stationary targets for our old adversaries. Sally says I could write another book. Unlikely. There's nothing more I want to say.

I've started sending small amounts of money back to two do-gooder organizations in Bangladesh, BRAC and Grameen Bank. Guilt, nothing more. (Herr Swindel took strong exception to this Lilliputian largesse.) I should send it all back, but so far the donations are keeping the guilt in the green part of the dial.

Tiffany figured out a way to divorce me without my presence or knowledge. On grounds of abandonment, or some such. Apparently news of the treasure never got back to her. I don't know, Tiff; if there were some way to send you a (small) part of the money without inviting litigation, I would. You did contribute – if we ignore your drunken revelations to Singh that a) blew our advantage, and b) led Singh to torture and kill Nawaz.

I'm trying hard to avoid past mistakes, but maybe those self-destructive tendencies are firmly ingrained and I'll screw this up. It won't be Sally's fault. She seems to be exactly what she is: a happy, easy-going, well-adjusted person. One of very few on the planet.

We don't talk of marriage. I've told her I'm infertile but she refuses to accept that as the last word. "Medical breakthroughs are announced daily," was her airy response. Sounds like she's thinking long term. Commitment, marriage, children? No objection to any of those. No need to rush though, is there? One relationship went disastrously sour and that should make a person cautious.

Neither of us wants another Vietnam meltdown and she's quick to steer me away from potential triggers. I'm equally alert to impending trouble. Sally's ex had some episodes; don't want to remind her of him.

And we've been able to have a series of conversations about my enduring preoccupation with the nature of God. She listens, asks a few questions, but I get the impression she thinks this is an academician's affectation. She's probably right, but I've revised, again, my stance on the identity of God. Everything in my new life points to the same conclusion:

God is love.

At least that's what I'm going with until a better idea comes along.

Glossary

You might fairly accuse me of a tendency to ornate expression, but it's been useful; that's how I kept Tiffany at bay until she could match me at my own game. That tendency acknowledged, I've never understood the motives of authors who delight in the *deliberately* obscure reference. Our answer – yours and mine – is, predictably, "We get it. You have a thesaurus or encyclopedia. Are we, the unwashed who buy your books, supposed to like you better for making us feel worse?"

In the interests of combating obfuscation, here are definitions of terms that draw on experiences (USAF, Bangladesh, born prior to 1970) or knowledge that not everyone may share.

Air America. Operated by the CIA, a 'civilian' air carrier that shouldered much of the logistics burden in Laos and Vietnam.

Air Force Song. Perhaps I should have paid more attention to the words. I expected the USAF to be a gentlemen's flying club.

> Off we go into the wild blue yonder,
> Climbing high into the sun;
> Here they come zooming to meet our thunder,
> At 'em boys, give 'er the gun!
> Down we dive, spouting our flame from under,
> Off with one helluva roar!
> We live in fame or go down in flames. Hey!
> Nothing'll stop the U.S. Air Force!

In point of fact, the USAF has *never* turned back from a mission because of enemy action. Can the jarheads claim that? No. Army grunts? No, again. Navy squids? Ha! I have to say it: The U.S. Air Force is the best military service. No reasonable person would deny it.

Albertsons, Aldi. Grocery store chains.

Amen-Ra. Egyptian sun god. If you examine the picture – a bas-relief from a temple along the Nile – you'll see how ancient sculptors chose to depict Amen-Ra's qualifications to be the original creator.

American Gothic. A popular painting by Grant Wood. The grim couple are the painter's sister and dentist. Am I the only one who finds significance in the sharp-tined pitchfork the dentist is holding? If you read up on this (but, why would you?) you will learn that Wood was more interested in the house than in the people. Early sketches were of only the house. The dentist and sister seem to have been an afterthought. You will also learn that the woman's face (sister Nan) is elongated, to her disadvantage. A sourpuss. I'm guessing Mr. Wood didn't get along with Nan.

Arthur Laffer. An economist who promoted the theory that higher income tax rates will undermine the incentive to earn income and depress both the economy and tax revenues. He reportedly sketched out a curve that illustrates the relationship between tax rates and tax revenues on a napkin. So far there seems to be no empirical evidence to support Mr. Laffer.

ARVN. Army of the Republic of (South) Vietnam.

ASQ. *Administrative Science Quarterly*. One of the more prestigious academic journals that publishes research on organizations.

Baht. Currency of Thailand. In the mid-80s the baht was trading at around 25 baht per US dollar.

Bajaj. More commonly called baby taxi. Tiff and I resisted calling them baby taxis. Since it was our primary form of transport were we opting for a grander name? As the picture attests, there isn't much 'grand' about them.

Baksheesh. The word used throughout South and East Asia for a small amount of money given as alms or a bribe.

Belle époque. French for 'beautiful era.' The period in French history from 1871 until the start of WWI.

Blighty. England.

Bought the farm. Crashed and died in an airplane. Perhaps derived from the compensation the government paid to a farmer if a military pilot crash-landed and destroyed the farmer's crops.

BRAC. The Bangladesh Rural Advancement Committee is widely respected for its work with the rural poor.

Brahma. The Hindu God of creation. He's most often depicted with four faces.

Brahmin. In the Hindu/Indian caste system the Brahmins sit at the top. You have to be born into a caste.

Brownie. A popular and cheap ($1 initially) box camera made by Kodak and marketed in various versions for over 80 years.

Buck-buck. Players keep piling on until the pyramid collapses.

Burma Shave. If you were born too late to see the roadside ads for this shaving cream, you missed one of the greatest advertising campaigns in history. Five small signs presented a poem that usually promoted the product, but also encouraged highway safety. The sixth sign carried the name of the product. They entertained highway travelers from 1925 until 1963 when the company's legal advisors had them removed. America's a glummer place for their absence.

Cart. A film cartridge.

Caterpillar Club. If you bail out of an airplane and the parachute – once made of silk, hence 'caterpillar' – saves your life, you're entitled to wear the Caterpillar Club shoulder patch. I didn't. It seemed an open admission of failure – that I'd lost a plane.

Chaff. Thin pieces of aluminum that appear as a target on radar.

C-note. One hundred dollar bill.

Clausewitz. Carl Philipp von Clausewitz was a 19th century Prussian general and military theorist.

CO. Commanding Officer.

Coupon clipper. Historically, investment bonds were issued with little coupons printed on them that had to be cut off and presented for payment. This, eventually, led to the term used here which denotes a wealthy and idle person whose most burdensome labor is clipping and cashing the bond coupons.

Dalit. Again, the Hindu/Indian caste system. These are the 'untouchables,' the bottom of the heap. I looked it up; they account for one-fourth of India's population.

DFC. Distinguished Flying Cross. This is a pretty important medal – although it sits seventh down on the list – and you may reasonably question my entitlement to the honor. It was first awarded to Lindbergh, then to Byrd for his trans-Atlantic flight. It was retroactively presented to the Wright brothers. Good company, don't you think? Officially it's awarded for 'heroism or extraordinary achievement while participating in an aerial flight.'

Deuxième Bureau. France's military intelligence unit through 1940. The title survived for many more years as a general label for any French intelligence service.

Đi tiêu. Vietnamese for shit.

Dissonance reduction. Cognitive dissonance, in psychology, is the mental tension a person feels when he holds contradictory beliefs or his behavior is in conflict with his beliefs. In my case, I accepted and wore awards that part of me felt were undeserved. The internal dialogue might include justifications such as the following to reduce the dissonance: I did almost get my ass shot off. Others are receiving higher awards for less. And so on.

DMZ. Created in 1954, the Demilitarized Zone was a ten-kilometer wide strip that separated North and South Vietnam.

Dunning-Kruger effect. Professors Dunning and Kruger conducted tests on undergrads at Cornell and documented what we've always known: dumb people are too dumb to realize that they're dumb. They don't recognize their own lack of skill; they don't grasp the extent of their incompetence; and they're unable to recognize actual competence in others. Doesn't this explain a lot?

E3, E-5. In the US military enlisted grades are preceded by an E; officer grades by an O. In Frank DiVitale's Army, E-3 was a Private First Class. When Frank left Vietnam he was a Sergeant (E-5).

East Pakistan. When the British Indian Empire was partitioned into India and Pakistan in 1947, the Muslims fled eastward and westward, creating two enclaves: the larger one in the west which survives today as Pakistan, and the smaller one, originally East Pakistan. Due to a host of differences, East Pakistan sought – and fought – for independence from West Pakistan. That independence was obtained in 1971 and East Pakistan became the sovereign nation of Bangladesh.

Fajr prayer. The first of five daily prayers required of Muslims. It's offered between dawn – in antiquity dawn was when there was enough light in the sky to distinguish between a black and a white thread – and 10-15 minutes before sunrise.

Farang. The Thai word for foreigner; it originally meant 'European,' but my Thai dictionary defines *farang* as 'a person of white race.' When R&Ring African-American GIs inundated Bangkok during the Vietnam war the Thais created *farang dam*, or 'black person of white race.' The etymology, as is often the case, is in dispute. Possibly from Franc for the French.

FIA. Federal Investigation Agency, one of several intelligence services in Pakistan.

Flight surgeon. A physician with a specialization in aviation medicine. Flight surgeons rarely perform surgery.

Frick and Frack. Originally two comedians/skaters with the Ice Follies. Over time, a term of derision for two nincompoops who are almost indistinguishable.

Gatwick. The second-largest airport serving London.

Glossolalia. Speaking in an unknown language. Gibberish. Meaningless speech.

Godown. Word commonly used on the subcontinent and in parts of East Asia for a warehouse.

Grameen Bank. The pioneering organization in Bangladesh that made small no-collateral, low-interest loans to the poor.

Greek chorus. A group of performers in the plays of ancient Greece who comment with one voice on the dramatic action.

Grey stone. A group of older – but not the oldest – universities in the UK, collectively named for the granite used in the construction of the principal buildings.

Grunt. Infantryman, used here for Army soldiers. Also dogface, doughboy, ground-pounder, hardleg.

Hanoi Hannah. The propagandist who broadcast three times daily on Radio Hanoi. Among other things, she'd read lists of recently killed or captured GIs and mention the location of US units.

Hanoi Hilton. The Hỏa Lò Prison was used by the North Vietnamese to incarcerate, interrogate and torture prisoners of war.

Hardleg. Army slang for a male soldier, with connotations of horniness.

Harry Reems. A generously endowed porn star who featured in the film *Deep Throat* with Linda Lovelace.

Hedonism. This philosophy is attributed to Aristippus of Cyrene, one of Socrates' students. Aristippus taught that pleasure is the highest intrinsic good. Very simply, the hedonist strives to maximize pleasure and minimize pain.

Hobson's choice. No choice. Thomas Hobson – 17th century England – ran a livery. A customer could take any horse as long as it was the first one. Take it or leave.

Ho Chi Minh. The leader of North Vietnam.

Hooch. A temporary or insubstantial dwelling.

HORSE. A basketball game usually involving two to five players. You have to match the shot made by the preceding player or you acquire one of the letters. You're eliminated when you become a HORSE.

Idi Amin Dada. The dictator who ruled Uganda from 1971-9. Spectacularly corrupt and brutal, his regime was believed responsible for half a million deaths. Among the colorful accusations: he practiced cannibalism; human remains were found in his freezer.

ISI. Inter-Services Intelligence; the lead intelligence gathering and coordinating agency in Pakistan.

Jarhead. A US Marine.

Jiggs and Maggie. From a newspaper comic strip of my childhood, *Bringing up Father,* that featured the partying stumpy Irish immigrant, Jiggs, and his rolling-pin wielding tall WASP wife, Maggie. While Tiffany was shorter than me, I wonder if the strip informed my expectations of married life?

Jolly Green. The Jolly Green Giant was a large search and rescue helicopter used by the USAF during the Vietnam war.

Jung, Carl. A psychiatrist who proposed, among many other things, that God had to go through the same process of growing up as humans. God's Old Testament behavior was that of a willful, and very strong, child. That explains why He messed with Job.

Kierkegaard, Søren. A Danish philosopher and the father of existentialism. In the same passage as the boredom reference ('root of all evil'), he wrote, "The gods were bored; therefore they created human beings." You may be surprised to learn that he was deeply religious. By that standard I guess I am too.

Lake Leman. Worth an entry as the lake goes by different names, depending on your allegiance. It started life on maps as Lacus Lemannus, a name bestowed by the Romans although they appropriated a Greek word (*limanos* = *port* in ancient Greek). By the middle ages it was Lac de Lausanne, after a city on it's northern shore. With the rise of Geneva, the Genevans labeled it Lac de Genève, and they've persisted in that usage. They're alone. The other residents around the lake's shores have gone back to Lac Léman. And, they think the Genevans have a *lot* of nerve!

LBJ. Lyndon Baines Johnson, 36th president of the US.

Left-seat pilot. Pilot in command.

Les flics. French policemen.

Lumpenprole. A word (the only one) of my own invention. The roots are lumpen (boorish, stupid) and lumpenproletariat which was coined by Marx as a label for the lower classes that compliantly went along with capitalism's raw deal. I would define lumpenprole as a person of the lower socioeconomic order.

Maghreb. The prayer required of Muslims offered between sunset and dusk.

Mark Antony. Refers here to the soliloquy given by Mark Antony in Shakespeare's *Julius Caesar* which begins, "Friends, Romans, Countrymen, lend me your ears." Antony turns the crowd against Brutus, Caesar's assassin, through a recitation of Caesar's virtues, each followed by, "Yet Brutus says he was ambitious, and Brutus is an honorable man."

Markov chain. A probabilistic process in which each successive step is dependent on the previous ones. The chain that Hasina and I were discussing is the probability of there being treasure (0.0625), followed by the probability of finding the treasure (0.02), followed by the probability of the losing side – Singh and Co., as it turned out – not killing off the winning side (0.01). If you multiply these you get a get a combined probability of 0.0000125 which is the same as 80,000 to one.

MIA. Missing in action.

Muschi. German for vagina.

My Lai. Site of the mass killing of between 347 and 504 unarmed civilians in South Vietnam on March 16, 1968. The massacre was committed by U.S. Army soldiers from Company C, 1st Battalion, 20th Infantry Regiment, 11th Brigade, 23rd Infantry Division. Victims included men, women, children, and infants. Some of the women were gang-raped and their bodies mutilated. Only the platoon leader, William Calley, was convicted. Sentenced to life imprisonment, he served three and a half years under house arrest.

It's generally agreed that the men of Company C were not sociopaths when they joined the Army. They were driven to commit insane acts by a criminally insane war. Were they accountable? That was the crux of the debate.

Nawab. This was the title given to the regional rulers of the vast Moghul empire. For the region that's now Bangladesh, in the late 17th century the Nawab was Khan Shaista. Or Shaista Khan.

OBE. The Order of the British Empire – subdivided into five classes – is the most junior order of chivalry in the British honors system. But still sought after. Paul McCartney, MBE, is on the bottom rung (Member of the Most Excellent Order of the British Empire); Elton John, CBE, is two classes up at Commander of the Most Excellent Order of the British Empire.

Occam's razor. The simplest explanation or argument – the one that makes the fewest assumptions – is correct. I'm not sure I buy this.

Operation Frequent Wind. The evacuation of Saigon as the North Vietnamese People's Army routed the last defenders of the city. Military historians are fond of telling us how many 'at-risk' Vietnamese, military and civilians, were pulled out, but by some estimates another one million were left behind who had worked with or for the US-led forces. No one expected the VPA would be gracious victors.

Oxbridge. Oxbridge is a portmanteau of the University of Oxford and the University of Cambridge. Portmanteau, if you're wondering, is a word combining two or more things or qualities. It's also a suitcase.

P'an Ku. In Chinese mythology, the first living being and creator of all. The universe was a formless chaos which coalesced into an egg. After 18,000 years P'an Ku, holding Yin and Yang, emerged from the egg. He separated Yin and Yang and spent the next 18,000 years creat-

ing earth and sky by pushing them apart – very slowly, obviously. Exhausted from the effort, he died.

Phi Beta Kappa key. Phi beta kappa is the oldest and most prestigious college honor society in the US. Each chapter has its own standards for selection. Members receive distinctive keys on a small chain; some of them wear the key for the rest of their lives.

Pince nez. Eyeglasses, very popular over one hundred years ago, that lacked ear pieces and were secured by pinching the nose. Here's the 26th President of the US modeling his pince nez.

Pinkville. The name GIs gave to the area around My Lai.

Poppycock. I'm sure you know what the word means. Do you know where it comes from? *Pappe kak* is Dutch for mushy shit. Given the obscurity of that etymology, the word doesn't qualify as elegant swearing as described in chapter 8. But it may be more fun to use now you know the original meaning.

Post restante. The term used in Europe for mail that will be picked up by the addressee at the post office. It's also the name of the department where such mail is kept. In the US this service is called General Delivery.

Potemkin village. Grigory Potemkin erected fake-front villages to deceive visiting Catherine II of Russia into believing that he was managing reconstruction in his region of responsibility better than he actually was. It's now any construction – physical, oratorical, etc. – erected to deceive others into thinking the situation is better than it actually is.

Privy. Outdoor toilet; an outhouse. In the unlikely event a person couldn't recognize a privy when it was urgently important to locate one, they usually had a crescent moon carved into the door.

Professorial ranks. Professors, as a general class, can be sorted into Assistant Professors (the lowest), Associate Professors, and full Professors. A decision to tenure a faculty member is usually made when he or she is an Associate Professor. Tenure is the equivalent of a lifelong contract of employment.

PTA. Prepaid ticket advice. A PTA is created when someone other than the passenger prepays for an airline ticket, usually from another location, and the passenger picks up the ticket at the airport he or she is departing from.

Quonset. A building made of corrugated metal, having a semi-circular cross-section.

R & R. Rest and recreation. Our squadron was shipped out of Vietnam before I became eligible for R&R to Bangkok.

Rasputin. Grigory Rasputin rose from Russian peasant to become an influential advisor to the royal family. His interference in politics is believed to have hastened the downfall of the Romanov dynasty and brought on the communist revolution. Hardly handsome, he was reportedly a relentless and often successful womanizer. He was not a discriminating lover, although he said he preferred city women because "they smell better." This cartoon depicts the malign influence critics claimed he had over the Tsar and Tsarina.

Rawalpindi. Often shortened to 'Pindi, and referred to as the capital of (West) Pakistan, although the official capital city is Islamabad, a few miles away.

Red brick. British universities established early in the 20th century in industrial cities.

Reverse Cowgirl. A coital position. The man on his back; the woman sitting astride, facing his feet.

Roscoe. Term used in the '30s and '40s for a handgun.

Rube Goldberg. A cartoonist and inventor whose cartoons depicted complicated machines that performed simple tasks via a series of convoluted processes. His self-operated napkin was memorialized in a US postage stamp.

SA-2. A Soviet surface-to-air missile deployed in Vietnam. The Soviet designation was S-75 Dvina. The SA-2 was radio guided and only one missile at a time could be controlled. A second missile was usually fired as soon as the first had completed its run. They were fast, reaching Mach 3 in 26 seconds, but accuracy was not great; on average they would only get within 75 meters of a target. This was a problem (for them; not us) as the *lethal* blast radius was 65 meters. Beyond 65 meters their detonation would pepper a plane with shrapnel that might damage it, but not bring it down immediately. The rumor that they had acquired heat sensors turned out to be untrue. Maybe planted by Hanoi Hannah? My heroics, shutting down both engines, were for naught.

SAM box. An airplane's radar detection device that signaled, with a rattlesnake-like sound, that North Vietnamese SAM guidance radar was scanning the skies. Lt. Ching – the generic name applied to all the SAM batteries – used his radar selectively as it signaled his location for our bombers to home in on.

Seabee. Members of the US Navy **C**onstruction **B**attalion that built infrastructure (ports, airports, roads, etc.) to support military operations.

SJ and **OP**. SJ (Society of Jesus) after a person's name means he's a Jesuit priest or brother. OP (Order of Preachers) identifies members of the Dominican Order.

SNCF. The French national railroad. *Société Nationale des Chemins de Fer Français*.

Spook. An operative of the CIA or other intelligence service.

Stepford Wives was a novel and a successful movie about women in a small town who were converted into docile, submissive robots.

Street Corner Society. William Foote Whyte lived for three years in a poor immigrant neighborhood of Boston and wrote a landmark book on life there, describing the gangs, those who sought upward mobility, the social structure, politics, and so on. His pioneering use of participant observation set the standard for sociological research for decades.

Subcontinent. Technically, a part of any continent, but over time the Indian Subcontinent has co-opted the term. Historically it was 'greater India,' a region now divided into India, Nepal,

Pakistan, Bangladesh and Bhutan. Sri Lanka is also included, although it's an island.

Swabbie, swab-jockey, squid. A sailor in the US Navy.

Taka. Currency of Bangladesh. In the mid '80s it was trading at around 33 taka per US dollar.

Telex. Text messages could be sent between telex machines (great clattering and slow typewriters) that were internationally connected via a network.

Termagant. An ill-tempered and overbearing woman. I include it in the glossary because it has a fun etymology. For many centuries Termagant was the name Christians gave to the violent and generally disagreeable god which Muslims worshipped. From there the name moved into the English theater as a turbaned stage-villain who would rant and threaten the audience. All parts were played by men and, it is speculated, since the actor wore long robes, that audiences wrongly assumed the character was a woman.

Theodicy. The attempt to explain why a good and compassionate God permits the existence of evil. This goes way back. Epicurus asked,

Is God willing to prevent evil, but not able? Then he is not omnipotent.

Is he able, but not willing? Then he is not benevolent.

Is he both able and willing? Then whence cometh evil?

Is he neither able nor willing? Then why call him God?

Tiff asked if my obsession with the topic made me a Theodick.

The Twilight Zone. A very popular TV series that ran from 1959 through 1964. Combining elements of sci-fi, drama, and social and political commentary, each episode was introduced by Mr. Serling who spoke in a flat, clipped voice.

T-group. Also known as a sensitivity-training group, human relations training group or encounter group. It was a popular form of group training in which participants – typically between eight and 15 people – learned about themselves and group processes through their interaction with one other.

Thud. The F-105 fighter/bomber. The name came from the sound the plane made on impact; it didn't have a great record for survivability.

Tourette Syndrome is a nervous system disorder manifested in repetitive movements or unwanted sounds. It's popularly associated with one of its less common symptoms: uncontrolled swearing and insults.

21. A version of street basketball, played on a half court, when only two to four players are available. Fouling is legal which leads to constant close contact. Close contact with Rev. Al was nothing any of us wanted.

UNFPA. The *United Nations Population Fund,* charged with reducing population growth through support for voluntary birth control measures. Formerly the *UN Fund for Population Activities.* They changed the name, but not the acronym. As you might guess, UNFPA had a lot on its plate in Bangladesh.

Van Dyck. A short beard; the cheeks are shaven. This portrait, painted by Rubens, is of Anthony van Dyck from whom the beard derived its name.

VC. Viet Cong. Literally translated: Vietnamese Communist. Commonly called Charlie and Gomer by GIs in 'Nam.

VPA. Vietnamese People's Army. Also North Vietnamese Army and Viet Minh. Some journalists used the abbreviation **PAVN** (People's Army of Vietnam).

Warm Springs. The Georgia town where FDR established the Little White House to which he retreated with his secretary, Lucy Mercer. Mercer's bedroom was across the living room from FDR's. Eleanor's room was at the back of the building.

Will the Real God Please Stand Up. A TV program, *To Tell the Truth,* has been around in various incarnations since 1956. Panelists on the show try to figure out which of three contestants is who he or she claims to be. After the panelists have voted, the MC asks, "Will the real XX please stand up."

Credits

The maps and illustrations are – thanks to their age or provenance – in the public domain.

Cover and title page. *Magni Mogolis Imperium* by Henricus Hondius. Amsterdam, 1636. Multiple copies in various galleries.

Football field. US Department of the Army, Office of the Chief of Engineers.

Sectional Aeronautical Chart, Atlanta, FAA. 1964.

Vietnam (Annam), drafted by Alexandre de Rhodes, S.J., 1651.

Tactical map. DMZ, Dong Ha, Cam Lo, Quang Tri, Dept of Defense, 1967.

Map of Cornell campus, drafted by Eva McCalley Heefner, class of '33.

Commercial and military carrier pigeon routes, 1890s. Published in *The Nineteenth Century*, 1899.

Softball diamond. US Department of the Army, Office of the Chief of Engineers.

Plan of Ancient Rome from *The New Student's Reference Work*, edited by C. B. Beach, 1914.

Map of Heaven from an illuminated manuscript attributed to Burgo de Osma, 12th century.

Treasure Island, from the German edition of the book, 1883. De-Wikipedia.

Bangkok Red Light Districts. bangkokredeye.com

Ganges delta area. *Asiae Unodecima*. 1540. Creative Commons license.

Dhaka City, 1850. From ancient pictures of Dhaka, found on ancientdhaka.blogspot.com.

Layout of Lalbagh Fort from *Banglapedia, 2003*.

Dhaka City downloaded from http://media-24bd.blogspot.com.

Swissair routes, from a timetable of the now defunct airline.

Kingdom of Love (*Royaume d'Amour*) by Tristan l'Hermite and Jean Sadeler, 1659.

My Lai, Quang Ngai Province, map of 16 March 1968 assault. This hand drawn map appears in several places, including a Congressional presentation. By one report it was drafted prior to the assault by staff of the 23d Infantry Division.

Hiking map, Gstaad to L'Etivaz. Extracted from topo series produced for Switzerland Tourism, 2008.

"Londinum" from *Civitates Orbis Terrarum,* edited by Georg Braun and Frans Hogenberg and published periodically from 1600 to 1623 in Cologne. A very popular map; there are several copies. This one is found in the British Library.

Stonehenge, drafted by John Speed around 1600 and reproduced in *many* publications. *English Heritage* has created an interactive version.

Detail of the île Saint-Louis from the 1550 map of Paris by Olivier Truschet et Germain Hoyau. Housed in the library of the University of Basel.

PFC Michael Bernhardt's (no relation to the author) quote on the My Lai massacre is from Seymour Hersh's article in *The Plain Dealer,* "Eyewitness accounts of the My Lai massacre." Published November 20, 1969.

American Gothic (1930) by Grant Wood. Currently in the collection of the Art Institute of Chicago.

About the author

Michael Bernhart is an award-winning author who has published extensively on international development and healthcare quality. This book is his first foray into fiction, although several funding proposals skirted the boundary. He lives in a yurt perched atop a mountain in northern Georgia with one ex-wife, two daughters, and three cats. He keeps a shotgun, not a pistol, for home defense.

CPSIA information can be obtained
at www.ICGtesting.com
Printed in the USA
LVHW091925170919
631381LV00004B/6/P

9 780997 616071